SHORT STORIES
1988–1991

by Stan Leventhal

Foreword by Sarah Schulman

ReQueered Tales
Los Angeles • Toronto
2022

Short Stories
1988–1991

by Stan Leventhal

Originally published separately as
a herd of tiny elephants and **Candy Holidays**

This edition: ReQueered Tales, May 2022

ReQueered Tales version 1.30
Kindle edition ASIN: B09RN9SC58
Epub edition ISBN-13: 978-1-951092-54-2
Print edition ISBN-13: 978-1-951092-55-9

For more information about current and future releases,
please contact us:
E-mail: *requeeredtales@gmail.com*
Facebook (Like us!): www.facebook.com/ReQueeredTales
Twitter: @ReQueered
Instagram: www.instagram.com/requeered
Web: www.ReQueeredTales.com
Blog: www.ReQueeredTales.com/blog
Mailing list (Subscribe for latest news): https://bit.ly/RQTJoin

Praise for Stan Leventhal

"Stan Leventhal was wonderful company: warm, honest, curious, engaging, and human. *Mountain Climbing in Sheridan Square* is the next best thing to hanging out with him."

—*Christopher Bram*

"A tender, honest novel about that moment between diagnosis and the decision to grow. Messy boyfriends and dreamy crushes set against the back-drop of daily life make Leventhal's characters vulnerable and familiar. His insider's view of the porn industry adds a comically surprising dimension."

—*Sarah Schulman*

"Stan was a literary activist who always gave to, built and endorsed literature and writers. On this Sunday morning, all these years later, I can still see Stan in his apartment window on Christopher Street, next door to the Stonewall Inn, overlooking Sheridan Square as he typed away."

— *Michele Karlsberg*

"Stan Leventhal's new novel, *Skydiving on Christopher Street*, is a startling attempt to capture the life of an urban gay man on the printed page. Leventhal's vision is clear and undaunted. For all of its somber chiaroscuro, it challenges us to see the world through new eyes and to revel in its author's ability to translate life into art, pain into understanding."

— *Michael Bronski*

"Leventhal's novel is powerful for unexpected reasons. This portrait of life at the crux of New York's gay community is excellent company."

— *Dennis Cooper*

Also by STAN LEVENTHAL

Mountain Climbing in Sheridan Square (1988)

A Herd of Tiny Elephants (1988)

Faultlines (1989)

The Black Marble Pool (1990)

Candy Holidays and Other Short Fictions (1991)

Skydiving on Christopher Street (1995)

Barbie in Bondage (1996)

Short Stories 1988–1991 (2022)

SHORT STORIES
1988–1991

by Stan Leventhal

Table of Contents

My Friend Stan Leventhal

My friend Stan Leventhal's work changed from his 1988 volume of collected stories, *a herd of tiny elephants* (Banned Books) to the collection *Candy Holidays and Other Short Fiction* (Banned Books) published in 1991. I don't know when he realized he was HIV positive, but by the time we were all having lunch outside at the OUTWRITE: Lesbian and Gay Writers Conference in San Francisco in 1990, Stan was out as a person with AIDS. At that table were Bo Huston, George Stambolian and a few others who would also soon be dead. Stan was involved in a power play with a gay literary agent hijacking his beloved child Amethyst Press out from under Stan's careful nurturance. He would soon lose the press to this new owner who would publish one failed volume and then shutter its doors. Amethyst author Mark Ameen was also sitting with us. Stan was very upset. I remember Bo saying "Stan has AIDS" as a way of expressing disbelief that those who could count on living would stoop so low as to pillage those who expected to die.

As he got sicker and sicker I remember a Chinese lunch with Stan alternately shivering and sweating so much that liquid rolled off his face onto his plate. He ordered a double Jack Daniels – it was noon. Then a visit to his apartment on Christopher Street overlooking the park where he was suffering from bad diarrhea. He had finished a monograph on his favorite author, Guy Davenport, and gave me a farewell copy.

But the world captured in *a herd of tiny elephants* is a laid back life of smoking joints, jerking off (which takes place in almost every story), playing the guitar, watching a lot of TV, and hanging out at bars having drinks, casual sex with friends and strangers while waiting for Prince Charming who never came. It was a cheap New York, with lots of young gay men with time on their hands and each other in their arms. And then every once in a while someone would suggest using a condom, or mention a sick acquaintance or even reference a memorial service. Yes, AIDS was creeping up coming closer and closer in Stan's life but still in the background of his characters' concerns which centered around finding a real boyfriend, and some kind of unarticulated artistic ambition. There is a lot of innocence here.

By the time *Candy Holidays* appeared 3 years later, everything had changed. In fact I remember Stan showing me the photograph he had chosen for the book's cover: a sleek, sexy shot of Stan, in a speedo, torso nude and smooth, stretched out by the side of a swimming pool, ass up. "This is the last photograph I will ever allow to be taken," he told me. This was how he wanted to be remembered.

From the start in *Candy Holidays* the writing is more ornate, there is more of an attempt to craft characters even though they remain autobiographical and mostly first person. But the stakes are higher, the language is more intense, and the very first story announces the author's HIV status. These characters have jobs and careers, they are in high density situations often filled with threat. There are gestures towards Science Fiction, urban life as a bondage nightmare, a surreal visit with family in Boca – trying out genres, trying out styles, searching for a mode of expression to meet his emotional life. The one constant is that Stan's characters are always thinking about men and finding something to read.

As the editor of Torso and a number of other "stroke books" – gay male porn magazines available at local newsstands, Stan took the opportunity to publish interesting fiction by gay men and lesbians. It was on the model of a queer *Playboy* with frontal nudes – somewhat on the tame side by internet standards – and quality fiction by up and coming writers. Some of Stan's stories are sexually explicit with cocks and jack-off contests and loads and wads being shot and all those words that we now rarely find in literary fiction. Our "gay and lesbian" fiction was sexually explicit partially because we published it, and partially because no one expected straight people to read it.

This leads me to the question we always have to ask about our friends who died of AIDS so young – what would have become of Stan Leventhal? Would he have kept writing? I think so. Would he have survived the transition from underground gay publishing to corporate mainstreaming? I don't know. Would he have gone back to school and ended up professionalized – as a social worker or music teacher or librarian? Probably. But cut down when he was just getting started Stan never got the two things he wanted the most: a for-real boyfriend and an edition of his own writing in hard cover.

– Sarah Schulman
July 2020

Sarah Schulman is the author of more than twenty works of fiction, nonfiction, and theater, and the producer and screenwriter of several feature films. Her writing has appeared in *The New Yorker, The New York Times, Slate,* and many other outlets. She is a Distinguished Professor of Humanities at College of Staten Island, a Fellow at the New York Institute of Humanities, the recipient of multiple fellowships, and was presented in 2018 with Publishing Triangle's Bill Whitehead Award. She is also the co-founder of the MIX New York LGBT Experimental Film and Video Festival, and the co-director of the groundbreaking ACT UP Oral History Project. A lifelong New Yorker, she is a longtime activist for queer rights and female empowerment, and serves on the advisory board of Jewish Voice for Peace. Her most recent work is *Let the Record Show: A Political History of ACT UP New York, 1987-1993.*

a herd of tiny elephants

1988

*For their friendship, creativity, intelligence, and support,
this book is dedicated, in memoriam, to:*

David Acker

Fred Cantaloupe

Glenn Person

Richard Umans

The Buddy System

"Conventional wisdom tells us that it is foolish to write about writers because *real* people do not wish to read about them, and to write about gay people is one step away from insanity because *nobody* wants to read about them. Us. So, I decided my next novel must be about a gay writer."

"Of course," I said and knew that we were going to be friends.

"More coffee?"

Lawrence turned to look for the waitress. We had been introduced only twenty minutes before at the office of a magazine that occasionally published our work. I had read several of his stories, liked them, and was stunned and pleased that he knew of me and had a similar opinion. When he asked if I had time for a cup of coffee at the diner down the street I didn't hesitate. One meets so few writers that one really likes. Besides, I thought he was very handsome. For a moment I considered making a pass but decided not to. Even though I have been told that I'm not bad-looking I figured I was not in his league. And I didn't want to louse up a potential friendship. So we did in fact become friends. Buddies, actually. I recall one night when we were out together – very drunk, probably holding each other up – that we were accosted by a gossip columnist of some acquaintance. "Darlings!" he oozed and pecked us on the cheek. "Lawrence, Stu, are you two, gasp, an item?" Lawrence glanced at me. The spasm of his left eyelid told me that he was going to say something very nasty, so I motioned him to remain silent.

"Henry," I placed my arm around Lawrence's shoulders, "we are *buddies.* In the pool of literature, when the hunky lifeguard blows his whistle, we pause, seek each other's hand and stand to be counted."

"That was very good," said Lawrence.

"You boys are terribly wicked … that's probably why I love you so. Off now!" He pecked us again and, preening, strutted back into the crowd.

It was shortly thereafter that Lawrence met Keith.

* * *

"The baths are not about *sex.* They're about fantasy."

"Come off it, Lawrence. You go to the baths to get your rocks off. When you want fantasy you usually head for a Spielberg movie or read something by Lovecraft."

"That's true," he sighed. "I suppose admitting that sex is the attraction spoils the fun."

"You were telling me about this guy you met."

"Yes, we had a wonderful night. I lost count of the eruptions but I'd be willing to bet there hasn't been so much lava since Vesuvius." I chuckled. "Anyway, he actually called the next night, that was Sunday, and we had, can you believe it, a date."

"Don't tell me you're in love."

"Of course, it's too soon to say anything, but what I'm feeling is not restricted to my crotch."

His name was Keith, and Lawrence described him as "… the perfect male. Designer pecs, great bod, boyish face, good skin. He knows who Gertrude Stein was, prefers Talking Heads to Puccini and leaves sweet messages with my answering service."

"What does he do?"

"Everything."

"For a living."

"He's the regional marketing director for a food con-glomerate."

"What does that mean?"

"When I find out, I'll fill you in."

Neither of us had a lover and I was glad that he'd finally met someone he liked. I can't deny, though, that I felt a twinge of envy. The problem was figuring out if it was because Lawrence had found someone while I was still very much on my own, or because someone aside from me had made him happy. I would be lying if I didn't admit my disappointment because he'd never been interested in anything other than my brain. I was eager for the companionship of another writer, however, and found it a great relief to have someone to call who would agree that editors are spineless; publishers, goons; and the general reading public, mostly moronic.

But I was not having much luck meeting men. Perhaps because I look a lot younger than I am and always say what I'm thinking. The ones who cruise me usually assume that I'm still a kid and lose interest as soon as they realize that I have a mind and am not easily manipulated. The ones who might enjoy my company never give me a chance because they think I'm too young and have nothing interesting to say.

And I'm terrible at sustaining a relationship. Three weeks is a major accomplishment. When a miracle occurs and I actually arrive at that elusive state of "seeing someone," one of us inevitably turns the other off by being too aloof or too eager. The last time I was "seeing someone" I would agonize over how many days to wait and call after a date. And if too many or too few days went by before hearing from him, I'd fear that he wanted to use me at his convenience, or imprison me forever. Perhaps I evoked a similar response in them. It just never seemed to work out.

Lawrence was always very supportive and managed to convince me that most of the time the fault was in the other fellow. I remember once, though, when he chastised me for letting a good one get away.

"All right, Stu, you're avoiding the issue. What happened with the geology teacher/bodybuilder?"

"Nothing, I simply never returned his calls."

"Why?"

"Because I got tired of always having to go out to Brooklyn. He never came to my place even once."

"Didn't you think he was worth the trip?"

"Well, yes, but aren't you the one who said if I made it too easy for them they'd just take advantage of me? If I remember correctly you said, 'The trout that leaps into the fisherman's boat is always thrown back; such willingness always creates suspicion.'"

"Dammit, Stu, that's not the way I put it!"

"Maybe, but that's the way I remember it."

"Anyway," he paused, "will you come to dinner on Friday? You must meet Keith." They'd been dating for several months and I had avoided an introduction.

"If I must, then I shall."

* * *

Keith proved to be a charmer. His curly brown hair, fetchingly unkempt, as if it had been dried by the wind after a swim, framed a gentle, yet masculine face. Quick with a smile, his large eyes possessed an innocence that seemed to whisper, "trust me."

I found it easy to relax with them. Lawrence was in a particularly joyous mood, so proud was he to show off his prize, and Keith, like a blank page that assumes the character of whoever is writing on it, could get along well with anyone. About half-way through the tortellini pesto, however, the conversation sagged. I attempted to shore it back up. "Lawrence, this is the best pasta you've ever prepared." He grinned. "So, Keith, Lawrence told me that you're not very keen on Puccini."

"Who?"

"Puccini!" said Lawrence, exasperated. "The opera composer."

"Oh," said Keith with a laugh, "I don't like opera."

"I understand you like to read Gertrude Stein."

"Read?" he asked, unabashed. "Wasn't she the one who gave that recipe for hash brownies to Alice What's-Her-Name?"

"That's right," I said, suppressing the urge to scowl at Lawrence. But I was determined to salvage the conversation. "What's your favorite thing in the whole world?"

"You mean, besides sex and food?" I nodded. "Scuba diving!" he said and proceeded to tell me everything there is to know about it. He described the sensation of drifting under water, immersed in a rainbow-colored world of fish and coral. It was poetic, heartfelt and enchanting. I had mentally deducted a few points from my evaluation for Puccini and Stein, but added ten bonus points for his description of the silent, kaleidoscopic sea. Keith emerged from my scrutiny as a good catch for Lawrence, so I gave their relationship my tacit seal of approval.

I would occasionally join them for a movie or a play. At first I thought that they felt sorry for me and invited me along because I was without a soul mate. But I soon realized that they needed me as a shock absorber so as not to wear each other out. Although they seemed to get along splendidly in most respects, they required a buffer because of the difference in their interests.

If we went to an escapist movie and Lawrence enjoyed it, Keith would say something like, "See, it wasn't Shakespeare but you liked it! Right, Stu?"

And I would murmur something like, "Man can't live by Shakespeare alone."

If we went to see an avant-garde play and Keith didn't like it, Lawrence would say, "If you saw more intellectual plays you would learn to appreciate them. Right, Stu?"

And I'd mutter something like, "You know what they say, one man's meat ..."

It reached the point where I started to feel like a

mediator. I was used to Lawrence's calls seeking comfort. Keith, however, began to call me as well. "I know that Lawrence is your best friend and I really shouldn't have called, but, well, we had another fight," as if I hadn't already heard, "and I thought if I could talk it over with you it might help."

I was as helpful as I could be. They usually argued over something like the fact that they'd already had Chinese food that week and one of them wanted it again. This would escalate into shouting and harsh words. They would not talk for several days and then make up. I thought there was some underlying tension that caused these rifts but had no idea what it was until Lawrence confided that he suspected Keith was cheating.

"And you're not?" I chided.

"No! I haven't been with anyone else since we started seeing each other."

"Did you make some kind of blood pact?"

"Well, no."

"How can you be sure he *is* fooling around? You don't know for sure. You'll just have to trust him."

"I want to."

"Innocent until proven guilty. It's the American way."

"Stu, I'm aware that Keith calls you to talk and you've been so good to us, I just want to thank you for all your support. Without you to keep us on an even keel, we wouldn't have lasted this long."

"Nonsense."

"You're a real buddy."

* * *

Lawrence completed his novel, *The Lavender Quill Conspiracy,* and his agent had no trouble placing it. Full of intrigue, romance and humor, I enjoyed reading it.

Dancing with some friends at the Anvil one night, I saw Keith in the backroom engaged in a ritual of non-verbal communication with someone other than Lawrence. I don't think he saw me. I kept quiet about it.

I was busily involved in an assignment for a national slick that required much research, in-depth interviews and critical analysis. I went out every night to have a drink and unwind. A conversation with a stranger would occasionally arise, but things rarely soared.

One night a met a nice guy. Marty. A carpenter. We exchanged small-talk for a while and he invited me to his apartment. Three dogs, Mandi, Sandi and Brandi, spaniels all, cavorted about like hyperactive children until Marty and I fell asleep. I awoke to find the creatures in bed with us, as though I'd been a part of some bestial orgy. I called a few days after and left a message on the answering machine thanking him for a nice night. He didn't return the call until three weeks later. He said that he had gonorrhea and suggested a visit to the clinic. I had, until then, managed to avoid contracting any sexually transmitted diseases. Angered at first, I eventually calmed down figuring that an imbalance had been corrected. I was long overdue. It was my turn. I made an appointment with my doctor.

Keith had gotten into the habit of dropping by my apartment unannounced. It started when Lawrence was preoccupied with the completion of his book and wanted no distractions. But it continued after things had returned to normal. We would chat, usually about movies or their latest spat. Once he brought me a book with beautiful color plates of saltwater tropical fish. If I ever had the desire to go scuba diving, he'd be glad to guide me along, he said.

The three of us attended the Holly Near–Ronnie Gilbert concert and our spirits were lifted so high, we left the auditorium with our arms around each other, Lawrence in the middle. We ran into Henry in the lobby. "Darlings!" Peck. Peck. Peck. "Is this a brazen attempt to revive the lost art of the ménage à trois?"

"Don't be silly," said Keith with a smile.

"Fuck you," said Lawrence, his eyelid beginning to squirm.

I pretended I hadn't heard the remark. "How are you,

Henry, and what's the hot scoop?"

"Those rumors about Richard Gere and William Hurt, all *untrue*."

"That's a relief," I sighed.

"The rumors regarding a certain writer and his perfidious lover, however, are *very* true."

Lawrence's eyelid began to shimmy and Keith's jaw dropped to his knees.

"Henry," I pushed him aside, "words simply won't do. Onward," I said to my companions.

* * *

I went to the doctor and was tested for gonorrhea. I was poked, scraped, given a prescription and told not to indulge for a few weeks. Going about my work, I began to notice a peculiar rash that itched like nothing I'd ever experienced. When I called for the results of my test – which turned out to be negative – I told the doctor about it and he suggested another examination.

"Do you have any pets?" he asked.

"No."

"Curious. I must inform you that you have a rather advanced case of scabies, which is usually gotten from animals."

So as blind luck would have it, I'd escaped infection from Marty, the carpenter, but Mandi, Sandi and Brandi had given me a souvenir of the encounter. Getting rid of the scabies was not easy, but I followed instructions until every trace was gone. Thanks to the supposed gonorrhea, the reality of scabies and my own paranoia, I was kept out of the sexual arena for more than three months.

It was during the afternoon, on a Thursday as I recall, that Keith dropped by. I offered him a beer.

"I never kissed you on your birthday last month," he said as if he had to apologize.

"I wouldn't let *anyone* kiss me on my birthday this year, let's not go into the details."

"I'd like to make up for it now," he insisted. Loosening his tie, he walked over to where I sat. I turned my head, expecting a quick one on the cheek. He held my jaw, forced his tongue down my throat and rubbed my groin. It felt heavenly but I pulled away.

"Do you know what you're doing?"

"Yes," he said, unbuttoning my shirt.

"If Lawrence finds out about this he'll kill us both and commit suicide."

"Then let's make sure he never finds out." He winked. I'd gone without the touch of a man for too long to resist.

Sex with Keith was a lot less than I ever would have imagined. He knew all of the appropriate maneuvers but after a few minutes I was so overcome with guilt that I divorced myself from the act and switched on my automatic pilot. Perhaps he felt guilty as well because when it was over I could tell that he wasn't any happier about it than I was. He left without another word passing between us.

Certain that our encounter would never get back to Lawrence, I forgot about it. I began work on my first novel and eased myself back into social activities. The first time I had dinner with Lawrence and Keith, I half-expected conspiratorial looks from Keith and suggestive remarks about treachery from Lawrence, but my fear was unnecessary. Lawrence's book was doing very well, critically and commercially. Keith had gotten a promotion. Everything was as smooth as possible.

One day, soon after that, Lawrence called and said that he had to see me right away. The degree of anger in his voice unsettled me; I was trembling when I answered the door. He waived the formalities with the palms of his hands and planted himself on my couch.

"The most important thing here is the truth. I've got to know. Keith told me something that I can't believe. Now I'm asking you. Did you and Keith ever sleep together?" I didn't know what to say so I didn't say anything. "You probably think I'll go haywire if you say 'yes'. But please, I'm begging you, the truth is what I'm after."

I had trouble getting the words out. "If you mean what you asked the answer is 'no'. We never slept together."

"Did you ever have sex?"

"Yes. Once." I felt like I was on trial; the anxiety while waiting for the verdict was killing me. Lawrence just sat there looking blank. I wanted to shout, "Hit me, hate me, tell me that you never want to talk to me again, but please, please end this torment." I couldn't say it. The best I could manage was, "Why did Keith tell you?"

"Because he wanted to hurt me. He told me that he seduced you right here on this couch about two weeks ago."

"It's true."

"But I didn't believe him. So he said that the two of you had been getting it on behind my back for a long time. I knew one of his statements had to be false. You're not going to believe this, Stu, but I could have handled it. I mean, he was fucking everyone in sight. But when I realized that he'd lied, just to hurt me, I told him it was over."

"Is it over between us too?"

"It doesn't have to be." He moved closer.

"You don't hate me?"

"I'll never hate you. But there's only one way to make amends." I was greatly relieved. "What's that?"

"Can I fix us a drink?"

"Of course," I said.

He filled two snifters with brandy and we toasted silently. Placing his hand on my knee he said, "I want what Keith got."

I almost choked, then giggled. "You're joking. You don't mean ..."

"Yes I do." He drained his glass and removed his shoes.

"You're serious?"

"Uh huh." He nodded and began to unbutton his shirt. "I never thought you were interested," I said softly. He stopped and looked up. "I thought I wasn't good enough for you."

"I can't believe this," I confessed, "I thought that I wasn't good enough for *you*!"

Our eyes met and fused into a single vision. We stared at each other. It lasted a moment but seemed longer. Leaning forward, our lips came together; we tasted each other slowly. I unbuckled his belt and then my own.

* * *

My first novel, *Ménage,* centered on the shifting relationships of three gay men. Published by a small press, it garnered some complimentary critiques from serious literary types and sank like a barbell. Lawrence's novel was nominated for the Endicott Award for Suspense Fiction.

We moved in together. A large loft in Tribeca with a panoramic view of lower Manhattan and the Jersey coast. Lawrence said that he wanted to adopt a puppy but I managed to talk him out of it. He settled for a tank of saltwater tropical fish.

In his weekly column, Henry wrote, "Two up-and-coming authors have tied the matrimonial typewriter ribbon and have set up word processing in a spiffy downtown loft, certain to be the scene of this year's most delectable literary soirées."

I thought that finding a lover and settling down would solve all my problems. Silly me. Everyone warned us that two writers could never live together because rivalry would create too much tension. That's not the case, however; Lawrence and I are still supportive of each other's work and we share all of our triumphs and defeats. I guess that's possible when friends become lovers.

But in our zeal to achieve greatness, or at least, goodness, we have become very critical and protective of each other's mental activity. He gives me a hard time because I prefer Ellington to Wagner. And I have to admit I berate him on occasion for spending too much time with Agatha Christie when he should be reading Tolstoy.

And the jealousies. We chose to establish a monogamous relationship and as far as I know, we've succeeded.

I've been faithful, though at times I almost crossed that line. And Lawrence says that he hasn't strayed either. But ever since we started living together the temptations have multiplied. When I used to go out I was usually ignored. Now I find myself having to reject a lot of attractive offers. Lawrence is experiencing the same thing. Ironically, since we're no longer available to the cruising public, we're very much in demand. When we go out together it's very flattering. If one of us is out alone, however, the other can't help wondering whether he's succumbed to a flirtation.

It's not easy to be someone's lover and buddy. Both of us will readily testify. The only thing we really fight over, though, is the word processor. We're both gluttons when it comes to monopolizing it. So, after much deliberation we decided to order another. It should arrive any day.

"The Buddy System" first appeared in *The James White Review*

Tax-Free

Sometimes it's the garbage trucks, sometimes the drunks. The early morning noises that explode on the street just over his windowsill wake him up every day. Unless he's been hired for an all-nighter. Usually he's in bed by three and up at around eight. When the weather is so cold that his window is shut and caulked, the street sounds are muffled but they still wake him up. He lies in bed, unable to slide back into dreaming, unwilling to leave the security of his mattress on the floor.

Every morning he has about two hours of "free association" time, a phrase he picked up from a movie he sat through twice. He replays the highlights of recent events or puzzles over the strangeness of a recurring dream. In the most frequent one, he wins an award – a gold statuette – and sees himself in a tuxedo, ascending a small flight of stairs to a stage with a podium. An enormous audience of faceless people screams and applauds as he leans into the microphone and thanks them for taking notice of him. He awakens feeling good all over. In another, he's hiding in the cabinet beneath the kitchen sink, praying that his parents and teachers – who are ransacking the house – won't discover his whereabouts. This dream always leaves him with a sense of fright. He awakens wondering why they are looking for him; the dream always ends before he can find out.

His cock, always at its hardest in the morning, beckons his hands or commands a roll-over so that it can be wedged tightly between his stomach and the hard mattress. Sometimes he'll cum like this, picturing himself in an auditorium clutching a microphone, moaning and sweating, hips shaking at the eager young faces that hover at the edge of the stage.

He goes to the bathroom and checks his face before pissing and showering. His skin is usually pretty clear, except sometimes a pimple will appear on his forehead due to a hair clogging up a pore. He curses and slams his fist down on the sink. All day long he washes it and checks it out in mirrors wherever he is to see if it's grown or shrunk. If the pimple seems unusually large, he hides himself in movie theaters near Times Square. Slasher films, as some people call them, are what attracts him lately. He fondly remembers the scene in *Mother's Day* when the victim, presumed dead, stabs the bad guy in the back with an electric carving knife. The blood, so much more colorful and abundant than in real life, splattered all over the screen leaving permanent stains in his memory. When he saw that scene for the first time, his cock snapped to attention. Now all he has to do is replay the scene on the monitor in his brain. His cock stiffens and doubles in size before the bad guy keels over, the knife still vibrating, buzzing like the drills that tear up the streets. Afterwards, he wonders what it would be like to die. He pictures cartoon versions of heaven and hell, with angels strumming lyres or devils with pitchforks. He can think of hundreds of reasons why he should end up in each place. When he balances his good and bad deeds, they cancel each other out in a one-to-one correspondence. He figures it could go either way. He'd prefer to be with the smiling angels, but he's prepared to accept the devil's anger. He did, after all, run away from home.

He smokes a joint while sipping his morning coffee, light and sweet, while the small black and white television set – at least fifteen years old – he figures silently thrusts flickering images at his face. The coffee mug empty, another roach in the ashtray, he listens to a record on the small, portable stereo with fuzzy-sounding speakers. One of the four albums he owns, all lifted from a secondhand record store, is a two-disc set by Bob Dylan. "Absolutely Sweet Marie" is his favorite song. "Your railroad gate, you know I just can't jump it/sometimes it gets so *hard,* you see," he sings along in a voice that is higher and less cracked than Dylan's.

In the early afternoons he occasionally goes to the bars. All over town they fill up with businessmen and as yet undiscovered artists who take lunch hours that frequently don't require food and often last longer than sixty minutes. He orders a club soda and manages to strike a deal before having three sips and lighting a cigarette. His customers are usually younger and better-looking than the ones he gets through the escort services. And they don't ask him a lot of questions or show him photographs of their families. It's strictly wham-bam-thank-you-Sam and then they go back to their offices. A blow-job is ten dollars. He finds a suitable spot nearby at no extra charge. To fuck will cost twenty-five dollars plus hotel fee or fifty dollars at his place. For kissing, add another twenty-five. He can easily clear fifty dollars per afternoon on his own and at least a hundred any night by putting himself on call with one of the escort services that he is registered with.

The man on the telephone gives him the name of a hotel and a room number. Then says, "Pretend you're a college student," or "I told him you're interested in sports." He journeys to the hotel and knocks on the numbered door. It's usually opened by a heavier, older guy. "I'm a college student working my way through school," are his first words. Or, "I'm really into sports, 'specially baseball." He gets paid before he takes his clothes off. And usually gets a good tip while putting them back on.

There's a lot to be said for the "three-day work week," a phrase he learned from from his ex-friend Billy. They'd go to movies together, smoke joints, talk about their customers. Once they were hired to have sex together while someone watched. Afterwards they promised that they'd never do it together again unless someone paid them. One time they were hanging out at the bar on 9th Avenue and Billy accused him of trying to steal a customer. Billy punched him in the stomach. Then pulled out a knife and cut his arm. The sight of his own blood terrified him. He ran home and didn't leave his room for three days. It wasn't a very deep cut, but it took months for the scar to become almost invisible. He wore long sleeve shirts until you had to put your eyes right next to it to see it. Now his only friend is Ken, the bartender. Sometimes he gives him free drinks. When he sees Billy, they pretend they don't know one another. They pass quickly without any sign of recognition.

Always home by around six o'clock, he showers and, every two or three days, calls in. The television, with the volume turned up now, shouts a list of news events at him. He shakes his head when he hears something about the value of the dollar decreasing. He's afraid that he will have to lower his rates and his tips will lessen. That would mean more working hours and less time for himself. Hostage situations can make him put down his fork. He pictures Arabs with machine guns, splattering the walls of tents in the desert with the blood of American women and children. After the news, he prepares dinner. His favorite food is Kraft macaroni and cheese. It's fast and easy to make, fun to eat. He lets the taste linger in his mouth before rinsing it away with Coke or Pepsi.

Reruns of old comedy shows – like *Laverne & Shirley, Gilligan's Island,* and *Three's Company* – help the time move along while he waits for the telephone to ring. Smoking another joint, his memory replays tapes of incidents from his childhood and years at school. He can never control these thoughts; they seem to have a rotation all their own.

Laverne comes in with a bag of groceries and he recalls going to the supermarket with Mom, when he was young enough to ride in the shopping cart. She'd hand him boxes of cereal, cans of beans, cartons of milk and he'd arrange it all very neatly against the sides. As the wall of food grew up around him, he'd imagine himself in a fort, fighting off the

Indians. When they'd get home Mom would say, "Good boys always wash their hands and face after hard work," and he'd run to the bathroom, work up a lather between his palms, scrub his face clean, then run to the kitchen and announce that he was a good boy.

Gilligan is on the beach with the Skipper and he remembers going to Virginia Beach with Dad. They'd wade out to where it was waist deep and he'd leap from his father's shoulders into the salty water. Then they'd swim out to the orange buoy and race back to the wet sand. Dad would buy him hot dogs with lots of mustard, soda pop, and allow him a sip or two of beer. "But don't tell your mother," he'd warn him.

Jack comes out of the bathroom with a towel around his waist and he thinks of Coach Sebretski, who hated him because he refused to shower with the other boys after gym class. The first time he took off all of his clothes and headed for the shower room, they'd looked down at their own hairlessness and pointed to the wiry bush sprouting from his crotch, laughing and joking. After that, he'd dress while they showered. One of the other boys, usually Drew, would go to the Coach and rat on him. The Coach would storm into the locker room and demand that he strip and shower. He'd refuse. They'd argue. And he'd always need a late pass for American History. When he thinks of Coach Sebretski, he always remembers Miss Parkins, his third grade teacher, the best he ever had. She was nice. And she said that he was the most handsome boy in the class. He thought that Todd was the most handsome boy in the class but didn't want to argue with her because he liked her so much.

When he thinks about the past, the thing that stands out most of all is the day he ran away for good. Mom and Dad barged into his room while he lay on his bed, naked, playing with his cock. They yelled at him; told him that he was evil, hell-bound for sure. They locked him in his room. He busted the window and escaped with a knapsack full of clothing and some *Silver Surfer* comics. On the turnpike, his thumb stuck out, he hitched a ride north with a fat, smelly trucker. He arrived in New York and stumbled around until a skinny Puerto Rican kid started talking to him; told him how to get to the Port Authority building and how he could earn easy money there.

The telephone jerks him back to his room and the cackling television. He turns it off and answers the phone, reaching for his pad and pen so he can write down the necessary information: which hotel, the room number, and who he's supposed to pretend he is.

He showers again and carefully selects what he thinks the customer will like. It's usually the same pair of snug jeans with one of his dozen or so white t-shirts. He makes sure that he has a few imported rubbers and recalls the first time a customer insisted that he use them. "Haven't you heard about the health crisis?" asked the heavy-set, jowly man with glasses. He didn't want to admit that he hadn't so he said, "Sure." Lately, it seems that all that Ken, the bartender, wants to talk about is the health crisis. He'll never forget the first time he stretched the sheath of latex over his cock. It felt good. Like a delicate hand caressing him, making him harder.

A hotel room with the shades drawn, a large bed, the lights dim, is where he finally finds himself. More often, the better ones and not the flophouses he occasionally endures. Most of the time the customers are fat and over fifty. They have uncommonly large cocks that he can barely get his mouth around, but accommodation in his deceptively small ass is no problem. Many of them pull out pictures of their wives and children to show him. He can't understand why they think he wants to see the pictures, or why they need his ass if they have a wife at home. But he gets fifty dollars an hour, two hundred and fifty for an all-nighter, tips and there's no extra charge for kissing. He can earn over a hundred dollars a day, almost any day he chooses. Tax-free. Pretty good, he thinks; no one that he knows can do as well.

He returns home and clicks the light on. Strips and looks at himself in the mirror. His body is still hard and slim, his face boyish with green eyes and parentheses around his mouth when he smiles. His hair is straight, the color of wheat and almost touches his shoulders. He turns and looks at himself from several angles. Grabs his cock like a microphone and poses. He turns off the light and plops onto the mattress, covering himself with the blanket. On his side, he brings his knees up to his chest, clutches the pillow with his left arm and closes his eyes. He hopes that he will dream about the gold statuette and adoring audience. He prays that he'll spend eternity with the smiling, musical angels and not the silent, smirking devil.

The Showdown

When Walker asked if I wanted to go to the jack-off finals I hesitated because it was, after all, a Friday night and I couldn't stand the thought of missing an episode of *Miami Vice.* Watching Don Johnson in action while massaging my cock was my usual activity on Friday nights between ten and eleven.

"I have plans for Friday night."

"Look," said Walker, "the contest doesn't start until midnight. You can jerk yourself off and have plenty of time to shower and meet me so we can see some real pros at work."

"Do people really jerk off professionally?" I asked, giggling.

"At the Dungeon they do. The winner of the tournament gets five hundred dollars in cash and a round trip ticket to Key West."

After my Friday night ritual I met Walker. We had a beer and then made our way to the Dungeon, located in the heart of the meat packing district of the West Village. A black door with the address and the word "private" is the only indication that one has arrived at the right destination. Beyond the beaded curtain which separates the club from the reception area is a staircase that descends to the darkly-lit main area. Low-ceilinged with gray concrete walls, the rectangular room boasted a rack, guillotine and stocks. Other instruments of torture hung on the walls illuminated by indirect red lights.

Standing around the perimeter of the room were a variety of guys – young and old, fat and thin – all waiting with anticipation as the master of ceremonies checked the masking tape that marked the area for the contest. An oblong of about eight feet by four feet had been created with a gauge indicating feet and inches. The two contestants were to stand opposite each other with toes touching – but not going beyond – two parallel red strips which were set about five feet apart.

The loud music which had been pummeling everyone's eardrums suddenly stopped and a handsome Hispanic man with a clipboard strode to the center of the floor and opened his arms in a gesture of welcome.

"That's Carlos Ramirez," said Walker, "he's the manager of the club."

"Men and boys, friends, fiends and fun-lovers," said Carlos, "this is the final round in the First Annual Dungeon Jack-Off Classic." Scattered applause emanated from various sectors of the club. "As those of you who have been with us from the beginning are aware, the finalists have demonstrated their extraordinary abilities in their previous bouts, and tonight they face each other to compete for the coveted prize."

"Let's get to the action," someone yelled.

Walker nudged me and whispered, "That guy lost last week by an inch and a half."

"Too bad," I sympathized.

"And now for the contestants," bellowed Carlos. "To my right, weighing one hundred and ninety-five pounds, from Scranton, Pennsylvania, Geoff 'Powerman' Morganstern!"

The spectators applauded as a strapping blond man with beard, moustache and diamond stud in his left earlobe, sauntered to the center of the room. He tore off his white t-shirt, pulled down the black 501s and gingerly stepped out of his piss-burnt jockstrap. He twirled it on his index finger and tossed it into the crowd. A knot of onlookers jostled to claim it. The competitor flexed his bulging arms and jiggled his pectorals, strutting around the oblong, flaunting his mightily developed torso, narrow hips and enormous thighs. His cock, long and limp, sprouted from a mass of wiry bronze hair and his low-hanging balls swayed with his swagger.

"And his opponent," intoned Carlos, "from Eau Claire, Wisconsin, weighing one hundred and fifty-two pounds, Al 'Monster Dick' McKenna!"

Dark and lean, the other contestant slowly walked into the competition area pulling off his football jersey. He unzipped the bleached jeans and they fell to his feet revealing a well-defined stomach, perfect ass and sinewy legs. His thick cock hung to mid-thigh and would not have looked out of place on a man twice his size.

"You gentlemen know the rules," said Carlos, smiling. "Lubrication!" he commanded and a lovely young man appeared with a can of Crisco. He approached each contestant and spooned out a handful. They began application to their dangling cocks.

"All right. I'm going to start the countdown to the showdown. Five, four, three, two, one – GO!"

The athletes began stroking themselves. "Monster Dick" McKenna's organ responded first. It stood out perpendicularly, his dark shaft reflecting the light in all directions. It grew to approximately eleven inches as his scrotum tightened and his thighs began to quiver. "Powerman" Morganstern grimaced as his cock began to elongate, the balls of his feet pivoting on the floor. The rapidity of his pumping caused sweat to appear on his face as his nipples hardened, pointing slightly down and out.

The audience began to root and cheer.

"Go 'Monster Dick'," someone shrieked.

"Cream 'im 'Powerman'," screeched a fan.

The contestants eyed each other and increased the speed of their pulling. Sweat began to drip from all over their bodies. The golden down on Morganstern's buttocks caught the light as his meaty buns bounced up and down. The lean butt of McKenna, hard and well-rounded, remained firm and moved in tandem with the jerking of his hips.

Suddenly "Powerman" Morganstern started to groan and his body shook as his eyes disappeared into his head. He let out a low growl and his entire body vibrated as he let loose a jet stream that landed about a foot and a half from his toes. "Monster Dick" McKenna glanced at the floor and smirked. He began to thrust his hips to and fro, increasing the speed of his strokes. A high-pitched moan arose from his throat. As his back arched he shot a huge gob that landed right between Morganstern's feet.

The crowd was jumping and screaming as Carlos entered the oblong and raised McKenna's dry hand in victory. The two competitors shook hands as the various audience members began to disrobe, summon the Crisco boy, and enjoy for themselves the pleasure they had just witnessed.

"Let's go," said Walker.

"Are you kidding? The evening's just started."

"I was hoping you'd say that," he grinned.

We stripped, greased ourselves with Crisco and spent the next couple of hours testing our distance and stamina.

"The Showdown" first appeared in *16 Tales*

Orange Sunshine, Purple Rain

There is only one way for me to measure the success of a sexual encounter, and it has nothing to do with the intensity of the orgasm. Some are light and fast, others long and fierce, but I'm not sure what variables determine this. My mind, however, is the perfect indicator. If the only thing in the region of my conscious thought is the sexual play at hand, I have achieved the sought-after escape that signals success. If, however, my thoughts roam around, touching on memories or anticipations, then I know that sex, in spite of the orgasm, has not diverted me sufficiently.

Am I having fun? I ask myself.

Could be better, I reply.

Which is how I know that the scene I'm experiencing right now is devoid of everything except a sense of duty; that is to get through this without hurting my partner's feelings. My partner being Dennis Michael Walker, my ex-lover. He's working me with his mouth as I think of this, while Prince sings "Purple Rain" in the background. I'll probably explode at the proper moment and he will think that he has conquered me again. But it's only a chemical reaction. My body must defer to nature. Reason does not signify. But my mind remains independent and I can't stop thinking of my boyfriend in New York, or my parents, who live about thirty-five miles from here. Here is Dennis Michael's apartment.

He's looking at me now. Smiling. Flashing that goofy grin that asks: aren't I terrific? Don't I do it great? I smile back. I don't want to hurt his feelings, ruin his evening. But just before I offered my phony approval, I had been thinking about Tim, the man I met four months ago. The man in New York who I miss so much while I'm on vacation in Florida. Visiting my folks. But I haven't told them about Tim yet. It's too soon. You never know how long these things will last.

I met Tim – in a bar, of course – and we talked for a long time before deciding to go to my apartment for sex. Safe sex. An expression I didn't have to explain. It was understood that we would use condoms and refrain from the kinds of things we'd both done a million times before without a moment's hesitation. Licking ass. Swallowing cum. We had a wonderful time and began to get together about three nights a week. Eventually, we'd meet for dinner or a film and gradually crossed the line that separates the fuck-buddies from the boyfriends. And condoms – the straight man's defense against fatherhood – became a mandatory accessory for our activities.

When Dennis Michael and I were both naked I produced two condoms. I demonstrated my agility with them and he looked at me sourly. "You're kidding."

"Nope. It's the rage in New York. For anyone who wants to see the far side of thirty-five."

"Just 'cause some guys died?"

"That's reason enough for us."

"We Floridians don't think about that kind of stuff."

"Maybe it's time you started. You're taking a big risk just having sex with me, you know. This is for your own good."

He grudgingly slipped the other one on and modeled it, something I would have enjoyed more if he hadn't let his body go. What used to be firm and sleek was now soft and loose. He's still attractive. Such a youthful face. A bit chunky, though. And still a little slow in the snappy conversation department. We hadn't seen each other in a year and when I asked how he was doing, he replied, "Great."

"What's new?"

"Nothing."

When I ask Tim what's new, he can go on for two hours. At first I thought I was just fascinated by his work. He's a theatrical set designer and he knows lots of interesting people and hears all kinds of funny stories. I'm never bored for a moment. But Dennis Michael is different. A man of few words who never uses more than one at a time – unless he has to – and so tired of his job that he has to remind himself what he does.

"So, how's work?"

He thought about it for a while. "Okay."

I didn't press it, but I wanted to talk. It seemed like the logical thing to do, considering that we were sitting together with a table between us. I started telling him that I haven't yet overcome all the obstacles in the way of a fledgling singer-songwriter, "... so I've gotten four more songs published, but the record companies are still doing their damndest to pretend I don't exist."

"Gee."

"I guess I'm in kind of a malaise."

"Yup."

I'd be willing to bet that Dennis Michael has no idea what that means, but is too cowardly to ask. When I'd used that line on Tim, he smiled and said, "Well, I'll spread mayonnaise all over your malaise and lick it off from now 'til dawn."

It's that kind of stuff that makes Tim so endearing. And I try to remember what was so attractive about Dennis Michael when we were lovers. He was cute. Beautiful, actually. But no personality. Back then I wasn't too big on personality, just looks. Guess I've come a long way.

But now it's time to get this over with. If I concentrate on Dennis Michael nothing happens. Zero. But I think about Tim's blue-gray eyes, his sense of humor, and that helps me enter phase two. And picturing Tim's firm, meaty ass and tapered thighs moves me into phase three. Pressure's building. I recall the sound of Tim's laughter in my ear and I'm soaring, holding onto the headboard now. Just a few seconds more. And there it is, faster than sound, moving like a wet torpedo. Droplets now. A calmness overtakes me as I'm emptied of all tension and strain. Thank you, Tim. Fuck you, Dennis Michael.

"How are your parents?" he asks.

"Fine," I say, wondering why he didn't ask during one of the long silences that joined us at dinner. Oh, now I see. He doesn't really want to know how my parents are. This is his way of indicating that it's my turn to service him.

We switch positions and I begin to work him over. It does not require much effort. I know this man's body. The original parts, anyway, not the new additions. Besides, I've had a lot of practice. This is easier than getting drunk and passing out. I wonder if Tim is fooling around in New York while I'm getting it on down here. We haven't signed any papers or drawn any parameters. Yet. The only thing that's been discussed and decided is that safe sex is the *only* sex. For now, anyway.

"These goddamn rubbers spoil the fun," says Dennis Michael. If my mouth were not otherwise occupied I would tell him that the distance between fun and death grows smaller every day. But that's too abstract for him. So I just chow down with more force. He groans. That ought to hold him for a while. God, but this is boring. Why do I get such a kick out of this with Tim? I used to enjoy this with Dennis Michael, but it's not the same. Everything's changed since I met Tim. Dear Tim. What will I pick up for Tim as a souvenir? A t-shirt that says Beach Bum? A sack of oranges? A Welcome To Fort Lauderdale piggy bank? The possibilities are astonishing.

He groans again. Or was that a moan? It's getting harder to tell. But at least he's responding. Perhaps to the acid? I can't believe people still *do* acid. I thought that went out with the Strawberry Alarm Clock. Are the Grateful Dead still together? I lose track. Time is so elusive. Thinking of time, I can probably be back to watch the 11:00 news with Mom and Dad. Who are sitting at home this very moment knowing that I'm having sex with Dennis Michael. They are too good to be true.

When I told them I'm gay I was prepared for the possibility that they might disown me. Or murder me on the spot. But Dad said, "I always suspected."

What a relief. Then I told Mom.

"It'll kill your father."

"No it won't. He already knows and he just played eighteen holes."

As soon as Mom had talked to Dad and realized he wasn't going to have a heart attack over it, she accepted me and my preference without reservation. Once a year I leave the winter of New York to visit Mom and Dad in sunny Fort Lauderdale. At night, when I'm going out they both say, "Have a good time." The next morning they ask, "Did you have a good time?"

"Yes."

"Did you meet anyone interesting?"

"Yes."

"What's his name?"

Just hearing them use masculine pronouns when enquiring about my evenings makes my heart jump up and down with joy. It was worth the risk of telling them my secret. They are an endless source of love. Last night, when I casually mentioned that I wouldn't be home for dinner tonight, Mom asked, "Got a date?"

I nodded.

"Anyone we know?" asked Dad.

"Dennis Michael Walker."

"The geometry teacher," said Mom, "the one who moved down from New York a few years ago."

"Right," I said.

"Your annual date," said Dad.

"Yes."

Then Mom said, "You've heard about this AIDS thing?"

I nodded.

"And you're taking all the necessary precautions?" added Dad.

"Yes."

"Have a good time," they said.

The fact is, I wasn't *that* eager to see Dennis Michael again. But he's the only person I know in Florida who's under sixty-five years old. So when I arrived I called to see if he wanted to get together – just for dinner and dancing. He said he couldn't wait. That was Monday. Today is Friday. And his cock is in my mouth. He appears to be writhing a bit. Good for him.

Dinner was fine. A place called the English Pub. After we'd established that I'm still working at the factory, performing on weekends, shopping demo tapes around, and that he's still teaching suburban brats how to slice up circles and sub-divide angles, the conversation simply stopped. I brought up all the recent national and international headlines I could think of, but he had nothing to say about anything. Maybe he spends too much time in the sun? Perhaps he's taken a few too many acid trips? It's probably just that he's so good-looking he can get whatever he wants without trying too hard. Like all human ornaments. The brains turn into oatmeal through lack of use. But they can't help it. No one is held accountable for their genes.

After dinner he took me to some disco. I forgot the name already.

"Do you wanna drop some acid?"

"No. Thanks."

He swallowed a hit and we started dancing. After six songs I drove us back to his apartment. And here we are shedding sweat onto his designer sheets.

Acid! I couldn't believe it. I haven't done any in about ten years. There was a time when orange sunshine was my favorite thing in the world, and I would trip out a couple of times a week. But that was when I was a kid. Then it didn't matter if I wandered around in a daze for forty-eight hours after coming down. These days I have responsibilities. A job to hold onto and a career to build. And even though I'm on vacation, I've still got to get back to my folks' place with me and their car intact. This ain't New York. Can't just hail a cab.

He groans again, but that might be because the stereo just clicked off. Thank God. It's not that I don't like Prince. It's just that "Purple Rain" is one of those songs that I heard several million times too many on the radio at work. And now I've just heard the entire album. Not bad. But not my idea of ideal fucking music. I prefer instrumental stuff. Vocalists are too distracting.

Was that a groan or a moan? I remember when Dennis Michael could come before my jaw muscles loosened up. He sure is taking his time. Maybe it's the acid? Or that he's getting older? Perhaps he needs the voice of Prince to keep him in the proper frame of mind? Should I turn the record over? As I recall, he used to get excited when I squeezed his nipples. I'll give it a try. There he goes. Here it comes. He's smiling. Breathing fast and hard. I guess I did all right.

"Would you turn the record over, please?"

"Sure," I say and get up to do it.

"That was great. Haven't lost the old touch, have you?"

"Guess not."

I lay down alongside, resting my head on his chest. I wonder what Tim is doing right now.

"You know, these rubbers aren't so bad. Takes some adjusting, though. Still, I could never get used to them on a regular basis."

"You just might have to, at some point."

"Humpf," he says.

I smooth down his hair.

"Have you been seeing anyone?" he asks.

"Yeah. Sort of. It's been about four months."

"What's his name?"

"Tim. And you? Seeing anyone?"

"Anyone I want."

"And what about love?"

"Love wasn't made for guys like us. I'm too particular and you're too romantic. I like it that we get together once a year and fuck. Gives me something to look forward to."

Did he always get this chatty after sex, or is it the speed

in the acid? I'm not sure. Maybe next year at this time I'll still be seeing Tim and he'll come to Florida with me and I won't have to see Dennis Michael. That would be great. Because the question that's been straining for recognition in the back of my mind is growing more insistent. Ever since we got down to sex I've been afraid to focus my inner ear in that direction. But I can't ignore it for another moment.

Do I ever want to have sex – safe or any other kind – with Dennis Michael again?

No.

How should I tell him?

Don't tell him.

But when he finally figures it out – say two or three years from now – it might hurt his feelings. What then?

He'll get over it. Eventually.

Schoolmarm

The usual afternoon crowd gathered in Ruby Rae's Saloon. Because the sun was high and the dust had parched everyone's throats, business was good. Ruby Rae McDaniels, the attractive proprietress, served drinks and the best food in the territory. In her burgundy gown with black velvet ribbons crisscrossing the bodice, billowy sleeves and bustle, she moved among her customers with style and charm.

Luke Hanson gulped his second bourbon. When Ruby Rae headed toward him with the bottle, he waved his arm in refusal and politely tipped his hat. She moved over to where he stood at the end of the bar and asked, "What do you have planned for this afternoon?"

"Well," he replied, "the branding's all done and the cattle's grazing, so I thought I'd ride over to Slattery's Pond for a swim."

"That sounds heavenly," she sighed. "Will you be around this evening?"

"Most likely. There's not much else to do around here at night." He turned and slowly sauntered away as she placed her elbows on the bar and supported her chin in the palms of her hands. Watching the retreating figure, she noted the assurance of his step and the way his musculature shifted against the straining denim. As the swinging doors slowed to a standstill, she imagined herself embraced within his powerful arms. Her reverie was shattered, however, by the caustic voice of Trade Watkins.

"Hey, Ruby Rae! Quit daydreaming and fill up this here glass. Pronto!"

"Listen here, you. Be patient. You're not the only customer in my place. I may not be there when you want me, but I'm always right on time."

"What's a man gotta do to score points with a woman like you?"

She glanced at his greasy hair and the stubble on his face. "A bath and a shave might be a good place to start."

Luke Hanson untied the reins and patted the piebald stud that he'd raised from a foal. Swinging up into the saddle, he adjusted his boots in the stirrups. He removed his hat to wipe the sweat from his forehead with the back of his hand, and the harsh sun glinted off the gold ringlets that framed his tanned face. With his broad shoulders and straight back, he looked like he was born to ride high in the saddle.

He spurred his mount and rode west at a moderate pace until he reached the pond. Located at the foot of Rocky Point, the surrounding patches of scrub oak and larkspur gave it the appearance of an oasis.

After tying the reins around the trunk of a small tree, he stepped up onto a rock perched above the clear water. The first thing he noticed was that there was someone, already immersed, who had the same idea as himself. Sure enough, there was a horse nibbling the short grass across the pond, and a pile of clothing on a rock nearby. Luke stepped back and climbed to a higher position where he could observe unseen. He sat down and removed the small pouch containing tobacco and papers, and proceeded to roll himself a smoke.

The silence was broken by the splashing sounds of the swimmer who had finally surfaced for air. It was Richard Mannering, the temporary schoolmaster, who instructed the youngsters of Deep Gulch. As Luke inhaled deeply and watched the form moving athletically about, his mind drifted back to the day when Mannering had arrived at the small, wilderness town.

Up until a week prior to that day, Laura Mannering had been teaching at the one-room schoolhouse. She had travelled west from her native Boston to take up the position and had lived there happily until she had become unaccountably ill. Doc Preston advised her to stop working and get plenty of rest, so she summoned her brother, asking if he would help with the teaching chores while she recuperated. Her condition had finally improved and Richard, greatly relieved, decided to stay until recovery was complete.

When he stepped down from the stagecoach that day, Trade Watkins, the scoundrel of Deep Gulch, had confronted him in front of Ruby Rae's Saloon. "Stranger, who are ya and what do ya want?"

Looking a bit uncomfortable and out of place in his gray tweed four-button suit, starched collar and cravat, he offered his hand. "My name is Richard Mannering and I'm here to assist the school teacher, my sister. And whom, sir, do I have the pleasure of addressing?"

Trade ignored the outstretched hand. "Well, now don't you talk just like a reg'lar professor. So, you're the new schoolmarm, eh?"

The face of the young stranger became serious and he drew his frame up to its full height. "Sir, before you insult me any further, let it be known that I am well-practiced in the art of pugilism, and will give you a demonstration should your attitude persist." He crouched slightly and readied his fists.

Trade spat on the ground and taunted. "Pugilism? Is that some fancy style of French cooking?" He laughed and patted the piece of iron that hung threateningly at his hip. "This here gun does all my fightin'. You best stay clear. Y'hear?"

By that time a crowd had gathered in anticipation of a showdown, or at least a brawl. But Ruby Rae forced her way into the throng, took the stranger by the arm and led him to the teacher's cottage behind the schoolhouse at the end of the street. Luke had watched the scene and admired the way the young stranger had stood up to the town bully.

Luke ceased his reminiscence, stubbed out the tiny cigarette butt and jumped from the promontory to the ground. He made his way to the other side of the pond and stood on the rock by Richard Mannering's clothes. When the younger man emerged from the pond, he stood stark naked on the rock and stared into Luke Hansons' eyes.

"How's the water?" asked the overheated cowboy as his gaze took in the lithe, sculpted body that stood defiantly before him.

"Refreshing," said Richard.

Luke slowly unbuckled his holster and let it drop. He unbuttoned his plaid shirt, removed boots, trousers, skivvies and asked, "You feel like swimming some more? It looks like it could get mighty lonesome by yourself ... wanna race?"

"Okay. To the far end and back?"

Luke nodded.

At the count of three, they dove into the cool water. Richard was back at the starting point waiting, with a look of mock superiority in his eyes, when Luke finally caught up. "Guess I'm out of practice," he chuckled.

"A little training would make you a great swimmer."

"Maybe someday you'll give me lessons?"

"I'd be glad to." Richard grinned. He splashed water at Luke's face and dunked his head, holding him under for a few seconds. When Luke's head bobbed up and his mouth gulped for air, Richard splashed him again and yelled, "Catch me if you can!"

He swam away while the other attempted pursuit. Looking back over his shoulder, he slowed his pace, allowing the cowboy to overtake him. Luke dove under, grabbed Richard by the ankles and pulled him down. They wrestled playfully in the middle of the pond until an overpowered Richard gave up. "Okay," he said between deep breaths, "you win."

As the two tread water, Luke placed his hands on Richard's shoulders, then brushed his cheek with the backs of his fingers. Smiling, Richard touched the golden down on Luke's chest. He moved one hand lower to feel the tense muscles of

Luke's washboard stomach, while the other hand gripped the firmness of his thigh. They embraced for a moment, then Luke said, "Let's go." They swam back, climbed out of the water and lay down on a blanket that Luke spread over the hot rock. When completely dry, they moved behind the formation and sat in the shade. Their eyes met. Luke took Richard's hand and held it. One thing led very smoothly to another and by the end of the afternoon, they had attained an intimacy that both had hoped for, but neither had ever thought possible.

* * *

When Laura Mannering had become ill, Widow Turner volunteered to help out. She moved into the teacher's cottage, sleeping on the couch in the front room, to nurse the ailing Easterner. Doc Preston, not certain at first as to the nature of the illness, finally ascertained that it was simply exhaustion. Constant attention and lots of rest were what Laura required, and Widow Turner was an experienced prairie healer.

The afternoon session concluded and the children dismissed, Richard stopped by the cottage, a small A-frame trimmed in white, with shutters, a porch, and a garden in the backyard. Laura was sleeping and Richard gazed at her pale face and long auburn hair, noting that her breaths were long and easy. Quite a change from just a few days before. He leaned over and kissed her forehead, being extra careful not to awaken her.

Widow Turner poured a cup of tea for him and patiently answered all of his questions in the front room, the door to the bedroom slightly ajar. "She's sleeping less and eating more – a good sign. Yesterday she only ate some broth, but I got her to eat a soft-boiled egg this morning." She pulled a strand of gray hair from her forehead and smoothed the folds of her apron.

"And her sleep," asked Richard, "is it restful?"

"Most of the time. She's having fewer nightmares. She

should be fine in no time at all."

Richard thanked her and patted her hand.

The sky was intermittently cloudy that day as Richard left the cottage and made his way down the plank walk. The street was deserted and the town locked in quietude as he approached the bank. Suddenly he heard someone scream for help and a gun shot rang out immediately thereafter. He was about to enter the bank when a man, clutching two large money bags, backed out the door. Richard grabbed him by the shoulder, spun him around and drove his fist into the robber's belly. The felon dropped the booty and fell to the ground, gasping for breath. Richard turned toward the door as another crook, with a six-gun in each hand, walked backwards out the door. Silently coming up behind the gunman, he seized his forearms from the rear and pressed his thumbs into the insides of the man's wrists. He dropped the guns and whirled around, only to have his jaw broken by Richard's swift uppercut. Rubbing his sore knuckles, Richard retrieved the money sacks and walked into the bank to return the loot and conduct his business.

Later that day, Luke strolled into Ruby Rae's, leaned against the bar and waited to be served.

"Hi there, handsome," called out Ruby Rae, her brown eyes sparkling, "the usual?"

"Yes'm."

Before she could get to him with the drink, Trade Watkins, who stood nearby, turned to Luke and smirked. "D'ja hear what happened?"

"No," said Luke, not particularly interested.

"You missed all the action. The schoolmarm beat up on two bank robbers," he chuckled.

"You want to step outside and repeat that?" asked Luke, a look of fury creeping onto his face. Trade realized something was wrong and went for his gun. But Luke, a lot quicker on the draw, shot it out of his hand. He placed his smoking revolver on the bar and said, "Outside."

They stood facing each other on the dusty street.

"You were saying something about –"

"Yeah," said Trade, "the schoolmarm –"

Luke grabbed Trade by his vest and hammered his fist into Trade's mid-section. He pushed him to the ground and fell on him, beating him with his tightly-clenched fists. Trade grabbed a handful of dirt and flung it at Luke's face. Tears obscured his vision and Trade's fist connected with his right eye. They rolled on the ground, kicking and punching, but Trade was no match for Luke and was quick to concede.

Luke slowly stood up, his fists still balled. With a stern voice he said, "The next time I hear you refer to Richard Mannering with anything less than respect, we can pick up where we left off. I'm warning you." He scooped up his hat, dusted it off and re-entered the saloon. After finishing his drink he returned his gun to its holster, tipped his hat to Ruby Rae and strode over to Richard's hotel room. He knocked and entered. "I hear you were a real hero today."

Richard gasped. 'What happened to you? You look like you got into a scrap with a polecat."

"Trade Watkins has a big mouth. I just shut it for him, that's all."

"That's the biggest shiner I've ever seen! Come and sit down over here."

Luke sat on the bed and Richard tended his wounds. He asked what happened and Luke told him. Shyly. Richard laughed. "Words can't hurt me ... you shouldn't have gone to so much trouble."

"I couldn't help it. I, uh, think I love you."

* * *

Jason T. Starrett, the bank president, gave Richard a reward – which he accepted reluctantly – and also insisted that Richard and a friend have dinner at Ruby Rae's, courtesy of the bank. Richard protested. "I just did what any honest person would have done."

"You must accept our acknowledgment of your noble

deed. Just think, Mr. Mannering, it may cause others to become as conscientious as yourself." He clasped his hands and rested them on his rounded paunch.

Richard finally gave in, thanked the man, and invited Luke to dine with him on the following evening.

A large, noisy crowd was assembled in the smokey saloon. There were weary cowpokes, hungry travellers and fast women. Some folks were eating and drinking, some gambling, while others were just listening to L. Washington Jones, the piano player. Recently arrived from St. Louis, the thin man with the gold tooth knew all the latest ragtime tunes.

When Ruby Rae placed the food before Luke and Richard – who sat adjacent to one another at a small, corner table – she eyed the cowboy and said, "I'm not doing anything later. Yourself?"

Luke looked away, embarrassed. "Aw shoot, Ruby Rae, you don't ever give up, do you?"

"Well, I just think a man like you could use a woman like me."

Luke blushed and struggled for something to say. Ruby Rae turned to Richard and said, "See if you can talk some sense into this fool."

"Madam," he almost choked, "I'll see what I can do."

When she turned to walk away, Richard winked at Luke. Luke deliberately dropped his spoon on the floor. The two men bent down to fetch it. When their faces came close together, their lips met for a brief, unobserved kiss. They sat upright and Luke tucked his napkin under his chin.

"How's Laura doing?"

"Growing stronger every day. I guess she was probably working too hard. That and the new territory must have been quite a strain. Widow Turner says she'll be up and around in no time."

Luke cut into his thick steak. "And what will you do when she's back at the schoolhouse?"

"Look around for work of some kind. I'm thinking of settling here for a while."

"To keep an eye on Laura?"

Richard casually sipped his wine and gestured toward Luke's swollen eye. "I was thinking about keeping an eye on you!"

Luke grinned. And winced. "Ouch," he said, and nodded at the bandage around Richard's knuckles. "You want me to cut up your steak?"

Richard laughed. Then smiled. They slowly ate the large meal – occasionally holding hands underneath the table – until they finished their coffee and were ready to depart.

"Schoolmarm" first appeared in *Mandate*

Hammerthrower

Tom looks at the computer and waits for the screen to change. He senses Bentley staring at him, still angry because he was late. He'd had to stand in line at the post office. When he'd finally reached the window, the woman rummaged in the back for what seemed like an hour, only to return and hand him the package claim slip.

"It's probably been misfiled," she'd explained. He wanted to scream. *You stupid bitch! I'm late for work already ... doesn't anything in this fucked-up city ever work?* But he'd smiled, given her his phone number so she could contact him when the package was found. "Thank you," he'd said and marched out the door. He muttered four-letter words and cursed the whole of civilization while racing to work. And finally ceased his ranting when he realized that people were looking at him the same way he looks at the ones who stand on street corners or sit in subway cars mouthing unintelligible nonsense. He quietly hummed an old song his grandfather used to sing while rapping on a banjo, "I'll Be Glad When You're Dead You Rascal, You."

"Code Entry" flashes on the screen and Tom wants to turn and look at Bentley as if to say, *See how fast I'm working, making up for lost time.* But Bentley is unaware of him, too busy cackling into the telephone, telling one of his friends about the utterly fabulous, too hot to mention – you won't believe it, darling – opening he'd been to the night before. When Tom had entered the business office, Bentley looked at his wristwatch, smiled lecherously and said, "If you had woken up with me, you wouldn't be late." Tom wished he had the nerve to reply, *If I'd woken up with you I'd have slit my wrists.*

Tom concentrates on the screen and begins to enter the new computer codes. He is halfway down the list when Bentley hangs up.

"Oh, Tom?"

"What."

"Did you see the memo about new code construction? We have to start using a new system so that the income earned from subscribers, general public and donations will be differentiated from each other, according to the run of the play, in quarterly segments."

"Oh?" He feels like smashing his fist through the computer screen but turns and fakes a smile. "There was nothing in my box about it," he pleads innocently. *Why didn't you tell me before I started, you dumb jerk.*

Bentley shuffles some papers on his desk and holds out the memo. "Here it is. I'm sure you'll be able to understand it without any explanation from me. I have a meeting with the Big Cheese in fifteen minutes, so let me tell you about the wonderful new play I saw last night. It's about a mother of six who's dying of cancer and she wins the New Jersey lottery and ..."

Bentley's voice drones on and Tom seizes key words like 'comic,' 'intermission,' 'farce,' and 'direction,' but doesn't really listen, while thinking about how lonely he was when he woke up that morning. So lonely that he'd thought of Palmer Whittington for the first time in years. He began to evaluate his prospects and realized that the only person who has any sexual allure for him is the carpenter renovating the administrative offices above the off-Broadway theater. He'd started calling him Hammerthrower – too shy to try and find out his name – and as he thought of the hard, beefy body that always passed by his desk, his cock had woken up and reminded him that it had been a long time since he'd been naked with any-one. Brad, one of his best friends, is dying from AIDS and Tom is afraid for Brad and himself. The health crisis terrifies him. Moreover, he hasn't met anyone interesting for quite a while. And Hammerthrower, six feet, one hundred and eighty-five pounds of animal grace, passes by dozens of times every day and smiles. But so far nothing has been said. *He's probably straight anyway.*

"... and at the end I didn't know if I should laugh or cry. It's that good. Best play of '85. Mark my words. I think I can get you a pair of comps. Interested?"

"A farce about cancer and lotteries? I'd rather watch a pineapple rot."

"Bitch! I try to be a nice guy ..."

Asshole.

"... and offer you two free tickets ..."

Just so you can get me into bed, you miserable old queen.

"... and you sit there making fun of a strong contender for the Pulitzer Prize ..."

Shut up already, fatso.

"... well, that's what I call gratitude."

"I'm sorry," says Tom, "just doesn't sound like my kind of play. And you know me, I'll say anything for a laugh."

"Well, I'm not laughing."

"I said 'I'm sorry'."

Tom turns to the computer terminal as Bentley walks out of the office, shaking his head. The phone on Bentley's desk begins to ring but Tom ignores it, preparing the new codes. He works it out so that each of the twelve possible financial entries can be immediately identified and retrieved with a series of six-digit numbers that indicate quarter, year and source. Satisfied that Bentley will find nothing to correct or complain about, he steps out of the office to fetch a cup of coffee. He spots Hammerthrower by the coffee machine and ducks into Claire's office.

"Good morning, Claire. How's Frick?"

"Impossible, as usual. How's Frack?"

"Obnoxious, as usual." They both grin.

"How about a cup of coffee," says Claire. "Rasputin and Scrooge should be in their meeting for at least a couple of hours."

"I'd love some. But you'll have to get it."

Claire removes her glasses and shakes out her hair. "Why me?"

"'Cause Hammerthrower's hanging out by the coffee machine and if I tried to pour a cup with him so close I'd probably scald myself."

"Gimme a break!"

"I mean it. He really turns me on."

"He turns *all* of us on."

"Claire, do you know anything about him? Anything at all?"

"Nope. But if you want I can find out his name, address and social security number."

"Would you? Find out his name, I mean?"

"No problem. Coffee?"

"I'll answer your phone and take messages."

He sits at her desk, looking at her plants and ceramic knick-knacks. Why can't I meet a guy who's as nice as Claire, romantic as Palmer and sexy as Hammerthrower?

The phone rings and Tom grabs the receiver. "Hello?"

"Where's Claire? This is Mrs. Goldstein and I'm a subscriber and I just wanted to let you know that me and my husband – he's a doctor – really didn't like the last play and if you want us to subscribe again you're going to have to –"

"Excuse me, Mrs. Goldstein, would you hold please?" Click. "Hello?"

"Is Claire around?"

"She stepped out for a minute, can I take a message?"

"This is William."

The phone rings again. "Hold, please." Click. "Hello?"

"This is Robert down at the theater and our temperamental director just slugged out our temperamental leading man and they are consequently not talking, so I was wondering if Claire could come down and –"

"Hold, please."

Claire enters with two steaming styrofoam cups.

"Thank God you're back. I've got an angry subscriber on one, your boyfriend on two and a flustered production manager on three. How do you make it through a whole day of this?"

"Sex and drugs don't hurt."

"I leave you to your calls."

"How about lunch?"

"I'll stop by around 12:30."

"Becky," she says into the receiver, waving goodbye, "hold my calls for a while." Click. "Mrs. Goldstein? This is Claire. How are you today?"

Tom walks back to the business office with the coffee and begins to sort out the previous evening's box office receipts. A few minutes later he hears a knock at the door.

"Hi," says Hammerthrower, smiling.

"Oh, hi," says Tom. *Oh my God, I can't believe it, he spoke to me.* Tom clears his throat. "C-C-Can I help you?"

"Yeah. My name's George." He walks over and extends his hand.

"Tom." They shake.

"I've been doing some renovating around the office ..."

As if I hadn't noticed.

"... and there was a slight mistake on my paycheck ..."

I'll fix it, I'll fix it!

"... Look, see here? The decimal point is in the wrong place."

Tom looks at the check, then at George's bulging biceps, then back at the check.

"It's no problem. I can't change it, but Bentley can as soon as his meeting is over. Would you like to wait?"

"Thanks. Don't let me distract you."

"You can sit down right here," says Tom, indicating Bentley's chair. He turns to the terminal. *Oh, God, he's sitting right there. I wonder if he's looking at me? Okay, calm down, back to work. How can I work? I want to tear his clothes off and lick every inch of his body. Probably not even gay. But maybe.* Tom swivels his chair and faces George. "I've seen you around the office with your hammer and leveler and everything. How's it going?"

"Level."

"Huh?"

"It's called a level, not a leveler."

"Oh, I never knew that ... so, how's it going?"

"Not bad. I should be done in about three weeks."

Three weeks. Gotta move fast. He tries to think of something clever to say. While stammering, waiting for inspiration, George suddenly speaks up.

"You know, Tom, I've been wanting to meet you."

"Me? Why?"

"Ever since I saw you dancing at the Manhole a few weeks ago I've wanted to meet you."

"You go to the Manhole?"

"Sometimes. When I feel like dancing."

Okay, so he goes to the Manhole. That doesn't mean he's gay.

"Since I broke up with my lover I've been getting out more."

He said lover, not girlfriend. Could this be true? "Oh, you just broke up," says Tom sympathetically. "I hope it wasn't too messy."

"Actually, I think he'll turn out to be a good friend."

I can't believe it. He's gay. What'll I say? Tell him how horny and lonely I've been? No. I'll ask him if he wants to see a movie with me next –

"I was wondering if you'd like to go dancing sometime?"

"You mean, with you?" Tom almost chokes.

"Of course."

"God, that would be great, how about –"

Bentley suddenly appears at the door. "My, my, party going on?" He looks at Tom, points to the computer and walks over to George. "Good day, Sir. I'm Bentley, the business manager. What can I possibly do for you?"

Tom turns to the computer and tries to ignore the conversation, with little success.

"... so I just have to get my paycheck straightened out and everything will be fine."

"Hmm, let me see. Oh, this is easy. I'll make out a new one right away. Oh my dear, such arms! Which gym do you go to?"

"I don't go to a gym."

"I guess you naturally athletic guys don't have to."

"Actually, I'm not very athletic. Pretty handy, though."

"I'll bet you are. There you go."

"Thank you," says George.

"Perhaps we can get together sometime, lunch maybe? You can tell me all about how handy you are."

"Well, gee I don't know, Bentley? Bentley, well, that sounds nice, but I don't think my wife would understand. Bye."

Tom looks up and George winks at him as he exits. Bentley sits down and sighs, "Not a bad piece of meat, eh Tom? Too bad he's not on our team."

* * *

Tom grasps the familiar doorknob with a trace of anxiety, not knowing what to expect. *Maybe a circus? No, it's a week night. A morgue, perhaps ?* The door swings out, the red lights and loud music dancing out onto the sidewalk as he steps inside, glances around. The door closes behind him, imprisoning the sights and sounds within the bar's angular geometry. Not too crowded, but not dead either. There's a punk with studded ears and a tattoo of a scar on his cheek. *Thought they didn't allow those types west of Third Avenue.* Tom looks away before their eyes can connect.

Negotiating the bar. At the end near the door, pretty Derrick mixes a row of drinks with post-modernist choreography. *Too full of himself. Enough attitude to crash the sound barrier.* Tom makes his way to the far end of the bar and Arthur, *very nice, though he always seems so nervous,* hands him a light beer. He smiles and Tom smiles back, handing him a five. He waits for the change, leaves a twenty-five cent tip and walks to the jukebox.

Bruce Springsteen is moaning about "Dancing In the Dark" and Tom tries to imagine the rock star from New Jersey without clothing. *Nice.* Springsteen is replaced by Gloria Gaynor shouting, "I Am What I Am" as Tom moves to his favorite spot, near the cigarette machine. The speaker above thrusts slinky bass lines that keep his hips gyrating even when he's not crazy about the song itself.

He sips the beer and pictures Palmer Whittington right beside him. Married to Elizabeth. Probably has two kids. Hires skinny hustlers and fucks them in motels in and around Baltimore and Washington. Waiting for Papa Whittington to die and leave him the undertaking business. Shit.

Tom lights a cigarette and surveys the crowd. Plenty of flat stomachs and round butts but some are too young, too old or too hairy. Almost everyone has a moustache and beard. Tom likes the look but hates the feel of bristly hair scratching his face. He recalls the time his lips were scraped until they felt like sandpaper.

He notices a cute guy with a hard, compact body leaning against the bar. His moustache looks soft, like corn-husk fibers. Not bad. I'll just stand here, try to look like I'm not too interested, but willing. When he glances this way I'll smile. He'll smile back. I'll wait a second to see if he makes a move. If not, I'll just walk right over and shake his hand. The name's Tom. Pleased to meet you. I'll tell him about the theater and look into his eyes, accidentally on purpose brush his hip with my hand. He'll kiss me and suggest that we go to his apartment –

A man with build, facial hair and coloring, all similar to Tom's intended, enters his field of vision and joins the man whom Tom is mentally seducing. They kiss, exchange a few words and are out the door, while Tom silently curses, wondering if they're friends or lovers. *Probably lovers,* he decides, grateful that he hadn't yet made the move that would have resulted in rejection and embarrassment.

The throbbing bass line that buoys the Supremes leaps out of the speakers and Tom's body is enslaved by the rhythm. "You Can't Hurry Love" he sings along in a silent falsetto, his free hand adding punctuation to the lyric. He throws the cigarette butt to the floor and stomps it out as two slim Hispanic guys enter the bar, whispering in each other's ear, tittering over some private joke.

He remembers being fifteen. Mr. and Mrs. Whittington were away for the weekend. Palmer invited Tom to spend the night. Tom told his parents the invitation had come from Mrs. Whittington. They danced together for the first time in Palmer's rich-kid bedroom. The soundtrack provided by the Supremes. Then they slept together. Waking up at short intervals all night long, tentatively touching each other's body. *Gotta stop thinking about Palmer, concentrate on Hammerthrower, I mean George. Maybe tomorrow I'll just walk over to him and –*

"How ya doin'? Sam's the name. What's yours?" Tom turns his head to the left, the direction the voice comes from. A short, balding man with a jelly-belly smiles and offers his hand. Tom refuses it and looks away. He almost delivers his lecture on cruising etiquette. *It's not fair to approach a stranger in a bar who has not had the opportunity to indicate whether he is interested. Attacks from the rear are an intrusion. Definitely not in good taste.*

"Fuck you," says Sam, wandering away like someone had just kicked his teeth in. Tom wonders what Sam's response would have been like if he'd delivered the lecture. He envisions him sobbing and is glad he's kept quiet.

He sips the beer and looks around. Not much to choose from. Derrick leans against the bar, as though posing for a Calvin Klein ad while Arthur, *nice, average-looking Arthur* pops beer cans and mixes cocktails. An older man – overweight, wearing a tacky toupée – hovers near the jukebox and Tom thinks that the sight of this man naked would probably make him throw up.

The Mutant Slime jump out of the speakers extolling the

pleasures of "The Road To Hell" amid the chainsaw buzz of decibel-crazed electric guitars. *This ought to wake everyone up.*

The door opens and Carlton, an ex-trick, enters. *Oh no!* Tom hopes that Carlton will not notice him. He remembers going to Carlton's apartment one night, expecting the usual kissin' and huggin', suckin' and fuckin', only to discover that Carlton's primary pursuit is having his face straddled. Tom, not wanting to appear rude, sat on Carlton's face, embarrassed, wishing he had not accepted the invitation to spend the night. When Carlton said, "Okay, let 'er go," Tom had no idea what he meant. "Bombs away!" urged Carlton and Tom, suddenly enlightened, got up, dressed faster than he ever had before and left in silence. If Carlton approaches, Tom will say I *don't shit on command,* a phrase he has prepared for such an occasion.

Carlton wanders past and Tom recalls the one time he was able to think of a clever, spontaneous rejoinder. Always terrific with snappy quips long after they could be useful, Tom fears that he is doomed to always thinking, *If I'd only said* ... But the muse had come to his rescue when his parents had found some physique magazines beneath his bed when he was sixteen. Confronting their son, Tom's father looked blank as his mother queried, "Are you a homo?" With matchless timing Tom answered, "All day, every day and all through the night." Shaken at first by his confession, his parents were reassured by the confidence with which he'd replied. As though he could take care of himself and handle any situation. The subject was never brought up again, however, his parents did not reenter his room until he'd moved away, and they acted like they'd never found out.

Tom leaves the beer can on the ledge that runs around the periphery of the room and Arthur has one ready for him when he reaches the bar. "Thanks," he says, handing the money to Arthur.

"On the house," says Arthur who taps the bar, smiles, and turns to refill the ice tray.

Willie Nelson sings "All Of Me" and Tom hums along even though Ol' Willie records too frequently and suffers from overexposure. Too bad. A handsome black man with a sexy bubblebutt and muscular thighs walks toward the jukebox, and though Tom likes his body and smooth skin, the beads and cowrie shells braided to the man's scalp cause his interest to subside. He's back at his usual spot and directly behind him, two men are talking a little too loudly.

"This is the third time in less than four months that someone I know's been diagnosed with AIDS. It's scary."

"I read something about a strain of virus recently detected in sheep and it said –"

"Sheep? Are you kidding? First it was pigs, now it's sheep ... I don't want to talk about it."

And I don't want to hear about it. Tom remembers all of the good times he's had with Brad, Steve and Patrick – dinners, discos and drugs before separating to search for sex – and now Brad is lying in a hospital bed, just waiting to die. *Life sucks!*

Willie Nelson is nudged off the turntable by Patti Smith and Tom goes to the john. He places his beer on the sink and pees, then takes a joint from his cigarette pack. Three large tokes are drawn and exhaled, the joint stubbed out and reunited with the cigarettes. He returns to his usual spot. "Girls Just Want To Have Fun" he sings and sways, the grass relaxing him completely. He peers at the crowd through new eyes and sees a handsome, thirtyish guy at the bar. He smiles. The guy smiles back. Tom is by his side.

"Hi. Tom."

"Jean-Hugh."

"Huh?"

"Jean-Hugh," he says very slowly. They shake hands.

"You come here often?"

"No, just visiting."

Shit! "Where are you from?"

"Montreal."

"That's nice." Tom looks at Jean-Hugh and thinks about

all of the tourists he's entertained since moving to New York. And how each one took a tiny piece of his soul away. *There's Guy in Chicago, Michael in Shreveport, Justin in Albuquerque, even Bruno in Zurich. But what good are they so far away?* He decided to get involved sexually only when there is the possibility for some kind of relationship other than a penpal.

"What do you do?" asks Jean-Hugh.

"I'm an accountant. It's pretty boring." Tom takes advantage of the silence between songs. "Think I'll go and play the jukebox. Nice meeting you." Tom slowly walks to the jukebox, pretends he's inserting some quarters and presses a few random numbers.

The Judds pop out of the speakers and ask, "Why Not Me?" their passionate yearning impossible to ignore. *Goddamn. Another lonely night.* He finishes the beer and walks to the door. *Do I want to go to Video Village and watch the pretty boys swoon over Alexis and Krystle, or do I want to go to sleep?* It takes two seconds to choose his bed over the video screen. He waves to Arthur, leaves the barroom, and embraces the cool night air that's been waiting for him behind the familiar door.

* * *

Tom chuckles to himself as he mentally composes a list of the absurd titles that have been produced at the No Exit Theater: *Moon Pie Gunner, Granny's Beer-Stained Shawl, Play Dead, Racing To Sleep, Things That Go Hump In The Dark.* As auditing time approaches, it's Tom's task to inventory all financial records for the three previous years. Every ledger must balance perfectly, every dime be accounted for, or the theater will lose it's nonprofit status. Each afternoon, Tom checks and double-checks the paperwork of a closed production. As Bentley has planned it, he will be right on schedule for the auditing team that will appear in two weeks. Bentley sits at his desk reading the reviews of the play about motherhood, cancer and the New Jersey lottery. Tom scans figures on the computer screen. The telephone rings and Bentley answers it. "It's for you." He puts the call on hold and hangs up as Tom lifts his receiver.

"Hello." Tom knows Bentley is listening, trying to figure out what's being said on the other end. "Hi, Steve, how are you." Bentley pretends he's still reading. "Fine. Everything's okay. What's up?" Bentley's ear strains to catch any sound that might escape the receiver. "No! It can't be." Panic spreads across Tom's face as he turns away from Bentley. "What time? Was he alone?" Bentley looks at Tom with sympathy. "What do you mean, 'private'?" A tear falls from Tom's eye. "When's the memorial service?" He reaches into his pocket for a hand-kerchief. "Thanks, Steve. I'll call you tonight."

Tom blows his nose. Bentley puts the paper down. "Your friend, the one with AIDS, what's his name?"

"Brad."

"Is it over?"

"Yeah, he died this morning. Christ, thirty-two years old."

"When's the funeral?"

"His family doesn't want any of his queer friends at the funeral. We're going to have our own memorial service next week sometime."

"Can I get you anything?"

"No. Thanks."

"Would you like to take the afternoon off?"

"No, I'm all right. Can't say I wasn't expecting it." Tom decides to change the subject. *Mustn't get too chummy with Bentley, he'd get the wrong idea.* "Besides, who'll go over the accounting for *Crapshit,* I mean *Slapschtick?*"

"Why do you always make fun of our plays? And why do you always tune me out? I want us to be friends."

We can't be friends because I can't stand the sight of you or the sound of your whiny voice. *"I never mix work and friendship."*

"You can come up with a better line than that."

None that I dare say out loud. He punches the keyboard, the green neon digits popping up on the small screen.

"I have a board meeting at three, Tom, and I have to have a quick conference with the Big Cheese beforehand, so I'm leaving now. Take messages and I'll return calls tomorrow morning."

"Okay."

He feeds the computer with one half of his brain and thinks about his career trajectory with the other. He'd started at the theater as a temporary receptionist, and was hired on a permanent, fulltime basis after several months. One year after that he'd been shifted to assistant to the Production Manager and eventually snagged the coveted post of assistant to the Business Manager. As soon as Bentley is promoted to assistant General Manager, Tom will be in charge of the business office. It's an easy job that pays well, and Tom can select his assistant from the pool of underlings waiting for a shot at promotion. After that he'll only have to find his perfect soul mate and life will be everything he could hope for.

He finishes checking the final numbers and returns the data to the memory banks. Lifting the telephone receiver, he dials for an outside line.

"Good afternoon. May I speak with Patrick, please. This is Tom calling."

"Hold, please."

He drums his fingers on the desk and hums a ditty from his childhood.

"Tom? Patrick here. Have you heard about Brad?"

"Yeah. Steve called a little while ago."

"I just spoke to him."

"How do you feel?" asks Tom timidly.

"Like shit. You?"

"Worse than shit ... you want to meet at the bar after work, try to drown it a bit?"

"That'd be good."

"See ya there." He buzzes reception and gets Becky on the line. "I'm stepping out of the office for a while and Bentley's at a meeting. Could you hold the calls, please?" He walks into Claire's office and sits down, waiting until she's off the telephone.

"Always a pleasure talking to you, Mrs. Goldstein," she wrinkles her face in disgust, "'bye now."

"Hi."

"I'm tired of that old bitch," sighs Claire.

"I'm tired of *that* old bitch," says Tom, hiking his thumb toward the business office.

"So, what's new? Quick, before the phone rings."

"You want the good or the bad first?"

"Hmmm, the good."

"I met Hammerthrower yesterday. His name's George and he's on my team."

Claire shakes her head. "That's a relief. I thought there was something wrong with my hair! And what's the bad news?"

"My friend, Brad, the one I told you about –"

"The one with AIDS?"

"Yeah."

Claire places her hands on Tom's knees. "I'm so sorry, for him, for you. All you guys. I know it must be rough."

"Thanks for letting me get it off my chest. It really helps."

"Tom? You wanna meet me on the roof later? We'll smoke a joint, talk a bit. Might help."

"What time?"

"Three-thirty. The board meeting should just be getting underway."

"Sounds great."

"Be there or be square," she intones.

"Later."

Tom steps out into the hall, walks to the men's room and enters. He's alone. He washes his face with cold water, and is drying his hands on a paper towelette as the door swings open.

"Tom, how are you?"

"George!" They shake hands, study each other's face and both begin talking at the same time.

"Go ahead," says George.

"I just wanted to apologize for Bentley, interrupting us that way yesterday."

"Is he like that all the time?"

"You mean pompous and overbearing? Yeah, it's what he does best."

"Doesn't he get on your nerves?"

"Yup, he drives me crazy. But I think he'll be promoted soon and then everything'll be okay."

George smiles. "I think we were talking about going dancing sometime."

Tom blushes. "I'd really like that."

"You free tonight?"

Tom almost spills the news about Brad, but quickly reconsiders. *There's plenty of time to compare AIDS notes.* "I can't make it tonight. But anytime after."

"How about tomorrow night?"

Tom wants to embrace George, lick his ear and press their bodies together. A slight shudder tiptoes up his spine. "Tomorrow night is perfect."

George hands Tom a business card. "My phone number. Call me after work tomorrow and we'll arrange something. You want to go to the Manhole?"

"That would be fun."

They both wait for the other to make a move or say something, but they remain still and silent. Tom leans forward as George wraps his arms around his waist and draws him closer. Breathless, they squeeze each other and bring their lips together, jumping apart as the door swings open. They both nod at the intruder, an auditioning actor, no doubt.

"Well," says Tom.

"Well," says George, "I'll stop by the office later and pick up that W-2 form."

"Right-O," says Tom, "see you later." He walks back to the office, touching the pocket that contains the card with George's number. *I hope there's a kind soul with smelling salts around when I realize what just happened and faint.* He throws back his head and laughs out loud. Entering the business office, he hums a happy tune that's been dancing in his memory for as long as he can remember.

73

Love's Jealous Fury

"This corset is *killing* me! There's a stay poking my right arm-pit ... and it hurts!" Alex walked to the mirror in the small, box-like room that reeked of unlaundered sweat socks. The mustard-yellow carpet and mayonnaise-white walls seemed to match the stale odor. Vincent sighed and struggled with the zipper, finally yanking it, in fits, to the neckline. "Can I breathe now?" gasped Alex.

"Don't you dare. There'll be sequins and bugle beads em-bedded in the walls, floor and ceiling."

Alex eyed himself in the three-way mirror and frowned. "Magenta is definitely not my color." He turned to the left and looked over his shoulder. "And this wig! It's all wrong. I should've brought the Veronica Lake."

Vincent removed the cigarette from his lips and stubbed it out. Grabbing the hairbrush which lay alongside the ash-tray, he advanced toward the mirror. "Perhaps if I tease it up a bit here and there. You know, you really don't look too bad. I've known *real* girls who would kill for your waist," he said, sucking in the stomach that bulged slightly over his jeans. "There! Is that any better?"

Alex turned to the right and scrutinized his image. "Hmmm, that's not too bad ... maybe a bit more rouge. What do you think?"

"I think you're nuts, but don't let that stop you. Did I tell you this was crazy? Did I?"

Alex waddled to the vanity table. "This girdle is too tight."

"You don't even have the heels on yet and you're moving like a Mack truck."

Alex sat down very slowly and groaned.

Vincent grimaced. "Successful women authors, when they are sitting down, do not open up like the gates to Buckingham Palace. Put those legs together!"

Someone pounded on the thin door. "Five minutes!"

"Thank you," said Alex. Vincent pinched his arm. "Er, thank you," he purred, stretching his voice two octaves higher.

"You've got to be more careful," whispered Vincent.

"I know, I know." Alex stared wistfully into the light bulb-encrusted vanity mirror. "And I still have to get these gargantuan feet into those tiny shoes. Would you give me a hand?"

"Of course. That's why God created literary agents."

* * *

The three-piece band attempted a Vegas fanfare beneath the burning kleig lights and Don James, wearing a blue serge suit with a plum-colored ascot, beamed a smile into Camera One. The studio audience roared on cue.

"And now, ladies and gentlemen, my next guest is the lovely and tantalizing author of the book that *everyone* is talking about. The woman who created *Love's Jealous Fury,* Antonia Harlequinette!"

The applause sign lit up and the crowd clapped wildly as she sashayed to the empty chair by the host's desk.

"Antonia, you, of course, know Biff LeGrande."

"Why yes, we met backstage."

The football star/deodorant salesman stood up and pumped her gloved hand. "A pleasure."

"Oh Biff, the pleasure's all mine!" She waited for Don and Biff to sit and finally realized they were waiting for her.

Lowering herself into the plush chair, she smoothed the folds of her gown, tearing off a few hundred beads. They scattered on the floor and everyone pretended not to notice.

"So, Antonia, are you enjoying the success of your new book?"

"Well, Don, I'd be lying if I denied it."

"It's been a bestseller for months. Were you surprised?"

"One can never predict what people want to read. One simply writes and hopes for the best. Have you read it?"

"Well, uh, not yet, but it's right at the top of my list."

"That's such a comfort," she said, toying with the cameo that dangled in the hollow of her throat.

"Tell me, Antonia, what inspired you to write this story?"

"I'll tell you, Don, I just observe what's going on around me and turn it into literature."

"Are you saying that your book is autobiographical?"

"Not exactly. Helen Handworker, that's the heroine, she has some of my character traits, but mostly it's from my imagination. I mean, I would never shoot a man in bed. I'd at least wait until he got dressed." She waited for the yucks but the laugh sign did not flicker. The color slowly returned to the cheeks of Don James. He mumbled something that was inaudible and, retaining his composure said, "We'll be right back after this brief message."

All eyes focused on the monitors. Sandwiched in between the one about starving children and the one about dog food was a commercial for Secure. Biff LeGrande, grimy and sweating, sits down on the locker room bench and sighs. Then, he's taking a shower, the camera ogling his ample chest and arms. Now, he's standing in front of his locker, a white towel wrapped around his waist, holding a red and blue cylinder. "Be safe with Secure. Confidence in a can." Suddenly fourteen jiggly blondes surround him, pawing and shrieking. He appears to be enjoying the attention.

The bandleader signalled the familiar eight bars, and the applause sign flashed its message with urgency.

"Welcome back, ladies and gentlemen. I'm sitting here

with Biff LeGrande, who just gave one of his characteristically scintillating locker room performances, and Antonia Harlequinette, the author of *Love's Jealous Fury*. Tell me, Antonia, are you married?"

"No."

"Have you ever been?"

"Well, yes, I mean no, not in the legal sense."

"You've *lived* with men?"

"That's right. And women."

Don James shook his hand as if he'd placed it on a hot waffle iron. "Not at the same time, I hope!" He chuckled at his own joke and the laughter and applause signs roused the audience to hysteria.

"Gosh," said Biff, "that sounds pretty racy to me!"

Antonia cast him an icy glance.

"But sexy too!" he added.

"So, Antonia," said the host, "are we to assume that you don't approve of marriage?"

She tossed her hair over her shoulder and moistened her lips. "Not for myself. A great writer must have many love affairs. Marriage only gets in the way." She waited for a response but the laughter sign lay dormant and the audience remained silent.

"Well," said Don, "Antoniait'sbeengreattalkingtoyou hurrybackandseeusagainsometimeokay? Nowafterabriefmessagewe'll bebackwithournextguest."

* * *

"You were sensational!" A happy Vincent hugged a sheepish Alex.

"You don't think I blew it?"

"Blew it? You were on television! It'll sell books! This is America!"

Alex pulled the wig from his head and reached around to unzip his gown. "It's a good thing they don't have a sign that says *attack*." He removed the shoes. "Do you really think I was convincing as ... a woman? I mean –"

A fist pounded the dressing room door.

"Uh, who's there?" chimed Antonia.

"It's Biff. Biff LeGrande."

"Just a moment, please." Hastily replacing the wig, she strode to the door and flung it open like Loretta Young on methedrine. "Come in, come in. This is my agent, Vincent Spinetti. Vince, meet Biff LeGrande."

The two men shook hands as Antonia closed the door. Biff glanced around the room, then fixed his eyes on Antonia. "You may have fooled the bimbos out in televisionland, but you didn't fool me for one second."

Antonia stiffened. "Why, Biff, whatever do you mean?"

"Come off it, sweetie." He pulled the wig from Antonia's head and, pushing his hair from his forehead, put it on. Swaggering toward the mirror, he placed his hand on his hip and studied his reflection. "This is definitely more me than you."

Antonia gasped. Vincent looked stunned.

"Just between us," said Biff, studying the makeup on the table, "I won the Miss Drag San Francisco contest in 1982."

Vincent suppressed a giggle. "You?"

"Moi," he said, "and I could probably win it this year too, if I had the time. I have a collection of wigs and gowns that makes Antonia's –"

"Alex."

"Alex's wardrobe look like rags."

"I never would have guessed," said Vincent.

"Me neither," said Alex.

"When I retire from football I'm planning on opening a chain of drag boutiques: LeGrande Dames – feminine attire for the discriminating man."

Alex and Vincent looked at one another in astonishment. "Well, I've got to go now," said Biff.

"See you on the Carson show," said Alex.

"You bet." He departed, slamming the door.

Alex whispered, "He's very cute."

"He's not your type," said Vincent, "he's mine."

Alex moaned. "If I don't get out of this corset soon I'll kill myself. I feel like I'm in a Chinese finger trap."

"It's a good thing we brought the muumuu. Here."

Alex undressed and slipped into the comfy folds of pink and green cotton. "So, it's back to the hotel."

"Right." Vincent lit a cigarette.

"And tomorrow?"

"Baltimore. It'll be a snap. You're to be the Guest of Honor at a fund-raising luncheon for the Elks."

"Are you *serious?*" Alex sat down and put on his bunny slippers.

"No. Actually, you're going to address a group from Women Against Pornography."

"VINCENT!"

"Okay, okay, just kidding. It's a symposium on violence at a Romance Writer's Workshop."

"I think I can handle that."

"One thing, Alex?"

"Yes?"

"A bit less mascara, perhaps, and uh, no more bugle beads. Okay?"

The Bold Sailor

Time itself cannot touch you. It is the measurement, the containment, the stretching and contracting of the moments that leaves scars. My friends say that I will forget. Or that he will come back. As if the two were dependent. But something tells me he will never come back. And I know that I will never forget him. I can count on this – on myself. Not that I am so remarkably reliable. It just seems that everything else is much less so.

I had noticed him sitting across from me on the subway. He smiled and I imagined a terrific body beneath the loose-fitting designer jeans, but I looked away. I never smile on the subway or in bars. The consequences could be dangerous. That night he walked over to me at the bar. Was it a coincidence that I'd seen him earlier, or had he been following me around? I'm still not certain. Blond and balding slightly, his hard body packed into old Levi's, he had a tattoo on his right bicep: USN.

"What d'ya call that there you're drinkin'?" he asked.

"I don't call it anything, it's ..."

"Vodka and cranberry juice."

"That's correct," I said. I was surprised but tried not to show it.

"I been watchin' them makin' your drinks for a few nights now. I wanted to buy you one but didn't know what to call it."

"Vodka and cranberry juice."

"Right." He looked at me nervously, expecting me to say something, so I did.

"What's USN?"

"Huh?"

I touched his arm. "The tattoo."

"United States Navy."

"You used to be a sailor?"

"Still am. But I'm gettin' out soon. You?"

"I'm a painter."

"Pictures or houses?"

"Paintings. And I work at the library."

"The liberry?"

"No, the library."

I didn't make it easy for him; I never make it easy for anyone. A man's got to be careful. But I liked him and invited him to my loft. We spent the night together. I didn't find out his name until the following morning.

* * *

I'm always thinking about the time I spent with him. It's involuntary. I try to hold onto the good memories and not feel the pain. Difficult. Would I rather not have the memories at all? No, these are all I have to treasure, though the reminder of my present loneliness is the price. The sailor comes and goes, leaving behind a trace of salty sea air. I sniff and it stings my nostrils.

I know the songs of sailors. From before the steam engine. When ships sailed into the unknown on muscle-power and sweat. Men sang songs to make the work go easier. And the songs of home that lulled them to sleep at night. To dream about the loved ones. Some were content living among all that manpower. Others dreamed that the Captain's pretty cabin boy was a girl in disguise.

There among the barflies, so many hairdressers in cowboy drag, was what I'd been searching for. A man who loved men. I presumed he possessed all of the fine attributes of manhood: honesty, courage, ambition. Neither an intellectual or a disco queen. He'd never seen a Broadway show or been to the opera. I was amazed.

The morning after our first night together he nudged me with his knees and asked if I was awake. I turned and looked at his cheery face. I offered to make some coffee and he finally introduced himself. "By the way, m'nam Wayne. Wayne Bedford."

We shook hands. The first time I'd ever done that in bed. He hugged me. We kissed. He started to tickle me but it was far too early for laughter. I jumped out of bed and heated some water.

We got together again that night and the next morning I persuaded him to remove his belongings from the YMCA and spend the rest of his leave with me. There was so much that I wanted to discover about sailors and I figured he might learn a few things from me as well.

* * *

I know the songs of the sea. From before scientists started taping the sounds of whales and dolphins to be vivisected by musicologists. I have the records that Wayne bought for me. *Whaling and Sailing Songs From The Days of Moby Dick, Blood Red Roses.* And I found one at the library called *We'll Go To Sea No More.* Tough songs about hard work, squalid lives and treacherous companions. Gentle songs about love and separation.

Perhaps he joined the Navy because of some romantic dream about the old times. He knew that the days of piracy and adventure were over. But he'd been raised in a coastal fishing town in New England, originally settled by Portuguese immigrants. The tales and songs had been passed down from father to son for generations. But being out on the sea in the Twentieth Century was something different. The latest news, political and cultural, is not foreign to the modern sailor unless he chooses isolation in order to escape contemporary life. I was never certain about Wayne's motives. Every time I asked him to tell me about the Navy all he ever said was, "Drank a lot. More than you'd believe. Smoked a lot of hash. Had guys in every port. You can have an Eyetalian or an A-rab for a song." Then he'd wink and laugh. A deep, throaty chortle that would redden his cheeks and make his eyes shimmer. "But nothing like you," he would add and wrap his arms around me, kissing and squeezing, summoning something from within that would smolder and ignite until the two of us fell asleep, tangled together on damp, rumpled sheets.

* * *

I don't sell many paintings. That is, as many as I should. But I sell more than I did before I met Wayne. He taught me to be more aggressive. And that pleasing people is not sinful.

I remember the first time I showed him my work. My loft has stacks of canvasses everywhere, but I don't think he so much as glanced at one until I asked for his opinion. I selected four recent efforts and leaned them against the empty wall which serves that particular purpose. He lit a cigarette and carefully studied each one. "I don't know what they mean, but I like the colors."

"They don't *mean* anything."

"Then why paint 'em?"

"To create something that is appealing to the eye."

"I like paintin's of flowers and bowls of fruit. Oceans and hillsides. Y'know, stuff that's real."

"Well, my work is ..."

"Work? You call this *work?*" He snuffed out the cigarette and asked if I wanted to go for a drink. I declined and spent the evening reading. He returned a few hours later and made love to me as though atoning for some horrible crime.

The next night he insisted on taking me to dinner. He wanted to go to a semi-fashionable restaurant where the employees and clientele were gay males, and a Lacoste shirt and clean jeans were considered dressy enough. He said and did everything with great formality. I grasped that this was a big event for him and did not correct him when he mispronounced the wine he'd selected. I assumed his pose and acted as though we were at the Captain's table.

Over coffee he told me that he'd decided to terminate his naval career and look for a civilian job. "Could I stay with you and share the rent?" He reached for my hand, gallantly kissed it and smiled. I felt like the one who catches the bouquet at the end of the wedding. He looked like he'd just won the lottery.

* * *

He called last night, the first time in about three months, but he was too drunk to really communicate. I kept asking where he was calling from but never got a coherent answer.

I couldn't sleep. I pictured him stripped to his jockey shorts and recalled the sensation of his skin against my own. I changed positions, stomach down, and tried to think about something else but the images would fly at me, taunting like a horde of angry demons.

I called the library the next morning and told the branch manager that I had the flu. Lots of fluids and plenty of rest, he suggested. I couldn't face the strangers who passed in and out of the book-lined fortress that I fantasized as my own. The people who came in to read or escape the weather never bothered me. And the erudite souls who truly love books, reserve several at once and return them on time are so few. It's the others who occasionally rouse the monster in me. They break spines, fold corners and confuse John Ashbery with John Berryman. I despise them, and by extension, the job. Sometimes, when the library is completely empty and it's just me and all those words, I feel a contentment that I've never found anywhere else. The silence is a symphony of white noise and when I close my eyes I can hear the voices arising from the pages discussing love and death, arguing theories, trading juicy gossip.

My real work is altogether different. I try to capture shapes, colors and textures with oil and canvas. Then I must persuade some suburban harridan to buy the work by convincing her that after I die, which could be anytime considering the squalor of my existence, she shall have made a smart investment. Business is a pursuit that has never interested me, nor have I been successful in mastering its protocol. I suppose I could have found work that pays better than the library. But I probably would not have found the time to paint, and if magically found, not known what to do with it. Wayne said he wanted lots of money. In fact, he informed me, he was one of the few who would know what to do with a fortune, should he ever be in possession of one.

* * *

The money and hashish that he had accumulated for his leave were beginning to disappear; he'd spent two hundred dollars on a three-piece suit. Burnt sienna. I came home from work one day and found him sitting on the bed, his suit disheveled and sweat-soaked. He clutched the classified ad section of the *Times* with several positions circled in pencil. Leaning back, he tossed the paper aside and clasped his hands behind his head. "Well, I registered with an employment agency and they made me up a resume. Resume?" I nodded. "And I'm supposed to call tomorrow."

"How does it feel, job-hunting in the big city?"

"It's fun! Lots of good-lookin' guys everywhere. I got lost, though. Finally just got in a taxi and gave the guy your, I mean our address."

* * *

Ever since Wayne left I have kept myself so busy that time is something that is no longer part of my conscious thought. I cannot gauge or measure it and have lost the ability to control it. I seem to exist apart from – above or below, I'm not certain which – the rush of time. Haven't escaped it. I can feel myself aging. Slowly. But still, somehow, I am removed.

On the third day of Wayne's search for employment I returned home and found him cursing the heat and concrete sidewalks.

"What's the matter?"

"I called my sister to wire me some money 'cause it looks like I might not find a job as fast as I thought. Anyway, she told me that Mom is in the hospital."

"Is it serious?"

"Brain tumor."

"Oh, my God!" I hugged him and comforted him as best as I could.

"I'm gonna catch the 9:47 bus."

"Is there anything I can do? Do you feel like eating something?" He nodded. I glanced at the clock. "Just enough time to get some groceries. After we eat I'll help you pack and we'll go to the station together. All right?"

When I returned from the supermarket, however, he was gone. He'd packed his belongings and left the keys in the mailbox. I could not find a note with a telephone number where he could be reached.

The next day I received a call from the employment agency. Wayne had been accepted for the position of clerk at a "chic private hotel." I said I'd have him call as soon as I heard from him.

I went about my work, absentmindedly, for several weeks, wondering what was going on. Eventually I received my phone bill which registered a long distance call to somewhere in Massachusetts, "between Boston and the Cape," as Wayne had once said. I walked around for a few days with the bill in my pocket, anxious to call, afraid of what I'd find out.

Late at night, a few days later, I dialed. His sister answered. He wasn't there nor did she know where he was stationed. I introduced myself and she said that Wayne had spoken of me. "As long as I have you on the phone," I said, dying of curiosity but fearful that I was intruding, "I'd just like to find out how your mother is doing."

"What do you mean? She's fine, as far as I know."

"I see. That's a relief."

"Did Wayne tell you she was sick or something?"

"In a word, yes."

"Oh, honey, that's just Wayne's way. He's been making up stuff like that ever since he was a kid."

A few days later I received a hastily scribbled note from Wayne in which he apologized for having lied about his mother's health. He went on to explain that he was afraid he'd never find a job and would not allow himself to be supported by another.

I didn't really speak to anyone for weeks. When friends would call I'd say that I was busy and would get back to them when I was able.

I'm desperate to let him know that he'd been accepted for a job, but he usually calls when drunk and never lets me know where he is so that I can write to him. Although he stays in touch, communication is difficult.

All I have now is work, time and memories which function together like an automated Mobius strip. And I still have the records he gave me. There's one song in particular that constantly runs through my mind. It's about a bold sailor who leaves his lover to go to sea, each one keeping half of a broken coin. Years later when they meet, they do not recognize each other at first, but the parts of the coin match perfectly and they realize that they have been reunited. Sometimes I have a dream that is like a surreal film of that song with Wayne and myself as the main characters, mandolins and concertinas snaking across the soundtrack. Only when we meet again we recognize each other instantly. The two halves of the coin, however, do not fit.

"The Bold Sailor" first appeared in *Shadows of Love*

All About Eve

The Clothes Make the Man

Robbie and I were already in our pajamas and bathrobes when the first guests began to arrive. Mr. Williams appeared at the door as a football player, and his wife had on a bonnet, chewed a teething ring and had a plastic training potty strapped around the enormous diaper that clung to her waist. I took their coats as Robbie, fifteen months younger than me, led them into the living room.

"Who was that?" asked Father as I passed by my parents' bedroom.

"Pete and Rona," I said and deposited their outerwear on the bed in the guestroom.

"C'mere and help me," he called just as I was about to rejoin Robbie, sneaking cigarettes and canapes. As I helped Father fasten the large suspenders of his clown costume, he chuckled to himself in the full-length mirror and said, "The clothes make the man!" That was his philosophy of life, and it had been drilled into Robbie and I every time we went shopping for clothes or dressed to go out. This was the first time he had ever said it in jest, though, and I was greatly relieved to discover that he was capable of joking about it.

The doorbell rang again, and after dealing with the coats, Robbie and I stole upstairs to our bedroom, where we had hidden the forbidden booty. We were ecstatic because every year up until this one, we had been exiled to our maternal grandparents' home, while our house was the site of the annual New Year's Eve costume party that was inevitably the talk of the community for several days afterwards. We coughed our way through a cigarette, devoured a handful of tiny wieners, then crept back downstairs and, hiding behind the sofa in the den, watched the costumed figures arrive. Mr. Hurst showed up as Zorro, his wife as Rapunzel, and – we thought it was so funny – the Golds appeared as Steve Lawrence and Edie Gorme, Mr. Gold in a low-cut red lame cocktail gown and wig, Mrs. Gold with her hair slicked back, in chinos and a cardigan.

As the evening wore on and everyone got drunker, Mother and Father kept imploring us to go to bed, while their guests cajoled them into letting us stay. Eventually we were banished to our room, but that was after Barney Josephson let us each have a sip of his scotch and soda in the kitchen when no one else was around.

The next afternoon, Mother and Father insisted on dressing us up in their costumes and taking our picture. Robbie was completely lost inside of Father's clown get-up, but Mother's grass skirt and long black wig fit me perfectly. She demonstrated the hip and hand movements that are associated with Hollywood Hawaiians, and as I started to get into the groove – I was really enjoying myself – Mother said, "Very good, dear!"

I had an idea. "I'll be right back," I said. I ran upstairs and put on a t-shirt and placed two tennis balls between the cloth and my chest. Voila – tits!

As I sashayed down the stairs, hips swiveling and hands undulating, Mother squealed, "Ooo, that's good!"

But Father roared, "Yeah, TOO GOOD! Go back upstairs and change. NOW!"

The Morning After the Night Before

The first thing I remember is being startled into consciousness by the telephone. My first impulse was to roll over and pretend that I couldn't hear the piercing ring, but my effort was stymied by the comatose body that snored loudly by my side. I couldn't recall having invited someone over and figured if I went back to sleep, everything would eventually fall into place. But the phone didn't stop. It occurred to me that it might be important, so I jumped out of bed, which was a mistake, because my head started to reel. I had to sit down for a few seconds. Suddenly my guest sat up and said, "Hey, Cowboy! Aren't you gonna answer it?"

"Yeah, sure," I replied and stumbled across the room to pick up the receiver. It was Michael.

"So, how's the mad kisser of Christopher Street today?"

"Huh?" I managed to enquire.

"I suppose you don't remember anything."

"That's a fair assessment," I mumbled.

"Do you remember when Carl showed up as Mae West?"

"No."

"Do you remember seizing his lipstick and smearing it all over your mouth?"

"Nope."

"Well, you insisted on leaving your lip print on everyone's left cheek."

"Did I really?"

"You most certainly did."

"Are you putting me on?"

"Hell, no!" he replied indignantly. "You made everyone pull down their pants and you kissed all of us on our left cheek, repainting your lips each time."

"You're kidding."

"No I'm not! Even my straight cousin from Schenectady!"

"God! I'm sorry ... but I still can't believe it."

"Go back to sleep and call me later."

"What time is it?" I asked sheepishly.

"About four o'clock. Bye."

I hung up just as this very handsome man, with impeccable pectorals rose from my bed. "G'morning, Hotstuff." He smiled. "You sure know how to kick in the spurs and ride! Uh, which way's the john?"

I showed him the bathroom, and was putting on my robe when the doorbell rang. It was Carl, and he had apparently left Mae West at home. "I'm right on time, just like we planned. Boy, you really stole the show last night! I brought the lipstick along in case you want to do an encore." He stepped across the threshold, put down his bundles and closed the door. "Look, it was too cute to wash off. I put a Band-Aid over it when I showered." He turned around, pulled down his pants and, sure enough, there were my lips in bright scarlet. He refastened the buttons of the black Levi's and, heading for the kitchen with the packages yelled, "I hope you're hungry. I got everything from pâté de foie d'oie to smoked oysters. Champagne too!"

My stomach recoiled in terror and I decided to search for a cigarette. Super-Pecs emerged from the bathroom, winked and sprinted to the bedroom. I heard a loud popping sound and I vaguely recall sitting down on the couch when Carl came out of the kitchen with a bottle and three glasses. Just then, the hunky stranger – whom I still could not recollect meeting, let alone fucking – sauntered into the living room clutching a small mirror with six lines of coke in his right hand, and a fat joint in the other. I believe it was Carl who chimed, "Happy New Year," as we downed the first glass of bubbly, and I recall the aroma of the Columbian smoke as I accepted the joint and drew a large toke.

To be completely honest about this, I can't remember anything after that. But I can vividly recall getting to work the next morning. When I entered the reception area, Sheila stopped typing, scrutinized me from head to toe and, glancing at her watch, chided, "You are exactly seventeen and a half minutes late and you look like *death* ... but I bet you had one helluva better time than I did!"

A Herd of Tiny Elephants

I finished listening to the life story of a stranger, and he excused himself to go to the bathroom. When the doorbell rang, Mark turned away from the circle of people with whom he had been talking and looked at me. Sylvester, his lover, sailed in from the kitchen drying his hands on his pleated, khaki slacks and signaled to Mark that he would answer it. He darted into the foyer as Mark came over to the straight-backed chair where I sat, adjacent to the small, round table bearing family photographs in gilded frames. He reached down and touched my shoulder.

"Follow me," he whispered.

"Who wouldn't?" I asked silently.

He led me down the metallic, circular staircase to the lower level and into the bedroom, a part of the duplex to which I'd never been invited. The moon cast pale yellow trapezoids on the darkened floor. He closed the drapes, the light slowly receding into black, and turned on the light. The room looked like it had been decorated for Valentine's Day. The vermillion drapes were edged with white lace, the scarlet bedspread bedecked with a pattern of hearts and flowers. Cream-colored walls were connected by a crimson trim and the gray carpet flecked with splashes of fire engine red.

He leaned against me, furtively kissed my cheeks and ran his smooth palms up and down my bare arms. I couldn't believe it was really happening. His sharp features, milky complexion and hard body beckoned to me whenever we met, but I trained myself to look without reaching out to touch.

He bit my ear and I dared to grasp the solid arms clothed in off-white raw silk. I suddenly thought of Sylvester. Surely we would be missed. Although there was a party going on, the crowd was not that large that the disappearance of one of the hosts and a guest would remain unnoticed. I was about to say that I was getting nervous, but he shushed me and began to unzip my pants.

"Hmm, no underwear. Just like I thought," he chuckled. He removed a tiny vial of coke from his pocket and sprinkled some on the part of me that lay in his hand. Stooping, he took me into his warm, wet mouth and played me like a flute concerto. After the final cadenza he zipped me up, kissed me for what seemed like a long time and said, "Let's go. I was showing you my elephants." He pointed to the bureau which supported a herd of miniature pachyderms; ebony, jade, blown glass, onyx, ivory, and marble. He picked one up. "This is Jasper." Placing it in my pocket with care, he kissed me again, turned off the light and led me back upstairs.

* * *

I met Mark and Sylvester through mutual friends, Donald and Kirsten, friends of mine who lived down the street from the fashionable boutique where Sylvester worked. In spite of the difference in our sexual interests, Donald and I had become close in college and stayed in touch because of an undying interest in Jack Kerouac and Neal Cassady (actually, he wanted to *be* Kerouac and I wanted to *have* Cassady). Donald has a highly developed sense of fashion, unusual in one so hetero, and enjoyed buying clothes from well-dressed gay men. I went with him to the boutique once and sat in my t-shirt and jeans watching him model Italian slacks, English sweaters, French shirts (I suggested that we grab some tacos and catch a Fassbinder film, but he didn't make the connection). He loved discussing collars and cuffs with Sylvester and would ask for comments and suggestions. Sylvester, an average-looking guy with a small nose and thin lips, getting paunchy as he neared his late thirties, took great delight in dressing a straight man who looked like a teeny-bopper's heartthrob and had no qualms being around gay guys. The two became good friends and eventually introduced each other to their respective lovers.

One night Kirsten made a pot roast and invited me to dinner. She met me at the door of the small one-bedroom apartment in an untucked Oxford shirt (Donald's) and jeans, her straight blonde hair pulled up into a bun. Donald was dressed like a junior executive at his first board meeting.

The meal was wonderful and I complimented the chef. After asking if I was involved with anyone ("Not yet.") she suggested that I be introduced to her "favorite couple."

"Donald, don't you think that Joey should meet Mark and Sylvester?"

"Why?"

"They're married, right?" I asked.

"Well, yes, but they throw fabulous parties and there are always hordes of single gay guys. Have some more string-beans. Isn't that right?"

Donald drained his wine glass. "Yup."

"How about if I invite them to dinner next week? Joey can come too and I'm sure he'll be invited to their next bash."

"Sounds great," said Donald.

"Ditto," I agreed.

I was eager to finally meet some single gay guys. It wasn't often that I met people who were interesting and also available. So I was determined to make a good impression on Mark and Sylvester.

I was the last to arrive, having had to stand in line at the bakery, waiting to purchase a pound of assorted cookies. Donald looked chic in royal blue day-glo parachute pants and a bowling shirt with Dayton, Ohio embroidered on the back and Mona, in script, over his left breast. Sylvester looked like a country squire, so neat were his sweater-vest, tweed trousers, and wing-tips. Mark, Kirsten and I wore jeans and plaids.

Donald tossed a salad, Kirsten baked lasagna, Sylvester brought champagne and Mark stuffed our noses with coke.

"This lasagna is better than my grandmother's," said Sylvester, lifting an overburdened fork.

"Tell Joey about the time you were still a dresser and had to do Ginger Rogers," suggested Donald.

Mark sighed and looked bored. Sylvester ignored him. "She was in town to appear in a benefit for the Actor's Home and someone recommended me to dress and do her hair. First of all, I had to squeeze her into a tiny frock that could barely contain her, Darling, *she's multiplying,* and her hair was so limp I figured she'd been taking it to the cleaners, *literally,* and don't you know, that woman's face has been lifted so many times, she has to look down to look up!"

Kirsten laughed so hard, she fell off her chair and almost choked on a piece of celery. I helped her up and fetched some water. She was fine a few moments later.

When we were finished eating, Donald changed the music from Vivaldi to Steely Dan, then he and Sylvester sat on the couch to discuss *Gentlemen's Quarterly.*

I helped Kirsten and Mark with the dishes. I cleared, she washed and he and I dried. He patted my ass a few times and winked at me once. We rejoined Donald and Sylvester around the coffee table, sipping and snorting, ethnic jokes bouncing from one to another. At the evening's conclusion, both Mark and Sylvester kissed me goodbye and invited me to their next soirée. It was several parties later that Mark introduced me to his little elephant friends.

* * *

I was not at all pleased with the dance instructor whom I'd been over-paying for months, and Kirsten finally convinced me that we should take class together, her teacher being divine. She was right. Also, I didn't mind the trip from Sheridan Square to the Upper West Side and back; it gave me much welcomed reading time. And I got to know Kirsten a lot better. We would occasionally meet for espresso before going to class and began trading dog-eared paperbacks that each of us felt the other *had* to read. A more experienced dancer than I, she would sometimes get a part in an off-Broadway production. Both of us frequently got jobs doing small bits in Industrial Shows, usually for manufacturers of clothing or cosmetics. Between gigs she'd wait tables, walk dogs and babysit. I drove a cab.

It was about two weeks after the last party at Mark and Sylvester's. I had just gotten home from class and was leaving for work when the phone rang.

"Joey? It's Mark. How's Jasper?"

"Oh, just fine. He doesn't eat much, though."

"He'll only eat when you're not looking."

"Oh, I see. How're you, how's Sylvester?"

"Just great, we're both really fine. I called to see if you and Jasper would be available for lunch next Thursday?"

"Yes, we're very available."

"Why don't I drop by your place around noon?"

"Great!"

"Perfect."

Click.

I had to run to get to work on time. I was hailed by two hookers in mini-skirts, reeking of stale honeysuckle, their makeup looking like it had been applied by spray-can wielding graffiti artists. I picked them up at 60th and Park. Despite the loveliness of the evening, they asked to be driven to 55th and Park. After accusing me of taking "the long way" (I knew of no other), they jumped out of the car and ran into a posh building with a doorman. For the small price of twenty-five bucks, he said, he would tell me which apartment they went to. I told him to get fucked. Later on, I picked up a middle-aged man who passed out in the back seat after giving me a Bronx address. I got him there and woke him up. He rolled out of the car, handed me a fifty (thirty-three dollar tip!) and fell asleep on the sidewalk. Typical night.

When I arrived home it must have been around 4:30. I turned on the radio, smoked a joint, and fetched Jasper from my top drawer. I turned him over in my hands and held him up to the light. Carved out of jade, he measured about an inch in height. I noticed that most of Mark's elephants had their trunks to the ground, as if grazing, but Jasper held his heavenward, as though he were about to perform a trumpet solo. Tusks defiantly thrust forward, he stood with his right legs slightly ahead of the left, his tail curving upward, frozen in mid-swing. Tiny lines had been etched on his flanks to suggest the texture of hide and the ears were so thin, they looked like they might actually flap.

When I awoke the next morning he was still clutched in the palm of my hand, bathed in sweat, but no worse for having slept with me.

* * *

Upon arriving at my apartment, Mark hugged and kissed me, then stepped back to survey the space. He walked to the window and looked down at the street, turned and said, "What? No curtains?"

"Lack of disposable cash."

"How long have you been living here?" He looked disapprovingly at the stack of book-filled crates in the corner.

"Almost two years."

"And why haven't you unpacked?"

"Haven't had the time."

I invited him to sit down on my bed, which served as a couch during the day. Lighting a cigarette, he lowered himself slowly, smoothing the wrinkles in the bedspread on either side.

I turned on the radio and was about to sit down when he blurted, "I was going to suggest that we skip lunch and hang out here, but this will never do." His eyes swept my studio like a drill sergeant's, forced to rate barracks that were doomed to fail inspection.

"Are you hungry?"

"Yes," I lied.

"How about Clyde's?"

"I love it." That was true.

"Let's go then."

Somewhere between the salads and entrées we discovered that we both enjoyed the plays of Sam Shepard. Aside from that, we had little to say, much to my relief. When he asked what I thought of the fried mushrooms I said, "Delicious!"

"Wonderful ... superb, even," he rejoined.

"Excellent," I agreed.

"The best," he exclaimed.

The two of us could trade unnecessary words and phrases until their meanings were sucked into a vortex of nonsense. Thus did I welcome the silences.

Over coffee, brandy, and cigarettes he mentioned that Sylvester would be going away for a weekend the following month.

"Would you like to come over for dinner? It would give me a chance to cook something that he doesn't like."

"How do you know *I'll* like it?"

"We can discuss it ... I'll call you."

"Terrific."

"Wonderful."

He reached into his pocket and pulled out a small elephant of blown glass. "This is Rupert. I thought Jasper might be getting lonely. Would you mind babysitting for two of my friends?"

I smiled. "No problem. Tiny elephants don't make much noise anyway."

"Oh yes they do ... but only when you're not around."
* * *

We sat in the spacious, cluttered living room, the site of

Mark and Sylvester's entertaining. Vases, of differing shapes and sizes, festooned with an equally varied selection of cut flowers, had been added to all of the familiar bric-a-brac and it felt very much like a country garden. Sylvester had gone to visit his family in Cleveland for an extended weekend and Mark invited me over to dine on endive salad and chicken au jardin, a dish that he claimed took him all day to prepare. The chicken parts, mixed together with artichoke hearts, carrots, onions, and mushrooms, were moist and tasty, easily falling from the bones. Mark, after revealing the recipe, stated that Sylvester, strictly a meat-and-potatoes person, preferred to cook meals that required as few pots and pans as possible. He, on the other hand, liked to play in the kitchen and didn't mind the cleaning up if the food turned out as he expected.

"Have you heard the latest about Kirsten and Donald?" he asked with a coy expression.

"You mean their latest fight?"

He nodded.

"Kirsten called yesterday," I sighed, "she was upset, and Donald spent the night at my place." I sipped some jasmine tea. "He was pretty upset too."

"He has a jealous nature and he must be a bit paranoid too because I know Kirsten and she would never fool around." He put down his teacup like an exclamation point.

"I think he's afraid of losing her."

"I understand that."

"Also, he *hates* his job. Imagine if you had spent as much time as he did trying to build a career as an actor and wound up a gofer for a theatrical agent."

"That's no excuse. How about some brandy?" He went to the bar and half-filled two large crystal snifters and returned. We toasted and as I lit a cigarette, he poured a huge pile of coke onto the mirror which always occupied a central position on the antique coffee table. I was impressed.

"I've never seen that much in one place at one time."

He arranged the powder into several long lines, and without looking up said, "It's a living, like any other. Except

I can choose my own hours." He snorted half a line through a small glass straw and after handing it to me said, "Coke up!" I finished the line, dividing it between both nostrils, unlike Mark, who only used the one on the right because the capillaries next door had collapsed from years of abuse, as Kirsten had once said.

Moments later I felt a lightness in my brain and a half tingly, half numbing sensation spread to my hands and feet. He moved closer, started playing with my hair and rubbing my thigh. I wanted to kiss him on the lips and taste his tongue, but I was afraid to make the first move.

"How about some music?" I suggested.

"No sweat."

He walked to the stereo with an easy gait and slid a cassette into the deck. The room filled up with mellow cocktail jazz as his perfectly contoured thirty-five year old body, clothed in clinging Levi's and a ribbed, turquoise turtleneck, returned to my side. He lightly massaged my neck, kissed me and sought my tongue with his own. Our lips pressed together, we played a friendly game of hide-and-seek and I felt weightless, utterly free of gravity's pull. He drew back and did some more coke. I declined.

He removed his sweater, revealing the taut chest and stomach that I had hitherto only imagined. Unbuttoning my shirt, he unzipped my pants and stood up. I was ready to rise and follow him below to the bedroom, but he said, "I'll be right back." He went to the bathroom and came back right away with a stack of towels. After spreading them out on the thick carpet he asked me to remove the rest of my clothes and lie down. I stretched out on my back. He fetched a tray with small bottles and selected one with an amber fluid. "Smell this." He passed it under my nose and the scent of some unidentifiable wild flower engulfed me. Pouring some into his palm, he oiled my arms and chest, then my thighs and calves. He admonished me to roll over onto my stomach and worked it into my neck, shoulders and back. I started to groan and writhe, his firm touch sending me into spasms of sensation.

He worked his way down to my buttocks, the backs of my legs, the soles of my feet. He dried his hands and replenished the brandy snifters. "I'll be right back … don't go away!" He went to the bathroom and came back immediately, apparently forgetting to turn off the tap; the sound of running water tainted the music. He told me to roll over onto my back. Bending down, he placed one arm under my neck, the other beneath my knees and lifted me, cradling me like an infant. When was he going to get to the sexual part? I wondered while I was carried to the bathroom and gently placed in the tub, half full of warm water. I was bathed and then shampooed with some greenish gel that smelled like juniper. He towelled me dry from head to feet and combed my hair.

We returned to the couch, I completely naked, he, still in his jeans. He pulled a thick joint from his cigarette pack, lit it and passed it. I began to feel a little dizzy after the third toke.

"Shall we go down?"

I shook my head.

When he turned on the light I thought I was hallucinating. All of the reds were gone. The carpet was the color of astroturf, the curtains a satiny chartreuse, the bedspread a salad of cucumbers, avocadoes, and limes in free-fall. The elephants grazed silently on the bureau. He finally stripped.

"Love the new decor," I said, referring to his naked body.

"We change it from time to time," he gestured at the drapes. We got in between the cool sheets and held each other for a while.

"Are you tired?"

"A little," I lied. Spaced out would be a far more accurate description.

"So am I. Go to sleep, Joey, my pretty little … what does one call a male ballerina?"

"A dancer!"

That was the first and only time that I ever had the last word; he fell asleep before he could respond.

In the morning I had to leave early to warm up for an audition. Mark stayed in bed while I let myself out. Later that night I was going through the pocket of my denim jacket and found a small jeweler's box. Inside was a tiny elephant, obsidian I think, with a small card attached to its trunk that said, "Hi, my name is Cicero, what's yours?"

* * *

Two weeks later I called Mark and Sylvester to say hello and see how they were. Sylvester answered the phone.

"Hello? Sylvester? This is Joey."

"Oh. Hello. I suppose you want to speak to Mark."

"Well, not necessarily, I just wanted to say 'hi'."

"He's not here right now, I'll tell him you called." He slammed the receiver down.

Did he suspect that I had seen Mark while he was away? I wasn't certain. Perhaps he was in a foul mood.

Later that week, however, I was in the lobby of a movie theater with Donald and Kirsten. We were going to see *My Dinner With Andre.* They had greeted me a bit coolly, I thought, but didn't say anything. I returned from the concession stand with a coke and was about to share the good news that I'd gotten a call-back on my audition when Donald blurted, "How *could* you?"

"How could I what?"

Kirsten interjected, "Are you having an affair with Mark?"

"No."

"Are you sleeping together?"

"We did, once. What's the big deal ... and how did you know?"

"Well, Sylvester told us," said Kirsten.

"How did *he* find out?"

"Mark told him. He tells him *everything*," said Donald.

"Oh yeah? What's *everything*?"

"Jasper, Rupert, and Cicero," they said as if they'd rehearsed it.

We never did see the film. Kirsten stated that although she would never do it herself, it was okay, in principle, for two people who had been living together for a while to fool around. Donald disagreed. He insinuated that Kirsten had a secret lover stashed away somewhere and before I knew it, they were screaming at each other. I got them out of the theater. Kirsten hailed a cab and Donald and I took the subway. He crashed on the floor at my studio that night.

* * *

Mark called, he caught me at home between class and work, and asked if I would be interested in seeing Sam Shepard's *Buried Child,* dinner afterwards, with he and Sylvester. I questioned the wisdom of such a move. Wasn't Sylvester, after all, angry with me? Mark suggested that if the three of us had a good time together, the wound might heal faster.

When we met, Sylvester greeted me warmly, but grumbled to Mark throughout the production, Shepard plays not being his favorite entertainment. Glitzy Broadway musicals were more suited to his taste. Mark and I loved it, though.

We went to eat at Blue Skies and everything was very good. The pasta was not overcooked, the escargots buttery and well-garlicked, and the pianist-singer was actually quite pleasant.

When the waiter placed the check face down on the table, Mark immediately snatched it and reached for his wallet. I took out mine as well.

"How much do I owe for the theater and dinner?"

"Nothing," said Mark.

I looked at Sylvester, bewildered.

"Come on now, how much was the ticket?"

"I'm not telling. It was a gift. Please accept it."

I looked at Sylvester again. He stared ahead blankly.

"Okay, I accept, thank you. Now, how much is my part of the bill?"

"It's on me."

"Nope. I'd really like to pay my own way. Please let me see it," I indicated the check, trying to hide my embarrassment.

"No!"

Sylvester came to my rescue. "He wants to pay for his dinner. Let him."

"No ... it's on me."

"You give him elephants, cocaine, and your body, and now you want to feed him?"

I wished I could click my heels and disappear.

"What I do with my boyfriends is none of your business."

"Wait a minute," I said, "I'm not your boyfriend."

Sylvester smiled. "According to Mark, you two have been carrying on like sodomy was just invented."

"That's not true! We spent one night together and we didn't even do anything."

"Liar!" spat Mark. He placed a one hundred dollar bill on the table and walked out.

I looked at Sylvester. "I swear, we had one date and nothing happened!"

"Oh, I know ... don't worry about it. This is the fourth and last time he's tried to convince me that he was having a torrid love affair with a younger guy. It feeds his vanity. And I'm fed up."

We left the restaurant and Sylvester signaled a taxi. He hugged me and said goodbye, leaving me on the curb. I started to walk home, fingering the tissue paper wrapped around the miniature mammals in my pocket. They were quiet and still. I had intended to return them to the herd, but Mark's sudden departure and subsequent silence prevented my doing so.

A few weeks later, Kirsten left Donald and moved in with the guy whom she had denied she was seeing. "He's a dancer," she eventually confided, "the only straight one in the Greater Metropolitan Area."

Shortly thereafter, Sylvester moved out of Mark's duplex and roomed with Donald until he found a place of his own.

I resolved to never again get involved with a married man. The potential for touchy situations is too great, the opportunities for getting hurt and causing pain, too numerous.

Besides, who wants to be a training wheel on a sixteen-speed racer?

Jasper, Rupert, and Cicero get along very well together and have comfortably settled in on the night table by my bed. Their food budget is easily within my grasp. They clean up after themselves. If they make any noise it's only when I'm out of hearing range. And if they ever have sex, I've not been around to catch them at it.

"A Herd of Tiny Elephants" first appeared in *Blueboy*

Gang of Five

1

Joel and Gerry sat in Professor DeFranco's History class and exchanged glances of boredom. The old fart was going on and on about Abelard and Heloise and concluded the lecture by saying, "… and so Abelard paid for his so-called crime by having the thing with which he did his wrongness cut off." He leered and frowned. "Read chapter twelve for the next time. Class dismissed."

Gerry, short and thin, with hair that looked like it had been styled with an egg-beater, stood up and whispered in Joel's ear, "Hey, I just scored some red Lebanese. You wanna try some?"

"You gotta ask?" Joel reached for the cigarette pack in his faded work shirt. He lit one and exhaled a large plume of smoke. They were making their way out of the old brownstone on Beacon Street when they were waylaid by Chip.

"Joel, it's here. I was sorting the mail this morning, and you got it."

Joel glanced at Chip's crotch, then raised his eyes. "What?"

"Those records from the Columbia Record Club."

"What's he talkin' about?" asked Gerry, crossing his arms over his thin chest.

"You know those ads where you join a record club and get ten free albums for a buck?"

"Yeah."

"Well, I joined. As Joe Nobody."

"No shit," said Gerry. "What d'ja get?"

"A bunch of weird junk," said Chip.

Joel grimaced at Chip, noted his muscular thighs, and said, "Well, I figured if I was gonna get some free albums, I'd get stuff that I wouldn't ordinarily buy. You know, explore around a little."

On the top floor of the boys' dormitory, in the room that had been dubbed "The Penthouse," Gerry was breaking up hash into his stone pipe, Chip was admiring his biceps and pectorals in the mirror and Joel was opening the large package.

"Far fuckin' out. Brand new music for my hungry ears."

Searching for a book of matches, Gerry said, "Are you ever gonna tell me what you got?"

"For starters, there's *Brilliant Corners* by Thelonius Monk."

"Who?"

"Thelonius Monk. Jazz pianist."

"Oh."

"*Then there's* Tammy Wynette's Greatest Hits, Volume I."

"The country singer?"

"Yes."

"How bizarre."

"And *La Mer* by Debussy."

"All right, I get the picture. No rock, huh?"

"No Hendrix, no Cream, no James Gang, no Stones, just crap," said Chip.

"Not even any Band or Small Faces?" asked Gerry with mock incredulity.

"Nope. Brand new tunes for jaded goons."

Gerry lit the pipe, took a large drag and passed it to Chip, who sat on the bed. Joel placed a record on the spindle and touched the automatic switch. He sat on the floor and took the pipe. The three of them looked at each other as the intro to "Stand By Your Man" filled the room. They passed the pipe around several times and by the song's conclusion, they were somewhere between Jupiter and Uranus.

"Interesting," said Gerry, staring at the picture on the album cover.

"Too weird," said Chip, crossing his legs.

"Far out," said Joel, noting the way that Chip's stomach never bulged out over his jeans, even when sitting.

Tammy Wynette was halfway through "Apartment #9" when Gerry began to refill the pipe. Joel rose to change the record and cued up Thelonius Monk. When he sat down, he felt the rush from the smoke. He glanced at Chip's pretty-boy face and the halo effect of his golden curls. As was his habit when stoned, Joel's mind wandered through his memory.

He could remember his first day in Boston. It was the beginning of orientation week, and when his parents deposited him and his belongings at the dormitory on Beacon Street, he had at first tried to be brave. As soon as they were out of sight, however, he felt a slight choking in his throat, and a rush of nostalgia for the small, suburban town he had been so desperate to leave. He unpacked slowly, hoping that his roommate would materialize so they could meet, but finding the task completed and having nothing else to do, he decided to take a stroll and explore the immediate vicinity. When he had walked down the six flights of stairs and emerged onto the street, he saw many young people saying good-bye to their parents.

A pretty girl with long, black hair stood on the corner of Beacon and Berkeley, smoking a joint with a guy whose hair looked Dylanesque. Joel walked past and they smiled. He smiled back, but quickly walked on, unsure in the light of such friendliness. He had heard that the big city was tough and cruel and had prepared himself for it. But these people seemed nice. "I've got a lot to learn," he said to himself.

Heading up Berkeley Street toward Commonwealth Avenue, he passed staid brownstones that seemed to harbor ancient secrets. Cars went whizzing by and strangers came toward him, mostly youthful, all looking very hip. The faded jeans and long hair made him realize that his chinos and semi-crewcut would have to go if he was going to fit in.

It was like getting out of prison. His parents, whom he jokingly referred to sometimes as "the wardens," would never let him dress like the other kids. But now he had his chance. He smiled inwardly and lit a cigarette.

He walked on, lost in thought, occasionally distracted by a passerby or an odd building, when he came to a large park he later found out was called "the Common." He passed a small lake with boats shaped like swans. Sitting down on a bench, he lit another cigarette and leaned back. A young couple came over, placed their jackets on the bench and proceeded to dance. Not like in a ballroom or discotheque, but choreography such as a chorus line might do. It looked like they were rehearsing for a stage production of some sort, when out of nowhere, a drunk appeared, staggered over to the dancers and attempted to join in. They were doing high kicks, first to the left and then to the right, when the derelict fell on his ass. The dancers laughed, gathered their things, said goodbye and departed. He applauded their effort and waved.

Stamping out the cigarette, he stood up and began walking again, when a middle-aged gentleman accosted him. "Excuse me, can you tell me how to get to Washington Street?"

"I'm sorry, Sir, but I'm new in town and have no idea."

The stranger eyed him up and down. "I've never been to Boston before either. Where are you from?"

"New York. Actually, Long Island. I'm just starting college. Well, I hope you find Washington Street."

Joel turned to walk away.

"Wait a minute. Perhaps you can still help."

"What do you mean?" asked Joel.

"Would you be interested in, possibly, I mean, do you ever think about sex?"

Joel blushed. "What are you, some kind of pimp?"

"No, no, you've got it all wrong. Why don't you come over to my hotel room and we can discuss it?"

Joel never ran that fast in his life. He ran until he could not go on, and turned to make sure he had not been followed.

Plopping down on the grass, he held his head in his hands until the labored breathing began to subside. "Goddamn," he said to himself. He had always hated the overprotectiveness of his parents and the isolation of the suburbs. If he had grown up in a city he would have the street smarts to recognize an old queer on the make. He hated himself for his naivete and for handling the situation so awkwardly.

He was walking back to the dormitory when he saw the pretty girl again and crossed the street so he could smile at her when he passed by. She surprised him by introducing herself. "Hi, my name's Martha, what's yours?"

"Joel."

"You want to smoke a joint?"

"Sure."

They walked down Beacon Street toward Kenmore Square, talking about the Rolling Stones. He didn't really care for them, but did not want her to know that, so he pretended to be a big fan. "Yeah, I saw them at the Forest Hills Tennis Stadium a few years ago. I think Jagger's fantastic," he lied.

"I grew up in Forest Hills."

"Really? I'm from New York too."

They played the game of "Do You Know?" and when they realized they had no friends or acquaintances in common, they turned and walked back. The young man with tousled hair whom Martha had been with earlier came over to them and she introduced him as Gerry. They shook hands and Gerry asked Joel if he wanted to buy a hit of orange sunshine.

"No thanks," said Joel, "maybe some other time. I'm gonna go back to the dorm and see if my roommate checked in yet. Take care."

As Joel turned and walked away, Martha swallowed the bright orange pill that Gerry had placed in the palm of her hand.

Climbing the six flights up, Joel passed room after room with chattering young men – some preppy, some hippy – and reflected on a conversation he had with his best friend back home. He prayed that his roommate would be anything but a jock. He cautiously turned the key in the lock and found a body stretched out on the lower berth of the bunk beds. Jumping up in surprise was a guy wearing only his jockey shorts. He looked like a model. Sculpted body, chiselled features, curly blond hair and green eyes, the color of pistachio ice-cream.

"Hi, I'm Chip."

Joel detected a mid-western accent. "My name's Joel. I'm from New York. Yourself?"

"Indiana. I see you play guitar. Mind if I look at it?"

"No. I sing and write songs, too. You play?" Joel tried to keep his eyes from Chip's perfect torso.

"The only thing I play is football. I was team captain last year."

"No shit."

"Yeah, but my main hobby is girls."

He chuckled and playfully punched Joel's arm. Sitting back down on the bed he sighed and added, "Ah yes, girls. Can't live without 'em."

"You mind if I play a record?"

"Not at all. Nice stereo. What have you got?" asked Chip, twirling a gold curlicue around his index finger.

"Oh, a little of everything. What do you want to hear?"

"Anything."

Deciding to play it safe, Joel extracted *Rubber Soul* by the Beatles and played side two at a moderate volume. He sat down in the chair near the window and asked Chip what subject he planned to major in.

"I have no idea and couldn't care less. You?"

"Well, I really want to be a musician, but to be realistic, I'm gonna go for a B.A. in English Literature and maybe I'll minor in Education and teach."

Chip bounded from the bed and lit a cigarette. He pulled a trunk out from under the bed, opened it, and took out a rolled-up poster. "It's Hendrix. Mind if I put it up on the wall over here?"

"Go ahead. Nice colors."

"Hendrix is so cool it's scary. You got any pot?"

"No, but I was thinking of buying some. Maybe we could split a lid?" Joel attempted to pry his eyes from Chip's thighs and calves.

"Great. You hungry?"

"Yeah," said Joel, looking away.

"I'm starved. Why don't we go over to the cafeteria and check out the grub?"

"Sure."

Chip put on a plaid shirt, tight faded jeans and sneakers. Reaching for his Varsity jacket, he checked himself in the mirror, and finding the image flawless said, "Let's go."

They walked slowly down the street and Chip pointed out the attractive women. He had a comment for every female that passed by. Some were too old, too fat or too cheap-looking. But every now and then he would say, "Wow, I could go for that." Joel just sort of agreed with everything, but it was more in the spirit of being friendly than any actual similarity of opinion.

They stood in line with trays and accepted the overcooked food. It did not look very appetizing. They finally found places to sit, opposite one another at the end of a long table. Chip attacked his food, while Joel tasted it with apprehension. He decided he was less hungry than he thought. Looking past Chip, he noticed Martha and Gerry sitting two tables away. He noted that they could not take their eyes away from each other.

"What are you staring at?" asked Chip.

"Oh, these people I met before. Martha and Gerry, two tables behind you."

As Chip looked around, Martha smiled at Joel. He nodded back. "I could go for that," said Chip, hitching his thumb toward Martha. "I'm gonna get some more milk. You want any?"

Joel was startled from his reverie of the past when a pack of Bambu smacked his cheek and landed in his lap. Chip ginned and laughed. "Hey, why don't you roll us a joint? I'm gonna put on some *real* music." Chip sprang to his feet and moved to the stereo. Joel sighed as he watched Chip's tightly jeaned ass flex right, left, right, left in syncopated rhythm. He spilled some grass onto a album cover and rolled a hefty joint. Licking it, he sighed again as Chip sat down. Joel looked down at his own body, boyish and undefined, glanced at Gerry's anorexic frame, then ogled Chip's athletically tapered torso. He lit the joint, passed it to Gerry and tried to imagine having sex with Chip, as Deep Purple shot out of the twin speakers.

2

Thoreau College was a small, private institution, located in the Back Bay area of Boston. Most of the school's buildings were on Beacon Street, one block away from the scenic Charles River. Dividing the metropolitan area into two distinct camps – Boston and Cambridge – the river snaked it's way between the sister cities, with long, slender strip parks running parallel to the polluted water. The park on the Boston side was called the Esplanade, and it was there that the Thoreau students would go on warm, sunny days to study or get high. At night, the Esplanade served as a cruising area for the many gay students that had emigrated to the city of schools for either educational or recreational fulfillment.

While it was clear to Joel that Chip's main pursuit was women and Gerry's principle hobby was drugs, Joel was uncertain about himself. He felt divided. No longer a child, but not yet an adult, interested in learning, but eager to experience the pleasure he had been denied while growing up. He was torn between furthering his education and satisfying his lust for men. At an early age he'd known he was gay, but was unable to explore this facet of life while living at his parents' home. Besides, the small, suburban town offered no apparent opportunities.

Suddenly, he'd been thrust into a living situation that seemed to mock everything he'd known until then. His dormitory was packed with horny, young guys, much like himself. And though a handful were unquestionably gay, many of the others were more than willing to experiment. And the presence of certain drugs in the bloodstream only diminished some people's already lax inhibitions. Joel had become infatuated with Chip's body, but Chip was so obsessed with women that Joel was terrified of even suggesting any kind of physical involvement. Still, the sight of Chip naked always made him erect.

Joel thumbed through *Rolling Stone* while Chip occupied the bathroom. He came across an article on aging blues singer Son House and chuckled at the glaring inaccuracies. When he heard the toilet flush, he put the magazine away and cued up his Robert Johnson album. When Chip emerged, blowing his nose into a tissue, Joel turned up the volume, entered the bathroom and shut the door. Chip laughed to himself, thinking that Joel couldn't even take a shit without listening to his old blues records.

Meanwhile, Joel's cock was on fire. He had stumbled upon the secret of masturbation while very young, and had become addicted to the feeling. But as he had grown older, he feared that he might be making moaning noises at the crucial moment, and usually indulged himself only when his parents and sister were away. Even then, he'd fallen into the habit of playing loud music and running the shower to conceal any sound that might result from his clandestine activity. When he had gotten to college he did not care who heard what, but he retained the old habits.

The sweet anticipation was over. Anointing himself with Vaseline, he stepped into the shower stall. His thighs took up the pulsating Mississippi Delta rhythm. Letting his thoughts roam freely over Chip's well-contoured body, he closed his eyes tightly and worked himself until his loins tightened and he reached ecstatic release. He opened his eyes, shook out the last few drops and soaped himself all over. After showering, he emerged, still toweling himself dry.

"You sure take a lot of showers," said Chip.

"You noticed, huh?"

* * *

Martha and Gerry had begun to hang out together on their first day in Boston. At first, their relationship centered around their mutual interest in drugs. One day, after a few weeks into the first semester, he had invited her to spend the night in his room at the boys' dorm. His roommate, a nerdy guy whom he referred to as "Poindexter" to his friends, had gone home for the weekend.

Martha, wearing a flamingoed caftan, lounged on the bed eating Oreos while Gerry sat at his desk studying a Mass Communications text. She got up and walked over to the bookshelf, selected a volume of William Blake's poetry and returned to the bed. Her silky, dark hair, parted in the middle, flowed down the sides of her face to her breasts. She had barely begun to read when Gerry turned the stereo on, boogied over to the bed and sat down beside her. Putting the book on the floor, she pulled herself up to get next to him and allowed her breast to rub against him. Clad in a dashiki with concentric diamonds outlined in tan, black and white, he touched her cheek. She ran her fingers through his bushy hair and whispered, "Hi there, cutie."

"Let's get high," he said. "I got some new stuff and it's better than purple haze. Wanna check it out?"

"Does the Pope shit in the woods?" she said, checking her hair for split ends. He broke the small tablet in half, reached for the coke can on the night table, and handed the acid and soda pop to her. He waited until she had swallowed hers, then took his and tapped a joint out of his cigarette pack. "This oughta send us merrily on our way."

They passed the joint back and forth ever so slowly. Staring into space, they took deep hits and exhaled cumulus billows of aromatic Colombian smoke. The reefer and record ended simultaneously and she blurted, "Can we hear Carole King now?"

"You really want to listen to that wimpy shit?"

"Yes."

"All right, but then we gotta hear Hendrix or something equally quintessential."

"What's fair is fair. Kiss me?"

He pecked her on the cheek and got up to change the disc.

They had actually fallen in love with each other a few days before, but neither was really aware of how the other felt. Although they hadn't had real sex yet, they had made out a few times.

The acid started to kick in and they lay in each others arms, indulging their private fantasies. "What are you thinking about?" he asked.

"If you really want to know I'll tell you, but it's dumb."

"Tell me anyway."

"I'm moving through space," she began. "Completely tripped out, hurtling through the cosmos. My body feels light and supple. I can smell gardenias and patchouli. There are asteroids and meteors racing by. It looks like there's going to be a collision every second, but it all seems to work out just in time. My skin feels all tingly and you feel like you're a part of me. I mean, I feel like a part of you. You know what I mean. I feel like I'm sailing in outer space and it's never gonna stop. I don't want it to. It feels too good."

There was silence. The record player had turned itself off and except for the faint sounds from the street that penetrated the window pane, it was very quiet.

"Your turn. Where are you?"

"Somewhere in a jungle. Probably Africa. It's dark except for this enormous bonfire. Black natives are dancing around it. There's a million conga drums tapping out rhythms. I feel like I'm vibrating to the beat. I can smell ganja and taste exotic liqueurs that no white man has ever tried before. A short distance away, there's an orgy. A swirl of arms and legs and the smell of sweat. I'm dancing around the fire and every time I pass the writhing bodies I'm tempted to join in, but I haven't yet."

"Why not?"

"Chicken, I guess."

"You won't know if you like it or not unless you try it," she said. He kissed her on the lips. Their tongues met. Gerry hugged her tighter and her breath grew short. They held to each other tightly as he explored the interior of her mouth.

"Are we gonna do it?" he asked.

"Yes."

"Wanna smoke another joint first?"

"Sure. Anything. Can we hear Carole King now?"

"Of course. I'm an easy guy to get along with," he grinned.

"Shut up and kiss me."

He was happy to comply. He lit another joint and passed it to her. Martha placed the fiery end in her mouth and gave him a shotgun. Receiving the joint, he did the same for her. Then she inhaled a huge cloud of smoke, told him to exhale, and blew the smoke into his mouth. His face lit up. "What a great idea," he said and returned the same cloud of smoke to her waiting mouth.

He tentatively undressed her, very slowly, as though she might be an infant in swaddling. She stroked the fine hairs that sprouted from his bony chest. He cupped her rounded, but smallish breasts in his hands and felt them all around. Taking her left breast into his mouth, Gerry sucked at her nipple like a toothless baby. Martha let her hand slide along his slender thigh as she felt for the warm bulge encased in briefs. When she touched the mound of his flaccid, curled up cock, it began to pulsate and grow. Their breathing quickened as their tongues met in midair and they fell back on the comforter in a tight embrace. He removed the stiff dashiki and they both wriggled out of their underwear.

Martha sighed and stroked his cheek. Taking his cock in her warm hands, she leaned over and flicked the tip with her tongue. Gerry arched his back and moaned. He began to writhe uncontrollably, surrounded by her mouth like an arrow in a quiver. He pulled out slowly and lay her on her back, showering her face with wet kisses. Their mouths locked and their tongues fought as he eased his full weight onto her. Martha, in a frenzy, took hold of him and guided him into her. She felt a thousand tiny electrical sparks igniting inside, and a million shooting stars ricocheted through her mind. With deep but gentle thrusts, Gerry established an accelerating rhythm pattern that soon erupted into volcanic cataclysm. She screamed and bit his ear.

They slowed and stopped. They kissed. Their eyes conversed silently as they lay side by side on the damp sheet.

* * *

As soon as they'd entered the room, Chip locked the door and checked his wristwatch. Forty-five minutes to go. Nancy threw her coat on the bed and sighed, "It's too hot in here."

Chip flung the window open. "We can't control the heat from here. The thermostat is in the basement, where the house director lives, and it's always cold down there. So we sweat and he freezes."

Nancy, a tall girl with large breasts and brown hair styled in a page-boy, checked her make-up in the mirror. She erased a smudge of lipstick with the end of her pinky.

"Come over here and sit down," said Chip.

She swivelled to the bed and sat down. Chip put his arm around her shoulder and kissed her.

"What's the rush?" she pulled away.

Chip glanced at his wristwatch. "My roommate will be back in exactly thirty-seven minutes. It's the only class he always goes to."

"I get it," she said, unbuttoning her blouse. Chip leaped out of his own clothing and hastily unhooked her bra. She wriggled out of her slacks and panties and Chip, already hard, lay down on top of her and started pumping.

"Take it easy."

"Sorry."

He ground his hips up and down, while keeping an eye on the watch, poised for viewing just beyond her field of vision.

"You're gonna take me out one of these nights?" she gasped.

"Uh huh."

His motion accelerated and sweat formed on his brow. Her back arched up and he dug deeply. A shudder ran through his body as he exploded, moaning at peak volume.

"Shh," she cautioned. "You'll wake the dead."

"Uh, sorry," he said.

He rolled off of her. "Gee, uh, Nancy, that was great." He looked at his wristwatch. Eleven minutes. "Why don't we get dressed and go for some coffee?"

She slipped her arms through the straps of her bra. "Hey, big spender, do you think you can afford it," she said, as sarcastically as she dared.

"Gee, I think so," he said, pretending not to notice.

He locked the door behind them with three and a half minutes to spare.

3

Martha's dormitory was located a few blocks south of the boys' dorm on Commonwealth Ave. Presided over by Miss Allerton, a heavy-set woman with sagging breasts, the building was older and more ornate than its male counterpart. And the rules for the girls were much more strict. Although the boys could come and go as they pleased and were allowed female guests, the girls had curfews and males were not permitted beyond the reception desk where Miss Allerton kept watch.

Martha's roommate, Jacqui, was a short, lithe black girl with an Afro hairdo, high cheekbones and wistful eyes. Jacqui and Martha had become friends immediately, but at first did not spend much time together because Jacqui was more interested in poetry than drugs. She ignored her class schedule and spent most of her time at the school library reading her favorite modern poets. When the library closed she returned to her room and wrote poems of her own.

A few weeks after arriving in Boston, she'd sent off a

poem she'd written called "Black Mama," a rambling meditation on black American women. The poem had been accepted by a literary journal published at Boston University. Elated at the prospect of seeing her first poem in print, she began to spend more time with Martha and eventually learned about the pleasure to be had getting high. She was eager to meet "The Guys." So Martha organized a picnic at the Esplanade to celebrate the arrival of spring.

They spread blankets on the grass, placed the food in the shade of a sprawling tree and smoked a couple of joints. Gazing at the sailboats and skiffs that moved back and forth on the waters of the Charles, they listened to rock music on a transistor radio. Chip suddenly jumped up and declared, "It's frisbee time!"

Everyone except for Joel got to their feet and ran to a clearing. Reaching for his book, Joel turned the radio off, stretched himself out on an aqua blanket and turned to chapter seven of *Daniel Deronda* by George Eliot. He was absorbed in his reading, mesmerized by the coquetry of Gwendolyn Harleth, when he was distracted by the voice of a child who had wandered over to where he lay. He looked up and grinned just as the toddler's mother came along to apologize and whisk the youngster away.

Having finished chapter seven, Joel debated the wisdom of starting the next one, not wanting to be interrupted in the middle. He unpacked his guitar and strummed a few chords. Then the hungry frisbee players pounced on him, shrieking with laughter. Jacqui proceeded to open a bottle of wine while Gerry foraged for a fig newton. Martha crumbled some hash into a well-resined pipe. She lit it and passed it to Jacqui who took a small hit, passed the pipe and filled five paper cups with rosé. Students and teachers wandered by as the sun glittered through the leaves of the overhanging tree, casting shifting jewels on the grass.

"Martha said you just got a poem published," said Gerry.
Jacqui nodded. "My first."
"I understand you write a lot."

"It's the only thing that really interests me."

"Shit," said Chip, "I hate poetry. It's too hard to understand." He turned the radio on. "Wordsworth and Longfellow and all those guys make me sick."

"Me too," said Jacqui. "Irrelevant ranting and raving. I prefer poetry rendered in modern language."

"You mean, like Rod McKuen?" asked Gerry, sarcastically.

"Who's Rod McKuen?" asked Chip.

"Forget it," said Joel with a superior air. He looked at Jacqui. "How do you like living in the dormitory?"

"It's almost like a prison, but Miss Allerton is okay. I can live with it."

"I prefer the boys' dorm," said Martha. She winked at Gerry. "It's much cozier than Miss Allerton's Internment Camp for Young Girls."

"You mean women," said Jacqui.

"Right, women," said Martha. "I have to forge a note from my mother saying I'm going home for the weekend every time I sleep over with Gerry."

The bottle of rosé and baggies of dope emptied as the five stomachs were filled with cheese, bread and fruit. As the sun began its descent, the gang packed up the remains, folded the blankets, and headed back to their respective dormitories.

* * *

Halfway through the second semester, Chip had noticed a girl hanging around school, and her grace and loneliness completely overwhelmed him. While most of the female students were fairly adolescent in their appearance and behavior, she had the air of a sophisticated woman. He wasted no time trying to meet her and asked for a date. Her name was Genevieve and she readily agreed to have dinner with him. They started dating regularly, and Chip was so proud to be seen with her that at first he didn't mind that she wasn't willing to put out. He was certain that she was interested. She would flirt shamelessly in public, but always parried his quests for satisfaction when they were alone. Chip, to alleviate his horniness, would occasionally fuck some other girl who desired him, but he always felt above these easy conquests. He eventually grew tired of bestowing his favors on underlings while his entire allowance was squandered on Genevieve's expensive tastes.

One afternoon, Chip's libido got the best of him and he had a boisterous argument with Genevieve on the sidewalk in front of the Student Union building. Martha happened to be sitting on a stoop across the street, trying to memorize some lines for her Voice and Articulation class. When Chip stormed away from Genevieve with a look of defeat, Martha intercepted his path. "Can I buy you a cup of coffee?"

"Sure. Why not? Take pity on the miserable."

"Cheer up. You can tell me all about it."

They walked slowly towards the coffee shop down the street. Martha chatted about nonsensical trivia in an effort to distract him. It worked. When they sat down at a small table for two, he was relaxed enough to talk about his problem rationally.

"So," began Martha, stirring sugar into her coffee, "she's a real cockteaser, huh?"

"Yeah. Fuckin' bitch. Playin' with my head. I've got a lot to learn."

"Don't say that. It's not your fault. Don't blame yourself for her shortcomings. You're an attractive guy. Women will always find you desirable and you can do a lot better than stuck-up, snotty Genevieve."

"You really think so?"

"I know it."

"I guess I set my sights too high."

"Au contraire. You were deceived by a wolf in sheep's clothing. It can happen to anyone."

"Yeah ... thanks ... you're right ... I was too involved to see what was happening ... shit ... I'm such a fool ... okay ... I'm over it ... don't want to bore you ... let's change the subject."

"All right."

"Sorry I couldn't make it to see your play. How did it go?"

Martha sipped her coffee and gazed at Chip's radiant eyes. "Great. I loved doing it. The character I played says and does things that I never get to do or say in real life. I got a lot off my chest. Good therapy. The audience seemed to like it and my drama Prof, complimented me. I guess it was successful. You know, while we're on the subject, you know a lot more about me than I do about you. Like, for example, what do you want to do?"

"What do you mean?"

"You know, with your life? Your career? I mean, I want to be an actress and Gerry wants to direct films. What about you?"

"Well," he confessed, twirling a blond curlicue around his index finger, "I have this fantasy that I want to be an actor."

"Why don't you take any acting classes?"

"You're gonna think this is stupid, but here goes. I want to be discovered. I want to just have a regular job and have somebody look at me one day and say, 'Hey kid, I'm gonna make you a star.' You know, like Lana Turner. Or better yet, Mark Frechette. One day he's walking down Charles Street and Antonioni is driving by in a limo and the next thing you know, he's starring in *Zabriskie Point.*"

"That's quite a romantic and far-fetched notion." She pulled her hair from her shoulders and flung it back. "The chances of that ever happening are very remote."

"That's what makes it so attractive. It's a real longshot. It may never pay off, but if it does, I'll be immortal."

"Good luck," she said with a sigh. "I guess anything is possible."

"You mean, *everything* is possible."

* * *

The hip, long-haired English teacher, Mr. Blakely, talked about the Black Mountain school of poetry. He went on and on about Charles Olson and Robert Creeley, completely unaware that the class would much rather be discussing the Beats or the significance of poetry in rock lyrics. Jacqui and Joel sat in back of the classroom and pretended they were taking notes on the lecture.

"Jacqui," he wrote, "you've gotta do it. It's an opportunity to communicate your thoughts to other people. You work so hard on your poems. What's the use if nobody reads them or hears them? To write just for yourself is Literary Masturbation."

"Joel," she wrote back, "this is no ordinary poetry reading. All of us are black lesbians. I'm not into pigeonholes. Besides, I'm not ready for the world at large to find out my little secret. It's okay that the gang knows. But it's not something I'm ready to advertise."

The class was dismissed and they could talk.

"Does Martha know you're a lesbian?"

"Of course."

"She never said anything about it."

"Why should she?"

"I don't know." He touched Jacqui's arm. "I'm gay, but I haven't said anything yet to Chip or Gerry."

"What are you afraid of?"

"I'm not sure."

"Well then," she said triumphantly, "that settles it. I'm definitely going to participate in the reading."

"Great. What changed your mind?"

"You and your uptight attitude. If there's one gay person at the reading who is able to feel more secure about herself after hearing me read, it will be worth it."

"Can I come?"

"I'd love to have you there, Joel, but it's for black lesbians only."

"Oh, I see."

"Maybe someday we won't have to have so many restrictions."

"Yeah, I hope so," he said.

* * *

It was a warm spring evening, and Chip sat on his bed smoking a joint. He decided to turn the radio on. The mellifluous voice of Eric Jackson smoothly segued from Little Feat to Fairport Convention on WBCN, the reigning free-form rock station. Opening a box of animal crackers, he began to chew on a sweet rhino when Jackson cut the song short and announced, "Police urge all citizens to avoid Harvard Square, as the antiwar demonstration has erupted into violence. Again, Harvard Square is off-limits until further notice. Now, back to the music."

That was all Chip needed to hear. He grabbed his keys and was out the door seconds later, forgetting to turn off the radio and extinguish the light. Flagging down a taxi was easy and he instructed the driver to take him to Harvard Square, "the sooner, the better."

The car crossed over to Cambridge via the Massachusetts Avenue Bridge and he commanded the driver to let him off a few blocks south of the square. There were police everywhere. Students were running around in a thousand directions and several overturned cars were engulfed in flames. He was trying to get the sense of what was happening, when a tear gas canister exploded a few yards away. He was instantly overwhelmed by the billowy fumes and began to cough. A voice from out of nowhere shouted *"Come with us!"*

The next thing he was aware of was racing down Dunster Street with a man and a woman on either side of him. The three ducked into an old clapboard house after running for several blocks. The interior was cluttered with potted plants, drug paraphernalia and dozens of cats. The couple offered Chip the use of the bathroom. He washed his face and waited for his heart to stop pounding. When he emerged, his rescuers offered him mu tea, raisins and Screaming Yellow Zonkers.

Chip tried to talk like a revolutionary. "We've got to make our feelings known. Just 'cause we're students they think we don't have anything to say, or have the right to express it. Meanwhile the destruction goes on. It's too fucked-up."

"Fuckin' pigs," said the woman.

"Yeah, fuckin' pigs," said the man.

Chip's brain reeled in disbelief. His brother was a policeman. He did not like hearing them referred to as filthy barnyard animals. He felt like telling these two stupid hippies a thing or two, but remained silent. "I have to get back and study for an exam," he lied. He thanked them for their hospitality and sighed with relief as the door closed behind him. "Lousy creeps," he said to himself as he went looking for a cab to squire him back to his dormitory.

4

Joel had fooled around with several guys at the dormitory, but he found the encounters to be less than satisfying. He'd once sucked off Kenny, a tall, effeminate type, who'd fallen asleep as soon as he'd come. And overweight William, who'd sucked off Joel, wouldn't allow any kissing. "That's for faggots," he'd snorted. Joel was looking for affection and the kind of sex that went deeper than a fast orgasm.

It was about the seventh attempt that Joel had made to cruise in a gay bar. The first few times he had been too nervous when he entered. Several pairs of eyes had stripped him down as he walked through the door. He felt like a piece of meat being inspected by housewives in a supermarket, and he'd turned and left moments after arriving. He had worked up his courage, though, to the point where he made it to the bar, but he was still too self-conscious to look at anyone. One night an exceptionally good-looking young man approached him and said, "Smile. You look uptight and there's no reason to be."

"I'm not uptight," said Joel, "just mildly terrified."

After that, the conversation flowed so easily that Joel relaxed enough to feel comfortable in the unfamiliar surroundings. He knew very little about gay life and was eager to learn more. He decided he would try to seduce this stranger, just to see what would happen, but when the stranger kissed him on the lips and inserted his tongue, Joel became aroused and thought it would be best if he let the stranger seduce him. The young man invited him to go home with him, and Joel felt it was time for a formal introduction.

"By the way, my name's Joel, what's your's?"

"Michael."

"Pleased to meet you."

"The pleasure is all mine."

The full moon cast its glow through the naked windows of the darkened apartment. The two lay pressed against each other. While Joel savored Michael's mouth, their hands massaged each other's backs.

"You feel so good."

"So do you," whispered Michael. "Do you like getting fucked?" Joel hesitated, afraid to expose his lack of experience. "I – I've never done it before," he finally confessed.

"Would you like to try?"

"Yes."

Michael kissed him. "If at any time, you're not into it, just let me know."

"I will."

Joel was on his back with his legs in the air. He looked up at the sculpted silhouette that hovered above, and when their eyes met, he smiled dreamily. After the lubricant had been applied – to plug and socket – Michael delicately eased himself in. When penetration was complete he whispered, "How ya doin'?"

"I never felt anything this good."

His body relaxed and his mind whirled as Michael tensed his muscles and slowly began to thrust. The strokes grew longer and more forceful, until Joel imagined a locomotive piston driving a fast-moving train. When he felt the eruption, it was electrifying and he fought tears of joy. Michael smothered him with kisses and tender words, and when his breathing became normal, suggested they change positions. Joel was amazed that Michael wanted to reciprocate. As Joel entered Michael, he thought it was too good to be true. When he came he could not believe how grand it felt. He whispered, "Did I hurt you?"

"No, it was great."

"It felt like the earth moved."

"It did."

He lay alongside Michael. They fell into a tight embrace with arms and legs all tangled up and eventually drifted into peaceful slumber. When Joel awoke the next morning, he realized that he'd finally found what he'd been looking for.

* * *

In a downtown theater, Chip sat in the balcony absorbed in the incredible parade of big-breasted women who inhabited the latest film of Russ Meyer. He absently smoked a cigarette and when one unusually well-endowed actress made her appearance, the container of stale popcorn that had been nestled against his crotch fell to the floor between his feet, due to his uncontrollable tumescence.

* * *

Jacqui sat in a corner of the Boston Public Library next to a stack of books she'd carefully selected: Adrienne Rich, Marianne Moore, Sylvia Plath, and Gwendolyn Brooks. As her eyes scanned each line, her memory tried to hold onto every word, analyzing, theorizing, juxtaposing, dissecting until her concentration wore down and she permitted her brain to cease its dizzying flight.

* * *

On the roof of the boys' dormitory, Gerry and Joel were sunning themselves, in the raw, to the accompaniment of a transistor radio.

"I'm speedin' my nuts off," said Gerry. "Feels good, though."

"Feels great," said Joel.

"What are we gonna do about Dr. Walton's class?" asked Gerry.

"Good question. I've never failed anything before. I sure don't want to start now."

"Failing ain't so bad. Getting busted is worse. So's falling in love."

"I wouldn't know about that," said Joel with an exaggerated sigh. He lit a cigarette and thought about love. He had heard and used the expression all of his life, but he never really knew what it meant. Of course, he loved his parents and sister. But that wasn't the same thing as falling in love. He wondered what it was like.

* * *

Martha was Medea. She was Hedda Gabler, Madame Bovary, Camille, and Anna Karenina. Sarah Bernhardt, Katherine Cornell and Bette Davis. She reached down into the depths of her soul, summoned a demon from she knew not where, and terrified her acting partner into leaping off the stage. Breathless and pale, he ran to the lavatory and threw up before he could reach the toilet.

"Very good," said her Drama coach. "But don't waste it on rehearsals. Save it for the eighth month of a run when your interest is beginning to wane."

"I'll remember," said Martha as she exited triumphantly, stage left.

* * *

Every possible flavor was available that evening at the Pewter Pot Muffin House on Boylston Street. Gerry was devouring a blueberry/corn, while Joel buttered his orange/cinnamon. With his mouth stuffed to overflowing, crumbs falling into his lap, Gerry said, "What the fuck are we gonna do about Dr. Walton's class?"

"I seem to recall you asking the same question just this afternoon."

"There's no way on earth I can do the paper, take the exam and expect to pass. I've waited too long. It's impossible."

"Same here."

They looked at each other blankly.

Gerry smiled tentatively. "We could always phone in a bomb threat."

"What?"

"A sinister plot is taking shape in my mind."

"Let's hear it," said Joel, reaching for another muffin.

"College campuses across the country are closing down because of the Kent State massacre."

"Right," said Joel, buttering a bran/currant.

"There's been a lot of pressure on the Dean to do the same here, but so far everything's status quo."

"I'm listening."

"One little ol' bomb threat would do the trick."

"You really think so?"

"Sure. One call to the Dean, one call to the police. It's too easy. And there's no danger. There won't even be a bomb. Just two phone calls."

Joel wiped his lips with a paper napkin. "Can't we be caught?"

"I don't see how. We won't be on the phone long enough for a trace, and we'll call from a booth."

"What about voice prints?"

Gerry grinned. "How many people do you know who automatically tape all their calls?"

They paid the bill and sauntered off to Kenmore Square. Walking up to a row of phone booths, Gerry said, "I'll call the Dean."

"And I'll call the cops," said Joel.

* * *

Chip, Martha, and Jacqui were gathered in the Penthouse, listening to the first posthumously released recordings of Jimi Hendrix. They were scattered about the room, in various relaxed postures, when the first buzzsaw notes of electric guitar screeched through the speakers. At first no one could differentiate between the music and the street noise, but it quickly became obvious that something was wrong. The stereo was turned down and they gathered at the windows just in time to see the police cars, firetrucks and ambulances turn the intersection below into a carnival of swirling red lights and droning sirens.

Chip ran downstairs to find out what the commotion was about, and breathlessly returned to blurt, "There's a bomb in the Student Union Building!"

"That calls for another joint," said Martha.

Just then, Joel and Gerry entered casually.

"What's up?"

"Bomb in the Student Union."

"No shit."

Joel glanced at Gerry, who looked away. At that moment they silently agreed never to reveal themselves as the culprits.

The tumult in the street below eventually subsided, and the gang turned their attention to the latest from Hendrix.

"It's kind of like robbing his grave," said Jacqui. "I mean, what if he didn't want this stuff to be released?"

"Yeah, but shit, it's here," said Gerry. "Everyone else is gonna hear it, why not us?"

"Do you think there's much more unreleased stuff?" asked Martha.

"Couldn't be," replied Chip, "he was very particular and didn't record that much."

"We'll see about that," countered Joel.

When the record had been played twice, the conversation drifted back to the bomb and speculation ran high as to the consequences.

"They just might shut the campus down because of it,"

said Martha.

"No way," said Joel. "One bomb scare?"

Gerry stared him down and said, "Humpf!"

"In the meantime," said Chip, "let's get high. Higher than we've ever been before."

"You mean," said Gerry, "a bona-fide journey to outer space?"

"You got it."

The gang dispersed and everyone went back to their rooms to fetch their drugs. They were all reassembled in the Penthouse fifteen minutes later.

The music was loud and the smoke grew thick. There were over fifty small vials scattered everywhere containing every imaginable kind of smoking dope: hash, grass, ganja, opium, Turkish primo with streaks of white mold, and even Nepalese temple balls. Some of the vials had labels listing the contents, date purchased, and last date smoked.

It wasn't long before everyone surrendered to an attack of the munchies. Phone calls were placed and in a very short time pizzas, heroes, and Chinese food started to arrive. They stuffed themselves like it was the last meal before their execution, washed it down with cans of soda pop and once again lit up in search of that highest of highs.

They all fell asleep right where they sat, amid the overflowing ashtrays, greasy paper, sticky cartons, empty cans, pipes, papers, and roach clips.

In the morning, a mimeographed announcement was posted on every bulletin board on the college premises:

ALL CLASSES ARE SUSPENDED FOR THE REMAINDER
OF THE SEMESTER.
ALL STUDENTS WILL RECEIVE A 'PASS' IN ALL SUBJECTS.
CLASSES WILL RESUME IN SEPTEMBER.

5

"Let me drive for a while," said Chip. He was getting restless, sitting in the back seat with no one to talk to. Joel was reading a book about the music business while Jacqui wrote a poem in a stenographer's notebook. In the front seat Martha was asleep and Gerry commanded the steering wheel.

"When I stop for gas you can drive for a while if you want to." He turned the radio up and sang along with the Stylistics' "I'm Stone In Love With You."

Martha's parents owned a house in Provincetown and apart from the summer, no one used it. A large colonial structure, it was perched right on the water near the outskirts of town. Since Gerry's parents had allowed him to take the family's second car back to Boston for second semester – and the house was empty – Martha and Gerry had planned a special weekend trip for the gang. Since school had been unexpectedly recessed and everyone hadn't planned on returning home for several weeks, a trip to Provincetown seemed like a good way to kill some time.

It was a sunny Friday afternoon, and before they went to the house, Martha wanted to stop at the market for groceries. She directed Chip, now in the driver's seat, to the supermarket, and they all tumbled out of the car and foraged in the brightly-lit food complex. They loaded up a shopping cart with mostly junk food and got in line to pay the cashier.

Standing in front of Martha was Mark, a young man with a moustache whom she had met a couple of summers ago. When he turned and saw her there he politely inquired as to her parents' health.

"They're just great. I spoke to them on the phone a few days ago, told them I was bringing some friends down for the weekend."

"By the way, what are you doing this evening?"

"Oh, we have nothing special planned. Just gonna hang out."

"A friend of mine is having a party and he told me I could invite some people. Why don't you and your friends join us?"

Martha thanked him and accepted the small slip of paper with the address. "It's supposed to start at ten, but it probably won't get really hot until around midnight. See you later."

Martha's parents had told her that there would be a construction crew working in the backyard and that she should make her presence known to them when she arrived. When they drove up to the sprawling house there was a truck parked in the driveway, and the distant sounds of hammering and clanging hung in the briny air. After unlocking the front door and depositing the suitcases and bundles in the hall, Martha told everyone to make themselves comfortable in the living room while she went out back to talk to the men who were building the new seawall. She asked them what time they quit and invited them to come in for a beer before they left the premises. They accepted her offer and promised to knock at the back door at five o'clock.

Jacqui and Joel found the kitchen and were stocking the refrigerator when Martha returned, and subsequently took everyone upstairs to their rooms. The large house could easily accommodate them all, and the hostess insisted that they all have their own room, except for Gerry and herself, who took the master bedroom. While her guests unpacked and visited the bathrooms, Martha collected the white sheets which were draped over every item of furniture.

Eventually the gang reassembled in the living room and got down to some serious ingestion of beer, wine, and grass. The stereo played loudly, and they were all fairly stoned, so no one heard the workmen's knock which occurred punctually at five. After waiting several minutes and knocking again, the four men entered the house and followed the sound of the stereo until they found the living room.

Chip had been giving Jacqui a shotgun when the strangers hesitantly entered the large, ornate room. Taken by surprise, he became flustered and burnt his tongue with the reefer. Gerry tried to hide his stash, but it was too late. Everyone had seen. One of the men, a handsome, well-built black man stepped forward and gestured amiably, "Don't worry 'bout that stuff. We've been known to smoke it too. Sorry for the intrusion, but we were invited."

Martha stood up. "No, it's my fault. But let's forget it, okay?" Introductions were made all around, and Martha went to the kitchen to obtain four cans of cold beer. The man who had spoken appeared to be, if not the leader, then the highest in the pecking order. He introduced himself as J.T., short for Jonathan Taylor. "Everyone always called me J.T. Ever since I was a little bitty boy."

The assemblage began to relax. J.T. explained the processes involved in constructing a seawall. The gang listened attentively. Joel nudged Gerry, glanced from the stash box to the men and back to Gerry. He got the idea, but hesitated until Joel nudged him again. "Uh, you guys want to get high?"

"Love to," said J.T., "and I'm sure my friends wouldn't mind either." They nodded in assent. Gerry rolled two enormous joints, while Chip changed the record and Martha went to get more cold beer. As an afterthought, she grabbed some potato chips, pretzels and peanuts and reentered bearing a large tray. The pot-bellied man named Sam sprang to his feet and helped her. The two joints were lit simultaneously and passed around the circle in opposite directions. Sam found himself being handed both at the same time. He put them both to his lips and drew deeply, criss-crossed his arms and kept them going in their respective directions. The Lovin' Spoonful's *Greatest Hits* bounced from the speakers as the two clans drifted higher.

Sam stood up, walked over to Joel and whispered, "Where's the john?" Joel jumped to his feet and said, "Follow me."

He led him to the downstairs bathroom, adjacent to the front hall. Joel returned to the living room as the Spoonful disc was ending and replaced it with Sly and the Family Stone. When "Everyday People" came on, J.T. rose and began bumping and grinding. He danced over to Jacqui, bowed and asked her to join him. She accepted and the two were getting down in the middle of the circle when Sam returned. He walked over to the stereo, turned the volume down, spun around and shouted, "FREEZE!" In his left hand he held a badge and his right hand brandished a gun. "Here I am smokin' somethin' which is highly illegal, with a bunch of draft card and bra burners. You're all under arrest."

Gerry freaked out and bounded to his feet.

"You take one more step and you're a memory."

Gerry stood still and sheepishly put his hands in the air. Sam had an evil look in his eyes as he pointed the gun at each of them and asked, "Who'm I gonna take in? The whole bunch or just the one who owns the stuff?" Martha began to speak but Sam barked, "Shut up!"

He pointed the gun at Gerry and deliberately squeezed the trigger as Jacqui leaped to her feet and screamed, "DON'T!"

The hammer fell and made a slight, plink as Sam's evil gaze melted. He dropped the gun, laughed and slapped his thigh. "Really had ya goin', huh?"

Gerry, who had almost fainted, slowly sat down, shaking visibly.

J.T. retrieved the gun, grabbed the badge from Sam's hand and went over to Gerry. "Look, the gun's empty and the badge is a fake. Relax, kid. That's just Sam's sick sense of humor."

Sam, still laughing, went to Gerry and shook his hand. "Friends? You can take a li'l ol' joke, can't you?"

Gerry accepted the outstretched hand and shook his head in bewilderment. "Either you're a brilliant actor, or I'm one uptight motherfucker."

Martha, greatly relieved, said, "Or perhaps a little of both." With everybody back at ease, Martha said, "Hey, Gerry, roll another one, just like the other one." The music was turned up and the room became enveloped in a smoky haze. J.T. looked at his watch and announced that he had to go. Sam interjected, "Ya got another hot date?"

"That's right."

"Ol' J.T. here always has a date on Friday night, ain't that right? And you know what? She must be uglier than hell or more beautiful than Miss America, 'cause none of us has ever seen 'er."

"I don't kiss and tell," said J.T.

"Maybe she's married."

"Drop it, Sam." He thanked Gerry for the grass and Martha for her hospitality. The two shy men who had not said a word until they said goodbye, and Sam shook hands all around. They left the house, got in the truck and were soon out of sight.

Joel and Jacqui went around the room collecting empties and dumping ashtrays while Martha prepared an enormous pot of spaghetti and tomato sauce which yielded portions that were big enough to leave everyone feeling that they had eaten too much. Afterwards they went for a stroll along the dunes.

* * *

It was approximately eleven-thirty when the gang arrived at the address which Martha had obtained at the supermarket earlier that day. She rang the buzzer and a tall, slim man wearing a sailor suit and cap opened the door.

"Good evening. Please come in and leave your inhibitions behind you." He bowed grandly and stepped aside as the gang entered and huddled by the door. Martha explained that Mark Thompson had extended the invitation and introduced her friends.

"Pleased to meet you all. Just call me Mary. I'm known far and wide as Provincetown Mary." He smiled broadly and continued as he led them into the parlor. "Mark said he might not make it 'til late because he and Bill might fuck more than usual. If you can imagine that."

Mary showed them to the bar and told them to help themselves. Eyeing Chip up and down, he said, "You're kind of cute."

Chip blushed and looked away.

"Let me introduce you around."

There were two boys on the couch, both dressed identically in LaCoste shirts, black Levi's and Topsiders. Their names were Jeff and Tony and they were both strikingly handsome. Sitting next to them were a well-muscled man and a heavy, short-haired woman. The man, Arnold, had an effeminate inflection in his speech and his eyes lit up when he was introduced to Joel. The woman, Phoebe, spoke with evenly measured tones and politely said hello to everyone. There were two women dressed in jeans and sweatshirts holding hands near the stereo and a very elegantly-dressed, emaciated man named Paul who replaced Smokey Robinson and the Miracles with the Broadway Cast album of *Company*. Mary moved around the room clearing away empty glasses, refilling the candy dish and fetching fresh drinks.

Gerry extracted a few joints from his cigarette pack and passed them around. Martha had started talking to Paul about Stephen Sondheim, while Joel and Jacqui joined Arnold and Phoebe in a discussion about oppressed minorities. Chip and Gerry stood near the bar. "Can you believe this?" said Chip.

"Too much. Every time I think I've seen it all, BOOM. This could prove to be very interesting. 'Nother cocktail?"

"You bet."

Martha followed Mary into the kitchen. "Can I try on your sailor cap, please?"

"Of course, darling. Let me help. Oooo, it really suits you." The doorbell rang, and while Mary went to answer it, Martha reappeared in the parlor, twirling the sailor cap on the extended pointer of her right hand.

When Mary returned with the newly arrived guests, Joel was the first to notice that one of the two men standing in the doorway was J.T., leader of the construction crew. Stepping over to Joel, J.T. shook his hand and said, "I'd like you to meet Stuart, my lover. Stuart, this is Joel."

They shook hands. "Pleased to meet you," said Stuart.

J.T. moved around the room shaking hands with everyone, except for tuxedoed Paul, whom he hugged and kissed. Mary, who was standing next to Chip and Gerry at the bar whispered, "Paul and J.T. were lovers until Stuart stepped into the picture. But they're all friends now."

"Oh, really," said Chip.

Martha was stunned because she did not think that a person could be a construction worker and gay, but she did her best to appear unperturbed. She tried to find traces of effeminate behavior in his actions, but he was the same masculine guy he had appeared to be before. She figured that J.T. must be the "butch" and Stuart the "femme," but she was unable to detect any feminine mannerisms in Stuart either.

Arnold had gone to the bathroom and Phoebe was giving Jacqui the eye. Embarrassed, Joel went over to the bar.

"Is there anything I can get for you," asked Mary.

"Well, actually," said Joel, "is there anyone here who could sell me a hit of speed?"

"Hmmm. Let me think. I don't speed anymore myself. Bad for the skin. Wait a minute. Fred and Robert. They should be here soon. They always do speed. I'm sure you can get some from them. I'll talk to them as soon as they get here."

"Thanks. It's a terrific party and I want to keep my energy level up."

"You know, a girl could kind of go for you."

Mary placed his hand on Joel's shoulder. Joel became nervous with this queen in sailor drag touching him in front of his friends, but he did not want his uneasiness to show. He forced a smile and said, "You're not exactly my type."

Mary feigned indignation and said, "That's the story of my life." He sashayed away in an exaggerated huff.

Chip and Arnold discussed body-building techniques, while Martha and Gerry chatted about theater, film and acting with the look-alikes Jeff and Tony, who it turned out, were lovers and had dramatic aspirations themselves. Mary fussed in the kitchen and replenished ice, canapés, and M&Ms.

Mark Thompson finally arrived with his boyfriend, a burly man of indeterminate age. They mixed drinks for themselves and circled the room, greeting their friends. Jacqui, Phoebe and J.T. sat on the floor in front of the large speakers and sang along with the Rolling Stones' *High Tide and Green Grass,* while J.T.'s current lover, Stuart, danced with his ex-lover, Paul.

The doorbell rang and when Mary answered it to find Fred and Robert, he remembered that Joel had inquired about some speed. He explained the situation to them. Mary ushered them in and after they greeted their friends, introduced them to Joel.

Joel's eyes widened. Fred, though not very handsome, was very sexy. In skintight white Levi's the tapered columns of his thighs and the bulge of his crotch made Joel weak with desire. Robert was as cute as the underwear models in the back of *Playboy.* He smiled at Joel. "If you like, you can come over to our place. It's only a five minute walk and we've got plenty of black beauties."

"You're sure it wouldn't be any trouble?"

"Actually, it would be a pleasure. Besides, we'll be back in no time." Joel explained the situation to Martha and left with the two young men. Paul drew Mary aside and asked, "When are you going to do your Judy Garland number?"

"Give me a few minutes to change."

"I'll change the record after a few more songs."

An entire wall of Mary's apartment was decorated with posters of Broadway musicals, and Martha and Gerry were looking at them, listing the ones they'd both seen. Meanwhile, the two women in jeans and sweatshirts were slow dancing cheek to cheek. They accidentally bumped into the TV tray which supported the potato chips and California onion dip and it went crashing to the floor with debris scattering in all directions. Mary couldn't hear the commotion with his bedroom door closed and thought it was time for his entrance. He bounded into the parlor in complete Judy Garland drag and stepped into a large mound of onion dip. He slipped and fell, spattering the red gown, pumps and wig with stains that he was never able to remove. He sighed, got to his feet, and went back to the bedroom to change. Jacqui cleaned up the mess and Mary returned wearing the familiar sailor suit.

* * *

When Joel entered Fred and Robert's apartment he was struck by the beauty and sophistication of the decor. The vases of flowers, paintings in gilded frames and uniform leatherbound volumes made a tremendous impression. Robert asked if he'd like to sit and offered him a drink.

"Are you going to have one?" asked Joel.

"Yes."

"I'll have whatever you're getting for yourself."

"Rum and coke?"

"Fine."

Fred, meanwhile, returned from the bedroom with a joint and a vial of pills. "Smoke?"

"Sure," said Joel, "Why not?"

The three of them sat on the sofa, with Joel in the middle, and when the joint was finished, Robert picked up the vial and handed it to him. "Help yourself," he said as he patted Joel's thigh. He opened the vial, took out one capsule, placed it on his tongue and washed it down with a swig of his cocktail. Fred had his arm on the back of the sofa behind Joel's head and he eased it down so that it cradled Joel's shoulders. Joel glanced down at Fred's crotch.

"Would you like to hear some music?" asked Fred.

"Sure."

Fred mussed Joel's hair, stood up and played "The First Time Ever I Saw Your Face" by Roberta Flack. Robert had shifted his leg so that it was leaning against Joel's and the tentative touching of his thigh had graduated to a regular stroke. Joel became nervous, gulped his drink and glanced at Robert. When their eyes met, Joel shuddered. He felt a sinking sensation in his stomach. Robert took his hand. His palms became sweaty and he blushed with embarrassment. Fred sat down and dropped his arm around Joel's shoulders.

"So, Joel, what are you into?" purred Robert.

"Well," said Joel, clearing his throat, "I write and sing and would someday like to make records and give concerts. But right now I'm majoring in English Literature."

"That's wonderful. Do you like Jane Austen?"

"I haven't read her yet."

"You should read *Pride and Prejudice* and *Mansfield Park.* They're both excellent." The three sat and listened to the music. Fred played with Joel's hair and Robert held his hand. Beginning to relax, Joel suddenly felt his cock begin to stir. He hoped that they wouldn't notice, but it felt too good to suppress. He turned to Fred and asked, "What are you thinking about?"

Fred smiled. "Kissing you."

Staring into his eyes, Fred touched his cheek and slowly brought his head forward until their lips met. Planting his mouth firmly over Joel's, he gently drew Joel's tongue into his mouth and sucked it as though it were something precious and rare. Joel felt himself growing more erect as his body began to tingle all over. He slowly pulled away and was still looking into Fred's eyes when he felt Robert's grip on his hand tighten.

"It's my turn," said Robert as he turned Joel's face to his. The deep, lapis lazuli eyes riveted his gaze as he received Robert's eager tongue. Robert explored Joel's mouth as Fred's hand closed over his stiff cock, straining against the faded denim. Joel began to breathe faster. He allowed his body to roll with the flow. Seconds later, his warm fluid sprang forth and collected on the fabric of his snug, white briefs.

* * *

When the three returned to the party at Mary's, several guests had already gone. Those remaining were all offered capsules from the tiny vial. Everybody took one. They all sat in a circle on the floor, smoking, drinking, and speed rapping until dawn, while the same Santana album played over and over.

6

The gang splintered into five individuals for the summer

break and regrouped at the beginning of September. Martha, Gerry and Joel worked as a waitress, cab driver and summer camp counselor, respectively. Jacqui taught reading and writing for a Head Start program and Chip tooled around Indiana in his new MG.

Living arrangements for the third semester were slightly different from the previous year. Joel and Chip rented a small railroad flat on Marlborough Street. Martha and Gerry moved into a tiny studio on the same block, a few buildings away. Jacqui was back at her dormitory, this time with a room to herself.

Thunderous applause greeted Jacqui as she stepped down from the podium. The reading, her second, had gone exceedingly well. The audience loved her. She was deluged with compliments and thanks from the largely female, mostly feminist crowd. Among her admirers was a statuesque black woman who moved with antelope grace. With beribboned braided hair and warm, brown eyes, her name was Elaine and she had cried when Jacqui read her epic verse, "Hecate's Clock."

After the throng had dissipated somewhat, Elaine approached Jacqui. She took her hands, locked her gaze on Jacqui's eyes and profusely thanked the poetess for sharing her sensitivity and insight. Jacqui was too overwhelmed to say anything. When Elaine finally broke the silence, Jacqui accepted her invitation. They walked to Elaine's small, but nicely furnished apartment. African ceremonial masks decorated the walls, and wicker chairs were grouped around a circular, mahogany coffee table.

Sipping brandy, they listened to Sarah Vaughn and Nina Simone. They talked about poetry, the women's movement and bebop. Elaine finally admitted that she wrote poetry and Jacqui insisted on reading some.

"Not now. I can loan them to you. Read them when I'm not around." They moved closer. And found themselves touching each other to emphasize their thoughts and words. They kissed and when Elaine asked if she would care to spend the night, Jacqui was enthralled.

The two lithe forms lay together on the bed. They whispered silly things to each other. "Chocolate Lover." "Ebony Princess." They kissed and hugged and played with each other's breasts. Their breathing became deeper, their passions merged. They satisfied each other with their mouths, every so often substituting their fingers while they rested their tongues. When each was completely spent, they tried to sleep, but were far too excited. They talked and touched, hugged and kissed, until the first motes of sunlight danced over the windowsill.

* * *

Martha, Jacqui, and Joel were sitting in a tiny movie theater on Boylston Street when Gerry rushed over to them and breathlessly asked, "How much time 'til it starts?"

"A few minutes. You still have time to get some popcorn," said Joel. "What's the name of this film again?"

"The Seventh Seal," *said Jacqui.*

"Fellini or Truffaut?"

"Bergman," said Martha.

"Oh. Where's Chip?"

"He only goes to movies that have dumb broads with big tits," chuckled Joel.

* * *

The old television set that Gerry's parents had given him was broken again, and he was scribbling in his notebook. Martha wanted to watch *Casablanca,* so she called to see if Joel or Chip was at home and if their television was available. Joel answered and told her to come over.

Martha, Joel, and Chip sat in the living room sipping beer, while Humphrey Bogart and Ingrid Bergman inhabited the small screen. About halfway through the film, Joel yawned, stretched and went to his room. Martha and Chip watched the entire film. As the credits were rolling by, Martha donned her jacket.

"Don't leave yet," said Chip. "Stay and smoke a joint with me."

"Okay."

He turned off the television and they quietly entered Chip's room. He closed the door.

They passed a Jamaican joint laced with Panama red back and forth, sitting next to one another on the mattress on the floor. Emboldened by the fragrant smoke, Chip began to flirt. "I hope Gerry knows what a helluva woman you are." He stroked her long, dark hair. "Such soft hair. I'll bet he's about the luckiest guy in the universe."

"Come off it ya big lug. You wouldn't even give me the time of day. My tits are too small."

They laughed.

"I wish I could develop my breasts the way you've developed your arms. I like a man with all his bulges in the right places." She winked.

"If you think my arms are good, you should see my calves."

Martha shuddered. "Well," she said, "are you gonna show me?"

"Let's make a deal. Do you want the box or what's behind the curtain. But seriously, folks, if you take off your blouse, I'll take off my pants."

"Sounds fair."

Chip stood up and unzipped his jeans. Martha unbuttoned her shirt. He sat down. They studied each other for a minute and then kissed. He pulled her down and licked her nipples. The remaining clothing was removed. They embraced and flew into a frenzy of wet kisses, their bodies writhing around on the mattress. The attraction was strong, but neither could completely erase the thoughts of Gerry that kept returning to interfere. Chip and Martha fooled around all night long, but neither achieved the heights of sensuality and release of which they were usually so capable.

The next morning, they awoke and could barely look at

one another. They spoke a few awkward words. Martha tried to leave discretely. But Joel emerged from his room just as she was leaving Chip's room. Immediately grasping the situation, Joel frowned. He glared at them as they stood by the door, Martha's usually perfect hair, dishevelled, and Chip in his briefs. Martha tried to explain, but Joel interrupted. "Don't tell me anything. I don't want to know."

Chip entreated him to let him explain, but he grew angrier. He moved toward the front door, trying to suppress his rage, when Martha blurted, "Please don't tell Gerry."

"He'll never hear about it from me," snapped Joel, "I can guarantee you that!"

When he slammed the door behind him, the small glass hash pipe that Joel kept on his shelf, fell to the floor and shattered.

* * *

Gerry had never been much of a reader, except, for magazine articles about his favorite blues singers and rock stars. One day he stopped by a bookstore to pick up a copy of *The Rimers Of Eldritch* by Lanford Wilson for Martha. He was very high and found himself wandering around the stacks, looking at the illustrations on the covers of paperbacks, when he stumbled upon *Confessions Of An English Opium Eater* by Thomas DeQuincey. It had never occurred to him that there might exist a body of literature on the subject of transcendental drugs. He bought it, devoured it and was hungry for more. He subsequently discovered *Artificial Paradise* by Charles Baudelaire, *The Doors Of Perception* by Aldous Huxley, *M'Hashish* by Mohammed Mrabet, *A Separate Reality* by Carlos Castaneda and *The Yage Letters* by Allen Ginsberg and William S. Burroughs. Gerry became a lover of books, seemingly overnight, and began to haunt the cluster of tiny book stores that pepper the streets around Harvard Square, in search of any and all material that pertained to his newly-discovered literary genre.

7

Bring 'em home, bring 'em home.
Stop the war and bring 'em home.

Thousands of people had gathered in the Common to protest the continuation of the war, and the gang, plus Elaine, all stood beneath the Black Lesbians For Peace banner. The park was packed with flower children, militant students, and the National Guard.

Jacqui had convinced the gang that they should all march together and decided it would be the perfect opportunity to introduce Elaine to her friends. When the march had ended and the rally began, Elaine unpacked her picnic hamper and passed around alfalfa sprout sandwiches and thermoses of apple cider.

"This is great," said Chip, maneuvering a few stray sprouts into his mouth. "I'm glad you like them," Elaine smiled and her perfect white teeth sparkled. "Try some of this," she said, handing him a thermos. He swigged freely.

"Wow, this is hard stuff."

Elaine giggled and passed the thermos to Martha. Jacqui took Elaine's hand and kissed it.

"That's so sweet," said Gerry, raising Martha's hand to his lips. The speaker, a well-known civil rights leader, droned away in the background. Joel strained to hear the words but they were inaudible.

"Elaine has asked me to move in with her," said Jacqui.

"No kidding," said Joel.

Martha swallowed. "And you accepted, I hope."

Jacqui and Elaine beamed at her and nodded their heads.

"When's the big day?" asked Gerry.

"Soon," said Jacqui, "very soon."

"Can I have another sandwich?" asked Chip.

"Of course," said Elaine, reaching for one.

"Swig o' cider," said Gerry, taking the thermos from Martha.

Just then, a skinny dude in patched jeans came by hawking Peace & Love t-shirts. Gerry bought six and handed them out to the picnicking peaceniks. He ripped off his plain t-shirt and donned the new one. Jumping to his feet, he started chanting. *Peace now, peace now,* punctuating the air with his fist. The gang leaped to their feet and joined him. Soon everyone nearby did the same and eventually the chant was seized by everyone gathered in the park.

* * *

Joel stepped off the tiny stage to the accompaniment of scattered, but enthusiastic applause. Carefully placing his guitar in the plush-lined, hard-shell case, he sat down and ordered a coke when the waitress came by. He had been spending more time with his guitar, perfecting his picking style, developing his voice and composing folky pop songs. Finally working up the courage, he had come to the Sword In The Stone on Charles Street to try out his new material. He was pleased with his performance and satisfied by the audience's response. He lit a cigarette when his drink arrived and wondered if he should approach the club owner for a booking. His thoughts were interrupted when a stranger came over to his table and addressed him in a quiet voice.

"You're really good. I loved your stuff. Especially the last song. Did you write it?"

"Yes. I wrote 'em all."

"That's amazing ...would you mind if I sat down for a minute?"

Joel took in the sensitive green eyes, thick waves of brown hair, and pouting mouth. He gestured at the empty chair. The stranger ordered a Seven-Up and the two fell into animated conversation that centered on Tim Hardin, Tom Paxton and Phil Ochs. Feeling that the stranger's eyes were trying to probe his innermost thoughts, Joel looked down at the table, trying to avoid the intense gaze. The stranger lit a cigarette and inhaled deeply. "Have you ever heard of Bruce

Mackay? He has an album out on ESP?"

"I don't think so," replied Joel.

"I live right around the corner, and I thought you might like to come over and listen to it."

Joel pondered the suggestion for a few seconds, then explained that he would gladly go over, but first he wanted to talk business with the club owner. When he returned to the table he found that the bill for the two sodas had been paid.

"Thank you."

"Well, are you gonna work here, or what?"

"The guy said he was busy when I was on, but he noticed that the audience's response was positive, so he told me to come back next week and he'd give me a solid listen."

"Do you believe him?"

"Do I have a choice?"

They sat on the couch in the stranger's shabby apartment, listening to the Bruce Mackay record. Joel was enjoying it and began to relax when the stranger abruptly turned to him and introduced himself, apologizing for not having done so before. "The name's Zack."

"Joel."

"Yeah, I know, they introduced you at the club, remember?" Zack ran his finger along Joel's cheekbone and kissed him. Joel buried his hands in Zack's thick hair as they scoured the insides of each other's mouths. Gripped in a bear-hug embrace, they rolled around on the couch. Stripping themselves, they lay down alongside one another on the couch. Zack propped some throw pillows against the armrest. As Zack nibbled his earlobe and played with his cock, Joel closed his eyes and pictured Chip.

* * *

The Drama Department's production of *Hamlet* opened a few weeks before the end of the third semester and Martha's Ophelia was dazzling. The college paper's theater critic singled out her performance as the strongest. The gang sat together on opening night. Joel and Chip threw a party at their apartment afterwards, and Martha was buzzing with excitement.

"You're going to be a great actress," said Chip.

"You're already a great actress," said Elaine.

"Here, here," said Jacqui, raising her glass in tribute.

"You were sensational," said Joel.

"Thank you," said Martha.

"I love you," said Gerry, kissing her cheek.

Martha sipped her champagne and smiled at Chip. He grinned, toasted her, then looked away.

* * *

Jacqui was the first to drop out of school. Elaine had encouraged her to send a sheaf of poems to a small publisher and when she received the notice of acceptance, she decided to quit and start writing full time. She moved into Elaine's apartment on St. Botolph Street. *Circle Of Stars,* her collected poems, was published six months later. It was dedicated to "The Gang Of Five."

* * *

Martha and Gerry's studio, usually saturated with loud music, and thick smoke had become very quiet and sober. A layer of dust had settled over Gerry's record collection. Most evenings, Gerry lay on his stomach on the bed reading, and Martha sat in the easy chair memorizing lines.

One night she put down the script, walked to the bed and pounced. "Not now," he said and rolled away.

She tickled him.

"Quit."

She moved away from the bed and brushed her hair.

"I'm sorry, it's just that I'm obsessed with this stuff," he said, slapping the book with his palm.

"I know," she sighed.

"I have an idea," he said, sitting up. He crossed his legs

and pushed his hair from his forehead.

"Oh, what's that?"

"I'm gonna make a film."

"Really," she said haughtily, "can I play the femme fatale?"

"A documentary. About famous writers who wrote about drugs."

"That sounds interesting. I've been thinking about a few ideas myself." She put the brush down on the dresser.

"Like what?"

"Like finding a school with a better drama department."

"What's wrong with the one you've got?"

"It's always classics. We never do anything modern."

Gerry lit a joint and offered it to her, but she waved it away. "I've been checking out some catalogs and I'm thinking about applying to the Academy of Dramatic Arts."

"That's in New York?"

"Right."

"Funny," he said, "I've been thinking about moving back there to try and raise some money for my film."

* * *

It was a cold, blustery day, the wind slipping through the chinks in Joel and Chip's apartment. Joel had just returned from an audition at a folk club and Chip was sitting in a tattered armchair, listening to Led Zeppelin. Joel turned the stereo down.

"We have to talk."

"Shoot."

"Well, I've been thinking about it a lot and I decided I don't want to study English Lit anymore. I'm going to apply to a music school and learn piano and composition. You can find another roommate or keep the place by yourself, but I'll be out by next semester."

Chip lit a joint and passed it to Joel. "Strange you should bring it up, ol' buddy, but I think I'm gonna go too."

Joel inhaled and handed the joint back. Chip sucked in

a large toke and said, "With Martha and Gerry in New York and Jacqui writing all the time, it's not as much fun as it used to be. Besides, I feel like forgetting all this bullshit and going back home. There's a good job waiting for me at my father's radio station."

The night before Chip was to return to Indiana, he invited Joel to join him for dinner at The Crossroads.

A modest place with red and white checkered tablecloths and Chianti bottle candle holders, the restaurant featured a large menu of Italian dishes. Chip and Joel ate garlic bread and sipped red wine while they waited for their lasagna.

"I'm gonna miss you, buddy. The others too. But I guess it's time to get serious. Settle down to a good job. Get married. The whole damn thing."

"I know what you mean. I've had a good time, learned a few things about myself," he hesitated for a moment, "and now I know what I really want to do. Be a professional musician. And Jacqui getting her book published made me realize that the longer I put it off, the longer it's gonna take."

They ate in silence and finished off the bottle of wine. Chip bought another on the way back to the apartment and uncorked it as soon as they were inside.

"Vino?"

Joel put his hands to his head. "I think I've had enough."

"Not me."

They sat and watched television until Joel noticed that Chip was snoring. He turned off the TV and tried to rouse Chip. He was unreachable. Joel struggled to get Chip to his feet and dragged him, stumbling with the weight, to bed. Joel looked down at the body sprawled on the bed. He unbuttoned Chip's faded work shirt and lifted his torso to get the arms through the sleeves. Unzipping the jeans, he peeled them from Chip's muscular legs. The jockey shorts and sweat socks were easier to remove. He looked at Chip's perfect body, wished that he could lay down alongside and hold it tight, but silently said goodbye and brought the blanket to Chip's throat.

The next afternoon, Joel helped Chip carry his luggage to

the waiting taxi. They embraced on the sidewalk and promised to stay in touch. Joel watched the car disappear into the traffic and went back inside. He unpacked his guitar and strummed an e minor chord until the sun had gone down and the moonlight had transformed the room into shadows.

T.N.Y.C.G.M.F.W.

(The New York City Gay Men's Fiction Workshop)

"You know, Mort, I've said it before, it's really not a good idea to write about writers." Lighting a cigarette, the man with orange hair glared at his victim. "People don't like to read about writers. They're interested in characters with *real* jobs."

The older man blanched, cleared his throat and shot back, "What makes you think that being a lawyer is more interesting than being a journalist?" He nervously looked around the room.

"Hey, now Mort, calm down. I'm not attacking your profession, just this ridiculous story ..."

"Excuse me for interrupting, Red," said James, the slim young man who sat next to Mort on the sofa, "but according to Beckett, in his famous book on Proust ..."

"Proust again?" said Daniel, playing with the left shoulder strap of his white tank top. "Who the fuck is this Proust, anyway? I thought we were talkin' 'bout Mort's short story ..."

"Proust," snarled James, "happened to have been one of the great ..."

"Wait a minute," said Red. He paused dramatically and sipped from his coffee mug. "Before we get into a long digression about that pedantic French bore, let's get back to Mort's story. Okay?"

Mort looked down at his manuscript while Daniel forsook his shoulder strap to scratch his crotch. James shot a disapproving look at Red and snapped, "God'll get you for failing to appreciate the foremost non-living litterateur of the Twentieth Century ... now, about Mort's story ... I think the characters, plot and tone are all fine, but the description is too sketchy. Now take Proust, for example. He could describe the leaf of a tree in several thousand different ways."

"James, darling," said Mort, "I'm not trying to write like Proust. I'm more of a Hemingway nut myself and ..."

"*Hemingway*! Barf-O!" chuckled Red as he put his finger down his throat. He stood up and stretched. "I think it's time for a break. More coffee, anyone?"

"Thanks," said James, "just a half a cup this time."

"I gotta pee," said Daniel. His springy body uncoiled and glided into the hall as Mort fingered his toupée to insure its position.

"Mort?"

"No more for me, dear, how about some water?"

"Coming right up." The red-headed hulk sashayed into the kitchen as Mort's gaze settled onto James' boyish face.

"So, how are things going at the book store?"

"Terrific," sighed James. "I just got a raise."

"That's nice ... my interview with Dustin Hoffman was just published in *Film Comment*."

James offered a phony yawn.

"You're looking very well these days, James. It gladdens the heart of an older man just to look at young, attractive males."

Ignoring the compliment, James looked away. Daniel entered the living room and strode to the bar. He poured himself a shot of Black Label and lowered his body into the paisley easy chair. Just then, Red returned bearing a circular tray, his damp t-shirt clinging to his overly developed torso. "It's getting hot in here. Think I'll close the window and turn on the air conditioner."

"Fabulous idea," chimed Mort.

The telephone rang and Red charged into the bedroom to answer it. Daniel burped and stared straight at James' face as though it were a target. "Strange runnin' into *you* at the Saint!"

"I go there from time to time," said James.

"I didn't think that high-brow lit'rary types had time for somethin' like dancin'."

"Who goes to dance? I like the parade."

"I saw you talkin' to Scott Calisher ... y'know he usta be *mine.*"

James wound his index finger into the bronze curlicue that dangled over his left ear. "Don't you think it would be far more accurate to say that you were *his*?"

Daniel took a sip of scotch. "We're discussin' the first chapter of your novel next week?"

"Yes," James nodded.

"Good," grinned Daniel.

Red jogged into the living room. "Sorry, gents, but it was a rather *pressing* call."

"Oh?" said Mort. "Did your boyfriend's gerbil crawl under the refrigerator again?"

Red laughed. "No, actually, my sister's getting married next month and ..."

"Look," Daniel interrupted, "I don't give a flyin' fuck about your sister's sex life and I gotta split by ten."

"Can we get back to my story now?" pleaded Mort. "All these interruptions ... I lose track."

"If I'm not mistaken," said James, "it's Daniel's turn to share his lit'rary expertise."

Daniel lit a cigarette and glared at Mort. "How d'ya 'spect me to finish a story with no int'restin' characters or plot? I got to page seven and nothin' happened, so I quit."

"What do you mean, *nothing happened.* In the first paragraph the narrator receives a telegram from his brother who has been presumed dead ..."

"What Daniel meant," interjected James, "is that there

were no hot studs or steamy sex scenes, therefore his attention was not sufficiently engaged. Is that correct?" He looked at Daniel and faked a yawn.

"Yeah, somethin' like that."

"I think what Daniel is trying to say," said Red, "is that your story does not contain any characters or turns of plot to which he can relate."

"But I didn't write this story for illiterate disco bunnies. It's supposed to be a tender look at what it means to grow old as a gay person combined with a suspense angle ..."

"Yes, Mort, we figured that out," said James, exasperated. "Your writing lacks solid exposition. You need to describe things more metaphorically and ..."

The doorbell rang, surprising everyone. Friends were told to stay away when a writer's group meeting was in progress.

"Excuse me!" Red bounded to the hall and stalked to the door. Shushing Clifford, he guided him to the bedroom and closed the door. He fetched a wad of bills and traded it for a glassine envelope. Dipping into the alabaster powder with his long pinky nail, he fed each of the four nostrils present, which flared eagerly like the beaks of newly born birds at feeding time. Shushing Clifford again, he led him to the door and closed it behind him. He returned to his guests. "Sorry for the interruption but the Super had to check out my fire escape. Now, where were we?" Red looked at Mort.

Mort looked at James.

James looked bored.

Daniel looked at his wristwatch. "I gotta go ... we can meet at my place next time."

The others froze. Simply walking down Daniel's block was like confronting a construction crew with the possibility that they might be something less than Real Men. Daniel rose and Mort whined, "But we're not through with my story!"

"Look," said Red, "who wants to read a story with a clichéd inheritance scam involving an old, gay man? A *writer* yet!"

The Crystal Storm

Sitting on the sofa, upholstered with the dyed pelts of native beasts, Mahr gazed out the window and wept. His long hair, the color of mother-of-pearl with highlights of pink, gray, and blue, ran in rivulets down his neck. They tumbled across tanned shoulders that were too broad and powerful to belong to anyone but a Warrior King. A gauze tunic with narrow shoulder straps loosely hiding the hard torso was cinched at the waist with a gold chain. It hung to mid-thigh, concealing the iron codpiece that protected the ruler.

A large wooden door opposite the sofa creaked open and Sergon, the ruler's godfather, slowly entered the chamber. A domesticated beast raised itself in the corner and growled menacingly, the black fur around its snout bristling with fury.

"Silence, Shogar! Sit!" Mahr's voice, weak and weary, displayed none of the power for which it had become known. But the beast relaxed and rested its head on its paws.

"And how is my master this evening?" asked Sergon, his voice cracked and reedy.

Mahr, blinking away a tear, looked at him and replied, "Nothing has changed. The crystals look particularly threatening tonight. I am lonely. That is all."

Sergon rubbed his bald scalp with his upper right hand, an unconscious gesture that indicated concern. "Is there nothing I can do?"

Mahr looked away and watched the crystals exploding against the windowpane.

"Will my master not eat this evening?"

Mahr offered no reply.

"If my master needs me, surely he will ring." Sergon left the study and returned to his suite.

The crystals – tiny symmetrical shards of ice – shattered against the stone walls and glass windows of the fortress of Mahr. Long were the shadows on the surrounding gardens, cast from the stars and moons that glimmered in the dark sky. Gale winds sent the glinting crystals, some tinged cerulean, some scarlet, swirling around the naked trees and shrubs. They danced in the lights from the sky until collision with any solid object caused them to shatter in kaleidoscopic explosions. And the winds were unusually fierce that evening, despite their artificial origin. The dancing fireworks made auras around the trees, shrubs, and walls that encircle the fortress, itself the target of a million shimmering crystals.

Within the fortress were many chambers; some barren, some practical, and others ostentatious with finery and technology. One such room, the ruler's study, was lit from within by hundreds of candles, each in its own sconce, situated variously about the walls. A large screen, studded with many colored light bulbs, hung on the wall adjacent to the sofa, the lights flickering in an unvarying pattern. A light show that signalled no danger from predatory enemies, no chinks in the defense mechanism of Mahr's regime. A strange primitive style of Earth music – inverted clam shell marimbas, bowed catgut strings and conch trumpets – filled the study with primordial song.

Mahr lowered the volume of the elaborate sound system and walked to the bookcase, his calf muscles clenching like fists, and selected a large leather-bound tome. *Tales Of Bold Comrades In Combat, In Love* by Landragon. A standard text of the warrior class, lyric prose poems of homoerotic love. Mahr sat and began reading the words which had taken him away so many times before. Away from the pressure of owning land, ruling a planet, leading a race, fighting a cold war. Away also from the loneliness that comes with too few opportunities to meet suitable love partners. When Mahr was younger and still in training, there were always sturdy lads with whom he could gambol, wrestle, lock loins. But having risen to responsibility, his time was spent serving his transplanted tribe. The precious leisure time lost to staying in shape, reading reports and plotting strategies.

Mahr's eyes, clearer now that the tears had stopped, plunged into the story of Drango and Vixley – a heroic sea captain and his cabin boy. The legend says that it was only Drango's unyielding love for the handsome boy that gave him the strength and will to defeat the invading armada. As Mahr approached his favorite part of the tale – the description of the two disrobing – his reading was suddenly interrupted by the tolling of the visitor's bell which echoed through the corridors of the fortress. Confident that Sergon or another of his retinue would admit the guest, repel the insurgents or give direction to one who'd lost his way, Mahr resumed reading. A few moments later, Sergon entered the chamber and Mahr closed the book with a sigh.

"Master, you have a visitor. He is unknown to me, but the weapon detector and brain scan reveal that he is unarmed and most definitely not hostile."

"Find out what he wants and report back."

"You might want to interrogate this one yourself. It is long since one as handsome as he has crossed the threshold of this place."

Mahr returned the book to its shelf. "Summon the stranger. Prepare some food and drink."

The techno-winds changed direction and the clinking of the crystals on the window ceased. Mahr reached for the cylindrical scepter that rested in a contoured box lined with green velvet. He turned it over in his hand and studied the bizarre hieroglyphics etched into the ceramic heirloom. "Oh, scepter of my family's power, symbol of all that is good and evil, focus me. Mother of nature, Father of time, help me to find peace for my people, solace for myself."

He returned the dream wand to its case and wiped the sweat from his forehead. Just then, the massive door creaked open and the stranger entered the candle-lit chamber.

"Welcome," said Mahr.

"Thank you," replied the stranger. His fine features and dark, brown skin formed the perfect setting for the black eyes that shone like polished ebony. His thick, curlicued hair cascaded over the white headband that circled his forehead and could be glimpsed intermittently all around his delicately shaped skull. Mahr took note of the tight-fitting trousers and shirt cut from a metallic fabric, the raiment of a scholar. "My name is Vraylok. I am humbled to meet Mahr, whose deeds are known throughout the galaxy."

"Won't you sit? This sofa is most comfortable." Vraylok stepped around the table before the sofa and lowered himself. "You are humanoid," said Mahr. "Much like myself except for the coloring."

"Yes, we are both descended from Earth refugees."

"You know of Earth?" asked Mahr incredulously.

"Yes. I know the history of the Earthlings, for it is my ancestors' history as well."

"My godfather is preparing nourishment. Say that you will share our bounty."

"I accept your generous hospitality and will someday reciprocate."

"That is not necessary," said Mahr as he increased the volume of the music. "It is my pleasure to offer you the comforts of my home. I have food and liqueurs, game rooms, sights and sounds for amusement, a library for research. Stay as long as you like. Sir, you are most welcome."

Vraylok looked about the cavernous room, glanced at the growling beast in the corner, the shifting pattern on the defense screen. Mahr looked at his guest, the sinewy musculature and intelligent eyes, trying to suppress the sensation of lust that was spreading throughout his body. The codpiece suddenly felt too tight and confining.

Sergon reappeared and placed a large tray on the table. With his two left hands he deftly maneuvered food and utensils before the guest. With his right hands he performed – with perfect symmetry – the same preparations for his master. Bowing, he retreated silently. Vraylok was amazed at the display of manual dexterity.

"This man you call 'godfather', what are his origins?"

"He is humanoid, like ourselves. But descended from a mutant strain which developed from overexposure to radiation. Through selective breeding and genetic alteration, a race was created that has full use of four upper body limbs. Sergon is, like myself, the last of his family. He has looked after me since my birth. A more devoted ally would be difficult to find. Now you must eat."

Vraylok hungrily sampled the fresh fruits, carbo-nitrate casserole and meat pies that Sergon had served while Mahr – ignoring the more substantial fare – nibbled some small lozenges that taste like rock candy laced with mint. Vraylok bit into a succulent pear. "Where do you get summer fruit in the middle of winter?"

"We maintain a greenhouse with artificial climate control that provides fresh produce."

Mahr looked at Vraylok's white teeth and smooth skin. He experienced the nervousness of one who is in the presence of a desirable humanoid. He could think of nothing to say of substance, so commented on Vraylok's apparel.

"I see by the nicks in your travelling boots that you have been long in the crystal storm."

"Yes."

"I myself do not venture out anymore. The memories are too painful." Vraylok swallowed. "But that is why our ancestors created the domes, the crystals, the artificial seasons. So that we would not forget the mistakes of the past."

"Yes, this is a truism." Vraylok patted his lips with a silken napkin and looked at Mahr with sympathy. "One hears a great deal about you, Mahr. That is why I have come. To see if the rumors are true and if I can be of some assistance."

"What rumors are these?"

Vraylok's eyes, flashing like jewels on fire, betrayed his carnal interest. "I hear that you have not given your flesh to another man for over seven orbits. Can this be true?"

"Yes."

"Why?"

"If it were easy to explain, it would be easy to rectify."

"Is it the pressure from your immense responsibilities?"

"There is that. Also there is the burden of my lineage. I am the last of my line and incapable of heterosexual coupling, as are all of the Warrior Women I know."

Vraylok thought about this and smiled. "What would you say were I to offer help?"

Mahr chuckled. "And what can you do to help me?"

Vraylok pushed his plate away and took a sip from the mug of cold ale. "I have traveled a great deal and communicated with many creatures from all parts of the galaxy. I have read widely and have been trained as a scholar. Moreover, I have studied your life and exploits to the degree that I know you better than you might think possible. Including your sexual interests, which my information battery tells me, mesh perfectly with my own."

The artificial winds shifted again and the clicks of the crystals exploding against the window reverberated through the chamber. Shogar awoke, growled a few times and resumed his slumber. Mahr looked at the handsome visitor – the high cheek bones and broad, flat nose – and could no longer ignore the stirring in his body. The heart within that had cried for so long wailed like a siren in his ears. He could no longer feign deafness to the crying of his soul.

"I am listening."

"Mahr must heed my words. The device that creates ever-larger weapons must be destroyed."

"But what of our enemy's weapons?"

"When they learn that you are without, they will come to realize that they no longer have the need."

"And what of our defenses?"

The look of Vraylok's eyes changed from desire to concern. "The defenses must remain. It is your offensive armaments that must be destroyed. Once it is known that you are prepared to defend, but unwilling to attack, the others will follow and dismantle their offensive weaponry. Unnecessary armaments are too costly to maintain."

"My teachers taught me that the best defense is a good offense," argued Mahr.

"That is a myth that began in the arena of sport and wound up on the field of battle. An unfortunate occurrence that changed all of our fates."

"Could so many be so wrong for so many orbits?"

"Apparently. Has the cold war decreased at all since the time of your father? Since the time of your grandfather?"

Mahr eyed Vraylok with a suspicion that was beginning to crumble. Even if he was an emissary from the enemy, he made a lot of sense. "No," admitted Mahr.

"Then perhaps it is time for a different plan." Vraylok placed his slender hand on Mahr's thigh. The ruler shuddered and the warmth of Vraylok's touch caused the last of his doubts to melt.

"If you will permit me," said Vraylok, "I shall pleasure your flesh and feed you the entertainments of my own. I shall walk by your side and help you to keep clear the large issues and small details. As to the continuation of your lineage, I know of Warrior Women who would be pleased to bear your child."

Mahr gazed into Vraylok's eyes and smiled.

"Come," said Vraylok. "Let's walk through the crystal storm. You have, perhaps, forgotten that the crystals melt when close enough to the warmth of a humanoid. We will watch the crystals collide and create fireworks inches from our eyes, then disappear into mist as they touch our skin."

Vraylok ran his fingers through Mahr's silvery hair and lightly massaged the back of his neck. Mahr seized Vraylok about the waist and pressed his bulging musculature to the lithe man's frame. Mahr felt his blood careening through his veins. He hugged Vraylok tightly for a time and then pulled away.

"How do I know that I can trust you?" asked the ruler.

"How do you know that this planet will remain in orbit?"

"It is one of the things in which I must maintain faith."

"And I too."

The ruler stared at the ceramic dream wand, the symbol of power and instrument of war that had been handed down from father to son for millions of time units. Although each man in the chain was aware that it was simply an object of clay, to acknowledge this would be like calling one's father a liar. Whoever held the scepter was supposed to telepathically receive battle plans and ideas for new weapons, but the men of Mahr's family – although never admitting it – knew differently. Like a silly superstition that everyone was afraid to let die, the scepter had allowed the ruling family to retain their position because everyone believed that whoever possessed it held some magical power. Mahr, however, knew that it was just a piece of baked clay with no more significance than a stone in his garden. Would he betray his forefathers and destroy the instrument of aggression that had tyrannized his race for so long?

In his mind's eye, Mahr saw himself seize the dream wand and hurl it to the floor. In his imagination it shatters into a thousand pieces, awakening Shogar. The beast growls and ambles to the debris, sniffing and snarling. Mahr goes to Shogar and smooths his mane, cooing nonsense into his ear. Shogar, breathing easier, salivating less, returns to his corner and gnaws a chunk of rawhide. Sergon appears looking highly distressed, his arms all aflutter about his beefy torso.

"Master, I heard a crashing sound. What happened?'

"Nothing to worry about. Just a pile of broken dreams that must be swept away."

"Master, the dream wand!" The godfather's hands flew to his head, which he shook in disbelief.

"Do not be distressed, Sergon. I will accept the consequences of my act."

For the first time, Mahr realized that he could destroy the dream wand. Once a picture had been created in his mind, the realization was then possible. Someday soon, the cold war would be brought to an end.

Mahr pressed the button on his console that summoned Sergon. He appeared a few moments later. The ruler draped his arm around Vraylok's shoulder.

"Would you prepare my bedchamber for my guest and myself? We shall return shortly."

"Yes, master."

Sergon scampered out the door. Mahr turned to Vraylok and said, "Come, we shall walk through my garden though winter it still be."

Arm in arm the two men – a Warrior King and a scholar – exited the portals of the massive structure. Artificial sunlight emanating from the dome overhead signalled the dawning of a new rotation. Vraylok cupped his hands and caught the moisture of a thousand melted crystals. He offered the libation to Mahr who thirstily drank his forefathers' bitter tears.

"The Crystal Storm" first appeared in *Gaylactic Gayzette*

Word Into World

"You are what you read," he said and I readily agreed. I was standing in a bar with some stranger – he looked like he could throw a good cuddle – and he was trying to impress me with the agility of his mind, the dexterity of his tongue.

"Wasn't it Emily Dickinson who said, 'Poetry is language that makes your hair stand on end'?"

"Something like that," I said.

"Well, then the first time I heard real poetry was when I was walking down the street and this alkie bag lady came over and said, 'Be glad I'm not your mother, I would've raised you wrong.' It blew me away."

"I guess it would."

"Then there was the time I was applying for a job, I was completely hard up – debts and bills to pay, nothing in the bank – and I'm desperate for this job and the guy, instead of just saying 'no', delivers this never-ending litany on his philosophy of business, concluding with the sentence, 'So that just goes to show you, you don't fuck with success ... the job's been filled'. That was poetry, man. Not only did my hair stand up, but my stomach felt like it was juggling half a dozen ball bearings."

He looked at me with expectation but I couldn't think of anything to say so I just sipped my drink and cruised a cute number who looked like he'd never even heard of Emily

Dickinson. Tousled brown hair and sneering lips, his tight-as-a-glove bleached jeans had a familiarity and intimacy with his body that I hoped I could attain. But probably never would. Worth a try, though. I struggled to pay attention to the guy I was talking to.

"Words, words, words," he said. "Do you know the difference between a word and a world?"

He looked at me like I was supposed to give him a serious answer, but I had no idea what he was talking about.

"The letter l. Get it? Word. World. L."

"Oh."

"Not o – l." He laughed for a while. I glanced at the cutey leaning against the bar.

"And the difference between butch and bitch," I said, "is u and i."

"You and I?" he asked, jabbing his thumb at me and himself.

"No, u and i," I said, drawing the letters in the air between us.

"Oh," he said and laughed.

I excused myself and went to talk to the guy at the bar. He told me right up front how much it would cost. Way beyond my budget. I looked around to find that the guy I'd been talking to was gone.

I went home alone that night and reread all the collected poems of Emily Dickinson. Then I jerked-off and fell asleep.

"Word into World" first appeared in *Exquisite Corpse*

The Star of David

"I really felt like I needed a change and just had to see your reaction." Placing his beer on the bar, he stepped back, posed, pivoted, and rejoined me. His eyes quizzed my face as I gulped down the rest of my drink.

"You look fabulous, as usual," I said, "what's the big deal?"

"The problem is that I wanted a different look, and I think maybe I went too far."

I had heard that line before. Over the years I had seen Kenny go through his preppy phase which eventually turned into a flirtation with the jock look. After tiring of that, he had become a construction worker, a cowboy, and had finally settled into basic clone. Now the moustache, plaid flannel shirt, and work boots were gone and he sported a red tank top, tight faded denims, and tennis sneakers. He looked like a suburban teenager on a Saturday afternoon at the shopping mall.

"You look great in anything, and you know it."

Running his fingers through the thick, brown mane that framed an affected pout, Kenny shifted his weight and whined, "Well, I don't know if I should say 'thank you' or 'fuck off'! Was that a compliment or have I just been read?"

"Take it any way you want – it's your turn to buy the drinks." I surveyed the crowd while he angled for the bartender's attention. The kinds of guys that usually came to the Alley ranged from college-aged pretty boys to mature macho men. Every major style of dress and attitude mingled freely, and whether one's tastes were specific or eclectic, Mr. Right For The Night could easily be found. No wonder the place was always so crowded.

"Here y'are, pardner," Kenny slid into his cowboy drawl, "let's drink to a fine herd, strong fences, and that good ol' Texas moon."

"You forgot shootin' straight and lovin' hard."

His attention focused on a swarthy bodybuilder with the stance of a bulldog who stood several feet away.

"If you had your gear," I whispered, "you could just lasso the guy and drag him over."

"I was just thinking the same thing." The drawl was gone. "See you later."

I wandered over to the jukebox, checking out the other customers on the way. Reaching into my pocket for some change, I discovered that I had none and was about to return to the bar when someone touched my arm and said, "Excuse me, my name's David, what's yours?"

"Bill."

We exchanged the expected questions, but the words were more than just automatic on my part because this man looked like he'd just stepped out of my fantasies. Suddenly, there were four quarters in my hand. A smile appeared on his face and he said, "Play me some music, okay?"

He placed his hand on my shoulder and gently turned my face toward his own. That incredible smile. His teeth were as perfect and bright as any I'd ever seen, and the lines that formed parentheses around his boysenberry lips were mesmerizing. I inserted the coins in the slot and asked what he liked to listen to.

"Oh, anything." His hand moved down in between my shoulder blades and he rubbed my back in an ever-widening circle. He asked if I'd like another drink, but before I could tell him what I was drinking, he whispered, "I know."

I watched him walk away, quickly pressed some random numbers, and waited for his return. The jeans, faded to a powder blue, stuck to his body like a veneer of paint. The fabric adhered to the two perfectly formed globes in the rear that were joined together like Siamese twins, with a straining seam. In motion, they seemed to sneer defiantly, gracefully propelled by sturdy thighs that pumped rhythmically like the pistons of an engine. His purple t-shirt stretched across hard nipples, and the muscles of his upper arms threatened to sever the sleeves.

I was about to say something, I can't recall just what, when he glared into my eyes as though he could read my mind. The next thing I knew he was holding me, so very tight, that I wanted to melt into his body. I don't think he said anything out loud, and I'm fairly certain I was equally silent, but we moved, as in mutual agreement toward the door and emerged into the balmy warmth of a summer night.

The penthouse apartment had a splendid view of the Hudson River from the high-ceilinged room with wall-to-wall book cases. It seemed like an amazing coincidence at the time because David's library contained every book I could remember reading, plus all those for which I had not yet had the time.

We sat in the living room, he in an overstuffed easy chair, and I on the peach-colored sofa. Between us, an antique mahogany coffee table supported a *TV Guide* ensconced in a Gucci leatherette cover. A state-of-the-art stereo setup and many shelves of records and tapes took up an entire wall. As soon as we'd arrived, he pressed a button and we were surrounded by a Beethoven piano sonata.

"So tell me, Bill," there was that bewitching smile again, "how's your composing coming along?"

"How did you know I'm a composer?"

"I've had my eye on you."

"Are you serious?" I laughed. "I find it very hard to believe that I never noticed *you* before. Do you go to the Alley often?"

"Occasionally, but I travel a lot."

The sonata ended and was succeeded by the sinewy trumpet of Miles Davis. Another favorite. I was really intrigued.

"Yes, Bill, I know what you're thinking. I've been aware of you for some time and asked some questions here and there."

I felt a bit uneasy. The thought of a stranger checking up on me was disturbing, and this man's assured manner and sexy appearance made me a little nervous. He must have sensed it because he came over and sat by my side. Cupping the back of my head with his hand, he pressed his lips to mine and rubbed my stomach. My senses reeled and my cock, fully aroused, strained against my jeans.

"Do you like to play games?" David asked.

I hesitated. "Sometimes."

"What do you think about acting out fantasies?"

"What did you have in mind?"

Leaning over, he playfully bit my neck. "How about a little game of vampire and blood donor?"

I was amused. "You'll be Count Dracula and I'm to play the part of The Victim?"

"Something like that."

"I must confess that I wasn't prepared for this. I left the garlic and wolfsbane at home."

"Perfect."

"Besides, I'm Jewish and don't have a crucifix."

"That's another coincidence," he chuckled, "I'm Jewish too, so a crucifix wouldn't do you any good anyway!" Mimicking the voice and accent of Bela Lugosi, he intoned, "Before de night is over, my pet, you vill find dat ze creatures of de night know everyt'ing about human anatomy. It's a subject dat is very close to our hearts!"

We rose and embraced (such incredible strength) and taking me by the hand, David led me to the bedroom. The indirect crimson lighting gave an eerie quality to the black velvet spread that draped the double bed. White satin-covered pillows were gathered haphazardly by the gleaming brass headboard, and a tiger-skin rug ominously guarded the entrance.

"What, no coffin?"

"There's a layer of native soil between the mattress and box spring."

"I see."

There were no windows. Not even a skylight. I was instructed to undress, get into bed, and pretend I was asleep. He closed the door and left me alone, explaining that he would return momentarily. As I began to disrobe I got the chills. The room seemed to harbor a threatening atmosphere and the cool satin sheets raised goosebumps on my arms. Just as I had found a comfortable position and closed my eyes, he burst through the door, literally tearing it off the hinges. The wooden slab made a dull thud as it hit the floor, and there stood David, naked, breathing heavily. His eyes ablaze, teeth flashing, he slowly made his way to the bed.

"Pretty melodramatic entrance, I'd say. Do you always break down the door when you play this game?"

"You're supposed to be asleep, remember?"

I closed my eyes. I could feel him savagely tear the bedclothes away and an angry snarl leapt from his throat. He lay down on top of me and rubbed his cantilevered, downy chest against my own, skinny and hairless. His arms and legs pinned me, spread-eagle fashion, and his lips and tongue flew about my face, neck, and shoulders. He released my arms and took my cock into his warm, wet mouth. At first it felt like a million tiny feathers tentatively reaching out and teasing me. I started to squirm and he swallowed me whole. I groaned, writhing in a weightless vacuum, my heart beating like a bass drum. I noted, with satisfaction, that I had not once felt his teeth, and finally, unable to hold out any longer, surrendered to the wild spasm that signalled the release of all tension and anxiety. He raised his head and beamed a smile that engulfed me like the blast of warmth from a furnace.

He stroked my thighs, raised my legs and stared into my eyes. My mind suddenly felt like a radio receiver. He seemed to telepathically ask if he could continue.

"Don't stop now," I silently affirmed.

"Message received," he seemed to reply.

His tanned, sculpted torso hovered above as he tenderly, slowly penetrated me. I don't recall that there was any lubrication, but it was blissfully free of pain. He filled me so completely, so snug was the fit that my shriveled cock naturally began to expand and throb again. He played with my nipples and sucked my tongue as he drew himself in and out, massaging my inner being. Every muscle in his arms and chest stood out, taut, as he worked himself into a frenzy. Suddenly, he bit the side of my neck with such intensity that I must have screamed.

He lay down alongside me, our chests rising and falling in perfect harmony. Turning, he smothered me with kisses and drew my tongue into his mouth. For a second, I thought I tasted a hint of blood.

David stood up and sighed, "That was delicious." I began to feel a bit light-headed. My stomach churned audibly. "Are you hungry?"

Before I could answer I was sitting in a high-backed chair at one end of a long table in a room that I hadn't seen before. On the sideboard were several chaffing dishes, a large bowl of greens, and a decanter of white wine. The room was lit entirely by purple candles. David filled a salad bowl, poured a chunky white dressing onto it, and placed it before me.

"Eat!" he commanded. I was in no condition to argue. Skewering a leaf of spinach and a large mushroom with the intricately engraved silver fork which he placed in my hand, I commenced.

"Blue cheese, my favorite. How did you know?" He slowly poured a glass of wine which he set in front of me, and from a different container, fixed himself a large mug of odd looking tomato juice. "Haven't you figured it out yet? I know everything there is to know about you."

"Really?" I mocked, chomping away. "What was the last book I read?"

"*Tar Baby*, by Toni Morrison."

This guy was pretty good. "The last movie I saw?"

"*Raiders Of The Lost Ark.*"

This was getting weird. "What's my brother's name?"

"You don't have a brother. Your sister, whose name is Gayle – with a 'y' – is twenty-eight, and the weekday afternoon DJ at WLAC in San Diego ... would you like some more salad?"

"Are you clairvoyant?"

"Would you like me to tell you what you're thinking right now?"

"Sure, fill me in."

"Aside from your obvious bewilderment about my mind reading abilities, you had just flashed on the title of William Burroughs' *Naked Lunch* because you've never eaten a meal without your clothes on before."

He stalked over to the sideboard, every muscle defined, the candles casting taffeta patterns on his smooth skin. He deftly tossed noodles, cream, butter, cheese, pepper, and parsley. A generous portion was placed before me.

"Okay, Mr. Wizard, would you like to tell me what's going on?"

"I'll talk if you'll eat."

"Aren't you eating anything?"

"I rarely eat solids these days, bad for my digestion." I twirled some fettucini on the fork and brought it to my mouth. "Bill," he said seriously, "I have powers that you will never be able to understand. Look at the salt shaker."

I glanced at the small crystal container. It rocked back and forth for a few seconds and became a small frog that jumped off the table. In mid-air it changed into a screeching bat that circled my head, then settled on the table, right next to the pepper, turning back into a salt shaker.

"Did you put acid in the salad dressing or are you some kind of hypnotist?"

"Neither. I am unlike anyone – and anything – you have ever met before. I have, er, special abilities." The lazy speech pattern was gone. The tone had become clipped, imperious; the accent, Eastern European.

"You're as good with dialects as my friend, Kenny."

"Oh yes, Kenny. Cute kid, but fickle." He paused. "My name is David Ben Zvi. I am over eight-hundred-years-old and come from a place that has long been forgotten. I belong to a secret cult which dotes on young males who happen to be gay – Jewish virgins. SILENCE! You were about to inform me that you were not a virgin. When I use that word I am speaking of those whose jugulars have not previously been defiled. Remember when I bit your neck? I nearly drained you. That is why I had some nourishment prepared."

I was beginning to doubt my sanity. Or his. He sipped his drink. "It is not tomato juice. It is blood. Human. Delectable. To continue, I can read your every thought and can place images in your mind. You see me as young and attractive. I am, however, quite old and unpleasant to look at. I believe the word 'troll' is the current popular description."

It was not easy to believe that this gorgeous stud was what he claimed.

"You will fall asleep in my bed tonight, but you will awaken in your own apartment. You will remember everything."

I was not convinced but decided to play along. "Won't I become a vampire?"

"Hardly ... you have seen too many bad movies."

"Will I ever see you again?"

"No. You are no longer a virgin."

"So, how about if we skip the transfusion and just have sex? You were wonderful."

"I am afraid that is not possible. Having forfeited your status as virgin, you are no longer attractive to me. But I will protect you from the fangs of others. Now that I have had you it is my wish that no one else shall ever drink from your jugular again. When you awaken you will be in possession of a small amulet of protection which will be invisible to all mortals, except yourself. It is my gift in exchange for the exquisite taste of your blood."

I decided this guy was a terrific actor. There was probably some acid or mescaline in the food. He was probably a professional mesmerist, as well.

He led me back to the bedroom, the door having been miraculously restored to its hinges. We clung together in the dark until he rolled away and began to snore. I slipped into a deep slumber and had a terrifying dream.

David and I ran down a long stretch of beach; the ocean, a clear turquoise. We stopped to catch our breath and, confident that we had escaped our pursuers, sat down to rest. After a prolonged necking session, he went for a swim while I stretched out in the sand, the sun painting my skin a reddish brown. Suddenly, I felt two powerful hands circle my neck. I opened my eyes to find a huge salivating creature with rancid breath bearing down on me. I yelled for David as the hands grew tighter around my throat. I choked, gasping for air, then woke up.

I was in my bedroom. There was the poster from the 1967 World's Fair on the far wall. My bookshelf, crammed from top to bottom with music scores and dog-eared paperbacks stood near the bed and my clock-radio, old faithful, sat silently on the night table, the second hand slowly making the usual rounds.

My neck felt strange. As if someone or something had been trying to strangle me. I raised my hand to feel the skin and touched a metallic chain. I do not own any jewelry. Never have.

I ran to the bathroom, switched on the light and looked in the mirror. A small six-pointed star, suspended on a fine chain, dangled in the hollow of my throat. A closer examination revealed six tiny amethysts, one at the apex of each point. I blinked in disbelief. Working my hands around the chain I discovered that it did not have a clasp. I tested its strength. It would not break. I was still admiring the way it lay against my skin when the telephone rang.

"Good morning, Bill. I hope you had as good a time last night as I did."

"Kenny," I had to clear my throat, "I have to show you something and tell you a story that you will not believe. But you must!"

"How about brunch? Peter's Pavilion in about an hour?"

I showered and shaved, faster than I ever had before. I wanted to arrive at the restaurant before Kenny so I could see his reaction when he noticed the star.

He didn't. I sat, head held high, trying to show off my new acquisition. He immediately started to rattle off all the sordid details of his night with the bodybuilder. I listened patiently, craning my neck, but he did not notice.

"... and then we woke up and did it again. Can you believe it?"

I sipped my coffee. "Kenneth! Will you please stop for a second and say something nice about my star?"

"Huh?"

I grasped it between my thumb and pointer.

"The only thing I see on your neck is the biggest hickey ever. What did you go home with last night, a rattlesnake?"

I told him everything I could remember about David, his apartment, and all of the bizarre things that had happened. I had no appetite whatsoever and my eggs Benedict remained untouched. Kenny shoveled his into his mouth like a fireman stoking a steam locomotive.

"If I were you, dear," he swallowed the last of it, "I'd cut down on the booze and poppers ... anyway, to change the subject, I was thinking of getting one of those spiky haircuts, like the New Wave rock stars. What do you think about a streak of green, right here on the side?"

"You'll never be satisfied with the way you look," I said, exasperated.

"At least my reputation as the Chameleon of the West Village will be intact."

After paying the bill, we strolled to the pier. I found myself constantly checking the star. I touched it. Ran my fingers around the chain. I was certain that it was there.

Two years and four months later, on a freezing December night, I walked down Christopher Street bundled up with gloves, ear muffs, and a scarf. No one had acknowledged my star and I never mentioned it to anyone, fearing that I would be labelled crazy. I noticed a figure walking toward me. In the distance I could not make out his features, but as he drew closer I could see that he was just my type. He walked right over and introduced himself. We chatted for a minute or two, but it was far too cold to talk on the street so I invited him to my apartment.

"Make yourself comfortable."

"Nice place." He walked over to the piano and played a few chords. I removed my scarf just as he turned to look at me. He stared at my throat and scowled. Shrinking away, breathing deeply, he screamed something in a language I could not identify. He pointed at my neck and backed toward the door. Turning, he grasped the doorknob with both hands and yanked it off. Still screaming, he hurled it to the floor, and with both fists, pounded on the door until the entire frame splintered noisily apart and crashed out into the hall. He ran down the stairs faster than I had ever seen anyone move.

Getting my door repaired proved to be one of the major hassles of my life. Gayle flew in from the coast to help me stand guard until my apartment was secure. It took three days. We both drank lots of coffee, took turns sleeping, and ate countless chocolate bars. The story I told her to explain my predicament did not contain one shred of truth and she had no trouble believing it.

When I told Kenny (hair shaved off, black leather and studs from head to toe) what really happened, he laughed at me. But I can still feel the star and chain, and mirrors confirm its presence. At least, to me.

"The Star of David" first appeared in *Torso*

Body Language

Looking down at the dry stain on the blanket, Roger remembered spitting out the semen and saliva after Charlie came in his mouth. Recalling the foul taste, he handled the blanket at arm's length, as though it were diseased. Folding it, making sure that his fingers did not touch the soiled part, he tucked it into his laundry bag.

Roger had planned to suck Charlie's cock. All of the gestures and signs he had developed to attract attention to his own cock were sublimated so that the focus would be on Charlie's. The message was obvious, the language – though silent – clear and direct: I want to suck your cock. Tease it, devour it, feel it grow.

The pleasure would be mutual. Roger would enjoy making Charlie writhe and groan, as Charlie would revel in feeling his cock harden, the nerve endings stroked until almost numb, the tension and release of a satisfying orgasm. But Charlie tried to take what Roger wanted to give, and a gift is robbed of all meaning if it's stolen.

Charlie had not understood, was unable to distinguish between two acts which look similar but are completely different. Cocksucking may look like facefucking, but anyone who's tried either knows that they have little in common. A cocksucker takes the active role by manipulating his partner, who remains passive. A facefucker ignores the artistry of the cocksucker by thrusting his cock into the mouth and throat as though it were merely a convenient orifice with nothing special to offer.

Roger and Charlie had knelt on the bed, face to face. Bending, Roger embraced Charlie's cock with his lips. He provided saliva, worked his tongue, created vacuums, caressed with his cheeks and palate. Charlie responded by seizing Roger's hair. He rammed his cock into Roger's mouth. Forcing him to lie down on his back, Charlie straddled his head and pumped his face like a jackhammer.

Roger did not resist. He could not bring himself to deny Charlie the pleasure of an orgasm, even though he suddenly found himself not enjoying what had, a few moments before, been sublime.

To explain the difference between giving and taking, sucking and being fucked would destroy any vestige of propriety, mystery, sensuality. The sperm, which would have tasted pungent and creamy was rendered bitter, slimy. The mouthful that Roger had planned on savoring and swallowing was instantly spat onto the blanket in disgust.

Roger locked the door and slung the laundry bag over his shoulder. Leaving the building, walking up the street, he could still recall the awful taste on his tongue. He exchanged the bag for a ticket at the launderer's, wishing he could erase the memory from his mind as easily as stains can be removed from blankets.

"Body Language" first appeared in *Exquisite Corpse*

Telesex

"Good morning, Harry, this is Computer Central. Here is what you have to look forward to today: at 10:00 the paintings you wanted framed will be delivered; at 12:00 noon you have a luncheon appointment at Venus' with Joan; at 3:00 you have a Telesex date with #4017; and at 10:00 this evening you and Frank are expected at Eugene's party. It will be warm and sunny all day with temperatures in the seventies, and this evening will be pleasant with the temperature going down to sixty-five. Have a nice day."

Pressing the button that raises the metallic window shades, Harry turned and looked at Frank. Blond and brawny, he lay fast asleep as the morning sun filtered into the room. Harry waited a few seconds to see if Frank would respond to the warm massage of the solar rays, but his dreaming and steady breathing went undisturbed.

Harry pressed the Fuzak button before sauntering over to the bathroom, and the sound of synthesized polyrhythms gently permeated the three-room apartment. The bathroom light switched on automatically upon entrance. Harry slowly examined his body in the full-length mirror and smiled, grateful that he could maintain his trim physique without ever thinking about diet or exercise.

His hips kept time with the electro-pulse during the soaping, rinsing, and toweling dry. He switched on the sunlamp and, after exposing himself for a few micro-seconds longer than necessary, strapped the U-test-it onto his arm. His heart beat faster and his breathing quickened until the needle pointed to "normal."

He entered the bedroom to find Frank, awake now with headset and goggles in place, stroking himself vigorously. Harry walked over to Frank's terminal and picked up the cassette case: *Chet Fucks Luke In The Barn.* He grimaced. Making a mental note to pick up some new cassettes, he pressed the breakfast button. Moments later Frank came, moaning and sighing. He removed the headset and goggles and watched Harry zipping up his electric blue leisure pants.

"Good morning, handsome," said Frank, wiping himself off. Harry walked over to the bed and kissed him on the forehead.

"Breakfast will be ready in about ten minutes."

As Frank headed towards the bathroom, Harry noted that the well-developed body he had fallen in love with was now doughy flab. Picking up the *Chet Fucks Luke In The Barn* cassette, he ripped out the Vicel, broke the plastic in two, and dumped the remains in the garbage receptacle.

The radio in the kitchen was tuned to the all-talk station, and discussion centered on whether a thirty-year-old rhythm and blues star could be taken seriously as a presidential contender. Harry buttered an English muffin and reached for the jam jar.

"So, who are you doing today?"

"Well," yawned Frank, "Mrs. Vanderkamp is coming in at eleven. She's a total bitch, but her hair is easy and she always has terrific gossip. Early this afternoon Peter Stone is coming in. He made a special request *pour moi!*"

"No shit? Tell him your lover adores his Fruit-Of-The-Loom ads. Especially the one where all he has on is the white briefs with the hard-hat and work boots. Hot stuff!"

Frank reached for a second helping of scrambled eggs. Harry swallowed the last of his muffin and scowled.

"Must you have more? You're turning into a real pig."

"I always have seconds."

"Yeah, but you used to work it off."

Frank's cheeks reddened.

"I used to have a good reason to work out. I didn't mind the sweat and strain because I wanted to look good. For you."

He stood up and threw down his napkin.

"If you ever decide to kiss on the lips and have sex without Fucksuits or computers, I'll rejoin the gym."

He grabbed his yellow windbreaker and left the apartment, cursing the sliding door panel that closed quietly no matter how hard you pressed the button.

* * *

Joan, in a white crepe de Chine blouse, purple spandex slacks and patent leather heels was already seated at the table when Harry arrived.

"Am I late?"

"No, I was early and couldn't stand the thought of sitting at the bar."

Harry surveyed the view of Central Park, told Joan how well she looked, and signalled the waiter.

"I'd like a bourbon and water ... ready for another?"

"Absolutely!"

"And another for the lady ... so, how're things at the shop?"

"Not quite the same since you became a millionaire and quit."

"Is it my fault the old man had the King Midas touch and died so young?"

"No, of course not. But just because you don't *have* to work doesn't mean you should just sit around all the time doing nothing. You must really be bored."

"I am," he admitted.

"So, take up a hobby. Do volunteer work. Write a book, take a course, weave baskets, but do *something*!"

"I'm still getting used to the idea of being alive."

The slim waiter with Tenaxed black hair appeared with the drinks.

"How much longer are you going to use that as an excuse? The scare is over and you, like countless others, survived."

"I know … it's just that I'm still terrified. I thought I would be dead by now."

"But you're not. And the crisis is over."

She paused and watched him sip his cocktail. "How's Frank?"

Harry sighed.

"We had another fight this morning. It was my fault but I couldn't help it."

"You're too much. Let me remind you that he stuck by your side through the entire ordeal. He *loves* you. You shouldn't be so hard on him."

Joan checked her lipstick in the mirror of her compact and closed it slowly as the waiter returned and handed them menus.

"The soup of the day is gazpacho and the vegetables are broccoli and summer squash. I'll be back in a few minutes to take your order."

Harry tried to alter the course of the conversation. "So, what do you think about Michael Jackson running for president?"

Joan sipped her sherry.

"If a lousy actor can be president, then why not a great singer? But anyway, getting back to the subject, the doctor says you're fine, the Center For Disease Control has declared the emergency over, no doubt you tested your blood this morning and it's normal …" Harry looked away, embarrassed, "… so what are you so afraid of?"

He gulped the last of his drink.

"Dying."

"You're going to die someday whether you like it or not and sex will probably have nothing to do with it."

Avoiding her penetrating hazel eyes he picked up the menu. "I'm starved. What looks good to you?"

"You are one helluva lucky motherfucker. You get cured of a strange disease and turn around to find yourself suddenly rich. You live with a good man who loves you. Get over yourself, darling, and start living again. It'll be a lot easier on all of us."

"The only reason the old man left me anything at all was because he thought I'd never live to claim it! He never gave me a dime when I needed money for treatments."

"I guess you showed him, huh?"

Harry, defeated, avoided her gaze.

"I think I'll have the gazpacho and lobster tails ... how about you?"

Joan stopped playing with the ends of her long, straight hair and, flipping the strands over her shoulder, glanced out the window.

"I'm not that hungry. I think I'll just have a salad or something."

***

The pink and magenta Mini-rob rolled over to Frank's chair on command.

"Ms. Simpson would like some coffee, please."

"How would you like it?" asked the soothing, androgynous voice of the mechanical slave.

"With just a touch of cream, as usual."

A white styrofoam cup with steaming coffee materialized as a side panel slid open and a metallic tentacle slowly propelled it toward Ms. Simpson's outstretched hand. Her chalky cheeks cracked revealing a tentative smile.

"Thank you, dear," she said to the machine.

"You're quite welcome," it replied.

"Rollers and clips," said Frank.

The Mini-rob repositioned itself by the stylist's side and a platform bearing the requested objects rose from the top of the mechanism until it was within reach. Frank started brushing and separating the wavy strands of pimento-colored hair.

"I want to know everything," said the aging spinster. Frank nimbly clipped a roller into place.

"I did Mrs. Vanderkamp this morning and she's positively certain that Brooke and Mick are going to separate and divorce ... and *he's* taking custody of the child. Could you just die?"

"I knew it would never last. I was just saying to Ernestine the other day that it was the most unlikely thing to happen since Streisand agreed to a concert tour to raise money for AIDS research."

Frank, who had never really liked the singer until she generously donated her talent to the fund-raising drive, had gone out and purchased all of her records. The Beatles had always been his favorites, but he began to hum "People" under his breath.

"Frank," said Ms. Simpson between sips, "I happen to know that you did Peter Stone, just a few hours ago, and I want to know what he's like."

Spraying a clump of hair with the atomizer that hung from his utility belt, he cleared his throat.

"What, exactly, would you like to know?"

"I've heard that he is as stupid as he is handsome."

Frank suppressed a wicked grin. "He's not what you would call an intellectual, but he's a nice person, definitely not spoiled by his success."

"And his next project?"

"He just signed to do the magazine campaign for the new line of Club Baths jockstraps."

The mere thought caused a sensation in Frank's crotch. He excused himself, walked to the reception area and absently looked at his schedule. He returned when the swelling had begun to subside. Observing his approach, his client remarked, "My dear, you really are putting on a lot of weight. You used to look so athletic."

"One of these days I'm going to start working out again ... I've just been too busy lately."

Ms. Simpson eyed him suspiciously.

"And how is Harry these days?"

"Oh, he's just fine."

"Are you two getting along any better these days?"

"Oh, yes ... everything's terrific ... would you like some more coffee?"

"No, thank you, I think I've had quite enough!"

* * *

Harry looked up at the monorail above as he walked downtown. He had sent the chauffeur and limo home, wanting to take the opportunity to walk and think. Computer Central had, as usual, been correct. The sky was cloudless, the sun strong, and a gentle breeze played with his hair. En route he purchased a new copy of *Chet Fucks Luke In The Barn,* and also picked up a new cassette for Frank's collection.

Entering the apartment, he paused to admire the paintings in their new frames and proceeded to the bedroom. He stripped and fetched the bulky Telesex uniform from the closet, zippered himself into it, and sat down on the bed. He donned his headset and goggles, plugged the suit into the computer, and switched on his terminal.

"Ready!"

"Good afternoon, Harry. You will make contact in exactly one minute and eleven seconds."

He lay down and started to think about #4017. The blond hair, finely honed torso, massive arms and thighs and meaty buns reminded him of the way Frank looked several years before. And soon, hunky #4017 would be his. Sort of. With their touch-sensitive suits on and the audio and video strictly controlled, it would almost be like real sex, with no danger of actual contact. He had examined the catalog very carefully and was thrilled when #4017 had agreed to a Telesex date.

Suddenly a test pattern appeared before his eyes and a low hum entered his ears. Moments later the computer spoke.

"Many apologies, Harry. I am sorry to tell you that we

have a malfunctioning computer chip in our circuits. This date must be postponed until full repairs can be made."

"Shitfuck! Are you sure?"

"Yes. There is no way to circumvent it. Many apologies. An appointment with a repairman is being made at this very moment."

Harry tore off the headset and goggles and practically ripped the Telesex uniform from his body. He flung it against the wall, stormed into the living room, and poured himself a bourbon at the chrome and lucite bar. He quickly gulped two shots of the stuff and poured himself a third, to sip. Unwrapping a new pack of Columbian cannabis cigarettes, he lit one and inhaled deeply.

* * *

When Frank arrived home he slipped into the apartment and discovered Harry in the kitchen. Cleaning and chopping vegetables, casual in cut-offs and a tank-top, the running water prevented him from hearing Frank's entrance. Frank snuck up behind him, gathered him in his arms, and kissed him on the back of the neck.

"I was gonna suggest that we call out for Japanese/Cuban, but I see you have something else in mind."

"I got stoned and turned on the video and there was one of those cooking shows on and I realized I hadn't done any cooking in at least a century so I went out and bought some things and here I am." He flicked a piece of cucumber rind off his thumb and returned to his task. "Dinner will be in about a half-hour, okay?"

Frank walked past the newly framed paintings without even noticing their presence. He entered the living room, fixed himself a scotch, and drank it slowly while listening to a Beatles tape.

They sat at the kitchen table and ate by candlelight while the electro-pulse kept time in the background.

"This is the best tarragon chicken ever," said Frank,

wiping his mouth with a mauve cloth napkin.

"Thanks ... actually it's pretty easy."

"Ah, but the seasoning is so subtle, so perfect."

"Would you like some more?" asked Harry with a smile, hoping the offer would compensate for his attitude at breakfast.

"No thanks." Frank looked down at the belly that hung out over his belt. "It's really terrific, but I've got to start doing something about all of this excess baggage I've been carting around. You know, this is the first meal created by human hands in this apartment since before your illness."

"Yeah, I figured it was time to start getting back into things." He paused and stared into Frank's blue eyes. "I've sort of been toying with the idea of going back to work. Joan said I could probably get my old job back at Cartier's."

"That's the best news I've heard all day."

"Are you sure you wouldn't like some more?"

Frank shook his head.

"Can I help with the dishes?"

"Nope. I'm just gonna toss this stuff into the Steri-unit and deal with the rest tomorrow. We have a party to go to."

While Frank headed for the living room, Harry collected all of the dirty dishes and utensils. He knew that Frank would want to sit and digest for a while, and then go to the bedroom for his usual post-dinner yank session. Harry got the new cassette from the closet and handed it to Frank.

"Honey, while I was out today I picked up a little something for you."

He watched as the crimson ribbons and floral paper were slowly undone.

"*Tom The Sailor Strips and Poses!* I've always wanted this one. How did you know?"

Frank stood up and gave Harry a long hug.

Harry whispered, "I was wondering if you felt like, uh, you know, fooling around? We've still got two hours before we have to leave."

"Certainement, mon cheri. I must visit le pissoir, see you

in le boudoir," he winked.

Harry sat naked on the bed, nervously rubbing his palms together when Frank entered. Sheathed from neck to wrists and ankles in a sheer latex body condom, he clutched another in his hand. Harry rose, took the Fucksuit, and tossed it in the corner. Grabbing the back of Frank's neck, he brought their mouths together and touched his lover's tongue with his own. He stepped back, smiling, and peeled the hygienic garment from Frank's body. Guiding him to the bed, he lay down and pulled Frank down alongside. He rolled on top of him and gently kissed the parted lips of the man he loved.

"Telesex" first appeared in *No Apologies*

Candy Holidays

1991

This book is dedicated to:

Michele Karlsberg

Thanks to:

Charles Kerbs, Kris Lewallen,
Michael E. O'Connor,
Jerry Rosco, Susan Sanoff,
Benjamin Eakin,
Tom Hayes, Latifah Rabb,
The Publishing Triangle.

Oasis Motel

Like a jungle beast peering through thick vines and broad leaves, he watched me as I arranged myself beneath the gray sky. I wanted to dye my winter-white skin a tawny brown. He wanted me to notice him but did not want to seem too obvious. The courtyard in the center of the motel allowed a rhomboid of sunlight to enter and illuminate the area surrounding the pool. I watched the man watching me. But like a shy animal he was reluctant to approach the pool with me beside it, an antelope who would wait until the other animals had finished drinking and departed before emerging into the clearing for a mouthful of cool water. I could have smiled at him, invited him over with words and gestures. But I pretended I did not notice him lurking behind the garden palms, closed my eyes and prayed that the clouds would dissipate, the sun come forth, my body grow warm, my skin glow.

He walked, furtively, to the other side of the courtyard and observed me from another angle. I shifted position – belly down, ass up – waiting for the sun to respond to my brain waves. A cool, sharp shock of wind descended into the courtyard; I shivered. Goosebumps appeared on my arms and legs. The sunny warmth that I associated with Southern California did not manifest itself that afternoon nor the two that followed. My perception of things – like cities, hotels and men – is usually all wrong. I think I know something but eventually find out that I am ignorant. My expectations are rarely met, my predictions usually inaccurate. Too often I'm swayed by the cleverness of the packaging and I find out too late that what's beneath the ornate paper and colorful ribbons is not quite what I wanted.

At one time the motel probably looked pretty swank, its vaguely Spanish exterior washed in bright pastel colors. But these had faded over the years. The greens, once lushly verdant, now appeared sickly. The pinks, soft and serene, had acquired a brownish tinge like rust. A movie queen who never resorts to face-lifts, breast implants or hair extensions, the motel was aging naturally, the former ingenue forced to play supporting parts like shrikes, harridans and bag ladies. Aside from a scrapbook of dated movie stills and yellowed newspaper clippings, the glory is gone. The walls, floors and ceiling of the Oasis might retain some memories, some remnants of the past that resonate on certain frequencies and wavelengths. But a casual glance reveals nothing of the former stature. Today it is old and worn and uninviting. Damp, musty odors have permanently settled into the cracks and old furnishings. Vapors, dank and aromatic, seem to rise from the mattresses, blankets and pillows.

I thought perhaps that I could nuke my skin, conduct my business and indulge in a bit of mindless pleasure. But all my calculations and projections were like leaves that fall from a tree, soon to die if not already gone.

What you see on the large screen – with the benefits of ocular technology – is not what you see holding a strip of celluloid to the light, handling it by the edge, trying to make out the tiny, vague image. A length of film is not a movie; a movie is not just a series of photographs. I couldn't tell at first what he looked like. Just a sense of human form and color, movement and motion, rustling in thick, tropical vegetation. As he moved about, beneath the catwalk, lurking in the shadows like a private dick in a B movie, I was able to discern eventually that he had coppery skin over a plump, well-upholstered armature, the thighs and upper arms bunched up like overstuffed cushions. Dark hair, a moustache. He was Hispanic or Latino. Whatever it is called these days that is not considered derogatory. I've heard people call them Chicano. I like the sound of that. I don't know if the guy was Mexican or Mexican-American. I didn't know his name at the time. I probably wouldn't even be thinking about him except that he was the last man I may have infected, the final chapter, perhaps, in the book of my sex life.

There was something very unusual about the young men who worked at the Oasis Motel. I couldn't figure it out exactly at first, but when I walked in, suitcase in hand, I noticed that the guy behind the desk seemed strange. His motions were very fluid, more feline than human. His eyes had a deep-set faraway look. There was a glistening, oily patina on his facial skin and his hair looked like it had been lathered with Crisco. He checked me in, gave me the room key and explained everything that I needed to know such as check-in policy for guests' visitors and where the ice machine could be found. The next time I saw him he was wearing layers of red, pink and tan make-up, a large tiara clung to the top of a big red wig that dropped its metallic strands to the scooped, low cut of a clingy cobalt dress, the waist so slender I could have put my hands around it, with large breasts, like warrior melons, that seemed to move independently from the slim body they were lashed to, the whole package teetering on blue leather stilettos. He greeted me and smiled. Touched the silver and rhinestone pendant at his throat and sashayed past me. I took a sip of Jack Daniel's and watched his firm little buns punch the tight behind of the dress.

The man emerged from the jungle, lit a joint and moved to the far end of the pool, staring at me, inhaling deeply, sitting on a chaise. I looked up at the gray sky, searching for a break in the clouds, a schism in the smog. Then at the man, in black Speedos, folds of fat gathered at the waist, a surprisingly hard-looking chest, with arms like hams. His face seemed sinister, untrusting, yet he stared at me with an intensity that suggested desire. I smiled, looked away quickly, shifted onto my back and closed my eyes.

All of my friends are terribly concerned with appearances. Aside from the fastidiousness of their sartorial decisions, their haircuts, muscles and apartment decoration, they are particularly, fiercely finicky when it comes to men. A man passes us on the street – I have to admit he's handsome – and my friends believe that we have been in the presence of a god. Certainly, the stranger's hair is boyishly insouciant, his face symmetrically interesting in its configuration of lines and surfaces, contours and planes, his body moves jauntily with his balls, behind, thighs and calves all filling the snug jean-space like customized ingots. He is sexy. He is handsome. He probably knows it too, which only partially accounts for my skepticism. Does he know how to suck a dick like a lollipop? Is he reassuring and a comfort in bed, saying the right words, smoothing out the wrinkles on the sheets of sexual sacrifice? Does he have a good sense of humor? Has he anything interesting to tell you? Does he think David Copperfield is a Dickens novel, a magician who does one television special per year, or has he never heard the name at all?

These things are just as important as the body-face considerations. Yet you can't know about these things just by looking. My friends seem to equate hot looks with good times. But I've fucked enough beauties to know that this is not always the case. Still, I'm reluctant to tell my friends that I'm attracted to a guy who falls very short of their rigidly elevated standards. They would not approve of the hairy jungle beast stalking me at a sex motel in Los Angeles.

In my rented room I was belly-down on the bedspread, inhaling the rank vapors, the television tuned to a very bad closed circuit porn film. I don't know what's so great about close-ups of dicks going into orifices. I want to see the guys' faces as it's happening. When I wasn't at the pool I was in the room, reading, watching TV, drinking Jack Daniel's, smoking cigarettes and joints, eating burritos with super hot sauce from the Taco Bell across the street, jerking off, lying on the bed imagining the men I'd observed. They'd come into my room, I'd be splayed on the bed. They'd get on top of me, pressing me down. Letting go of everything, I'd watch their faces, feeling my body respond to their attentions, trying to note the exact moment when they reached the threshold of ecstasy and would, for a moment or two, seem to fly away from themselves to return happier, relaxed, wet and gracefully unburdened. Even beasts look beautiful for several moments at a time.

If the motel had more decoration, I could say that it looked tacky. But there was not really much of anything that would merit that distinction. In the lobby sat a nondescript table, a seedy couch and two potted palms. Beyond lay the pool, oval and not very large, a few scattered things to sit and lounge on, all surrounded by dwarf trees, scruffy bushes, lianoid tendrils, pointy swards, creating a fake rain forest within the horseshoe courtyard, surrounded by two tiers of small rooms.

I walked up the concrete steps, clutching the wooden rail, the paint chipped and stained, and moved across the catwalk of upper berths to room number seventeen. There were about twenty-four in all, I think. Just as I placed the key in the lock, a woman, short and slim, speaking heavily-accented English, ran up to me and said that the room hadn't been made up yet, would I wait for about ten minutes? I asked her if I could leave my suitcase in the room and wait by the pool. She didn't understand me so I smiled, walked into the room, put it beneath the television set and said, very slowly, enunciating with great care, that I'd wait downstairs by the pool. She smiled and I went down, into the thick greenery and sat in a chair of metal tubes and cross-hatched bands of multicolored, faded canvas. There was no one in sight. Nor was there any sunshine. I sighed and lit a cigarette. Just then, a door above opened and a young blond guy in cut-offs and tanktop emerged, hurried across the catwalk, down the stairs and entered the lobby. And a few seconds later a guy from a different room came down and joined me beside the pool. Medium of build, with dark hair, his face didn't look exactly stupid or nerdy but didn't display much awareness, intelligence or cool either. There was something in the way his eyes seemed to wander and a slackness about the mouth that communicated something to me that I can only call uninteresting. I was ready to extend my hand and introduce myself but before I did he asked, in a very nasal voice, if I had any rolling papers that he could borrow so he could roll a joint. I told him that there was a pack in my suitcase, but I'd have to wait until the cleaning lady finished in there before I could go and get it. He seemed very disappointed and started telling me (while I was wondering if I should have called her a chambermaid) about a bar he'd been to the night before. He'd been unable to score and couldn't afford a hustler. I asked where he was from. Las Vegas, he told me. I wondered why he could afford to book a room at this place but couldn't afford a hustler.

The lady came out of the room and hung over the railing. Señor, she called and beckoned me with her hands. I told the guy I'd be right back and ran up the stairs and into the room, opened the suitcase and got out the papers, but when I came back out and looked down at the chairs beside the pool he was gone.

The room had a musty odor, the walls were a yellowish green. Beneath a damp bedspread was a lumpy mattress with an end table at the side near the door. Opposite was a banged-up bureau and a television set on one of those mechanical arms that they have in hospitals that jut out from the wall and can move forward and back, from side to side. The small bathroom had a shower stall, sink, toilet and a window the size of a mass market paperback.

I stripped to my underwear and unpacked. Changed into a swimsuit, locked the room and lay in the cool air beneath the overcast sky.

I work for a firm that distributes office supplies. Acid-Free Microfiche Binders. Custom Engraved Plastic Signs. Pressure Sensitive Labels. Deluxe Heavy-Duty Steel Vertical Files. Lightweight Free Standing Mail Organizers. I'm on the road, actually, in the air, several months a year, a modern Willie Loman, visiting the company's largest clients. My first trip to Los Angeles, I asked a friend where to stay. He suggested the Oasis Motel. Told me it's a gay hotel and I'd feel very comfortable. I imagined it would be something like the gay resorts I've been to, where vacationers go to relax. But this place was more like a public transportation john, most people renting rooms by the hour, checking in and out like the trains arriving to and departing from Grand Central Station.

Before I got off the plane, before I stepped inside the Oasis, I carried in my mind a picture of Los Angeles, images in words from the minds of Chandler and Bukowski. But now, having been there and back, the memory I carry is closer in spirit and style to Genet and Burroughs. William S., not Edgar Rice.

The manbeast moved closer to me. I could finally see his face more clearly. Big eyes set closely together, a squat nose and thick lips. And his body. Large, in keeping with my earlier assessment. But not flabby. My beast, bulky but solid, would have been scorned by my friends, who upon taking in his presence would smirk and chortle, cackle and howl, white crows on the branch of a dead tree passing judgment on all who dared walk by. But this failure, this insult to the gym mentality, this truant from the school of gay male aesthetics turned me on more than any magazine or video model, more than any muscle queen I'd ever seen anywhere. He reminded me of those brutes on television wrestling with their huge chests, enormous arms, big butts, jutting baskets and massive thighs, hunkering in a crouch ready to launch an attack – either sexual or violent, maybe a combination of both. I was a little excited, but also a bit frightened. He sat in a chair beside me. I looked at him and said hi. He extended the joint toward me, his face in a tight, expressionless, but almost mesmerizing stare. I held up my hand in a gesture that said no thank you. He sort of grunted, got up and ambled away, moving like an overstuffed teddy bear, a slow, determined, low-legged gait. I wanted to bury my face between his thighs.

But I looked away and rolled over onto my stomach to conceal the swelling in my swimsuit.

I watched the motel guests come and go.

Sometimes a single man would enter a room and over the course of several hours be visited by a succession of young men. I assumed that what went on between them had very little to do with trigonometry or discussion about the Spanish-American War. In other instances, two men would check into a room together, stay for an hour or two, and then leave. In my three days at the Oasis, mine was the only suitcase on the premises, as far as I knew.

I was enjoying myself, watching the all-male parade, and I imagined what their lives were like beyond the walls of the motel. In certain cases I invented entire biographies. Some were, of course, in the entertainment field – movies and television – others belonged to street gangs. A few were businessmen, others were most likely teachers, drug dealers, cops, lawyers, politicians and doctors. They worked, ate meals, had homes, went to the beach, saw movies and watched television. Of this, I was certain. My brute worked as a blue-collar laborer, a plumber, a carpenter or construction worker by day, moonlighting as a masked Mexican superstar of television wrestling, grappling with other brutes in sweaty bouts that were held illegally in makeshift arenas on the poor side of town where the official rule book had been thrown out and each contestant would do whatever it took to defeat and humiliate the other combatant.

I called to confirm an appointment. With Jonathan Collins, Senior Purchaser for the accounting division of a large corporation. Collins asked if I'd meet him for dinner the next evening at a much-talked-about new restaurant and I eagerly consented. Then returned to my favorite chaise by the pool and observed, with fascination, the pageant of horny men.

It became impossible to ignore my own desires. I suppose I might have been able to forget the beast if the activities of the other guests weren't constantly bombarding my consciousness with thoughts of sex. And I didn't know exactly what it was that finally strengthened my resolve and induced me to take action, but I finally abandoned convention and tradition, responding to the call of a familiar and usually ignored voice from somewhere inside of myself.

The courtyard was empty except for me and my observer. I rose from the chaise, no solar rays binding me to it, and approached the beast, lurking in the shadows beneath the catwalk. I imagined his surprise as the distance shrunk between us. Told myself that he probably thought I was going to ask him for the correct time or directions to the La Brea Tar Pits. He looked at me expectantly as I asked if he wanted to play. To play, he said quizzically and I shook my head, yes, to play, your room or mine? Yours, he said with a tentative grin and followed me up the stairs and into the room.

The shades were closed, the only light coming from a small lamp on the end table. He stood at the foot of the bed. I asked him his name but he made no reply. He looked around but the decor failed to impress him; I could perceive no response. I'd never been so bold before, had never entered into a tricking situation without at least a few moments of small talk, a brief bout of verbal foreplay. I was with the bounty I'd wanted but wasn't sure what to do next. He helped me out by moving toward me in that deliberate, arms at the ready, haunches in a near-crouch stance just like the wrestlers on television. He touched my hair, tweaked a nipple, then wrapped me in a tight embrace. He bit my neck, squeezing me, rubbing up against me. He stepped back, pulled off his Speedos, then yanked mine down and crouched at my feet, breathing softly on my dangling cock. With the first rush of warm air I became erect and felt every nerve ending in my body become fully attentive, alert for any sensation that might be felt.

The following night I met Collins for dinner. We'd already reached an agreement pertaining to our business. This was to be a symbolic meal, not a haggling session, in which we'd cement that which had already been decided.

The restaurant, I think it was called Alberta's, is a large

establishment with a fancy four-columned entranceway where you leave your car with a gorgeous blond teenage boy and enter a huge place with a bar upfront – all sharp edges of chrome and glass, then an even bigger dining room like a large cave with chunks of terra cotta and remnants and swatches of burlap. As with most people and things in Los Angeles, the exterior is hard but it gets softer closer to the heart. The heart of this place is the kitchen whose chef managed to make some very tasty treats from disparate combinations. Some of the dishes reminded me of an odd recipe from a Flaubert novel: flamingo tongues with pepper and wine.

Collins brought two business associates. One, a slender blond fellow, Art Matewsky, an assistant Vice President, and my beast, Raymond Estella, Accountant-in-Chief. When I saw him sitting at the restaurant table, in a blue suit with a burgundy tie, I didn't know how to respond. Should I acknowledge our prior meeting? When Collins introduced us I could easily have said, we've already met, but I pretended I'd never seen him before. He acted as though he'd never had my cock in his mouth or ass. I relaxed but remained alert for signs that he might somehow reveal our brief but intense encounter. Perhaps another glass of wine might activate his tongue. But he remained very quiet throughout the meal, as taciturn as he'd been at the Oasis, only speaking when it was required, confining his statements to concise rejoinders.

When the meal was over, we all shook hands and said goodbye. The brute gave my hand an extra squeeze, but his eyes, his voice, revealed nothing.

I returned to the Oasis and sat in my room. I could hear the men's voices, footfalls on the catwalk, doors opening and closing just beyond my window. I stretched out on the bed wondering if I'd tell my friends, the disapproving white crows, that I'd been intimate with someone they'd quickly tell me was too ethnic, too old, too fat, too hairy, not good enough for me.

Shortly after my return to New York some minor medical

problems resulted in a test which proved my system to be HIV Positive. The first thing I thought of was the beast. I'd have to contact his firm, ask for Raymond Estella and share with him the most unpleasant message a person can ever be forced to deliver. I recalled how the brute had mauled me into a frenzy, sucked my body's essence until I was empty, how his aromas had made me feel tingly all over, the way his hairy and massive limbs had carried me to a mirage that is real among my memories, reminding me of the last time I was able to experience complete sexual release, something to hold onto until death like a phantom comes.

It's ironic and fitting that the last should be the best, that I finally experienced that which I'd been seeking and avoiding all my life. The California sun never touched me, but something far more satisfying held me close and gave me what I needed – cool water down a parched, gritty throat in a hot, dry desert.

Life is the Illusion

Not long ago before we noticed the coffee tasted strange, Ramona had begun to exhibit signs of unusual behavior. Eating little chocolates, for one. The first time I found the crumpled red foil of a liquid-center chocolate-covered cherry on the floor of her dressing room, I assumed it had been dropped there by one of the youngsters in the cast. Or perhaps a careless visitor. But soon after that I walked in, unintentionally surprised her, and she speedily licked the evidence from the tips of her fingers. She smiled guiltily, looked away, wiped her hands on her jeans, then gazed at me as though nothing out of the ordinary had occurred. But this was the woman who lectured us constantly about overeating, junk food, too much refined sugar, not enough fiber. Warned us about our teeth, our stomachs, our colons. Ramona had conquered every tidbit of knowledge on the subject of nutrition and health. And had herself become a paradigm of sensible eating and exercising. Always quick to berate one of us for indulging in a forbidden pleasure, it was more than a little disturbing to see her sneaking a bon-bon.

And she'd begun to expound to me a bit less. The play had been running for over eight months and initially we'd not gone through a single costume change together without Ramona lecturing me on theater, art, communication, linguistics, body language. "Life is the illusion, theater is the reality," she would intone. And she'd often say something to the effect that, "Art is what it's all about. Everything else comes second. One couplet from a Shakespearean sonnet is worth more than the entire population of Bombay."

"You don't really believe that," I'd say, zipping up the rear of her ballgown. "You wouldn't say that if you had a child living there, for example."

She sipped mineral water from a bottle, threw back her mane of dark curls and said, "Yes, I do believe it and even if I had a precious child – which I don't – who lived there, I would still believe it. If I didn't how could I go out there six nights and two afternoons a week and murder my mother?"

But this kind of talk had become intermittent, then sporadic, and finally, extinct. Ramona seemed listless, dissatisfied, more on edge, too easily upset. And perhaps, it did have something to do with murdering her mother eight times a week. Not actually committing a crime, of course. But feeling the pain, terror, guilt of such an act down deep in the molecules of her marrow. A truly great actress like Ramona Black would never fake it. And I knew of nothing in her private affairs that could induce the anomie to which she seemed to have succumbed. So I attributed her state of mind to the rigors of the play.

The Madness of the Hour by Tadeusz Wieniewska had been an underground "hit" in Cracow before the authorities closed it down after six performances. A manuscript had been smuggled out and translated into English. After eight months on Broadway – a serious drama in a sea of childish musicals – *The Madness of the Hour* brought as much respectability to the Barrymore Theater on Forty-Seventh Street as it did shame to the Polish officials who'd tried to exterminate it.

And it brought respectability to Ramona Black as well. Not that she'd ever been anything less than a true star, a genuine artist. But the television series she'd been signed to had not made it to the fall schedule, her last Broadway show had run for three performances, and the movie she'd spent nine weeks filming in Iceland had bypassed the theaters and gone straight to the video stores. She'd needed a great part, lots of attention, and the security of a big hit. And she'd found it playing the flamboyant freedom fighter who commits matricide. But the role, in addition to shoring up her confidence and stature, was whittling away at her psyche.

And others were beginning to notice. Like Harlan Taylor, the stage manager. And Dulcie Gillis, the young actress who played Ramona's daughter on stage. They'd become my buddies. The only people among the cast, crew, designers and management, aside from Ramona, whom I ever actually talked to – beyond the level of getting the job done. My work takes me to different theaters, introduces me to new faces, and whenever I hook up with a show that lasts for more than a few nights, I usually befriend two or three co-workers. We remain fairly close until the play has run its course. Then we move along and create new families.

Harlan Taylor, as big as a barrel, had only recently started working at the Barrymore. For many years he'd been a stage manager at the Metropolitan Opera. But after that had worn him out he'd moved to Broadway. "Sheeit!" he explained. "Smaller casts, fewer sets, less bull. Makin' less money than before but I'll live longer!" he said, scrunched up his big, brown face, and rolled his shoulders to indicate there was nothing more to be said. Friendly to me, occasionally cantankerous with a snotty actor or producer, Harlan could always be counted on to relate a scandalous backstage tale from the Met, or turn my face red with a truly gross joke. "Anthony," he'd say, and put his arm around my shoulder, "did I tell you the one about the Frenchman, the Englishman and the American who meet in a graveyard?" he'd ask. I could smell the scent of Camels on his breath.

"No," I'd reply.

He'd bring his mouth right to my ear and whisper the lewd punchline. Then I'd blush as red as a ripe tomato and exclaim, "Harlan!" and then I'd laugh so hard I'd be shaking and he'd join me and we'd finally have to stop to catch our breath.

It was Harlan who first befriended Dulcie Gillis and very

soon after, the three of us were inseparable between performances on matinee days. She was sixteen during her stay with *The Madness of the Hour* and at first, I thought she was too young to hang out with me. I began by masking my true activities whenever she was around. I'd never make reference to drugs or sex or anything else that might corrupt an innocent youth. But she was bright, wise beyond her years, and it soon became apparent that she was mature enough to handle my pot-smoking and my affairs with men. She asked me to get her some pot once but I declined. That would be going too far. And when she pressed me for details about my sexual experiences I was pretty vague, initially, until she made it clear that there wasn't much she hadn't heard or read about. And from that point on I felt comfortable discussing any topic with her that might arise.

"Did you get laid last night?" she would ask.

"Maybe," I'd say.

"Were you with Todd?"

"Yes."

"Did he fuck you silly?"

Hearing her say this, looking at her Patty Playpal demeanor, would loosen up my sense of propriety.

Then I'd giggle and she'd start to giggle and then she'd go to the coffee maker, fix two regulars, and we'd sip, talking about more serious things. Often, matters dealing with ecological catastrophes.

Ramona could have joined us. Without being too obvious about it, the three of us tried to pull her into our circle. We sensed that she would be sympatico. But she was aloof, ignored our overtures, so we joined hands without her. Though always pleasant and kind, she chose to observe the boundaries that separate the various factions of a theatrical community. Boundaries that, perhaps, Harlan, Dulcie and I should have observed too, but like the anarchists we fancied ourselves, chose to ignore.

Dulcie was the first to notice the coffee tasted odd. We sat in a changing room lined with costumes: a few articles of modern dress, plus frilly, bustly, spangly period things for the fantasy sequences. Harlan was telling me about a certain soprano he'd known. "Sheeit! She swallowed dick morning, noon and night but never strained her throat – never missed a high note!"

Dulcie was the first to bring a steamy mug to her lips. She tasted. Then her face crinkled like a peach pit. "Yuck!" she exclaimed.

I tasted mine. It seemed more bitter than usual.

"I've had much worse," said Harlan.

He finished what was in his mug. Dulcie dumped hers in a toilet. I just left mine on the coffee table.

The next day I fixed myself a mug and it seemed normal. But the day after that it tasted awful. I threw it out. About a minute and a half before her first act entrance, Dulcie grabbed my arm, pulled me into an alcove and whispered, "Don't drink the coffee!"

"Why?"

Her fingers dug deeper into my biceps. "I'm not putting you on," she said as severely as a sixteen-year-old actress can. "It's piss! Ramona's! I saw her pee into the coffee maker!" She stared at me with deadly intensity, defying me to doubt her.

'What do we do?"

"Nothing! Just don't drink anymore. Okay?"

"Okay."

She let go of my arm and the blood began to circulate in my fingers again.

I felt more than a bit uncomfortable dressing Ramona; unzipping the practical skirt, accepting the off-white blouse, helping her step into the eighteenth century French court gown. Was this woman, this brilliant actress, urinating in our coffee? And if so, why? My hands trembled slightly and my fingers fumbled a great deal. "What's wrong with you today, Anthony?" she asked with sweet sincerity.

"Nothing. Just being my usual klutzy self."

"Relax. There's no rush."

"Okay," I said, but my stomach felt swimmy and I had to

really work at it to keep my knees from colliding. I wondered if Dulcie could be mistaken. Or joking. Or – I didn't want to even consider it – just being cruel.

And then I found out the truth for myself one day when I arrived at the Barrymore a few minutes earlier than usual. The table with the coffee maker, sugar, milk, stirrers and mugs is in the green room. I was about to enter when I heard a strange sound. Like the clanging of garbage can lids. My body tensed immediately at the oddness of this noise and I cautiously peered around the door frame instead of just marching in. And there was Ramona, moving the large metal urn from the table to the floor. She glanced up to make sure no one was looking. I backed away in time. Then she surreptitiously took it into her dressing room. I ducked into an alcove. She didn't see me. A few minutes later she returned the coffee maker to its place. Although I hadn't actually seen her hike up her dress and squat, nor had I heard the pinging of her water on metal, I was very certain that Ramona was the culprit.

So, when the company manager accused Dulcie of this crime it was up to me to be the bringer of justice. Another youngster in the cast – Johnny Kincaid – was the first person the manager had accused. But at this point, no one knew that urine was causing the strange taste. It was determined that something was awry and it was assumed that the joker was a youngster. But when confronted and accused of this misdeed, Johnny somehow managed to convince them that he'd had nothing to do with it.

So the prosecutor turned to Dulcie. And, as she told us later, the interrogation went something like this:

"Young lady, have you been tampering with the coffee machine?"

"No."

"Someone is putting something in there that makes it taste funny."

"Urine."

"What?"

"Pee."

"Huh?"

"Piss. It's piss."

His face turned six shades of scarlet. "How do you know?"

"I just know."

"Then you must be the one!"

"No, I'm not."

"Then who?"

"Can't say."

She loyally and steadfastly refused to implicate Ramona. Upper management was convinced that Dulcie had done it and they took steps to terminate her contract.

Word spread through the theater's population like a nuclear chain reaction. Within hours of Dulcie's disclosure the oft-repeated message was: Don't drink the coffee. The theater owners instructed Harlan to buy a new coffee maker. And everyone, particularly the actors and actresses, began to whine and moan. How could this outrage have occurred? Isn't there something in the union regulations about this?

Ramona seemed oblivious to the entire affair. Tightening the bodice of her funeral outfit, my heart was slam-dancing against my ribcage as I cautiously asked, "What do you think of the coffee fiasco?" I fully expected her to slap my face, run from the room and have me fired.

But she slid into her grand diva mode and sighed, then casually said, "Of course, you know, I never drink coffee. And, never forget, a great artist must endure many a calamity to survive in this prosaic world."

I decided to see just how far she would take this charade. "Do you have any idea who might have done it?"

She looked me squarely in the eye and said, "Probably some poor soul who's desperate for attention."

I could see that a confession would not be forthcoming. So I went to see the company manager and told him what I knew. He acted like I had to be insane to make such an accusation. "Ramona Black is a star. She'd never do anything like that! Her behavior has always been exemplary!"

"I can prove it," I said and took him to her dressing room.

On the mirrored vanity table was an open bag of potato chips. I pointed to the evidence triumphantly. "See! A few months ago she'd have taken her own life before eating something like this. She's going crazy and the coffee maker is just one example of how far out there she's gotten."

He refused to believe me. Must have thought I didn't like Ramona and was trying to get her in trouble or something.

Harlan and Dulcie offered consolation when I told them that I'd tried to clear her name and had failed. Her contract had been terminated and she had less than a week to go before leaving the production. And things had not really gotten back to normal among the cast and crew. Some resumed drinking the coffee with no complaints. But others refused to have any – or if they did – said that it still tasted weird.

Everything changed the day before Dulcie's last show. In the morning, when the early edition of the newspapers became available, the front page headlines shouted the latest celebrity scandal. A Broadway star was named. Ramona Black. The trouble involved a jelly donut at a coffee shop on Forty-Eighth Street. Apparently there was only one donut remaining and Ramona had gotten into a fight with another customer over who would get it. The other person eventually tried to back down but Ramona slugged him. The owner called the police.

The Donut Riot story saturated the theater district before noon. At two o'clock that same day, the new *Playbill* arrived at the theater. The feature article consisted of interviews with actors and actresses who'd forsworn junk food and had gone macrobiotic. The lead quote was attributed to Ramona Black, currently starring in *The Madness of the Hour.* I don't recall the exact wording of the quotation but it was something like, "In a world gone mad how can one pollute one's body with sugar, salt and evil chemicals? The only way to purify the planet is to start with our own bodies."

The man who'd tangled with Ramona did not press charges. But when she arrived at the theater she was told that her behavior was creating a bad image for the show and she'd have to resign or be fired. Her manager had to be summoned to escort her from the Barrymore.

Dulcie's contract was resurrected a few hours later and the company manager apologized to her for his false accusation. The understudy to Ramona, Shelly English, took over the leading role and kept me on as her dresser.

Shelly was not as status-conscious as Ramona and eventually became a part of the Dulcie-Harlan-Anthony social circle. The show continued for only about two months after Ramona's departure, but we were a tight little group and had lots of fun between shows.

On the afternoon of the last matinee, the four of us sat in the green room, joking playfully, to dispel the on-coming gloom that is an appendage to any final curtain. "It's been quite an experience for me," Shelly quipped. "My first starring role on Broadway and my first taste of piss."

Harlan laughed so hard he finally had to stop just to catch his breath.

"I can't believe it," I said, "some of the cast and crew still won't drink the coffee."

"Really?" Dulcie looked at me, amazed. "Like who?"

I began to identify the wary individuals when Harlan harumphed and interrupted me. "Sheeit! This is ridiculous," he roared with a mocking grin. "Half these people got their tongue up somebody's asshole every Saturday night and they're upset about a little piss in their coffee? Sheeit!"

Razorback

Puddles.

I lifted my face from the gutter. Felt the sting where my jaw hit the pavement. Puddles right before my eyes. Slicked over with oil. Alternately yellow and black. Reflecting the stuttering neon sign. Over that doorway. Unfamiliar to me. The sign said "Cocktails." Off again. On again.

I got to my feet. Swaying slightly. I could still feel the pain on the back of my neck where he'd struck me. Karate chop, I guessed. I walked to the sign and peered through the window below it. Inside were rich people and their bodyguards. Talking and drinking. I could have used a drink. But had nothing to trade.

And where was he?

Then I heard the double click. It came from across the street. It was him. And his switchblade. Click. Click. Open and shut. All the time. He came toward me. And pulled aside his tattered lapels. To remind me of the machete suspended from his leather belt. As though I could forget. Involuntarily, my hand reached up to touch my slashed cheek. He held the knife against my other cheek. I felt the point pressing into my skin. I prayed that he wouldn't cut me again. He slapped my face and gestured with his head. That I should follow. I did. Willingly. For even though he was my enemy, he was also my protector. He provided food – well, nothing really tasty or substantial, but at least I hadn't starved to death. And his home – again, not much but four walls and a ceiling cluttered with debris – was where I stayed. And even though he was cruel and would hurt me sometimes, he would allow no one else to mistreat me. That's something, I supposed. But not much, I admitted.

He prodded me in the direction of home. I felt the blunt end of the knife handle between my shoulder blades. I obeyed.

We were crossing one of the broad avenues, dark since someone had shattered the streetlights. I couldn't remember how long it had been since they'd worked. Almost everything was dark at night since the creeps had taken over.

Suddenly, a loner jumped out at us from an alley way. Brandishing a broomstick. Click. The switchblade was opened. Moonlight glinted off the flat, shiny surface. The loner turned and ran down the alley.

We got home without further incident.

Home was a basement apartment somewhere in what used to be called the midtown area. That was before everyone began to leave. Prior to that, things had gotten steadily worse, but life was tolerable. Then the street gangs took over. They ruled the entire city. Except for a few rich folks who'd decided to stay and could pay for protection. And the loners who'd refused to join a gang or who had quit one. And what was I in this strange and primitive hierarchy? A prisoner and a slave. In service of and protected by a loner. An independent agent whose strength, speed, cunning and luck prevented his becoming another fatality; another unburied corpse in the city that looked like a ravaged graveyard.

We lived at the bottom of a metallic stairwell that led from the sidewalk to our door. Several dead-bolt locks were the only thing between us and the creeps. Upon entering, the first noticeable thing was the dank and moldy odor. A couple of stained mattresses on the floor. A naked bulb dangling from the center of the ceiling. Thick curtains over the high windows, taped to the frames so that no light could escape. And on the floor, amid the old clothing, empty cans and spent batteries, hundreds of cassettes and paperbacks.

He locked the door behind us. I sat on my pallet. He removed his raincoat. The kind that British spies always wear in the movies. But his was grimy, spotted, ragged. Just like my clothing. What little I had left.

Beneath the raincoat he wore the T-shirt I'd seen him take off only a couple of times. It was black and he had at one time had letters sewn on it that said "Razorback." I did not know what this meant until I saw his shirtless back one day. A herringbone pattern of scars ran in a broad ribbon from his neck to his waist. He'd either been in a ritual fight, held prisoner and tortured, or had once belonged to a gang. Some of which had pretty weird initiation rites. I never found out because he never said anything. Never even told me his name. So I started calling him Razorback. Not out loud. But in my mind. To keep things organized. I gave him a name just to make things easier for myself.

As usual the first thing he did was heat up a can of soup on the two-burner stove. I always thought that the gas would run out, but like the electricity, it was always available and there was never a bill to pay.

We ate the soup – split pea with ham, as I recall – then he sat on his pallet and put on his headphones. A Walkman, of course. I'm not sure what he listened to, but it was most likely underground rock. By some group with a disgusting name. It didn't make any difference to me. But, as usual, he pointed the machete in my direction, meaning that I should pick up a book and read. Which I did. He never cared what I read as long as the pages kept turning.

So he listened and I read and eventually we both fell asleep. A typical night for us. Not much fun as far as I was concerned. But at least I was still alive.

* * *

I thought I was a light sleeper, but Razorback was one up on me. If I ever tried to leave my mattress during the night, he was always on his feet with the switchblade open before I could make two strides. So I was unable to overpower him while he slept. It would have been foolish for me to even try because without him I couldn't have lived for very long.

The only thing I knew about was books. And they were as useful to a person in this city as a computer would be to a monkey in the jungle. At some point – how long ago I couldn't say – most people either forgot, or never learned, how to read. There were students like myself, though, who not only knew how but actually enjoyed it. So there came to be a class of "readers" who could be hired by rich people to do their reading for them. And that's what became of me. As soon as I graduated from school I was hired by Mr. and Mrs. Garrison McMartin. They insisted that I move in with them – I had my own room with a fireplace and an air conditioner – and all they expected of me was that I read as much as I could and tell them the plots to all the new novels so they could talk about them at dinner parties and other social affairs. It was heaven for me. But I often wondered about the literary chit-chat at those parties. I mean, if a book is to be discussed only by people who have never read it – well, I guessed a lot of those discussions were pretty funny. But not to those involved. As far as I knew, all of the McMartin's friends had readers too. I think I would have gotten a big kick out of eavesdropping on one of those talks, but I never had the chance.

The McMartins had a huge library of classics – all unread until I came along – and each week they'd pick up a dozen or so new novels. I was kept busy but loved every minute of it. Almost every evening after dinner I'd tell them what I'd read that day. They would listen and ask me to repeat the sexy stuff so they wouldn't make any mistakes when the talk came around to the juicier parts. Then I'd read them the important stories in that day's newspaper.

It wasn't easy adjusting from the McMartins to Razorback. I used to live in the finest of surroundings with excellent food and the literature of the world at my fingertips. And then quite suddenly I found myself in a dingy basement eating canned soup and forced to re-read the same books over and over.

I haven't quite figured out what Razorback hoped to get from me. Unlike the McMartins, he never asked me about the books I read. He was content as long as my face was pointed at small print and pages turned. Was I some kind of status symbol? Did he believe that having his own private reader would somehow make him better than the other loners? I didn't know. He never said and I never asked.

When he captured me and dragged me to his apartment I automatically assumed that he had something sexual in mind. I was correct. He fucked my ass with wild abandon. We were standing up with our pants bunched around our ankles. I've always enjoyed rough action. I jerked my cock as he pumped me. It was fine. Every now and then, without warning or preamble, he'd pull our pants down and do me. It was a change from our routine. I didn't worry too much about sexually transmitted diseases. He probably didn't either. There were greater dangers around most corners and behind many doors.

In the mornings I felt disoriented. Must have been the nightmares. I had grown used to pleasant dreams and idyllic mornings with hot coffee, buttery croissants and sunshine pouring through my window. But at Razorback's the mornings were dark and smelly. Breakfast simply didn't exist.

I'd open my eyes and Razorback would be sitting cross-legged on his mattress, polishing his machete. Actually, it was just a large butcher knife. But in his artful hands it became a machete, a sabre, a scythe. He'd glance over at me while rubbing the blade with a chamois, and gesture – with his chin – at the books on the floor. I'd pick one up and start to read. But it was so difficult to concentrate so early. I'd still be recalling bits and pieces of scary dreams, trying to figure what they meant and what caused them. Some of the images would keep returning.

I'd be in a car that was under water and all the doors and windows were locked. I couldn't open them and water was seeping in, rising higher and higher. It always ended with me kneeling on the front seat, my head thrown back, gasping for the shrinking bubble of air just beneath the roof. I'd try to breathe one more time and my lungs would fill up with cold water. Then I'd wake up.

Or I'd be standing with my back to a wall and a gang of creeps would be closing in. First they'd cut off one of my arms. Then one of my eyes would be plucked out. Toes were chopped off one at a time. Then the gang leader would hold his sword at my groin. He'd lift his arms in an upward arc. I'd scream. And wake up.

All this while I was trying to read about some wealthy Englishman attempting to marry off his daughters to obnoxious landowners. It all seemed so trivial compared to drowning and disembowelment.

* * *

I recall awakening. And the stench of decaying human flesh. A horrible odor. Almost certain to induce vomiting. That is, if there's anything in your stomach. I was lying in the gutter, my face pressed against a rotting thigh. Gender? Unimportant. How long since the demise? Difficult to determine. And besides I didn't care.

But I finally figured out Razorback's logic. It was the second time that he'd karate-chopped me into oblivion, leaving me sprawled in the street. It was a form of protection. Razorback, with his swift legs and street-smarts, could easily avoid the creeps and other loners. I, slow and ignorant by comparison, would have been killed instantly. Had the enemy not thought I was already dead. Razorback's method for keeping me alive while we were out scavenging was simple: when in the vicinity of enemies, he would knock me out and leave me sprawled where I dropped. Anyone passing by would take me for dead and leave me alone. Good thing he never hit me hard enough to kill me; just enough to immobilize me and fool the others. I could have pretended I was dead, but I guess that never entered his mind.

So I eventually got used to those strange awakenings. Sometimes in puddles of rain and excrement. Sometimes among slashed corpses. The waking was always brutal. But I was still alive.

Every day we'd venture out of the apartment to search for whatever we could find that might be useful – food, bottled water, batteries. The most costly and rare commodity was condoms but they were increasingly difficult to find. All of the drug stores had been looted a long time ago. An unused condom commanded a higher price than fresh vegetables or coffee.

After Razorback cleaned his weapons and I read for a while, we'd wander the streets. Enter burnt-out department stores and unlocked apartments. We'd find a few cans of food here, perhaps some usable clothing there. Razorback would tear apart any battery-operated toy or appliance he could find. He was hoarding size AA batteries for his Walkman. I assumed that the ultimate horror for him would be to run out of battery power and be left without loud music.

We'd ransack the streets and buildings, gingerly stepping over corpses with spilled entrails. Racing from shadow to shadow, ears cocked, listening for the sounds of hostile creeps approaching.

Razorback was an athlete of evasion. He could hear a gang of creeps from several blocks away and without even seeing them, decide if he should run, take cover or stand and fight. If it was another loner, he'd usually knock me out, ambush the guy and take whatever spoils he considered usable. Then he'd come and pull me from whatever carnage or garbage I'd been left in for safe-keeping.

But one time – I recall it so vividly – Razorback made an error in judgment. It was the beginning of his end. And perhaps mine as well.

We were steeling down a narrow street moving west. Running from doorway to doorway, returning home after a long day's hunt. All was quiet. The sky was gray and the air thick with mugginess.

When we reached the intersection, Razorback peered around the corner. He motioned with his machete that I should follow. We sprinted across the street and ducked into what was left of a burnt-out greengrocery. Razorback foraged in the darkness – I could hear him rifling through cartons, all probably empty – while I kept my eyes on the door. Above the rustling of cardboard we suddenly heard the sound of several pairs of feet on pavement. Razorback stood and cocked his head. Listening. Before we knew it, three creeps burst through the door. Most likely what was left of a ten-to-fifteen-member gang. I automatically got down to the floor and lay as though I were dead. I would have had as much success fighting those guys as a pampered poodle versus a pit-bull terrier. Through half-closed eyes I could see what was happening.

One of the creeps was tall and thin with a shaved head. The second had an average build and long, stringy hair. The third was fat, limped and was missing half of his right arm.

We were invisible in the dark. I lay on the floor in a patch of rotten fruits and vegetables – the odor was almost intoxicating – and Razorback crouched behind an overthrown table. While the creeps waited for their eyes to adjust to the dark, Razorback pounced. With one swift motion he took the head off the fat one-armed guy. Blood hissed out of his neckless torso and the head – with tongue lolling through clenched teeth – rolled until it stopped inches away from my face. I gagged. The tall one turned to see what was happening and Razorback plunged his knife right through the guy's stomach and twisted it clockwise. The creep dropped his knife, tried to hold his guts in with both hands, then tottered and fell. The longhair – quicker than the other two – realized what was going on and backed away, cutting the air with his knife. Razorback approached him, his knees bent, ready to spring. Their knives clashed and the scratching sound of metal on metal made my teeth hurt. While keeping the creep's knife busy, thrusting at him, Razorback reached into his pocket for his switchblade. He pulled it out, clicked it open and raked it across the other guy's face. He howled and licked the blood from his lips as Razorback moved in and drove his knife into the guy's chest. As he pulled it out and backed away, the creep – with his last burst of strength – thrust his knife deep into Razorback's leg. He fell and crawled away. The creep stopped breathing as Razorback slowly pulled the knife from his calf. Blood dribbled over the blade. He tore off his shirt and tied it around the gushing wound.

I got up and went to him.

He looked up at me. The pain in his eyes was unbearable. I helped him to his feet and draped his arm around my neck. We moved to the door. He gasped as he dragged his punctured leg.

I stuck my head out the door and made certain there were no others. We moved quietly from doorway to shadow. I prayed that we'd get back home without another attack.

We did. Finally. I locked the door behind us and helped Razorback to his mattress. He was shivering and sweating, his face contorted from the pain.

I tore off the bloody shirt and tied a fresh one around his calf. Then I covered him with a blanket and tucked it around him.

I went to sleep but kept waking up. Razorback was having nightmares and would scream something then clutch at his leg. I wished that I could give him something for the pain, but there was nothing. We both slept – on and off – for I don't know how long.

* * *

I'm not exactly sure how or why everything began to fall apart. Once I'd been installed at the McMartin's I was pretty much cut off from the general flow of life and information. Almost all that I knew was what I heard on the radio, saw on television or read in the newspaper. The rest I picked up from the McMartin's dinner conversations.

If I remember correctly, the decay sequence went something like this. It started with a bunch of newspaper offices and radio and television stations getting sabotaged. The rumors floating around suggested that employees of the various media companies were angry about the news reportage. They claimed it was inaccurate when not brazenly biased. The firebombs flew. The output of the established news sources became sporadic and a bunch of underground newspapers and pirate radio stations suddenly came into prominence. But most of that news was really propaganda.

Shortly after the news became even more of a joke than it had already been, groups of people began to move out. It was said that most went to the country where people were less threatening and you could grow your own food. First the politicians left, then the doctors. The police and firemen soon followed. The subways turned into danger zones where entry was an invitation to death. I supposed it was underground that a lot of gangs formed and trained themselves to become death squads.

The bus drivers eventually disappeared and the taxi drivers were next. It became impossible to get gasoline and a lot of surface vehicles were simply left where they stopped when their gauges pointed to empty.

Life with the McMartins slowly went from luxurious to austere. And the dinner conversations became guarded and scary. Eventually they stopped asking me what I'd been reading. It was plain that they were more concerned with where the next roast or pecan pie would come from. Mr. McMartin owned a chain of restaurants and was able to stockpile alcohol and food. But after he'd traded all of that away and Mrs. McMartin had traded her jewelry and furs for tranquilizers and analgesics, I knew something would have to happen.

One night while we were eating – an assortment of canned vegetables and stale breads – Mr. McMartin announced that we were to leave for the country in a few days.

The country! I was so excited. I packed up my clothes and started bundling my books. I dreamed about tall trees, flower gardens and mountain streams.

On the morning of our departure we gathered in the lobby of the McMartin's building with all our belongings in suitcases and cartons. A panel van with armed guards pulled up to the curb and we started moving our stuff down the steps and onto the sidewalk.

It was a wickedly uncomfortable day and after carrying several loads all of us sat down on the steps to catch our breath and cool off. I opened one of my boxes and took out a book. Mr. McMartin was wiping his forehead with a hanky, Mrs. McMartin was fanning her face with a pamphlet of some sort. I began to read.

Suddenly, I heard gun shots. I looked up in time to see one of the armed guards hit the sidewalk as a gang of creeps descended upon us. They killed the other guard and were taking Mr. and Mrs. McMartin as hostages when one of the gang members – Razorback – approached me. He clicked open his switchblade and carved a small crescent in my cheek. He picked up the carton of books and handed it to me, then held the blade at my throat while he led me around the corner. I guessed the other gang members were having so much fun torturing the McMartins and shooting up the van, they didn't notice that we'd disappeared.

The blood was dripping down my cheek but both hands were full and I couldn't wipe it away. Razorback took me to his basement apartment. We entered and he locked the door behind us. He gestured with his knife and I learned to respond. Quickly. I sat on the mattress that he indicated. He handed me a book opened to the first page. While I read, trembling, wondering what was to become of me, he did push-ups and sit-ups on the floor. Then he cleaned his weapons while listening to his Walkman. Later on he heated up some soup and we went to sleep soon after.

That was the first night since I was a child that I was tormented by nightmares. I haven't had a peaceful night since.

* * *

Someone or something tickled me. My foot quivered as something soft and wet moved against it. I opened my eyes. It was a rat. Dark gray and slimy. I yelled and kicked it. It scampered into a dark corner.

I lay there for a while. Trying to sort everything out. I realized that I hadn't heard any gun shots in a long time. No more ammunition, most likely.

I got up and looked at Razorback. He was in a deep sleep. I moved toward him and he didn't spring up at me like I expected. I felt his forehead. He was burning with fever.

I opened a can of soup and heated it. Then I woke him up and made him eat it. Afterwards he went to sleep again. I spent the day reading and worrying.

If Razorback died I would be on my own. The way things stood, I wouldn't last very long. I couldn't really defend myself. I was not very fast. And though I knew a great deal about literature, I knew nothing about survival in the streets.

Time slowed down. I had too much time to think. Would I dare to leave the apartment and look for bottled water? Perhaps I could find some medication so Razorback would get better. I thought about this but was afraid to go out alone.

One night I woke up after a particularly brutal nightmare – I was being attacked by an army of rats with sharp teeth and evil eyes. Sweating all over I got up and paced back and forth. I decided that I would try to become proficient with Razorback's knives. I practiced throwing them until they would lodge tightly into whatever targets I selected. I ruined a lot of paperbacks but I'd already read them and there were plenty more.

During the afternoons I did push-ups and sit-ups. At first it was a real struggle to do even one. But after a few days I could do several with no effort. Day by day I increased the numbers. My body began to harden and I grew more confident.

One morning after I'd served Razorback his soup, he sat up and looked around. His leg was swollen and his face was gaunt. A horrible odor emanated from his body and mattress.

He got to his feet and limped to the pantry. We had less than fifteen cans of soup by then. He gathered his weapons and moved to the door. I tried to stop him but he pushed me away. I tried to follow but he threatened me with his machete.

He left and I haven't seen him since. I waited for a few days, but eventually gave up hope. He was in no condition to protect himself and was probably lying in a puddle of his own blood somewhere.

Although I prayed for his return, I realized I was being foolish. He was gone. I was on my own. My body was stronger than it had ever been, but I didn't have any weapons. If I left the apartment I was most certainly doomed. If I stayed, I'd starve. But maybe, I thought, just maybe I'd get lucky. Perhaps I could travel from shadow to shadow and get out of the city. It was possible, but not very probable.

Then I began to think about the possibility that maybe someday I might be rescued. Perhaps there were people somewhere who were planning to return and re-claim the city. I mean, the city was still usable. Most of the buildings stood where they'd always been. Pipes and wiring were largely intact. The main problem, as far as I could see, would be to clean up the carnage in the streets. All the city really needed was some heavily armed people to come and make it work again.

On some days I fantasized about going to the country. On others I'd daydream about an army coming to restore the city to its former stature. And another possibility occurred to me: that if I waited long enough all the creeps would kill each other off, or at least reduce their numbers enough so that I might get out of the city unharmed.

Maybe tomorrow I'll try to escape. Or maybe a week from now. But I could get killed days or moments before someone might come to save me. My dilemma. To leave or to stay. It's hard to decide. There's not much soup left, but I've still got plenty of books to re-read.

Brotherhood

Gregory gets on a plane at LaGuardia airport in New York. A few hours later he lands in South Florida. Takes a taxi to his brother's home in Boca Raton. He is greeted by Candi, his sister-in-law.

After she kisses Gregory on the cheek he enters the house. "Theodore will be home soon from golf," she says.

"How have you been?" asks Gregory.

"Just great. And you?"

"Great. Everything's great."

"How's your ..." Candi does not know whether to say lover, roommate, friend, or companion.

"Darrell."

"Right. Darrell. How is he?"

"Fine. Where are Richie and Sherry?"

"Summer camp."

"Summer camp? Where?"

"Vermont."

Gregory thinks it's strange that people would send their kids to someplace other than Florida to have a good time. He thinks Florida itself is one huge summer camp.

They sit in the enclosed patio. Candi and Theodore call it a Florida room.

"Would you like a drink?" Candi asks.

"What are you having?"

"Nothing."

"I don't want anything either."

"How about some water?"

"Okay."

Candi rises to get two glasses of ice water. Gregory wanders about the house. It is a one-story structure with a large living room which fans out into the kitchen, dining room, bedrooms and bathrooms. Every square inch of the floor is plushly carpeted. The decor is a splash of tropical pinks, greens, yellows. Deft use of black and white makes it appear still more colorful.

Theodore arrives and greets his brother. Then his wife.

Dinner is served at six o'clock. Candi removes dishes from the microwave and brings them to the table.

"About tomorrow," says Theodore, one year and three months older. Gregory looks up expectantly. He's been avoiding this for over ten years, since Theodore and Candi left New York and settled in Florida to raise Sherry and Richie. "We rise when the rooster crows."

"No problem," says Gregory. He will visit the club his brother and sister-in-law have been boasting about. He will tell them how lovely it is. And with the obligation met, he'll never have to return. "What's new?"

Theodore grins. "New television, new car, new microwave, next month we're painting the Florida room."

"That's nice," says Gregory.

Everyone smiles.

In the morning they have breakfast in the sparkling white kitchen. Gregory, Theodore and Candi sit at the round table. Orange juice, poached eggs, toast and decaf.

Gregory looks helplessly at Candi. "Um, do you have any real coffee? You know, with caffeine?"

As Candi is about to apologize, Theodore says, "Don't you know what caffeine does to your system? It's poison! Why I read somewhere that every cup of caffeinated coffee you drink takes thirteen minutes off the rest of your life."

Gregory lights a cigarette. "If I want to take thirteen minutes off the rest of my life that's my privilege."

"I'm so sorry," says Candi.

"It's all right."

"I didn't know," she adds.

"Really, it's okay. I'll live."

"Not if you keep poisoning your bloodstream, you won't."

"Let's not fight," says Gregory.

They eat silently.

Afterwards Candi cleans up. Theodore has to go to the store to pick up a few things for dinner. Gregory goes for a walk.

The home of Theodore and Candi is located in a housing development called Palmetto Springs. But this is quite unlike any real estate configuration that Gregory has observed anywhere. In the center of Palmetto Springs is a Golf and Tennis Club which boasts four eighteen-hole courses and thirty-six courts. The homes are situated on plots of land bordering the green fairways. Built especially for golf and tennis enthusiasts, the homes offer them the advantage of being able to arrive at the first tee or court number one in the time it would ordinarily take you to reach the first of many red lights.

Part of the arrangement is that the homeowners never have to worry about their grounds. Teams of landscapers and gardeners continually work on everyone's lawns and backyards so that the entire development has a uniform look. Theodore likes the idea of never having to mow the lawn. Candi likes the consistency and never having to worry that the neighbor's yard will become overgrown and unkempt.

Gregory leaves the house and walks a few blocks, observes some lovely rock gardens, cobbled paths, man-made waterfalls surrounded by garlands of brightly colored flowers. The streets are named after birds. Shirtless, tanned, muscular young men run around with rakes, hoes, hoses and mowers. There are grapefruit, lime, and avocado trees, palms and knees of cypress. Gregory walks around to the backyard of his brother's house. There is a clump of trees he cannot identify. He approaches and hears soft human noises. Getting closer he can see movements within the shadows. Stealthily looking and listening, he inches closer and sees two young men on the ground, slurping each other's cocks. He watches for a few seconds, grins and walks back around to the front entrance of the house.

Candi asks, "Did you have a nice walk?"

"Very interesting."

Theodore returns home with bags of groceries. Then he and Gregory go to the clubhouse in the golf cart. "So, you're still living with Donald?" says Theodore.

"Darrell."

"Sorry, Darrell." Theodore sighs. "I know you have these urges, you just have to try to control them."

"They're not simply urges. They're the core of my existence."

"The core of your existence is making Mom and Pop spin in their graves."

Gregory becomes indignant. "How the hell do you know? Did they send you a postcard or something?"

Theodore does not respond. He knows that unless he is silent the discussion will devolve into a nasty argument.

The route to the clubhouse is like a fairytale illustration. Neat pastel homes nestled in green bowers with palm fronds swaying lazily and bright flower petals spicing the verdure.

The main building of the clubhouse – attached to the Pro Shop, cart shed, and caddy bench – is a large brick edifice with white columns and gingerbread trimming. They park the golf cart and enter. Theodore says, "This is the best that America has to offer. Everyone is honest, fair and family-oriented."

"By family-oriented you mean heterosexual?" Gregory asks as a man in a pink jumpsuit with a purple scarf sashays by.

"Yes," Theodore affirms.

"Interesting," says Gregory. "When I was in New Orleans I saw a drag show in which one of the queens was dressed just like that."

Theodore glances at the man in pink and purple. "The

latest in modern golfing fashion."

"Southern gutter drag circa 1977."

Theodore shoots a disapproving look.

Gregory smirks.

They walk through the lobby, down the hall lined with trophies in glass cases and enter the dining room. The host smiles and leads them to a table by the window, looking out over gracefully terraced lawns.

"This is very nice," says Gregory.

Theodore smiles triumphantly.

A waiter appears and hands out menus. Gregory stares at the waiter's eyes. The look is returned. Theodore stares at the menu.

"Our specials today include quiche à la Boca, mock turtle soup and steak au poivre."

Gregory can't resist the urge to be wicked. He looks at Theodore. "Quiche? At an all-American joint like this? I thought real men –"

"I'll have the quiche à la Boca," Theodore interrupts.

"A real man like you?" mocks Gregory.

"It's the latest thing," says Theodore.

"Steak," says Gregory. "Medium."

"Anything to drink, gentlemen?"

"Coffee," says Gregory.

"Perrier," says Theodore.

Gregory raises his left eyebrow. The waiter retrieves the menus and leaves.

Gregory smirks. "Pink jumpsuits, quiche à la Boca, Perrier ... what's happening to the land of the brave and the home of the free?"

"Just shut up! Okay? Shut up!"

The meal is consumed in silence. Over coffee, Gregory tells Theodore that the food is wonderful and thanks him.

Theodore shows Gregory the newly renovated mens' locker room. Rows of metal lockers, rows of benches, rows of shower nozzles, rows of sinks and mirrors, stacks of towels, shelves of deodorant, powder, shaving cream, aftershave, combs, razors, cologne, men in towels, men naked, men turning under spitting spigots, men slapping men's behinds, steam, tile, male camaraderie. Theodore raises his arms and says, "This is really something, huh?"

"Yes, Theo, it most certainly is."

Gregory drives the golf cart while Theodore plays nine holes. The terrain offers a smooth ride, the awning atop the cart provides relief from the sun. Theodore is happy chasing tiny white balls and Gregory is content to follow and relax. Theodore slices into the woods to the left of the fairway. While helping to search for the lost ball, Gregory observes a young caddy and an older player, jerking each other's cocks behind a tall hedge. He smiles and turns away.

"Got it!" shouts Theodore, holding the ball aloft. Gregory emerges into the sunlight. They continue to follow the course and eventually return to the clubhouse.

Theodore takes a shower.

Gregory wants to visit the sauna first.

As Theodore is soaping himself, Gregory is settling onto the wooden bench in the hot, steamy, tiled room. There are several men already there, in pairs. Gregory closes his eyes for a moment, then inhales deeply. He feels a hand tentatively pawing at his crotch. He opens his eyes and finds a man with a moustache pushing aside the towel, grabbing for his cock. Gregory looks around, and through the mist can see hands on cocks stroking furiously. He indulges in a quick one then leaves the sauna. He showers and towels himself dry. Then meets Theodore in the lobby of the clubhouse.

They drive the cart back home. "Quite a sauna," says Gregory.

Theodore is pleased that Gregory has said something complimentary.

"Do you use it much?" Gregory asks.

"I don't like the idea of a bunch of men sitting around with nothing on," says Theodore.

"Horrible thought," says Gregory.

They pass the Olympic-sized pool adjacent to the clubhouse. Theodore brags about the swimming competitions held there every Fourth of July. Gregory's attention drifts away from his brother's words and he notices a very well-muscled, very tanned, very sexy lifeguard by the pool. He looks at the man's blond hair, his sculpted features, his powerful body.

They arrive home by six. Candi serves dinner about forty-five minutes later.

Afterwards, Theodore asks Gregory if he'd like to watch *Woodstock.* They have a videocassette. Gregory politely declines and asks if he can borrow the car.

"Where would you like to go?" asks Candi.

"To a bar."

"Oh," she says, delighted, "which one?"

"Rawhide."

"I haven't heard of it," she says, eager to hear all about it.

Theodore punctures her balloon. "It's a gay bar, honey."

"Oh," she says, embarrassed, "that's okay. I don't mind."

Theodore sighs. "You don't understand, he wants to go alone."

"Oh! I see. That's okay. Really. I don't mind."

"See you later."

Gregory enters the darkness of Rawhide, about a ten minute drive from Palmetto Springs.

The first thing he notices is the lifeguard he'd seen earlier at the clubhouse pool. He's dancing with another sexy, blond, tanned guy beneath the whirling disco globe. Gregory looks around. This bar is unlike the ones he's been to in New York. It combines the high-tech decorative touch of a disco with the gritty raunch atmosphere of a leather bar.

Gregory drinks orange juice instead of scotch because he will have to drive back to the house. He almost goes home with a young local but decides it's too late, he's too tired, and so he leaves alone.

On Sunday morning Candi doesn't start breakfast until almost ten o'clock. When Gregory wakes up she's just begun. He can smell bacon frying. Wriggling into a shirt and shorts he goes to the kitchen.

"Good morning," says Candi.

"Good morning."

"Did you have a good time last night?"

Gregory lifts his hair from his forehead, stirs some milk into his coffee. He drinks it. "Hey! There's caffeine in here!"

Candi smiles.

"Thank you. I had a good time. How was the movie last night?"

"Still my favorite," she says. "In spite of all the mud. Everytime I see it I'm transported back in time. Those were wonderful years."

"They were."

A few minutes later Theodore appears, tying the belt of his Japanese print robe.

"Good morning," he says to no one in particular. Then to Gregory, "What time are you scheduled to leave?"

"If it's all right with you I think I'll stay for a few more days."

Theodore is shocked. "I thought you couldn't wait to check into that sex hotel in Fort Lauderdale. You have a reservation for today, right?"

"Right. But I thought I'd change it and stay for a while. Just a few days. If it's okay."

"Of course it's okay," beams Candi. We'd love to have you."

"Thank you," says Gregory.

"So," says Theodore, his chest puffed up with victory. "It isn't so bad here, is it?"

"No," says Gregory, recalling the gardeners fucking in the backyard.

"It's clean and wholesome," adds Theodore.

"I can't argue with that," says Gregory, thinking suddenly of the men in the sauna.

"So what are your plans for today?" Candi asks.

"Think I'll go swimming," says Gregory, picturing the hunky lifeguard.

Theodore sighs. "Water, sunshine, golf, tennis ... Florida's a far cry from New York."

"But not quite as far as you might think," says Gregory.

The Solar Hunks from Uranus

Captain Pulsar switched his hand-laser from coma to death, planted his legs firmly, aimed at the approaching solar hunk and fired. A needle of white light burned a perfect hole through his scrofulous chest and the solar hunk, emitting a piercing cry, fell forward and expired. As the vapor of life seeped from his prostrate form, the orange color of his lumpy skin began to darken and dull. But the radioactive aura, emanating from every muscled curve of the hunk's dead body, continued to glow, as it would until the half-lives of the radioactive particles were no longer detectable without sensory extenders.

"Damn Quarkbusters!" said Captain Pulsar.

His real name was Li Che Po; that was before he became an intergalactic superstar. Now he's known everywhere as Captain Pulsar.

When he first said the word – quarkbusters – I had no idea what it meant. Sure, I knew what a quark was and I imagined what the act of busting one might look like. I even tried to picture a being who would be occupied with such an enterprise. But, I confess, I wasn't really certain what this caper was about until it was almost over.

The Captain and I, trying hard to maneuver our way through the sprawled bodies of dead solar hunks without touching them, eventually got out of the smooth, shiny corridors of the alien vessel. We believed that if we'd touched – even for one nanosecond – the skin of one of those creatures, we'd be destined for early cremation. If an ordinary human had physical contact with a solar hunk, the radiation would slowly permeate – and eventually kill him, her or it. As attractive as the solar hunks could be, what with their superb musculature and all, if they managed to entice someone into a sexual liaison, the result would be a slow, painful death after a thrilling libidinal experience. Even though the skin of a solar hunk is not particularly enticing (at least to me), the muscles usually cause an ordinary mortal's resolve to dissipate. Then the hormones begin to flow. And like a meteor plummeting to a gravity enclave, the human locks loins with the solar hunk, experiences several moments of divine pleasure, then begins to expire like a bombarded neutrino.

The Captain and I managed to escape from this particular encounter uncontaminated. Not a single one of those overcooked mutants from Uranus managed to touch us even momentarily.

We entered the air-lock and strapped ourselves into our two-seater shuttle. The Captain maneuvered us away from the alien ship just quickly enough so that when it exploded we were far away; there was no serious damage to our conveyance from the fiery, missile-like debris.

When we docked and disembarked, we made our way to the conference room. I seated myself before the main computer terminal and booted the system as the Captain summoned the Executive Council.

Adam, the first to arrive, greeted us with warmth. "A bit too much," the Captain told me later. "We'll have to have his connections and circuits examined when we get back to Corporation headquarters."

Entering the quiet and cool, plushly decorated conference room with its large table and swivel chairs, Adam first addressed the Captain with a salute, then dropped his pose of formality and hugged him passionately. The Captain grimaced, and finally pushing Adam away said, "Adam, I'm happy to see you too, but I've only been gone for a couple of hours and I only have one set of ribs."

Adam faked a shudder and stood at attention. "Sir? Am I to understand that you do not wish to be hugged?"

The Captain grinned. "No. It's not that." He hesitated for a moment. The Captain had many Asian ancestors and it was part of his nature, a racial trait some say, to be as humble in one's speech as one is aggressive in battle. "You must remember that those arms of yours can crush a real human like a gorilla could a sparrow."

"Certainly, sir, and please accept my apologies."

Adam turned to approach me. Most of the earlier models from Adam's creators walked a bit stiff-legged. But his rolling gait was almost human. With his soft, blond hair, delicate features and intense eyes, he was quite attractive. For a cyborg. While I was conscious of his beauty I was not compelled to desire him because my few sexcapades with cyborgs had all been frustrating. Who wants to go on a date with a creature who can orgasm every thirty seconds? Kind of makes an ordinary guy like myself feel a bit inadequate.

"Bart," said Adam as he hugged me, mindful of the Captain's words, ever so lightly, "was it a successful mission?"

"Yes. We're alive. It was successful."

"Very good."

Adam moved to the far end of the conference table and sat. Moments later Lieutenant Lucille Hopkins and Sergeant Garcia arrived, completing the Executive Council. They sat and Garcia poured himself a glass of water. Lieutenant Hopkins, Lucille, signed to the Captain that she was ready. The Captain looked at Garcia and he nodded.

As the Captain briefed them on our mission aboard the alien ship, I sat and watched Lucille. She has been deaf since birth and is an excellent lip-reader, in addition to having the most graceful signing technique I've ever seen. When someone is speaking to her she watches every movement of the lips and mouth with her big, brown eyes and if you look at her face you see the sweetest most attentive expression you can imagine. I can watch her endlessly. Her face is like an angel's. Her hands are like a sculptor's. With her dark, brown hair and lithe figure, she is quite an attractive person. Sometimes I think that if she were a man or if I were a woman ... but I'm happy being me and she's content with herself so ... even though we easily could, I don't think either of us wants to make the change.

Anyway, the Captain told the Council how we managed to sneak aboard the solar hunks' vessel and just managed to escape, once they'd detected our presence.

"Regrettably," the Captain wound up his speech, "we were unable to locate the coordinates of their mothership but at least we got rid of about a dozen of them ... and we escaped without any injuries to the team or damage to the shuttle whatsoever. Right, Bart?"

"Yes," I confirmed. "And now that we've seen the interior of one of their ships, we'll be better prepared the next time."

Garcia, Security Queen, slammed his big fist on the table. "If I'd been with you, Captain, I'd've pulverized every one of 'em, and their little ship too!"

When he hit the table it felt like the whole room shook. Garcia is a big man, over three hundred pounds of fighting muscle. And when he gets angry it's best to be on his side of the disagreement, or if that's not possible, very far away.

"We needed you here," said the Captain.

"Aye, sir, but next time ..."

"What's our next move?" asked Adam.

"Uranus."

Adam blushed, his white android complexion turning to a vague pink. "Captain!"

"The planet Uranus."

"Oh," said Adam, abashed.

Garcia laughed. Lucille shook her head and grinned. I wasn't certain whether Adam had truly misunderstood or if he was just trying to be cute. With cyborgs it's often hard to tell. Captain Pulsar chuckled and ordered us to resume our duties. He called the bridge and asked the space mapper to find the best route to Uranus. After we filed out of the conference room, Garcia took me aside and asked if I was free to fuck for a while. I told him I had to log my report but could meet him about an hour later. He grunted and asked if he should come to my cabin or if I should go to his. I suggested that we meet in the aft air-lock because I knew that he was as fond of anti-grav sex as I.

"Good thinkin'," he said.

There is something quite special about fucking in zero Gs. Those little discomforts that result from sex in normal circumstances simply never materialize. Although I serve the Captain and the good ship Indigo in many capacities – historian, theorist, tale-teller, jester, philosopher and sommelier – I still have time for the occasional sexfest, so I'm not exactly what one might call virginal or inexperienced. Nor am I a profligate – but I'll leave all that to future historians. In any case, I know how it feels when your sex partner accidentally pinches a nerve or crushes a limb beneath his weight – intentional pain is an entirely different matter. When fucking in free-fall this ceases to be a problem. The only thing you have to watch out for is bumping into the walls, floor or ceiling. And it's hard to tell which is which once gravity is no longer a factor. When one is completely involved in a sexual encounter one tends to forget that one might be drifting head-first toward a wall of heavy metal. Sergeant Garcia and I wore helmets, in addition to tiny breathing capsules, and tried to stay at the center of the air-lock. We drifted of course, but never made contact with any undesired hard objects. Garcia's body is hard in all the right places, but his almost gymnastic expertise allows him to utilize his full strength without causing any unwanted bodily damage. After I did the best I could to satisfy myself with his various surfaces and orifices, he did the same with me. I like a guy who's strong and a little rough, so I was completely sated by the time he was finished with me. I felt like I'd been fucked into the middle of the next century, so I was feeling good all over when we felt the first tremors.

"What's that?" Garcia asked.

"Beats me," I replied.

He grinned. "All you ever think about is sex."

Before I could respond to his pun, an admittedly slight exaggeration, the Captain's voice surged from the ship's sound system. "We are under attack by another Uranian vessel. All hands to battle stations. Condition Crimson."

Garcia, trained to respond immediately to such commands, had grabbed his uniform and was gone before I could figure out where I should go. During attacks I was sometimes needed on the bridge, sometimes at my terminal and occasionally I was told to just disappear, be quiet and await further instructions.

After slipping into my uniform I ran to the bridge to see if I was wanted there. As I emerged from the sphincter the Captain shouted, "To the navigator's station! Channel computer dispatches!"

"Aye, aye, sir," I barked and left, running to carry out my orders.

The ship was vibrating from the blows of the enemy laser torpedoes as I reached navigation. Chief of Navigators, Mina Mtume, sat at her console, staring with menacing intensity. She is a short, olive-skinned woman, occasional lover of Lucille, and the best navigator to ever graduate from the Academy. It was her job to try to dodge the salvos from the aliens. With the aid of a computer, she must strategically maneuver our ship through short evasive paths – as during an attack – or plot vast routes that will take the Indigo to the far reaches of the universe.

I sat at the assist console across from her and tried to keep one eye on her, in case she had to signal me, and one eye on the assist screen in case any pertinent data arrived from the Captain, Security Queen, or from Corporation headquarters.

As Mina's fingers danced across her keyboard, I couldn't help noticing the shocks from the laser torpedoes were becoming less intense. Suddenly the Captain's voice thundered through the navigation room. "Armed intruders aboard ship!"

Mina glanced at me just long enough to say, "They must've blown the docking bolts," then riveted her eyes to her screen. A minute later two solar hunks with sub-atomic projectile dispensers entered the room and commanded us to move away from our terminals. I looked at Mina. She shrugged, rose and moved into a corner.

I was following her when one of the solar hunks came right over to me, grabbed me by the arm and led me into the corridor.

My mind raced in fear. Would the solar hunk's radiation kill me, or would he destroy me with his weapon first? In either case I was doomed. With a choking sensation in my throat and my heart pounding like a lunar smelting pump, I walked in the direction he indicated, my destination and fate unknown.

* * *

I woke up, in my quarters, on my bed, feeling a little groggy. As my eyes opened, I recognized the place and remembered who I was. Then, like a flash of solar fire or the kick of déjà vu, I recalled what had happened with the invader from Uranus.

First, he'd locked us in my room. Then, to my horror, he began to make love to me. I was terrified at first; the amount of radiation I was being exposed to would kill me in no time at all. But the solar hunk must have read my thoughts because he stopped and started talking to me. I presumed that he did not know Earthling, but had one of those instant translators built into his bandolier. The hunk sat on my bed. I watched his expressionless face, my eyes occasionally roving to take in his superb musculature as he began to speak.

"Bart," he began, "you will not die from the radiation."

I started to protest that I most surely would but he pressed on, refusing to allow me to speak.

"We are not your enemies! We have been ill-used by the crafty Kraveners. They are using us to get to your people. It's true they have mutated my people with their pellets of unstability. But the radiation is not contagious! They have tried to make you believe a falsity, and they have created many untruthful scenarios so that you would infer what they wanted you to believe. My fellow creature, we wish you no harm. In fact, I have been instructed to inform you that my people will not hold your people responsible for the raid you perpetrated on one of our ships. You were intentionally mis-informed and misled. It is my mission to communicate these thoughts to you so that your resources may be joined with ours to defeat the evil Kraveners."

As I listened to the alien's words, something instinctively told me that he was being honest. I wanted to believe him. What he said made sense. We'd had no prior quarrel with the Uranians. It was only when the Kraveners had begun to pil-lage the galaxy, bringing death and destruction everywhere they went, that our troubles started with our former friends.

The solar hunk went on to explain that after he left me, I'd fall asleep. Meanwhile, he and his comrades would leave. Upon awakening it would be my task to convince Captain Pulsar that he should cease fire and have a conciliatory brunch with the leader of the solar hunks. This I agreed to do. But before he put me to sleep, he taught me a few things about Uranian love that I'd never experienced before in life or study.

* * *

I relayed the message I was told by my Uranian captor.

"It's true," said the Captain. "I received a memo from headquarters. The renegades from Kraven are responsible for all of the death and destruction to the Uranians."

We'd convened – the Executive Council – in the confer-ence room. Lucille watched the Captain's lips, then shook her head in disbelief. The fingers of her right hand danced on her left palm, as though she were making a reminder to herself. Garcia just stared at the Captain, attempting to rearrange the furniture in his mind. He'd been told that the Uranians were our enemies. Now he had to create an entirely new mental context. Adam stood up and paced the length of the room – something he picked up from watching too many of those primitive Hollywood videos.

"And what of the radiation?" I asked, almost afraid to hear the answer. After all, just hours before I'd been exposed to a lethal dose. I could picture my life slipping away as I spoke.

"That, as well," said the Captain. "We were deceived. If you are struck by one of the Kraveners pellets, you will die in half-lives like the Uranians. But contact with a victim – even intimate contact – is harmless."

I was so overwhelmed by this news that I started to cry. Lucille came over and placed her hands on my shoulders, her cheek next to mine. She kissed me and her eyes told me not to worry.

"Damage to the ship was minimal," continued the Captain. "The docking bolts will be repaired in a matter of hours. There were no casualties to crew or interior. They simply wanted to have a heart-to-heart with you, Bart."

As Lucille seated herself, I wiped away my tears and looked at Captain Pulsar. "What's next?"

"We're going to connect Garcia with whoever's in charge of the Uranian's offense force. Perhaps our combined power will enable us to defeat the Kraveners."

Adam said, "Captain?"

"Yes?"

Adam stopped moving. "I think Bart and I should gather all of the data we can regarding skirmishes with the Kraveners. Perhaps we'll discover some salient point or flaw to target our attack."

"Good thinking, Adam."

We were dismissed.

I accompanied Adam to the ship's library. While scouring the tapes for possible clues, Adam suddenly locked the library door and led me behind the bank of terminals on the island in the center of the room.

"Have you found something?" I asked.

"Not yet," he said. "Just thought I'd ease your mind."

"About what?"

"Contamination."

He pulled me toward himself , and deep-tongued my throat. "There," he said when he was finished. "If you were contaminated – which you weren't – now I am too – which I'm not."

"But you're mostly machine," I protested, "what have you got to be afraid of?"

"I'm just as susceptible as you are. And don't you forget it."

We continued to search through the many banks of data. Hours later we still hadn't made any significant discoveries. Finally, Adam suggested that we take a break and he invited me to his cabin for some fast sex.

I accepted.

I guess now is a good time to mention that I'm a poly, which means that my genetic distribution is multifarious and unreconstructed. Most people descended from humans have one basic skin tone from head to feet. And some of those tones are downright gorgeous. From the darkest gleaming black to the brightest white – with a million shades in between including brown, olive, copper, orange, red, yellow and gold. But a poly is spotted. We're piebald. There is a patch of brown on my left arm, some red on my chest; my face is mocha but my ass is silvery white. I'm not attracted to other polys. I like well-blended skin tones that don't vary much. Why anyone would go out of his or her way for a tryst with me is beyond my comprehension. I'm not complaining. I'm simply amazed that anyone would find me attractive when there are so many others whom I feel are so much more sexy than I.

I had a great time with Adam. He's very imaginative and can do some pretty remarkable things with his body. For one thing, he can fuck your butt and suck your cock at the same time. I tried to reciprocate with him, once, and nearly snapped my spine. But for him it requires no effort at all. Whenever we dock at a Corporation starbase for some D & D

– Debriefing and Distraction – Adam is so busy making new liaisons, we never see him until it's time to depart for another mission.

* * *

Once we found out that it was the Kraveners who were responsible for the quarkbusting, everything changed. We had to re-think the entire situation. Suddenly, the solar hunks were no longer our enemies. And it was difficult to accept the Kraveners as quarkbusters. We'd been raised to believe that Uranians were bad guys and Kraveners good guys. Trying to change our attitudes became a paramount concern. It was a little like finding out that what we'd considered to be red was now blue and vice versa.

Quarkbusting had become one of the major problems in the galaxy. Everytime an astro-physicist bombarded a quark incorrectly it had an adverse effect on every other quark in the entire cosmic chain, thereby having an adverse effect on the stability of the universe. Since everyone these days is concerned about the future, the ecology of the universe is at the forefront of our collective consciousness.

We had no idea that the Uranians would not only turn out to be good folks, but that they were willing martyrs as well. It was with a sense of shock that I received my orders regarding the war on the Kraveners. According to the Captain's missive, the Uranian solar hunks had volunteered to deploy themselves as a diversionary force so that our attack platoon could score some crucial hits.

Once again I was assigned to assist Mina in the navigation sector. The Indigo was speeding toward a Kraven warship. It's sort of funny being in a starship during a space battle. Unless you're on the bridge or in the missile room, you have little sense of what's going on.

I kept my attention divided between my screen and Mina. After the solar hunks initiated their kamikaze run, we fired at the Kraven fleet, immediately knocking out three of their principal vessels. After that, the rest scattered and we had no trouble picking them off. A few escaped, but they would pose no threat with their mother ship reduced to space dust.

When the Executive Council convened in the conference room, I felt a little sad. As Adam recounted the events of the day I began to feel a rising in my throat. I realized that the solar hunk who'd made love to me had died so that others in the galaxy might live. The enormity of his sacrifice overwhelmed me and I felt awful because I didn't even know his name or anything about him.

Captain Pulsar could see that I was not well, and after the meeting was adjourned, asked me to meet him in his stateroom.

Very proud of his Asian heritage, the Captain had decorated his room with vases, tapestries and screens, handed down in his family for eons of generations. I was admiring the delicate artistry, the subtle coloring, the sensitive construction of these antiques when the Captain, dressed in a loose silk kimono, came up behind me and placed his hands on my shoulders. I turned.

"I want you to take me, Bart, act the part of the conquering hero and penetrate me."

He didn't have to explain any further. The Captain had a wonderful attitude toward sex. One which I could be comfortable with. Everyone is free to do what he/she/it wants, but if somebody doesn't want you to do it to them you can't. So you don't always get whom you want but you never have to do it with anybody you don't want to do it with either. I think it's the best we all can expect considering that we're all individuals with our own personal tastes, desires and dislikes. It's fair. Some societies that I've heard about or read about, had some pretty weird ideas about all of this. I'm happy with things the way they are.

And there I was with the Captain and he wanted me to relieve him of all responsibility, to take control, to let him feel the strength and will of another. It's not very often that someone as attractive and powerful as the Captain desires this of me, so I willingly complied. I thought of my dead Uranian lover, and of how much I loved the Captain and I channeled these thoughts into aggressive sex. I fucked the Captain with all of the passion and force of which I was capable. It was incredibly satisfying. When it was over the Captain smiled and sighed. I felt transcendent, like a transformation had occurred. There was a glow and a buzz that leapt from my body to my brain to my heart to my soul.

After the Corporation Mothers learned of our battle, they sent many congratulations. Not only for defeating the enemy, but for determining who was who. The Captain insisted that we hold a formal memorial ceremony for our slain Uranian brothers and sisters. It was a brief, simple, solemn gathering. I felt all weak inside and almost cried again. Lucille and Mina stood on either side of me, offering comfort. Afterward Lucille signed to me that I was a hero; that I'd helped immeasurably to defeat the evil marauders, that I should hold the dead solar hunk's love forever in my heart. I kissed her and hugged her, then she and Mina went off to be by themselves. Later on I heard that they'd organized a Centurian Tulip Grope.

Meanwhile, most of the male crew members gathered in the gym. We laid the tumbling and wrestling mats side by side and indulged ourselves in a wildly frenetic Alpha-Delta Clusterfuck. It was pretty sensational what with the high spirits and general energy level of all concerned. We fucked and sucked for hours, rested, and then began again. This helped to foster our sense of community and brotherhood. And it strengthened our emotional bonds, giving us the courage to face whatever might be waiting for us as we cruised the wild, mysterious ever-expanding universe.

Candy Holidays

This year Daryl was not a wizard, a vampire, or a telephone booth. Elvin was not a hippie, a clown, or a refrigerator. They sat in their apartment in the Village while a parade passed by just below their windows. Tots dressed up like Teenage Mutant Ninja Turtles waddled by. And a hundred adolescent girls from Brooklyn and Queens in Madonna costumes. Couples from Jersey doing Elvi and Marilyns, Lucys, Rickys, Ethels and Freds. The streets were lined with blue barricades and blue policemen and policewomen, a gauntlet to guide the slowly moving crowd, whistling, shrieking, laughing.

Daryl lifted a candy corn from a ceramic bowl, bit off the white part, chewed, then the yellow, chewed, and then the orange. He swallowed. "So, what are we going to do tonight?" He said it to the air of the room, his eyes gazing at no particular spot, certainly not at Elvin, who lit another cigarette.

"Why is it always me who has to make all the decisions? Your turn."

"I don't know. I never know."

Daryl rose and turned on the television set, increasing the volume until the parade sounds were gone. Elvin lifted a magazine and turned pages.

Halloweens past had been miraculous. Ritualistic. Tiny seeds planted long ago in the marrow of their genes had finally burst forth in a splash of awesome color. The gray and brown of childhood uncertainty, the black and white of teenage angst had been supplanted by the freedom of adulthood. As a grownup you might have to spend a lot of time pulling weeds from the garden. But the occasional blooming, the sporadic wild party made everything worthwhile.

Daryl and Elvin arrived in New York, separately, about seven years ago. They've lived together for the past three. Halloween had been a highlight of their tandem journey through the city. But lately, forward motion had become difficult. The travelers had not been connecting with their usual agility and finesse. The very terrain, the ecosystem and infrastructure of their environment was in decay. More violence. More homeless. More disease. More litter. When Daryl got off the bus from Maine, when Elvin had flown in from Georgia, they perforated their edges to mesh with the city's gears. Eventually they bumped into each other, found that they could blend together with ease, soften for one another the brutal blows of surviving. But they'd somehow lost the formula, accidentally bent a working part out of shape, and now sat idly, letting their annual bacchanal slip by. Little boys like Daryl and Elvin had marked time in the prison of youth, weathering the tortures of traditional family oppression, eager and anxious to escape parents, siblings, small-town gossip, to go to a big city and sample the forbidden flavors denied them all their lives. The trips from Penobscot, Maine and Whispering Pines, Georgia to New York were necessary steps to move beyond stigmatized beginnings and claim the glamour of a wild flower, a strange breed in a queer brood in a large, throbbing, loud and crazy metropolis.

"We could go to a bar and drink," said Daryl, shaking a handful of candy corn like dice.

"We could go to a club and dance," said Elvin.

"Too crowded on Halloween. Coat check would take an hour."

"Bars would be crowded too."

"Maybe there's something good on the tube." Daryl threw back his head and popped the candy corn into his mouth, then picked up the remote and sifted through the images. Elvin gazed down at the magazine in his lap, started tapping his foot lightly, intertwining the nervous fingers that seemed to want to leap from his hands.

The room, dim with the blinds closed and only the reading lamp providing any light, shrank before Elvin's eyes. He closed them. Then glanced around. And noticed the shabbiness of the couch, the worn-out spots in the carpet. Certainly not the beautiful surroundings with brand-new expensive things he'd seen in magazines and had daydreamed about owning. But this was not the source of his unrest. The apartment – not the cause, but a symptom – merely reflected the tattered and unkempt relationship of its occupants. Elvin looked at the Jeff Stryker dildo, wound in a double helix of Mardi Gras beads, like a shrine, on the mantel. Somehow Daryl had become less accessible, less agreeable, not fun anymore, and Elvin, though he still loved him, wanted to get away. Not completely. But at least move out. Get his own apartment. Try to keep Daryl as a friend and lover, but jettison the roommate thing.

"We should do something," said Daryl. "It's our night of nights."

Elvin lit another cigarette. Looked at Daryl with a cool, even stare. Asked himself why he and this very attractive person in the armchair had become like two magnets, one facing the wrong direction, pushing away from one another. "I don't feel like going out. Everything'll be too crowded and noisy. My life is crazy enough."

Daryl turned off the television set. And sat down, heaving a sigh. What is it with you, he wanted to say. What the fuck's going on? Why can't we just get along anymore? But he said nothing. Words would lead to an argument that would end in nastiness and anger. He looked at Elvin with eyes that attempted to send up a white flag of truce.

Elvin looked at those eyes and saw nothing but insolence and disgust. He tried to look neutral. Then stared down at the floor.

For several long minutes time became a rack upon which they were lashed at the wrists and ankles, stretching, stretching, with pain emanating from the heart to the limbs, burning, molten lava in every vein.

Daryl breathed deeply and very calmly, exceedingly gently said, "I need to go out. Come on. Let's try to have some fun."

Elvin let the magazine slide from his lap. Then bent to retrieve it and stood up in one swift movement. He yawned, said, "I think I'll take a nap. Go. Have a good time. Really. See you later." The words, the intonation, the inflection, weren't quite as he'd intended. Maybe it would be good for them to spend the evening apart. He'd tried to back down, see if a brief respite from each other might have a positive effect, but perhaps something undefinable from within had shaped the words to convey something else. When they were spoken Daryl heard them as sarcastic, challenging, a dare that could not go unacknowledged.

"Well. Fine. That's what I'll do. Right now." As he rose and his mind clicked into departure mode – jacket, keys, money – he could feel pressure, pushing his chest down, making him breathe faster, harder. He moved quickly, efficiently completing the circuit from the chair to the table to the coat stand, dropping the keys into his pocket, patting the other for his wallet, then, without a backward glance, opened the door and walked out.

Elvin watched the cute little buns pulsate away and then disappear, cute little buns attached to a manly body with an ever youthful face. He played a Sarah Vaughan album and flung himself onto the couch. He tried to listen to the music but his mind, not in the mood, bombarded him with images and impressions. Some felt good. Others pierced him like lances. The dream had not come true. Or, to be more accurate, it had come true but it didn't look like it was supposed to. He'd leave Georgia to go to New York. Become a famous dancer and choreographer. Fall madly in love. Live in a fabulous apartment. And all of this had occurred. But not quite. To

Elvin it seemed a cruel joke. He'd come to New York as planned, but just when the serious decay began. The dance gigs were few and he worked part-time as an aerobics instructor. He loved Daryl but was not happy. And the apartment, never quite fabulous enough, was even less so now. It seemed like his life was going on inside of a funhouse mirror, the correct images reflected but strangely distorted, shapeless and confusing.

Cute little buns, he thought, and I'm not even interested anymore. For a moment he considered going out to trick. Then remembered how much he'd hated having to search for sex in sleazy places – truck stops back home, backrooms and dungeons in New York. The three seconds of divine, transcendent pleasure were always rewarding. But the weirdos, the furtiveness, the rapidity, the germs and other microorganisms passed around like canapés were not appetizing. He'd been grateful when he'd met Daryl. Felt like he'd been freed from the bondage of torture. And now he did not want to return.

Sarah Vaughan sang and Elvin paid no attention, listening to the voices in his head, telling him everything he did not want to hear.

In a bar, which he hadn't visited in two years, situated in the Village near the river, Daryl stood, looking, watching, taking in all the sights like a camera, seemingly unaware that he was attracting as much scrutiny as the guys he himself observed. Unaware of his own appearance and desirability, he would have been unimpressed if anyone had acknowledged his presence. Some men have to work hard to look their best. To others good looks come easily and there are those who, doted upon at a very young age, develop a conceit, spoiled because their admirers demand so little of them. But Daryl, keenly interested in everything going on around him, eager to try everything, wanted to experience all the amazements of the world. And thought seldomly of himself. In bars he'd always be surprised when anyone addressed him. It was like being jerked from the air and placed on the ground. As though he was completely unaware that he could be analyzed just as easily as everyone else in the room. But it didn't matter. Daryl would stutter through the compliments, thanking the stranger profusely, become embarrassed, and quickly turn the conversation around to inquiries, focusing the spotlight on the other.

It was one of the newer bars that had opened on the near side of the plague curve. When the disease had first been detected and hysteria had mounted to a vomiting volcano of despair, many businesses had closed. But though the virus had not yet been conquered, a gradual return to a more normal mood had resulted in some new enterprises. Off to the right were a few scattered tables, to the left the bar, separated by a long wooden divider, waist high. At the far right corner, a screen played porn videos, on the right, another ran music videos. Hip Hop rhythms, in sync with neither screen, played loudly.

Daryl bought a drink. Stood close to the front near the entrance and surveyed the room. If Elvin had been there he would have remarked that it seemed like a nice place, good crowd. He realized that he was alone and for a moment felt uncomfortable. He hadn't gone to a bar without Elvin in a long time. He hadn't cruised, with serious intent, since meeting Elvin. Out of practice, out of shape. But he eventually relaxed. Whatever happens, happens, he told himself. I'm just going to have a good time.

There were corporate executives dolled up in high drag with makeup and feathers and wigs and sequins and accessories, and school teachers and doctors in serious leather with caps and vests and handcuffs and boots, a few people masquerading as media celebrities, and a few, like Daryl, who wore standard, urban cruising attire.

A hand gripped his left butt cheek and he spasmed and giggled and turned to look at who had grabbed him. A man, somewhat taller, with a saggy face, slack lips and a bloated belly said, "Hi there. Happy Halloween. You know you're very cute."

Daryl blushed, said thank you, and asked the man about his occupation, where he lived, are you a native New Yorker? He listened attentively, yet moved his eyes so they would not lock into the stranger's intense stare. Just when the man thought he might be making some progress, Daryl shook his hand, said it was nice talking to you, and walked away, sat down at an empty table and looked back and forth at the screens.

When a waiter came by and asked him if he wanted another drink, Daryl declined, then noticed a guy, pretty good-looking, watching him, smiling. He approached, grabbed the waiter by the arm and said, "Wait a second," then turned to Daryl and asked, "Can I buy you a drink?"

He nodded, said yes, the man sat down, they drank and talked, and when it came time to decide which apartment to go to, the question was quickly resolved.

The bed was large, the mattress hard, and Daryl enjoyed his nakedness upon it. An assortment of condoms, lubes, cock rings and dildos adorned the night table. The man, with large bones and dark coloring, was gentle and soft at first, nurturing, loving, then became rougher, tougher, sending Daryl into ecstatic transports of warm sensation. Each article of clothing he'd removed reminded him of the person at home. And before becoming completely lost to sensuous pleasure, each touch evoked past encounters, previous situations, many with Elvin, in which he'd reached new peaks of excitement, had felt so good he'd left his body and departed to some exquisite astral plane.

When they returned to themselves Daryl felt gratitude for the man who'd lifted him up so very high. And fought pangs of guilt when he thought of Elvin. The one who'd been a rock every time things became unsteady. The one who'd shared everything with him and overlooked his mistakes. Elvin meant so much to him, and he loved him, but Daryl felt that they could no longer communicate. He couldn't figure out exactly when it had gone wrong, or how they'd managed to slip away from one another. They never had sex anymore.

Hardly talked. Snapped at one another when they did. Never cuddled in bed. When was the last time they'd kissed?

He politely left the man, put on his clothing and told himself that when he arrived home he'd tell Elvin everything that had happened, all the thoughts that had lit up in his mind. They'd start communicating again and this would lead to a new, happier era in their lives.

Elvin had fallen asleep on the couch. When Daryl got home, at about 2:30 in the morning, he closed the door and moved about stealthily, removing his jacket and shoes, gently, silently, placing his keys and pocket money on the table. Too adrenalized to sleep, he sat in the armchair, eating candy corn in small sections, one tiny bite at a time. Elvin's gaunt face was beginning to show signs of age, tiny lines, a bit too much tanning. But Daryl was pleased to note that his lover's long, sinewy dancer's limbs, flat tummy and small waist, were still capable of making him want to reach out and touch. But this was not the time for sentimentality. Determined to vent his thoughts before he changed his mind and backed down, Daryl softly called out Elvin's name, attempting to awaken him without startling him. Elvin sighed, opened his eyes, immediately noted the awkward posture he'd melted into, and quickly sat up, rubbing his eyes, suppressing gap-mouthed yawns. "Must've fallen asleep," he mumbled.

"I'm sorry I woke you," said Daryl, "but I did a lot of thinking tonight and I think we should really have a serious talk. Now."

"About what?"

"About us."

"What about us?" Elvin could not help noticing that Daryl's hair looked slept upon, his pretty lips had that dry, chapped look, typical after sexual play involving the mouth, that his pants were not zipped up all the way.

"About us not getting along very well lately. We need to talk and figure out what the problems are, try to solve them."

"We should have talked before you decided to go out and play trick or treat with strangers."

Daryl flushed. He could never hide anything from Elvin. But what had given him away? Was it something I said, he wondered, or maybe just the way I said it? "I won't lie to you," he said humbly. "Yes, I fooled around. But it made me realize how much I love you."

"Right," said Elvin, a roiling head of steam inflating his anger, "you love me so much that you decided to go out and contract the virus so that we could die horrible, premature deaths!"

Daryl was so shocked at these words it felt like his heart had stopped beating. "I swear," he sputtered, "we didn't exchange any bodily fluids we simply –"

"I don't want to hear about it!" Elvin cut him off, rising, moving toward the bedroom. "I'm sick of you, I'm sick of this apartment, I'm sick of this city, I'm sick of my life! And nothing you can say will change anything!"

* * *

Daryl, after two days in Penobscot with his family, finally reached the point where he wanted to be back in New York. Coming home for Christmas was always exciting. Temporarily. Then boredom and restlessness would fight for dominance in his thoughts, he'd become edgy and brusque, distracted, tired from the deception, the subterfuge, the game he'd have to play to simply spend time with his family. He sat on the worn-out couch before the fireplace in the living room with threadbare carpeting. Unlike Elvin, Daryl's family were very relaxed about such things – chipped coffee mugs and cigarette burns didn't bother them unduly – and Daryl had never been able to fully understand Elvin's obsession, his fastidiousness – downright pedantic, annoying – when it came to furnishings and the care thereof. But it didn't matter anymore. As Daryl had told his sister, Denise, the only member of his family who knew about his relationship with Elvin, the first evening home when she'd taken him into her room, closed the door and asked him how things were going.

"I moved out," he told her. "Haven't told Mom or Dad or Aunt Belle yet. I figure I'll tell them before I go back. Make up some excuse about how the building was condemned or something. I can tell them anything; they don't care."

"What happened!?!" she'd asked, reacting as though something catastrophic could be the only reason why two people living together for three years would break up.

Daryl was quick to reassure her that there had been no particular incident, nothing specific that could bear the blame, just a gradual shifting, an unidentifiable set of factors that resulted in a new equation. "Really," he told her, imploring her to accept his story, "I'm happier now. We weren't getting along and I tried to make things work but they didn't and everything's much better now." For a moment he considered telling her about his infidelity but decided against it.

Denise looked at him – all solicitude – and patted his shoulder. "I want you to have the best Christmas ever. It's too bad we can't tell anyone else what's happened. Dad and Aunt Belle might go a little easier on you if they knew you'd just gone through a serious, emotional, traumatic experience."

Daryl wanted to reach out, pull her toward himself, wrap his arms around her and cry on her shoulder, tell her, yes, you've got it exactly, it was serious, emotional and traumatic. But he forced a smile, raised his hand in a gesture meant to convey sincerity, and assured her that he was fine, everything had worked out for the best in this best of all possible worlds.

"If I told the family I'm queer things would be a lot worse than they are right now, that's for sure."

"They know. They just don't want to talk about it." Denise scowled, "I hate that word – queer. When I hear people use it at work it makes me so mad."

"In New York that's what we call ourselves now. Gay is obsolete."

"Really," she exclaimed, brightening, "it's so hard for us country bumpkins to stay up-to-date with you fast-movin' city folk."

They laughed. And talked about Denise's boyfriend, Carl,

whom she'd been dating for several years and everyone assumed she would eventually marry.

Daryl spent his mornings chatting with Mom in the kitchen, with his brother Donald in the bedroom they'd shared while growing up, with Dad in his workshop in the basement. They talked about the weather, TV shows, the lawn and the neighbors. Donald's wife, Megan, and their daughter, Tanya, six years old, were usually in the guest bedroom, watching TV, dressing and undressing Tanya's dolls. Daryl had little to say to them and tended to pass them by as he made his rounds.

After lunch he'd borrow someone's car and drive around, into the center of town, out to the quarries where he'd sunbathed nude on a flat rock, then to the steep, winding roads that led to the foothills where he'd sneaked cigarettes and beer with his pals. In the evenings he'd call local friends to see if they'd returned home for the holidays, he'd watch television with the family. Then late at night when they were asleep, he'd revolve and shudder in bed, wanting desperately to talk to someone in New York, but there was no one he could call. Steve, Jerry and Bennett would all be out of town visiting their families. Elvin was out of the question. He wished he could speak to Jim, Enrique or Mark, but since they'd died he found it too painful to even think about them. Daryl would finally drift into a restless sleep, in the mornings feel slightly out of it. Although the excitement of Christmas was building fast all around him, he wished he was back in New York, in the tiny apartment he'd found after leaving Elvin.

Mom busied herself with turkey, ham and fixings, Aunt Belle was responsible for soups, salads, vegetables, Denise baked cookies and pies, Dad erected the tree and decorated it with ornaments that had been in the family for generations and only he was allowed to handle, Donald did the exterior decorating with plastic carolers that lit up, wreaths, flashing lights and a weather-proof nativity diorama. Daryl, the youngest, and of whom the least was expected, would listlessly help out here and there, attempting to capture the family spirit, but not succeeding, wanting to be elsewhere doing other things. He could not say, exactly, what these other things were, but he knew, for certain, that he'd find them eventually.

When his father and brother argued about the impending war in the Persian Gulf, Daryl feigned interest but soon found his mind wandering. When they briefly stopped shouting at one another and asked Daryl his opinion, he confessed that he hadn't been paying attention and had to be reminded what they were talking about. "I haven't had much time to think about it," he told them and they wondered to themselves how he could be so uninterested and so uninteresting.

He belonged here, but he didn't fit in. Although his chromosomes bore the imprints of his mother's and father's blueprints, this cozily shabby gingerbread house in the game of Life was not nearly merry enough for Christmas, for him. He felt like an alien who'd been planted in his mother's womb. He could talk to Denise. But the rest of them were like strangers. Even the ribbon candy that Mom would buy and set out on a folding tray near the tree each year didn't taste right anymore. The reds were not cherryish enough, the yellows not lemony.

It was the gap, he finally realized, as he'd circle away from Aunt Belle every time she came near. The gap that existed between Daryl's truth and the family's denial. Except for Denise, the only bridge, who bore the weight of her brother's dilemma.

Aunt Belle, his father's older sister, was the glue that held the family together, the sandpaper who wore everyone out. She was short and round, puffy-looking all over, her face like a dollop of mashed potatoes with the eyes and mouth scooped and filled with gravy. Attempting to keep things smooth, ultra-smooth, she bullied, manipulated, cajoled, withheld information, distorted facts. She made certain that everyone stayed in touch, got together often, ruddered the family ship through rough waters.

It was at a Christmas supper, back when Daryl was about

eight years old, that Aunt Belle had inadvertently stopped the conversation at the table, changing the delicate family balance. Daryl had risen to fetch the salt and pepper and returned. She watched him move to and from the table, then turned to her brother and said, "Light on his feet, isn't he?"

It was as though everyone at the table was a marionette on strings jerked by unseen hands. They stopped eating. All eyes locked onto Daryl's father. He looked at his sister in shock, speechless. Belle offered her brother a tender look that meant to say, I'm sorry, but it was too late to take back the words and pretend they hadn't been uttered. For a prickly second all eyes scanned around the table, avoiding Daryl's eyes, then everyone looked down at their plates and continued eating.

Since that moment, years ago, the subject of Daryl's gait has not been broached, except between Daryl and Denise. Aunt Belle, the navigator, would pinpoint reefs and shallows, smoothly maneuvering away from any potential danger zones. Should the subject of marriage arise, for instance, she would dominate the conversation, offering explicit instructions for Denise and Donald, but, then, changing themes, speak of Daryl's attributes and his potential to excel in any field he might choose. If the conversation should veer too closely to the exact details of her nephew's living arrangements in New York City, Aunt Belle would, in a mock-complicitous, winking manner imply that Daryl's roommate – if in fact he had one – is a private concern that no one should discuss or question, then alter the flow, praising the cultural plenitude and delightfully cosmopolitan nature of his new home.

Loving her for her concern, but hating her for creating this knot of silence that nothing could unravel, the worst of it, her overprotectiveness, always came after every Christmas supper when she would insist that he sit with her and they talk. A very one-sided conversation in which she would ask him if he still had that low-paying job, what-do-you-call-it, not for profit?

'Yes," he'd say, firmly, "I'm still working at the Lytton Foundation."

"That's the, uh, not for profit thing?" she'd ask, a slightly sarcastic tone creeping from her mouth.

"Yes."

"Well, Daryl, dear, you'll just have to explain it to me one more time. How can anything be not for profit? And how can you make a decent living at it?"

He'd explain to her the grants he administered that went to scholars, artists, hospices, day care centers, but she would cut him off and lecture without mercy about the cold hard facts of life, and nice guys finishing last and fat bank accounts and the survival of the fittest.

Daryl would want to shake her and tell her that he was happy with his work, thrilled with his life, deliriously in love with a wonderful man, but he sat there, pretending to heed her, mentally contradicting every word.

And this year's conversation with Aunt Belle would be worse than usual. Because this year he didn't have a wonderful man to hold as a prize in his thoughts. So, after supper, after he'd helped clear the table, when Aunt Belle attempted to corner him in the living room, he snuck downstairs to his father's workshop, where Dad and Donald would go to escape from the women, sat on a plastic milk crate near the bandsaw, listening to them argue about the arms buildup, the troops deployed, the financial factors and environmental considerations. He listened, offered his opinions, trying desperately not to think about Aunt Belle, Christmas, New York, his tiny new apartment or Elvin.

* * *

It was the loneliest, quietest, saddest Valentine's Day Elvin had ever known. He sat on the new couch, staring at the new carpeting, Christmas gifts to himself. He thought that getting some new things, rearranging the furniture a bit, would help him adjust to life without Daryl. And also, since he had nowhere to go for Christmas, that it might cheer him up as he sat by himself while the rest of the world celebrated mightily. He could have visited people for the holidays, taken the money spent on the apartment and gone traveling for a while instead. But there was no one he wished to visit in Whispering Pines, Georgia. When he'd been caught behind the filling station with a trucker from Alabama, word had spread through town like wildfire. And when his adoptive parents had said goodbye the day after he graduated from high school, they told him that the best way he could repay their generosity, the huge debt he owed them, was never to have any contact with them whatsoever, never again. He would not miss them. He'd learned not to love them. They fed him, clothed him and sent him to school. But that was all. That was all. That was all.

He could have visited Charlie in San Francisco or Sherry in L.A., ex-dance partners whom he'd speak with on the phone a few times a year. But Charlie had recently moved in with someone and Elvin would make the situation lopsided, the third, unnecessary wheel. Sherry and her husband and kids would be too sweet for words; they'd throw him into a deep depression as he would torture himself with cruel memories of his childhood, regretting everything, wishing he'd grown up elsewhere. And there was no one to hang out with here. Manhattan had simply become a graveyard. Over the past six years Elvin had lost eleven friends – three dancers, two musicians, two composers, a director, an actress, an ex-lover who'd become a good friend, and the guy who used to live next door who would look after Elvin's apartment when he was on tour as Elvin would do for him when he was on vacation.

Christmas had been awful. He'd gotten used to Daryl's annual trek to Maine every winter, but this year had been worse – there was no joyful return to anticipate now. On the most romantic day of the year, Elvin had only his new carpet and new couch for companionship.

Until the phone rang.

"Elvin, this is Paul."

He had to think for a moment. Who's Paul?

"Paul Bergman. I teach the aerobics class following yours?"

"Right. Hi, Paul. What a surprise. How are you?"

"Fine. Fine. You?"

"Great. Just ... terrific."

"The reason I called is, well, you probably have other plans but just in case you don't – and I hope this doesn't sound too crass or corny – but you're recently divorced and I'm recently widowed and I thought – why don't we get together and see if we can have a good time. You know, just friendly-like. Dinner, maybe a movie or something, then split. What do you think? Don't be afraid to say no, I can handle it."

Elvin didn't know what to say at first. This possibility had never appeared in his mind; he did not think that he'd ever get any closer to the other aerobics instructor than the briefest of greetings when they passed at the gym. And he figured he'd be spending the evening alone with his books and records. If this had been planned, if they'd made arrangements beforehand, by now Elvin would have thought of a hundred reasons why he shouldn't go through with it. Would have come up with some very plausible excuses to bow out. But having had no time to consider all the angles, and allowing for the possibility that this might be fun, he blurted, "Well, I think this is a great idea. I had no plans, really. It would be nice. Tell me where and when and I'll be there."

Elvin had entered a state of limbo, had ceased to feel any of the intensity of life since Daryl had moved out. The comforting solidity of things had given way to ground-rumbling instability, the threat that all support could crumble at any second, that he'd been overtaken by a void of isolation which threatened to turn him into a hysterical madman. The offer from Paul was the first sign he'd seen in quite some time that life could still hold pleasant surprises in store for the unsuspecting. And by the end of the evening, before he walked home, Elvin managed to piece together a vague picture of what he wanted; he'd finally broken through a thin, wet membrane and found what he wanted on the other side.

He stood in the back of the backroom club where Paul had taken him, after a late dinner at a French restaurant. Elvin could hear the slurping and groaning sounds, zippers opening and closing, sighs and whispers from the creatures cavorting in the dark. He thought back on his conversation at the restaurant with Paul. Colette's had just opened several months ago. Paul had raved about it. Elvin hadn't been there, hadn't been to any new any things since he'd started spending time with Daryl. Once they'd found a good Chinese restaurant, or a friendly bar where they could meet after work, they would rarely try any other, figuring why keep searching after you've found something that works well for you? Safe. Dull. And as Elvin sat in the warm and comfortable, nice but not pretentious atmosphere of the restaurant, enjoying escargots, duck, wine, he realized that this is what had happened to his wonderful journey with Daryl. They'd been trudging down the same roads day after day, at work, at play – particularly in bed – and they'd simply become bored with the same old routine.

Which is why Elvin was so agreeable, after they'd eaten and walked for a while in the chilly February windy air, almost eager to go to a backroom club that Paul had suggested. In the front, a juice bar with video games, pinball machines, a pool table, a jukebox, and a crush of men passing into and out of a dark passage. Paul had plunged into the black maw while Elvin hung out at the bar for a while, considering whether to go any further. This furtive, anonymous, sex-in-the-shadows thing was what he'd told himself he'd hated more than almost anything. And who would risk any kind of harmful behavior with all of those fatal microbes everywhere? But, he convinced himself, he could dip his toes in, splash around a little, he didn't have to dive in headfirst. He could touch and fondle, be touched and fondled – even get naked if he wanted to – with no further obligation. There was no rulebook which said that he had to do this, this, or that as a requisite for permission to depart. He could just listen and sniff and watch if he wanted to. So, with his shoulders back and his tummy tight, he passed through the corridor that led to darkness.

It was like a funhouse, a mysterious interior with nooks and crannies formed by groups of bodies in differing configurations. As his eyes slowly became aware of shapely presences he moved into an empty corner, two men beside him, one standing upright, one on his knees. When Elvin had relaxed into the sturdy confluence of two concrete walls, allowed his physical and psychic weight to slip away, he sighed and a flow of warm sensation began to tickle him all over. When the man on his knees lifted his hand to Elvin's crotch and started manipulating his cock and balls through supple denim, Elvin looked down at the man's face lunging against the other man's crotch and felt himself responding, clicking into a steady vibration that escalated in speed and intensity until he rocked back and forth with the motion and finally fell back against the wall, unloading the pulsating tension that had built up in his groin. He caught his breath, moved as though in a daze, exited the room and hit the sidewalk, the cold bracing air, heading home, hearing echoes of words that Paul had said to him at dinner. When the conversation had skirted too closely to the subject of Elvin's ex-lover and Paul's deceased lover, they'd cautiously, delicately, exchanged thoughts and offered assuring comments, making this exchange, which had the potential for disaster, a comforting and uplifting commiseration of two lonely souls. Elvin thought that Paul was dealing remarkably well with his tragic loss, felt that he was someone he could confide in. So he opened his heart about the breakup with Daryl and when Paul had listened and said, "If I were you I'd buy him a heart-shaped box of chocolates and try to win him back," Elvin thought that maybe this wasn't such a bad idea.

* * *

At a small desk in the living room, Daryl sat and paged through a thin newspaper, pausing occasionally to read or skim an article. There was a stack of thin newspapers off to one side and a scissors on the other, a small pile of articles that had been clipped, several strips of marginal paper carelessly strewn. The apartment, nicely situated on the fourth floor, due to its corner location, offered sun – when it cared to shine – in the morning and in the afternoon. Finding it was a lucky break, the cost not as high as some landlords would have had it. A sunny Sunday morning, Daryl's stacks of paper rose and fell, he felt contented, well-rested, and suddenly thinking it too quiet, reached to turn on the radio, lowering the volume to a softer level.

Elvin was the one who'd taught Daryl everything he knew about music, which wasn't much, but Daryl was grateful for the instruction. Unlike Elvin whose knowledge of music was vast, who could sing and play the piano, Daryl was the kind of American boy who didn't go to rock concerts and never owned a guitar, hadn't shown any interest in theater or opera, cringed at the suggestion of piano lessons or the church choir. He could rarely recall song titles and had trouble identifying the names of vocalists and groups. During the disco years there were songs he danced to hundreds of times which he could not name if the fate of the universe depended on it.

Daryl's awareness of how much he'd learned from Elvin deepened, broadened, and he'd begun to think of ways, subtle, small ways, to say thank you. Elvin brought a certain intensity to his life. Things were never quite as surprising and exciting when Elvin wasn't around. Alone, Daryl felt unplugged, unconnected in the dark. When they were together it was like being part of an electrical circuit with tingling currents zipping from fingers to toes and back, everything for your ears glorious and fascinating, everything for your eyes a wonderment of dazzling color and light.

Elvin slept late, almost reaching consciousness, then sliding back into nowhere, finally awakening, shifting onto his back, his hands clasped behind his head, looking, coming back into focus. His arms ached a bit, unlike his legs, unused to the workouts he'd had lately. But it felt good. He was in the best shape he'd ever been which made the first signs of aging – his hair thinning and receding, skin lined and leathery – somewhat easier to handle. When he'd finally taken an unflinching, realistic look at his life he knew that he would not be able to dance and teach aerobics forever. He'd joined Paul, taking a course in physical therapy, an occupation that appealed to him more with time and experience. He and Paul had become rather chummy, meeting every so often for drinks or dinner, chatting a bit before and after classes. When Paul would ask Elvin if he wanted to go to a sex club, he declined. Eventually he stopped asking. Neither had any family in New York. Both had lost numerous friends and acquaintances. It's a miracle, Elvin thought, that just when I really needed a friend, there he was. Feeling confident and centered finally, after such a protracted period of uncertainty, Elvin thought about breakfast. Or maybe brunch. Whatever.

Like the pieces of a puzzle falling naturally into place, Elvin and Daryl had overcome their previous mistakes. If they'd thought the picture had a few things wrong with it after living together for three years, it had seemed completely undecipherable after they'd split up. But like salmon who follow the dictates of their genetic code and fight the brutal currents to return to their place of birth, so too had Daryl and Elvin, first following the beacon that beckoned from New York, then following their hearts when they realized how much they'd lost by separating. Though things might not be perfect, at least there was something to hold onto, another person to share the tragedies and the miracles. Elvin, for the first time ever, felt a sense of security and continuity. To Daryl it looked like a gray film or dullness had been rinsed from his eyes, the world now much brighter and more colorful, vivid in ways it had never been before.

Daryl finished clipping, then sorted the articles into three piles, articles about gay legislation, gay bashing, gay outing, gay artists, gay policemen, gay soldiers, placed them in envelopes addressed to Mom, Dad and Aunt Belle. Then, cleaning up the mess, felt jabs of hunger and wandered into the kitchen. But instead of eating anything, he decided to wait for Elvin to wake up and scoured, rinsed and dried all the dishes from last night. Then sat on the couch, the new one Elvin had bought, the color of which – maroon – Daryl was not too crazy about, but, he had to admit, looked classier than the old one. First he ate some jellybeans from the candy dish, carefully avoiding the greens and blacks. Then, went to the refrigerator and got a few red, gold, silver and blue foil-covered chocolate eggs, returned to the couch and let them, one by one, melt slowly into his tongue.

The argument started after they'd finished eating, but the seeds were planted when Elvin finally emerged from the bedroom, greeted Daryl with a kiss, asked him if he was ready to go to brunch, and Daryl, having waited for so long became a mite testy and countered the idea with the suggestion that instead they go to lunch. Elvin wanted to know what the difference was. "You can order anything you like anywhere we go," he said.

When they sat at the small table in the omelette-waffle-ice cream emporium, and ate eggs Benedict, sipping Bloody Mary's, hardly a word was exchanged. They walked to the pier and sat in the breezy sunshine. Gazing at people passing by and at the Jersey shore across the water, they sat on a concrete ledge, in silence, until Elvin decided to try to break through the barrier, the thin walls of the twin bubbles that surrounded them, by asking Daryl what he thought of the film they'd seen last night. Atypically, they hadn't discussed it immediately after because the phone rang as the credits rolled and Elvin had talked while Daryl went to bed. Daryl praised the writing and the story but didn't care for the acting or directing. Elvin, dumbfounded, usually in agreement with Daryl about these things, voiced a differing opinion. They argued, calmly, reserved, each trying to cling to the top wrung, maintaining the cool, detached tone of he who is right. When Daryl said, "The only good thing about it was that it's politically correct," Elvin, exasperated, blurted, "You're getting so goddamned political lately. Lighten up!"

"Well, maybe I am. Maybe you should be getting more political too!"

The rhythm, the velocity of their interchange stopped short, then began again in a new mode, one that was easier, softer. Elvin looked at Daryl's eyes with humility in his own, placed his hand on Daryl's knee and said, "Maybe you're right."

They came together again, blending smoothly, creamily, finding things to laugh about as they walked back to the apartment, the sidewalks and streets still festooned with plastic leprechaun hats, beer cans, strips of green and yellow ribbon, shattered whiskey bottles, a tattered, rain-streaked sign that said **NO FAGGOTS IN IRELAND** and another that read **IRISH QUEER**. Back home, they listened to the messages on the answering machine. One was from Charlie, Elvin's friend in San Francisco, wanting to share the news that his cousin who'd been sent to the Persian Gulf was on his way back, safe and sound. Then, a message from Aunt Belle, wishing Daryl and his friend a happy Easter – and, by the way, what's with all these newspaper clippings? And finally, Paul, asking if Elvin and Daryl would like to go dancing later that evening.

"You wanna go dancin'?" Elvin asked, a leering grin on his face.

"Let's dance," said Daryl, picking up some jellybeans, tossing one at Elvin, who scooped some from the dish, popped one in his mouth and lobbed a couple at Daryl. Chuckling, they pelted each other, with handfuls eventually, a confetti rainbow of soft pellets flying and falling, then laughed themselves silly on the couch, tumbling into a tight embrace, heat growing between them, two horny Easter bunnies cuddling in a celebration of life.

Lubricity

Shafts of light and glowing dots gliding around. Out of shadows and dark crevices in the air, bullets of brightness slipped through the mists, illuminating patches all around me. I was still in my room, I think. But in a strange sector of time and space: different dimension, another reality. Floating and unfettered. Sliding about in a jarful of wet, warm satin. I had the sensation of containment, yet I was unbound. Nothing looked normal and my eyes were captivated by the vapors, the shadows, the trails and auras of light.

Earlier, I had been reading. Then I watched a video. And eventually, read some more. My room disappeared. I swirled in a vortex of Spanish moss and kaleidoscopic color. From out of nothing tactile, figures emerged. An elderly gentleman with hollow cheeks and sad eyes. He appeared to be seated on a large, ornate throne. As he hove into view I could see that he sat opposite another gentleman – middle-aged with tanned skin and a thoughtful countenance. The second man's chair seemed ordinary to me, modern and unexceptional. Between the two men, a three-tiered chess board floated above a squat plinth.

They maneuvered amethyst knights, onyx rooks, aquamarine pawns and they talked. The younger would describe the buttocks or genitals of a sensuous youth and the elder would smile and nod in agreement. The elder would relate a somewhat brutal tale, smirking.

I realized who these men were. Are. For earlier that evening I had been reading *The 120 Days Of Sodom,* after having watched several scenes of the videocassette. Shortly before these visions entered my room, or I was transported to a bizarre reality zone, I had placed the book and the videocassette – one atop the other – on my table. Had the union of these two objects somehow engendered this fantastical manifestation? I was as uncertain then as I am now.

The Marquis noticed me first and summoned me closer with his gnarled index finger. "You may watch," he said, leering.

Pasolini took notice of me, "... and listen," he added, then returned his attention to the chess set.

From behind me, as if on an invisible hovercraft, a heavyset man drifted into view. He leaned over and offered to shake my hand. Grasping his plump fingers I started to introduce myself. Before I could manage a syllable he said, "Phil, Phil K. Dick. PKD. Pleased to meet you."

I recalled that the day before I had finished reading *Ubik.*

The darting lights and wavering veils – lavender, lime, crimson, cerulean – settled and slowed a bit as the game proceeded. The Marquis and Pasolini were transfixed by the small figures before them.

PKD and I watched, rapt, in silence. I could hear the gentle clang of platinum bells and inhaled the scent of oranges and cloves.

This must be heaven. Or hell for divine sinners, I thought.

"Heaven!" scoffed the Marquis.

"Heaven and hell are one and the same," said Pasolini. PKD grinned.

The game resumed. But I had to interrupt. I could not stop myself. "Is this some sort of punishment?" I asked.

The Marquis looked up and Pasolini turned his head to face me.

"I mean, do you suffer much?"

"Constantly," said Pasolini.

The Marquis chuckled. "In suffering there is pleasure – in pleasure is suffering."

PKD smiled, as though very pleased.

I couldn't let this precious moment go to waste. I gathered my resolve and plunged ahead. "Why did they persecute you?"

The Marquis shook his head, as though in disbelief. "For daring to tell the truth and rub their pretty faces in it."

"Ah, yes," Pasolini agreed, "the truth."

PKD sighed, "There are so many truths." And then he almost faded from sight. But reappeared a moment later. I wondered if this was to be my fate. Would I spend eternity with these three? If so, what had I done to merit their company? I have accomplished nothing to compare to the man who viewed sex through a prism; the man who conquered beautiful and the ugly with his unflinching eyes; the man who balanced on the point where multiple perspectives intersect.

Faced with the possibility, I wanted to stay with these three. They would educate and amuse me, massage my mind.

But as these thoughts visited I could feel myself sliding away. Slipping into familiar mundanity. The lights were fading, the bells more distant, the incense became faint.

I realized that this could be the end. "And what of passion?" I cried.

PKD chortled.

Pasolini smiled.

The Marquis sneered.

"Not the object," I protested as the vision rolled away, "the method!"

"Passion is humiliation," quipped the Marquis.

"Passion is politics," countered Pasolini.

"Passion is individual, transient, and multifarious," insisted PKD.

And then they were gone. I was alone on my bed. Reclining like an odalisque. I glanced around. At the stacks of books, cassettes, discs. And eventually melted into a long, dreamless sleep.

Boys in the Sand

The President paces back and forth, sand beneath his shoes, in a large tent in the desert. He is in Saudi Arabia to negotiate a peace settlement. The entire world waits anxiously. Barbara, The First Lady, did not accompany the President, opting instead to remain in Washington to teach the alphabet to Dan Quayle.

It's a warm night in the desert and an Arab boy, aged twelve, waving large paper fans, flutters about the President, cooling his torpid brow.

"Can't you do that any faster, for gosh sakes?" he pouts petulantly. "In the great states of America we have something called air conditioning."

The boy does not respond, either with gesture or sound. When the President is not looking at him he crosses his eyes and sticks out his tongue.

"Gosh darn it, I'm lonely," says the President. "I wish they could have taught this poor unfortunate waif some English so I'd at least have someone to talk to."

The waiting makes him uneasy. He glances at his Rolex and sighs.

Just then, the flaps of the tent part and the President's secret envoy for Operation Desert Oblivion enters.

"How the fuck are ya, Georgie?" says Roseanne.

"You're finally here!" he clasps his hands in gratitude. "Gosh darn it, now we can begin!" The President grins and says to himself, *If Saddam Hussein has any kind of dick at all, the person to shrivel it down to size is Roseanne Barr!* He rubs his hands gleefully.

"Let's get this friggin' show on the road," she chirps. "Ya got your secret weapons handy, Georgie Porgie?"

The President beams, "Present and accounted for." He clears his throat, claps his hands and loudly says, "Gentlemen!"

The flap at the other end of the tent swings inward and two men, maximum muscle, wearing jogging pants and tank-tops, enter and stand at attention.

A tear wells in the President's right eye. "Roseanne, in case you haven't already met them, I'd like to introduce you to my dear friends. Sly Stallone and Arnie Schwarzenegger. Gosh darn it, I'll say it – America's finest!"

"Hey guys," she hails, "yo, how's it hangin'?"

Arnie smiles and says, "Veil, I think it be just fine."

Sly grins and says, "Duh, I'm ready and rarin' to go."

Roseanne places her hands on her hips. "Okay, boys, let's see what ya got."

The President looks at Arnie. Arnie looks at Sly. Sly looks at the President. All three look at Roseanne.

"You mean, here? Now?" sputters the President.

"Of course!" snaps Roseanne. "I gotta see what my fuckin' bargaining power is, don't I?"

The President dismisses the Arab boy, lowers his hands, squares his shoulders and salutes. "I guess it's time to get down to business, gentlemen."

"Vell," says Arnie, "I guess if ve must and ve have to, den ve vill."

Sly says, "Duh, yeah."

"Okay, Gorgeous Georgie," says Roseanne, "you go first."

"This is for God and my country and, of course, Barbara back home," says the President as he unzips his pants.

Poor Barbara, is Roseanne's first thought.

The Arab boy raises his hand to his mouth, hiding a grin.

"Dis is for de great American economy, and God and

country too you best belif it, and especially for Hollyvood, my new home," says Arnie as he pulls down his pants.

Uh oh, says Roseanne to herself, *strike two.*

The Arab boy raises his other hand to his mouth, the balls of his feet pivoting in the sand.

Sly pulls down his pants, says, "Duh, yeah, what dese guys just said."

Roseanne crosses her arms over her chest. "Well, I guess we really are in a recession! But what the fuck, I'll give it my best shot."

The President's eyebrows converge as he says, "We can do better than this! Gosh darn it, I know we can!"

He starts stroking himself, but not seeing any improvement, looks toward the corner for some assistance from the Arab boy, who just a moment before crawled out of the tent and disappeared into the night.

The President looks at his dear friend, Arnie.

"Veil," he says, "I'm a patriot and I vill do my best."

He gets to his knees and sucks the President's cock. There is no apparent change in length or diameter.

"Duh, maybe you're doing it wrong," says Sly, bending over to get a closer look.

Just then a SCUD missile tears through the roof of the tent, the pointy nose lodging in Sly's asshole, his jogging pants in smoking tatters at his feet. "Ouch," he says, glancing over his shoulder. "Hey, Mr. President, do you think this thing is loaded?"

The President pushes Arnie's face from his crotch and says, "Gosh. To tell you the truth we don't know very much about these particular weapons, military intelligence being what it is these days."

Roseanne looks askance, shakes her head in dismay and pushes out the flaps, exiting, shouting, "You guys are pathetic! I give up! This is a job for Roger Ailes!"

She commandeers a waiting jeep, guns the engine and roars into the night leaving a turbulent sand storm in her wake.

Excerpt from Transcription No. 910524-103

[DELETE:]

Again? Are you serious? I've told you over and over. I didn't do it. I swear ... Oh. Okay. All right. Really. Just don't hit me again, okay? I'm innocent. I swear. Really. Like I told you. The first time I did it I met this guy who said his name was Leon. You know? I was just driving by the pier, real slow, I knew what I wanted but I'd never done it before. And so he gets into the car and I, you know, did it and then paid him and that was it. But then the fourth, or maybe the third time it was Leon again. And he remembered me and I remembered him. So this time when it's over he tells me that I can have a phone number and call him and he'll set me up with all the young ones I want. You know? Avoid the possibility of picking up someone who turns out to be an undercover cop or a serial murderer or something. So I took the number. And whenever I called to make an appointment either Leon shows up or someone just like him. You know. Young, black, willing. I don't know why it is that I'm so drawn to the dark-skinned ones so much. I just know they excite me the most. You know? So everything is great. I call once or twice a week and the guys show up at any place I want and there's no trouble. You gotta believe me when I tell you it was ideal. I was never happier and less grouchy at work. It was the first time I was able to get my rocks off on a regular basis. I thought I never had it so good. But, anyway, that's how it all started. I wasn't expecting any problems. But then last night when I go to meet the guy he turns out to be a white kid. Well, I didn't want to seem impolite. I couldn't tell him he was the wrong color. I mean, I could never say such a thing. To anyone. But the thing is the kid was wounded. He said his name was Billy but he might have just been making it up. I'll bet a lot of the boys don't tell me their real names. You know? But, anyway, I was sort of confused as to why Leon sent me a white kid this time, but also, it was so unsettling, he had this gash along the side of his head, above the ear, and his hair was matted with dried blood and what looked like burnt sand or something. And I asked him if he was all right and if he was sure he wanted to go through with this. He said yes, so I, you know, unzipped him and leaned over and tried to do it, but I couldn't get that picture of his bloody head out of my mind. I mean, I made sure that he got off, I always do, but I couldn't get hard. You know? So when it was over I wrote down the location of the nearest emergency room on the back of my business card and gave it to him. I mean, I offered to drive him there but he said no. He just got out of the car and I drove home. I swear. That was the last time I saw him. Then the next thing I know you guys are bashing down my office door accusing me of murder, embarrassing me in front of all my employees. But I didn't do it. Really. I'm not that kind of person. I would never hurt anyone. There. That's my story. For the fourth time. You guys are really something, you know? I mean I've got better things to do than sit around and keep you entertained. You know, I've been thinking. All the time I've been sitting here I've had time to think. And you know what? I figured something out. Because, to tell you the truth, Billy isn't the first boy I had an appointment with who wound up dead. There was another one. Tobias. I saw his picture in the paper. Said he was a crack addict allegedly killed by a dealer. Something like that. Anyway, I recognized him. And the name in the paper was the same one he gave me. Tobias. And you know what? He was black. But the cops never found the killer. Maybe they never even tried. Because he was black. The only reason you care about Billy is because he was white. Am I right? Maybe his parents are rich and famous or something. The papers will keep hounding you to find his killer. But nobody cared when the black kid got killed. You guys are really something. I'm not a criminal. I live in a nice house. Hell, you could call me a social worker. I provide poor youngsters with an income. You guys should be giving me a medal, not torturing me with all these stupid questions. Can I call my wife now?

[END DELETE]

The Jack & The King

Diego stopped sucking Sammy's cock just long enough to say, "You've got quite a slab of meat there. Can I take home what I can't finish here?" He re-engulfed Sammy's thick rod and sucked it like a vacuum cleaner.

"I'm all out of doggie bags," said Sammy, grinning. "I guess you'll just have to eat it all now. There are people starving in Poland, you know."

Diego pulled away again. Took a long breath and said, "Speaking of poles, mine is getting hard and lonesome. Maybe you could pay it some attention?" He continued slurping while Sammy maneuvered his body, bringing them both face-to-cock. He pulled Diego's shaft into his mouth, circled his lips around it and slid them up and down. Ever so slowly.

Diego, the definitive stud, caressed Sammy's head between his massive thighs and fondled his dangling ballsac. Sammy responded by inserting his index finger into Diego's ass. He pushed it in as far as it could go, then gently drew it in and out. Diego sighed, quivered, then shook wildly and deposited a formidable load in Sammy's throat. As soon as Sammy tasted the salty cream, he favored Diego with a sample of his own succulent jism.

They rolled apart and waited for the spasms to subside.

Then Sammy – all lithe and wiry – changed position so the two men were lying head-to-head and toe-to-toe. They fell asleep and remained that way until the alarm clock rang out and awakened them two hours later.

* * *

They had met for the first time at the Backdoor bar earlier that evening. Diego, the coppery-skinned, pencil-moustached muscle-hunk had been shooting pool. Sammy, the well-defined, sinewy man with the unusually large endowment, had been leaning against the jukebox smoking a cigarette. Sammy had watched Diego bend over to score a double ricochet, and the bleached-out seam separating his meaty butt had beckoned to him like a long-lost friend. His cock began to squirm, growing larger by the second, as he imagined his throbbing rod exploring the cavern within. He'd bought another beer and strolled over to the green felt table. When the game had ended, Sammy locked his gaze on Diego's brown, puppyish eyes and smiled. Diego returned the gesture.

"Can I get you a beer or something?"

Diego glanced at Sammy's bulging crotch. "I know what I want, but I don't think it's on the menu."

"If you're as hungry as I am," said Sammy, "maybe we could find something good to eat at my place." He winked. Diego winked back and extended his hand.

"The name's Diego. Sometimes they call me the Jack of Diamonds."

Sammy grasped his hand in a firm clasp. "Sammy, also known as the King of Hearts."

"Not the broken ones, I hope."

"Not tonight," said Sammy.

They'd walked to Sammy's apartment through the balmy, starlit night, attempting to out-quip one another. But they seemed to be a pretty well-matched pair.

"I couldn't help but admire your back-seat upholstery," Sammy had said.

"It's difficult finding the right interior *dickorator* these days," Diego had countered.

Then, glancing at Sammy's tumescent crotch, Diego had said, "With artillery like yours, looks like you could win a war single-handed."

Sammy grinned. "With artillery like mine, I'm afraid it takes both hands!"

They'd chuckled and continued walking, until they'd arrived at Sammy's. Upon entering, he'd invited Diego to sit on his bed while he fiddled with his alarm clock.

"What are you doing?" Diego had asked.

"Setting the alarm. It'll go off every two hours. If we should fall asleep, it'll wake us up. This night's too good to waste. I can tell already."

They'd started out with a jack-off contest. On many previous occasions Sammy had challenged his guests to see who could shoot the most cum the farthest distance. But that night, with Diego, he wanted to have serial multiple orgasms, so the quantity was not nearly as important as the distance.

"How far do you think you can shoot your stuff?" Sammy had asked.

Diego looked at him and said, "So, you're a distance freak, eh?"

Sammy smiled and said, "Well, not to brag or anything, but once I was sitting right here on the bed and shot a load that landed on the far wall."

Diego estimated the distance. "Must be a good ten feet. You were in a sitting position?"

Sammy nodded. "Yeah. It would have been even farther if I'd been standing."

"I accept your challenge, champ."

Sammy fetched a roll of masking tape and laid a strip on the floor. Diego did a few deep-knee bends, as though warming up for the 50-yard dash. His thighs and calves tensed like an Olympic triathlete's.

They stood at the foul line with their toes almost touching it. Sammy scooped a handful of grease from the can and Diego followed suit. They wrapped their dangling cocks in their fists and greased them from base to tip. Stroking themselves – back and forth, up and down – their cocks began to lengthen and grow erect. Soon they were rocking to and fro, their cocks fucking their hands like the pistons of a super-charged engine.

Sweat broke out on Sammy's forehead and Diego grunted with each thrust of his pelvis. Faster and faster they stroked themselves until suddenly Diego let forth an arcing stream of jism that landed on the floor about seven and a half feet away. A few seconds later, Sammy shot his load and several dollops of cum sprang forth, hitting the floor just a few inches behind Diego's.

"I guess you win," said Sammy sheepishly.

"There's always next time," Diego grinned. "Come kiss the winner."

He pulled Sammy into a tight embrace, their cocks pressed up against their stomachs. Diego forced his tongue into Sammy's moist, warm mouth and pushed it to the back of his throat. Sammy had moaned with delight at that point and led Diego to the bed.

They'd followed that with blow jobs. The ingestion of pure protein would surely help them make the night an especially memorable one. Then they'd fallen asleep, recouping their strength, lightly dozing until the alarm clock summoned them back to consciousness and the possibility of more burning action.

* * *

Diego was facedown when the alarm sounded. His perfect buns – the size and shape of a halved basketball – looked as though they were desperately in need of some attention. When Sammy awoke, he couldn't help but notice the beckoning butt. His cock sprang to attention, standing up perpendicular to his abdomen. He greased his palm and moistened the throbbing shaft. It gleamed like a rocket, reflecting the light of the moon through the open window.

Sammy slid onto Diego's back. "Hey there, Superman," said the bottom, "you got a deposit for my savings account? Interest is compounded hourly."

Sammy chuckled. "I hope there's no penalty for early withdrawal. The night's still young, you know."

Sammy's chest hovered over Diego's back and his cock poked at the entrance to Diego's tunnel of lust. The burning tip, already sticky with pre-cum, parted the opening and entered cautiously – like a coal miner exploring a promising vein of ore. As Sammy's burning rod inched its way closer to the father lode, Diego groaned with pleasure. His nipples hardened and his buns tensed, increasing the pressure on Sammy's cock. He sighed and rammed his way to glory. Diego's cock, stretching out between his belly and the sheet, sent waves of delight racing throughout his body, causing his breath to quicken. Sweat broke out on his forehead as he raised his ass in perfect rhythm to the downward thrust of Sammy's pelvis. Balls knocking against Diego's spread thighs, he raised and lowered himself as though doing push-ups. He could feel the pressure building in his groin. Flames of tension rose higher in his lower stomach and upper thighs. The moonlight illuminated Sammy's creamy white ass as it rose up and down, driving his Louisville Slugger to a grand slam. Diego's cock began to throb and he moaned. "Give it to me! Harder! Oh yeah!"

"Happy to oblige, tough guy. If you think you can take it."

"I'll take whatever you got and more," he gasped.

The rhythm sped up, the intensity grew almost unbearable. Suddenly Sammy yelled, "Thar he blows!" and huge gobs of cum shot through Diego's innards. Feeling the hot, molten lava spreading through his insides, he couldn't hold out any longer. His own cock smeared the sheet beneath him with pearly cream – the proof of a job well done.

After slowly pulling out and away, Sammy rolled off of Diego and lay panting by his side. Diego rolled over and glanced at him.

"That was pretty fuckin' fantastic," said Diego with a

beaming smile.

"I've had lots of practice," Sammy smiled back.

"You can practice on me anytime."

"Shall I set the alarm again?"

"What are you waiting for?"

Sammy pressed the button and rolled onto his side. Diego wrapped his body around him – chest-to-back, cock-to-ass – and they tried to doze off as the earth slowly turned away from the moon.

* * *

Adrenalin was flowing, coursing through the circulatory systems of the Jack of Diamonds and the King of Hearts. Both had closed their eyes, but neither was capable of falling asleep at this point.

They lay there, pretending, until Sammy got up to pee. When he emerged from the bathroom, Diego did the same.

Staring at each other, they sat on the bed as the first rays of dawning light came through the open window, accompanying the soft breeze that felt so good on their naked skin.

Sammy glanced down at Diego's wilted cock, looked up and said, "My ass is feeling a bit neglected and I thought, perhaps, you would favor me with the touch of your jackhammer there."

Diego grinned. "I'm always happy to oblige a friend in need. You want to eat the pillow or put footprints on the ceiling?"

Without skipping a beat, Sammy replied, "The ceiling could use something to liven it up. Hasn't had a paint job in years."

Sammy rolled onto his back and threw his legs up over his head. Diego reached for the lubricant and lathered first his own cock and then Sammy's. He rubbed both cocks up and down – one in each hand – until they were as hard as granite.

Sammy watched Diego's sculpted torso hovering above him, an attractive sight at any time, but even more so in the pale light of morning.

Diego eased himself into Sammy's tight asshole. First Sammy groaned, then moaned and finally sighed once entry was complete. He grabbed his own cock and worked his clenched fist up and down the shaft from the tip to the base.

Diego began thrusting in and pulling out – not all the way, though – slowly increasing the speed and intensity. Eventually, the motion and impact was similar to that of a jackhammer, as requested. Sammy began raising and lowering his hips, following the pattern that Diego had established. Faster and faster, harder and harder, the motion intensified until Diego suddenly cried out, "Oh my God!" His body squirmed in uncontrollable spasms as he fired a load of sizzling cum into Sammy's eager ass. When Sammy felt the hot juice filling him up inside, he could hold back no longer. He squirted a stream of cum which looped into the air and settled in among the sparse hair on his handsomely chiseled chest.

"How was that?" Diego asked Sammy, grinning from ear to ear.

"Next time the city needs a street torn up, I'll recommend you," he smiled back.

"I'm pretty particular about how and where I use my tools."

"Good, I'd hate to think that you wasted your talents where they weren't appreciated."

Diego slowly pulled his still-hard dick from Sammy's firm butt. It made a slight popping sound as it cleared the entrance and flopped against his thigh.

"Do you think I should set the alarm again?" Sammy asked.

Diego looked at the clock. "Gee, I don't know. I have to be at work pretty soon."

"How about a shower?"

"Terrific idea."

They rose from the bed and moved to the bathroom. Sammy started the water, parted the shower curtain and they both stepped into the off-white porcelain tub.

Sammy picked up the bar of soap and stood away from

the shower head as Diego doused his firm body in the pulsing waterfall. Working up a creamy lather, Sammy began soaping Diego's sexy contours. First the broad shoulders and powerful arms. Then the hard chest and – turning him around – the smooth back. His firm, meaty buns and strong, muscular thighs were saved for second to last. The stomach, shaft and balls served as a grand finale.

"Ouch!" Diego protested. "I guess I'm a little sore at this point."

"Me too," Sammy confessed. "But it was well worth it."

"Agreed."

Diego spun around beneath the falling water, rinsing the soap from his tingling body. Then he seized the soap and lathered up Sammy's taut chest, sinewy arms, hard stomach, huge cock and dangling balls. He turned him around and soaped up the prominent shoulder blades, the tapering lower back and the high white-as-snow buns. Then stooping, he cleaned the ropy-muscled legs and finally put the soap in the tray and watched Sammy rinse off.

They toweled themselves dry, got dressed and sat in Sammy's breakfast nook. He brewed strong Colombian coffee and prepared some eggs and toast. They ate in silence, bathing in the afterglow of sensuality that pervaded every inch of their bodies. The FM radio played some soft rock music in the background.

Then, when they were finished eating, they hugged and kissed. Sammy walked Diego to the door and opened it slowly. "Anytime you'd like to play again, I'll be ready, willing and able."

"I knew we'd eventually find something we could agree on."

Seder

I sit at a large rectangular table in a huge Upper West Side apartment. There is a plate before me with a roasted lamb shankbone, a hard boiled egg, bitter herbs, charoses, karpas, glasses of salt water and goblets of wine. Also seated at this table is part of the family of my boyfriend, David, who sits beside me. I've never met anyone in his family before and I haven't been to a Passover seder in more than twenty years. I am slightly nervous. Partially because I'm in a roomful of strangers. Also, I don't even know why I'm here.

David's Uncle Harry is seated at the head of the table, this being his home. At the other end is his wife, David's Aunt Cel. The other places are occupied by various aunts, uncles and cousins. David's parents are absent, visiting relatives in Israel.

Harry begins to read from the Haggadah. "Blessed art though, O Lord our God –"

But suddenly Sol, sitting directly opposite from me says, "In Hebrew, Harry, please."

Harry stops reading and slowly looks up. He is a very large man, thick everywhere with a sprawling belly, a bushy moustache and big brown eyes. "Not everyone understands Hebrew," he says.

Sol, thin, darting eyes with a beak-like face, hands and arms always moving says, "I'm aware of that. But it's supposed to be in Hebrew!"

There is a bridge table a few feet away with four children, who for reasons I can't perceive, have begun yelling at one another. Judy, the young woman seated on my left is the mother of at least two of them, so she rises to quell the disturbance.

"He touched my matzoh," whines the blonde girl, Rachel. As Judy quiets them down, my attention returns to the argument at the adult's table.

"Hebrew!" says Sol.

"English," insists Harry. "This is America, not Israel."

"Hebrew," says Sol, with reverence, "out of respect for God."

"God?" says Harry, almost mocking. "What God? The one that slept through the Holocaust and is still, apparently, unavailable for comment?"

Sol mumbles something in Hebrew, then says, "If you don't believe in God why have a seder?"

Harry fixes him with a victorious stare and says, "Tradition!"

Barbara, Sol's wife, says, "Why don't we vote? Majority rules?"

David, sitting at my right, leans over to whisper in my ear. "We may be here all night and never get around to the food." I smile. His hand, under the table, behind the Indian madras tablecloth, squeezes my thigh then briefly clamps over my crotch bulge. I blush. Glance around to see if anyone has noticed David's action or my response.

Just then, Rhoda, David's cousin, strikes a pose like a comedienne and says, "What the fuck difference does it make?"

Barbara, her mother, scowls. "Watch your language!"

Rhoda, ignoring her, continues, sing-songy, "Hebrew, English, English, Hebrew. Words are words. Let's eat!" A very plump woman, she makes most of us laugh when she puffs up her cheeks and starts to shovel food toward her mouth, an invisible utensil and imaginary food.

Cel says, "Harry, why don't you read part of it in English.

Sol, you can read the rest in Hebrew."

They begin to alternate paragraphs and I recall that David has instructed me not to bring up the subjects of religion, sex, or politics, so my game plan was to keep my thoughts to myself. But I'd asked, "If your family won't discuss religion, sex, and politics what will they talk about?"

"Oh, we'll discuss them all right. Just don't you be the one to bring them up. In fact," he'd added, grinning, "you just might want to stay on the sidelines and avoid the verbal daggers which will be flying like airborne latkes." He'd laughed. "I exaggerate. It's not that bad. We'll have fun. You'll see."

I was extremely agitated, my nerves like misfiring spark plugs as we entered the home of his Uncle Harry and Aunt Cel. She'd answered the door and David had said, "This is my Aunt Cel."

"Aunt Seal?" I'd said.

She'd laughed. A tall, slender woman with cascading black hair, she wore a yellow caftan with a turquoise and silver medallion. "Cel, short for Cecilia."

"Oh," I'd said, my face burning, probably fire engine red, wishing I could shrink to the size of a cockroach and scoot away.

She'd taken my hand, led me down the hall. "I was bom Cecilia, called Celia through college and ever since I've been married it's just been Cel. Come, let me show you around."

It's an enormous place, my entire apartment could fit within the living room of this one. There is also a dining room, three bedrooms, a book-lined study and two bathrooms. A spectacular view of Riverside Park, the Hudson River and the Palisades, cross-ventilation in almost half the rooms.

In the dining room she pointed out the tablecloth from India, salt and pepper shakers from Nigeria, wine goblets from Switzerland. On the walls, folk art from Indonesia and South America. Harry and Cel travel a lot.

As we moved into the living room, David checked the Band-Aid on his neck which covers the only lesion on his body that is detectable when he's fully clothed. When I'd asked him if his family knew that he was HIV Positive, like myself, he shrugged and said he'd tell them when it became necessary to do so and not until. "Let's not get into a discussion about AIDS either," he'd amended his earlier instructions.

I was introduced to Rhoda, a squat woman in jeans and a long billowing shirt. And Mark, one of those extraordinarily handsome men with dark coloring, curly hair, sensitive but rugged face, hard and lean, the Mediterranean look – he could be from Spain, Italy, Greece or Israel. I thought David was attractive – trim body, earnest face, wild brown hair. But his cousin Mark is sensational. And Barbara, an aunt, wears a silk blouse, tourmaline, with a matching skirt, strands of lustrous pearls, huge gemstones on her fingers. Her hair, stiff and lacquered, looks like nothing could budge a single strand.

I'm never good at meeting a lot of strangers at one time. But I dutifully greeted uncles Harry and Sol, cousins Stuart and Judy, and a bunch of kids who ran from room to room, chasing, pinching, taunting, squealing.

We sip wine, dip parsley in salt water, then Harry breaks the matzoh and hides the afikoman. When he returns – I figure it's probably in the master bedroom – Sol mumbles something in Hebrew. We drink more wine. David snaps off a corner of matzoh and eats it. Stuart, husband of Judy, brother of Rhoda, son of Sol and Barbara – I'm finally getting the lineage – says, "You're not supposed to eat it yet."

David chews and swallows guiltily.

"How am I supposed to teach Judy and my children about Passover if you're going to break all the rules?"

Rhoda says, "Fuck the rules," and reaches for the matzoh.

"Watch your language," says Barbara.

I look briefly at Judy, a slim beauty with long blonde hair parted in the middle, then down at my plate.

I haven't had many Jewish boyfriends. It makes no difference to me. But this seems to be what David wants. Am I Jewish enough for him? Should I care? I haven't known him long enough to consider him anything more than a friend and fuck-buddy. A safe fuck buddy. I'm not sure if there's potential for more.

Stuart, somewhat dumpy-looking, with listless eyes and bad posture, says, "It's time for the Four Questions."

"Rachel's the youngest," says Sol.

"But she's not old enough to read yet," protests Judy.

"Jeremy will read them this year," says Harry, with grandfatherly pride.

The chestnut-haired boy – I imagine David looked like him at his age – stands, everyone looks toward the children's table and he begins to read, "Why is this night different from any other night?" His voice is soft and meek but he has no trouble with the words.

When I was born no one asked me if I wanted to be Jewish, if I desired any religious affiliation or would rather be without. I played the game for a while. It wasn't difficult. My family was not very religious. Assimilation was the goal. Now and then I was expected to be a good Jewish boy. But mostly, the all-American kid. Judaism offered a few pleasures but was never a way of life. Chanukah presents were nice, getting out of school for Yom Kippur added to the attraction, potato pancakes and stuffed derma made me proud. I can still remember the words to "Mi Y'Malel," and the way we puffed up our chests and sang from the heart in Sunday school, creating costumes for the Purim festival. But just as vividly I can hear the echoes of the words: kike, but you don't look Jewish; yid, but you don't act Jewish; Christ-killer; she's a typical JAP; he tried to overcharge me and I had to Jew him down; all Jews have a great sense of humor; she's got a big nose like a Jew.

These words used to jolt me like electric shocks, and they still do, to a lesser degree. These days I am witness to millions of slurs directed toward all kinds of people, coming from all kinds of people. I realize that everyone hates everybody. I hear black people bad-mouthing Koreans, Episcopalians putting down Catholics, the Kuwaitis don't like the Jordanians, the French despise the Germans, most of the world is unfair to women, mommies and daddies beat up their kids and everyone hates the queers.

We all sip wine.

Rhoda reaches for a matzoh but Barbara slaps her hand away.

We drink more wine.

A citizen of planet Earth is expected to swear allegiance to a religion, a race, a homeland, a doctrine, a role and at all times honor the traditional chains of opposition. But something inside me, my conscience perhaps, struggles against this, questioning, condemning. If being a Jew means accepting that the Arabs and the Germans are my natural enemies, that everytime an eye is plucked another must be plucked in return, then maybe I should search for something more civilized.

Jeremy completes his task and there is a sweet warmth in the room, as though some youthful effluence has permeated the air and intoxicated all of us. When he sits down and utters an audible sigh of relief, everyone smiles as Harry begins a call and response passage, the collective voices forthright and sincere. David goes for my crotch again. I reciprocate. We exchange conspiratorial expressions.

It's time for Sol to read about the plague. He carefully spills drops of wine while negotiating the intricacies of Hebrew articulation. Judy goes to the children's table and lists the plagues in English, softly, like a descant to Sol's oration. Blood. Frogs. Gnats. Flies. Murrain. Boils. Hail. Locusts. Darkness. Slaying of the First-Born.

"Kinda sounds like the next Stephen King novel," quips Rhoda.

I can't help laughing out loud. I stop myself, embarrassed.

Sol bangs both fists on the table, taking everyone by surprise. He turns to Rhoda. "Have some respect! Why do you torture me so?"

The atmosphere has vanished. As though a rush of cold air blew in from an open window.

"It was a joke, Dad, just a joke," she says apologetically. "I'm sorry."

She seems truly repentant. I sense that she didn't expect

he'd react so severely, didn't intend to upset him.

"You're always sorry!" he snaps.

She leans back, her chest suddenly heaving, holds onto the edge of the table with whitening fingers splayed. The look of contrition, with eyes wide and mouth agape, turns into anger, her face tight. "When are you gonna give me a break, huh?" she shouts. "I can never please you!"

"Why did you come here tonight?" his face is crimson.

Barbara looks horrified, as though he might have a heart attack any second. "Stop it! Both of you!"

Sol continues. "Did you come here to honor your family and your religion, or just to get a free meal?"

I wince and look at Harry and Cel. They appear calm, as though this happens all the time.

"You'll never forgive me for being me. Right, Dad? Face it. I'm a lezzie, a queer, a bulldagger, a dyke."

With each of these words Sol recoils as though slapped.

Harry claps his hands. "Okay, enough. Unless you two care to take it outside."

"I think it's time to eat," says Cel, rising and moving toward the kitchen.

I overhear Judy whispering to the children, "Because sometimes Aunt Rhoda does things that your grandfather doesn't understand." She smooths Rachel's hair, pats Jeremy's head and returns to the adult's table.

I avoid looking at Sol. If he can't understand his daughter's sexual proclivities, what chance is there that he approves of me? Or David? I turn to look at him. He squeezes my thigh.

"Uncle Sol," he says, "you never criticize my, er, lifestyle. Why do you always give Rhoda such a hard time?"

I'm too embarrassed by this unflinching honesty to look at either Sol or Rhoda, so I stare at a painting on the wall.

He scowls. "It's different for women. They should have babies."

"There's no law that says that everyone in the world has to have children."

"She's my daughter!"

"Sol, Sol," pleads Barbara, desperate to calm him, change the subject.

I turn to Judy. "You must really be religious to know all the plagues by heart."

"I'm studying. To convert. I was raised Presbyterian. And when I married Stuart I decided I wanted to have a Jewish home for my children." She smiles, then whispers, "Do you think that if you and David decide to live together that you'll convert?"

"Me?" I say, stupefied. "I'm Jewish."

A look of disbelief moves across her face. "Oh, I thought …"

I pat her hand and smile to let her know that I'm not offended.

If the goons were to come right now and forcibly herd us all into concentration camps, which would I prefer, the Jewish one or the gay one? In the former there'd be no obvious consensus, only genetic connections and certain doctrines to which some would subscribe. Relationships would be arbitrary. Like at family gatherings. Where you talk to people once or twice a year and have only mundane subjects to discuss because you and your relatives share no interests, linked only by blood. And, anyway, how does one really define a Jew? Does my birth make it automatic? If I don't believe and don't practice, then, am I even eligible for the Jewish enclosure?

In the gay camp there'd be no question of my credentials. I could easily summon eyewitnesses and produce written and videotaped evidence that I am a bona fide homosexual being. And because there are people like me from every niche of human society, I think the chances of finding people with whom I have something to get thrilled about are much greater. I'd probably be a lot happier. Of course, there are Jews from all sectors of the globe as well. This is something I found out after spending my entire youth thinking that Jews only lived in New York and Israel. Since then I've met Jews from Ireland, Texas and China. So I'd probably meet interesting people in both situations, but I'd most likely have more fun in the gay one. But there's also the possibility that I would be sent to a special camp for the HIV Positive. Anything can happen in America. My Japanese-American friends will readily attest.

David's cousin, Mark, the extraordinarily handsome one, hasn't said a word. He occasionally goes to the children's table and talks softly to them. He's probably the father of the other two kids, but where's the mother?

I'm suddenly overwhelmed by a coughing fit, something that I go through three or four times a day, a chronic post-nasal drip, a sign of my weakened immune system. I turn from the table, hacking, blowing my nose, wiping the tears from my cheeks. Cel asks, "Are you all right?"

Everyone looks at me with solicitude.

"Fine. Just my allergies," I lie, honoring David's request not to mention the plague that God didn't think of when the Israelites were in bondage.

Cel brings in platters and bowls and the clinking and tinging of forks, knives and serving spoons on plates begins.

Stuart asks David how long he and I have been together. David looks at me. "About three months?"

I nod.

"How did you meet?" asks Rhoda, leering.

"Well," says David, "we were at a – wait, you tell it," he turns to me.

I'd just forked some very tasty pot roast into my mouth and I have to finish chewing. I put down my fork and look up. Everyone is staring at me with – I'm not sure exactly, curiosity, interest – I feel like a klieg light is shining on me and ten million strangers are about to solemnly judge my every word.

"We were at a peace rally," I say cautiously, unaware of the ratio of hawks to doves.

David says, "Yeah, it was just like the sixties!"

I nod. "We were both with the ACT UP contingent and we introduced ourselves and started talking and then went for coffee afterwards. Eventually we started dating."

Rhoda winces and says, "Dating! Ugh!"

"Nothing terribly exciting," I add, "movies, plays, dinner."

"And a few other things, I'll bet," says Rhoda.

Everyone chuckles as I pick up my fork and resume eating, hoping that this line of conversation is over, that someone will jump into the void of silence which now wafts into the room like a fine mist.

"Peace rally!" says Sol. "I think we should have gone further. I'm with Schwartzkopf."

"*Dummkopf,* you mean," says Stuart.

Sol wipes his chin and places the napkin in his lap with dramatic deliberation. "I'll have none of your anti-Americanisms. Not now. Not on Passover."

"I don't want my children to grow up in a world full of violence and hatred," says Stuart.

"He's right, Sol," says Harry. "War begets fear which begets hate which begets war."

"Cock 'n' bull!" says Sol, starting to eat again, a fierce though distant look on his face which suggests he has dropped out of the conversation and intends to ignore everyone.

We continue eating.

David's relatives share certain traits and propensities with my aunts, uncles and cousins. And coincidentally, one of my cousins also married a gentile, except that ours has no plans to convert. However, the tension between Sol and Harry is just like that of my uncles on my mother's side, Harvey and Jacob, and the conflicts between Sol and Rhoda, very similar to my cousins Miriam and Jeffrey who engage in a perpetual one-upmanship contest about who has the tougher job and who earns the most money. But no one in my family knows I'm gay, and I don't think there are any others, with the possible exception of my cousin Laura who was very tomboyish when young and has been independent and single throughout her adult life. I imagine if David came to a family gathering of mine he would probably be as shocked and amused as I am.

David touches the Band-Aid on his neck and the distraction of seeing his hand rise, a blur of flesh from the periphery of my vision, pulls me back to the table.

"I cut myself shaving," he says to no one in particular.

Almost everyone has finished eating. I ingest one more forkful, pat my lips and tell Cel how much I enjoyed everything. I rise to help clear the table but Harry insists I sit. As the children go to search for the afikoman, fruit, coffee, tea and sponge cake are served. The wine and food have slowed everyone down. There is a lassitude hovering about the table.

It takes Rachel about two minutes to find the hidden matzoh. She triumphantly presents it to Harry who reaches into his pocket and gives her a dollar bill. He dandles her on his knees as the other children sulk at their table. Sol stands up, approaches them, slips them each a dollar instructing them not to tell Rachel, who is distracted by Harry. I gather this was pre-planned.

David clasps my thigh. Leans over and whispers, "I've had enough. You?"

I nod.

"Let's boogie."

As we say our goodbyes I shake hands with all the men, the women kiss my cheek. They all indicate that they hope to see me again soon. I feel like telling them the chances of David and I still being together by next Passover are pretty unlikely. There's our precarious health, of course. And I've never sustained any romantic or sexual relationships beyond a year. I'm not even certain why I came here tonight. I usually avoid contact with my friends' families. I don't know why I accepted this invitation. Perhaps I'm more involved than I suspected.

David and I walk down Broadway.

"You done good, kid," he says. "They loved you."

"I liked them. A lot. They reminded me of my own family, which I can only appreciate from a distance."

"Yeah, I know what you mean." He places his arm around my back. "Maybe we can do this again next year?"

"Sure," I say, not wanting to sound too pessimistic, unwilling to spoil the mood.

Suddenly David stops. I turn to see what's wrong. He tears the Band-Aid from his neck and tosses it into the gutter.

The Garden of Terra IX

It was on a warm and sunny afternoon, just a few weeks after the farmers had begun their work, that Mark came running to the planting field. Breathless and agitated, he approached Tony and Liz who were talking beneath the shade of a tree just a few meters from the garden.

"The Captain asked me to organize a meeting for tonight," said Mark, trying to catch his breath. "Attendance by everyone is mandatory."

"Oh?" said Liz nonchalantly. "What's up?"

"Yeah," said Tony, "did they fix the communicom or something?"

"No," said Mark, shaking his head. "I'm not absolutely certain but I think he's going to discuss ... compulsory procreation."

"Compulsory procreation?" queried Tony. He looked at Liz. She looked at him, then at Mark.

"You mean ..." she said.

"Yes. We've got to start making babies."

"Making babies!" said Tony. "Why?"

"To keep the continuity of our community going," said Mark, "until we can escape or someone comes to rescue us."

"Sounds pretty intense to me," said Liz.

"I don't know if I can handle it," said Tony.

"Same here," she rejoined.

"If the Captain orders us to, then we have to," said Mark.

"Wow," said Liz. She shook her head. "I knew things might get rough on this planet, but I never imagined anything so ... repulsive."

Tony and Mark nodded in agreement.

* * *

Like all of the others, Liz and Jana's hut had been constructed mostly of whatever could be salvaged from the wrecked Wayfarer. Many consisted of panels loosened from the hull, a chair or two from the recreation center and a thatched roof of twigs, vines and broad leaves. The crew members who were unattached ate and slept communally; couples had private domiciles. Liz and Jana sipped some tea and talked long into the night, past their usual bedtime.

"It could have been a lot worse," said Jana. "We could have crashed into a planet with no terraforming and we'd all be dead by now."

Liz sighed. "You're right. But still ..."

"I know it seems awful but we've all gotta do it. Look at it as an unpleasant but necessary task that you only have to do once and then never again."

Liz put her cup on the flat stone that served as a table. "That's easy for you to say, you've done it with men before. I thought I'd never have to."

Jana crossed her legs and straightened her spine. "That's true. I guess you might say I'm experienced a little." She grinned. Then her expression became serious. "But I find the prospect just as repugnant as you do."

"Is it as awful as I imagine it is?"

Jana snickered. "Well, there's a reason why I fell in love with you. What we do is more fun. But still – to be fair – I'd have to say that it varies from man to man. Some are more considerate than others. Or less obnoxious, as the case may be."

"I hope I get a pleasant one," said Liz with resignation.

"I hope we both get pleasant ones," said Jana. She moved alongside of Liz and draped her arm over her shoulder. "You'll see, it won't be that bad. I'm dreading the pregnancy more than the body contact."

"I hadn't even thought about that part," said Liz. "Nine months of sheer agony."

"Not to mention the delivery."

"Yeah," said Liz, "the delivery." She grimaced.

"Let's not worry about it until we have to," said Jana, kissing her cheek. "We should try to get some sleep."

They undressed and extinguished the candle. Then lay in each other's arms on the pallet they'd built just inside the doorway of the small hut.

* * *

The blue sun was setting over the treetops as Tony and Mark strolled through the woods before dinner. It was Tony's turn to cook and he always avoided it for as long as possible. Mark had gotten used to this and always snacked on wild berries to forestall his hunger. A squirrel scampered up a treetrunk and Mark said, "It's just like Earth here. Amazing."

Tony looked at him sharply. "On Earth men don't have to have sex with women if they don't want to," he said, making no attempt to conceal his anger.

"Look at it this way," said Mark. "At least you don't have to bear the child."

Tony sat on a log and picked up a stick. He poked it through the damp leaves that covered the floor of the forest. "A truism," he said. "And raising the kid might not be so bad."

"Sure," said Mark. "It'll be fun. You and I can still live together and the kids can spend half the time with us."

Tony looked at him incredulously. "You mean, you won't mind being a daddy? I thought you hated children!"

Mark shook his head. "I don't hate them. I just felt that I wasn't qualified to raise them. It sort of scares me ... all that responsibility."

The sun was invisible now. A violet glow along the horizon was all that remained. The forest was a labyrinth of shadows.

"How are they gonna decide who breeds with who?" Tony asked.

"Good question. Hadn't thought of that. But I'm sure Captain Shepherd and Officer Harker have something in mind."

"When do you think we'll find out?"

"Soon. Probably."

Tony asked, "Getting hungry?"

"To tell the truth, yeah. You?"

He nodded. "Might as well face the inevitable and fix us something to eat," said Tony, rising, tossing the stick into the shadows.

"Might as well," agreed Mark and followed him back toward their hut near the beach.

* * *

The garden was beginning to show the effort that had been put into it. There were small green tomatoes, young ears of corn and tiny orange petals on the marigold shoots. Tony and Liz had been working all morning and hadn't said a word to each other.

"I guess we're going to have to talk about this sometime," said Liz, breaking the heavy silence. She looked over at Tony who'd stood up, brushing dirt from his knees.

"Talk about what?" he said diffidently.

"Us," she said. "And our baby."

"What's there to talk about? Just tell me where and when and I'll do my best," he snapped.

Liz threw down her makeshift hoe and strode over to him. "Look," she said, "I'm not any happier about this than you are. But the least we can try to do is make it pleasant for each other. This wasn't my idea, you know."

Their eyes met. "I'm sorry," he said. "You're right."

They sat in the shade of a tall tree. A gentle breeze ruffled their hair as a rabbit poked its head through the tall grass then disappeared.

"You know what's really bothering me?"

"No," she said. "Tell me."

"I'm prepared to deal with the kid and all. I'll try to be a good father. It's just that ..."

"What? I can be very understanding."

"It's just that I don't know if we're supposed to ... make love or just do it fast and get it over with." His face flushed crimson and he looked away.

Liz smiled. "Any way you want. Just be easy with me," she said.

"You go easy with me, too," he said.

"We'll make this as easy for each other as we can," she said, taking his hand in hers. They smiled at one another. Then went back to work.

* * *

The reflection of the red sun rippled like a soft, flat disc on the surface of the ocean. It was late afternoon, on a small stretch of sand far away from the remains of the spacecraft, where Liz took off her shirt as Tony removed his shorts. She looked at him nervously. Then turned around to finish undressing. Tony took off his undersling and stood there, not knowing what to do next. Liz turned and looked down at the blanket on the sand.

"Maybe we should lie, I mean sit down," she said. Tony nodded. They knelt.

Tony inched toward her. "Well, here we are," he said.

Liz moved closer to him. He placed his arm around her neck. She turned her face toward him. Eyes closed, lips parted. He watched her face move closer, then closed his eyes and aimed his mouth at her lips. He lipped her nose as her mouth grazed his chin. She giggled. He laughed. They looked at each other and shook in spasms, slapping their thighs.

When she finally got herself under control, Liz said,

"Maybe we should skip the romantic foreplay and get it over with."

"Good idea," he said, grinning.

She lay back and closed her eyes. He mounted her and closed his eyes. With a little cooperation and some tactful suggestions, they were able to accomplish what they'd set out to do.

* * *

Jana was cleaning the area in front of the hut. She scooped up a handful of dried brown leaves and placed them in a small basket she'd constructed of bark and vines. A yawning sound emanated from inside of the hut and moments later Liz came to the doorway. Shielding her eyes from the sun, she looked over at Jana. "I've been sleeping more," she said, then smiled and walked over to where Jana stood. She kissed her. They hugged.

"How do you feel?" Jana asked.

"I feel marvelous. Like there's been a chemical change in my whole body. I feel charged with life; alive and glad of it."

"Good," said Jana. She placed her hands on her own stomach and said, "It gets more intense. I know exactly how you feel. That's how I felt the first few weeks. It's grand, isn't it?"

"Yes," said Liz, beaming.

"Am I showing yet?" Jana swiveled to accentuate her profile.

"Not yet. But you look wonderful."

They stood there for a few minutes, looking at each other. The ocean, almost indigo at that hour, made kissing sounds on the shore.

"Let's lie together for a while," said Jana and led her into the hut. They lowered themselves to the pallet and held each other close.

* * *

They were in the forest, sitting on their favorite log in their chosen glade. Tony was breaking a stick into tiny slivers. Mark gazed at a painted bunting perched on the branch of a mulberry tree.

"You seem awfully nervous," said Mark.

"I'm just wondering about stuff."

"What kind of stuff?"

Tony sighed. "You know. About the kid."

"What about the kid?"

"Well, you know. If it'll be normal, if it'll be a boy or a girl."

Mark nodded. "Yeah. I'm worried about my kid's health too. So's Laura. But who cares if it's a boy or a girl?"

"I care. And I'm also wondering if it'll be ..."

"Be what?" Mark asked.

Tony inhaled deeply and his chest expanded. "If it's a straight girl or a lesbian or a gay boy I can handle it. But if it's a straight boy – oh gosh – I won't be able to teach him how to chase girls or any of that stuff."

"You know," said Mark, taking his hand, "that's what I was always afraid of. But now I realize that's not what's important. You teach the kid what you can and he or she will learn the rest elsewhere."

Tony's face registered surprise. "I never thought of it that way. You're right, though. I'll just explain moral stuff like right and wrong and teach educational stuff like who Gertrude Stein, Tennessee Williams, Billie Holiday and Stephen Sondheim were and stuff like that."

"Right," said Mark. "This might even be fun."

"It's gonna be great," said Tony. "We'll be daddies together and I'll be an uncle to your kid and you'll be an uncle to mine."

Mark smiled. They kissed. Then embraced. A few stars began to flicker in the twilit purple sky.

Stan Leventhal (1951-1995)

STAN LEVENTHAL, author, editor, and publisher, lived in New York City in the 1980s through 1995 where he died of AIDS. He is fondly remembered as a generous, genuine and passionate advocate for social causes and other writers. He was nominated for a Lambda Literary Award three times: for the debut novel *Mountain Climbing in Sheridan Square*, *Faultlines* and *The Black Marble Pool*. He published one other novel and three collections of short stories.

He served as a judge for the annual Bill Whitehead Memorial Award and was a member of the Publishing Triangle Steering Committee. His short stories and reviews appeared in *Outweek*, *The Advocate*, *The New York Native*, *Torso*, *Mandate*, *Exquisite Corpse*, *The James White Review* and *Gaylaxian Gayzette*.

In addition, his work appeared in the anthologies: *Gay Life*, edited by Eric E. Rofes; *Shadows of Love*, edited by Charles Jurris; *The Stiffest of the Corpse*, edited by Andrei Codrescu; and *Sword of the Rainbow*, edited by Eric Garber and Jewelle Gomez. The author was actively involved in the fight for literacy. His message to his readers: "Literature is crucial to our lives; reading is fun."

About ReQueered Tales

In the heady days of the late 1960s, when young people in many western countries were in the streets protesting for a new, more inclusive world, some of us were in libraries, coffee shops, communes, retreats, bedrooms and dens plotting something even more startling: literature – highbrow and pulp – for an explicitly gay audience. Specifically, we were craving to see our gay lives – in the closet, in the open, in bars, in dire straits and in love – reflected in mystery stories, sci-fi and mainstream fiction. Hercule Poirot, that engaging effete Belgian creation of Agatha Christie might have been gay ... Sherlock Holmes, to all intents and purposes, was one woman shy of gay ... but where were the genuine gay sleuths, where the reader need not read between the lines?

Beginning with Victor J Banis's "Man from C.A.M.P." pulps in the mid-60s – riotous romps spoofing the craze for James Bond spies – readers were suddenly being offered George Baxt's Pharoah Love, a black gay New York City detective, and a real turning point in Joseph Hansen's gay California insurance investigator, Dave Brandstetter, whose world weary Raymond Chandleresque adventures sold strongly and have never been out of print.

Over the next three decades, gay storytelling grew strongly in niche and mainstream publishing ventures. Even with the huge public crisis – as AIDS descended on the gay community beginning in the early 1980s – gay fiction flourished. Stonewall Inn, Alyson Publications, and others nurtured authors and readers ... until mainstream success seemed to come to a halt. While Lambda Literary Foundation had started to recognize work in annual awards about 1990, mainstream publishers began to have cold feet. And then, with the rise of e-books in the new millennium which enabled a new self-publishing industry ... there was both an avalanche of new talent coming to market and burying of print authors who did not cross the divide.

The result?

Perhaps forty years of gay fiction – and notably gay and lesbian mystery, detective and suspense fiction – has been teetering on the brink of obscurity. Orphaned works, orphaned authors, many living and some having passed away – with no one to make the case for their creations to be returned to print (and e-print!). General fiction and non-fiction works embracing gay lives, widely celebrated upon original release, also languished as mainstream publishers shifted their focus.

Until now. That is the mission of ReQueered Tales: to keep in circulation this treasure trove of fantastic fiction. In an era of ebooks, everything of value ought to be accessible. For a new generation of readers, these mystery tales, and works of general fiction, are full of insights into the gay world of the 1960s, '70s, '80s and '90s. For those of us who lived through the period, they are a delightful reminder of our youth and reflect some of our own struggles in growing up gay in those heady times.

We are honored, here at ReQueered Tales, to be custodians shepherding back into circulation some of the best gay and lesbian fiction writing and hope to bring many volumes to the public, in modestly priced, accessible editions, worldwide, over the coming years.

So please join us on this adventure of discovery and rediscovery of the rich talents of writers of recent years as the PIs, cops and amateur sleuths battle forces of evil with fierceness, humor and sometimes a pinch of love.

The ReQueered Tales Team

Justene Adamec • Alexander Inglis • Matt Lubbers-Moore

More from ReQueered Tales

Mountain Climbing in Sheridan Square
Stan Leventhal

A series of discrete episodes among friends provide snapshots of one gay man's life. There are parties, concerts, dinners with everyday life – and death – interwoven in the rich story-telling. An actress, a painter, a set designer, a writer – all sweating and surviving in Manhattan, all scoring their first successes. Part autobiography and part documentary, artfully written, it details the lives of these creative people. Young and professional, they know there is more to life than money. There is trust and the sort of love that trades in deeds of kindness.

"Stan was a literary activist who always gave to, built and endorsed literature and writers. I can see still see Stan in his apartment window on Christopher Street, next door to the Stonewall Inn, overlooking Sheridan Square as he typed away." — Michele Karlsberg, LGBTQ publicist and friend

Leventhal's debut novel was welcomed warmly as a Lambda Literary Awards Finalist in 1988. This new edition features a foreword by Christopher Bram (*Gods and Monsters*).

And don't miss ...

The Black Marble Pool – There's a dead body at the bottom of a pool in the backyard of a guest house in Key West. Who is he? And what caused his untimely demise? Maybe it's suicide. Or an accident. But more likely – murder! And who's responsible? One of the guests, the people who run the guest house or one of those mysterious women in town?

"The pace is brisk: the plot keeps twisting, as no one is at all who they seem." — Keith John Glaeske, *Out In Print*

Skydiving on Christopher Street
Stan Leventhal

Like bookends, *Skydiving* returns to the characters and bustle of New York a few years after *Mountain Climbing in Sheridan Square*.

Stan Leventhal paints a picture of Christopher Street in the 80s and 90s. "The streets became ours again. When the fag-bashers began to get bold, to slither from their slimy lairs, the young gay guys and fledgling lesbians fought back. There was a new war to win, along with battles of fear, ignorance, and indifference ... We paid for it with our muscles, our brains, our bodily fluids. It has our names written all over it. Our blood fills the cracks in the pavement. It's ours and we're never going to give it up."

Against that backdrop, we see the pieces of an ordinary life. He's an editor for a porn publishing house – it's not glamorous, it's just work. His relationship is on the verge of ending. He is visited by the ghosts of friends he has lost to AIDS. In the midst of the familiar days, he learns from his doctor that he too has AIDS.

> "A tender, honest novel about that moment between diagnosis and the decision to grow. Messy boyfriends and dreamy crushes set against the back-drop of daily life make Levethal's characters vulnerable and familiar."
>
> — Sarah Schulman (*Let the Record Show*)

> "*Skydiving on Christopher Street*, is a startling attempt to capture the life of an urban gay man on the printed page. Read in conjunction with *Mountain Climbing in Sheridan Square*, the book moves us into a darker, more disturbing arena in which knowledge does not necessarily bring happiness, understanding does not bring relief. Leventhal's vision is clear and undaunted and, for all of its somber chiaroscuro, challenges us to see the world through new eyes and to revel in its author's ability to translate life into art, pain into understanding."
>
> — Michael Bronski (*A Queer History of the United States*)

Leventhal's final novel was produced in 1995. This new edition features a foreword by Paras Borgohain who is currently writing a screenplay for the novel.

Second Son
Robert Ferro

Mark Valerian, the second son in the Valerian family, is ill, but determined to live life to the fullest – and live forever if he can. When he discovers Bill Mackey, a young theatrical designer who is also suffering from this disease neither wants to name, he also finds the lover of his dreams.

Together they develop an incredible plan to survive that will take them to Europe, to rustic Maine, and finally to the wonderful seaside summer mansion of the Valerian family, where father and son confront the painful ties of kinship ... and the joyous bonds of love.

"*Second Son* is transcendently beautiful; exquisitely written, exquisitely restrained. Its skillfully drawn characters come alive with an incandescent power as they struggle to preserve the romance, the passion, the tenderness that is vital to body and spirit. The accomplishment of *Second Son* reminds us of what literature has always been about – the deep examination of the soul. Rich, poignant, unforgettable, it leaves one with a rare feeling of having been in touch for a little while with the things that really matter." — Anne Rice

"I admired *The Family of Max Desir*. I love *Second Son*. The surprising story of the love between two men threatened by illness is full of fine authentic details and broader realizations about the human condition. Ferro's new work is entirely original, affecting, and yet strangely upbeat and heartening." — Doris Grumbach

Originally published in 1988, it was Ferro's final novel, completed in the months leading to his death from AIDS as he cared for his lover Michael Grumley. This new edition contains a foreword by Tom Cardamone (*Crashing Cathedrals: Edmund White by the Book*).

Life Drawing
Michael Grumley

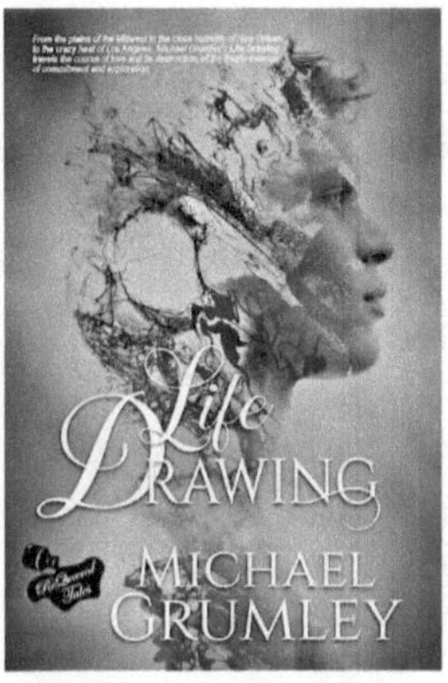

Born in Iowa to the sounds of Bob and Bing Crosby and the Dorsey brothers, Mickey grows up to the comforting images of his living room TV and the reassuring ruts of his parents' life. During the restless summer of his senior year in high school, drifting away from the girlfriend he could never quite love, Mickey spends a night with another boy, and his world will never be the same.

On a barge floating down the Mississippi, he falls in love with James, a black card player from New Orleans, and in time the two of them settle, bristling with sexual intensity, in the French Quarter – until a brief affair destroys James's trust and sends Mickey to the drugs and sordid life of Los Angeles.

"A simple, classic, engaging, and beautifully written tale of a boy who ran away from home, a man who didn't make it in the movies, an artist who found himself earlier than most and did it all west of the Mississippi, in places which, while very American, few Americans have ever been." — Andrew Holleran

"*Life Drawing* affirms the rich complexity of passion in the story of a small-town boy's difficult journey to manhood. Michael Grumley's crisp, direct language brings to life the demanding wonder of sexuality and the delicate tightrope of love between black men and white men." — Melvin Dixon

Originally published in 1991, it was Grumley's only novel, completed in the month's leading to his death from AIDS as he was cared for his lover Robert Ferro. This new edition contains the original foreword by Edmund White (*A Saint from Texas*) and afterword by George Stambolian (*Gay Men's Anthologies Men on Men*), close friends of the couple.

Like People in History
Felice Picano

Solid, cautious Roger Sansarc and flamboyant, mercurial Alistair Dodge are second cousins who become lifelong friends when they first meet as nine-year-old boys in 1954. Their lives constantly intersect at crucial moments in their personal histories as each discovers his own unique – and uniquely gay – identity. Their complex, tumultuous, and madcap relationship endures against 40 years of history and their involvement with the handsome model, poet, and decorated Vietnam vet Matt Loguidice, whom they both love. Picano chronicles and celebrates gay life and subculture over the last half of the twentieth century: from the legendary 1969 gathering at Woodstock to the legendary parties at Fire Island Pines in the 1970s, from Malibu Beach in its palmiest surfer days to San Francisco during its gayest era, from the cities and jungles of South Vietnam during the war to Manhattan's Greenwich Village and Upper East Side during the 1990s AIDS war.

> "It's the heroic and funny saga of the last three decades by someone who saw everything and forgot nothing." — Edmund White

> "Harrowing and sad, and very funny, *Like People in History* manages to bridge the unnerving chasm between the queer present and the gay past." — Andrew Holleran

In a book that could have been written only by one who lived it and survived to tell, Picano weaves a powerful saga of four decades in the lives of two men and their lovers, relatives, friends, and enemies. Tragic, comic, sexy, and romantic, filled with varied and colorful characters, *Like People in History* is both extraordinarily moving and supremely entertaining.

Published to acclaim in 1995, winner of the Ferro-Grumley Award for Best Novel, this 25th Anniversary edition for 2020 features a new foreword by Richard Burnett and an afterword by the author.

The Genius of Desire
Brian Bouldrey

Hopelessly drawn to the romantic notion of a double life, young Michael Bellman spends summers in Monsalvat, Michigan, coming of age in a loving tangle of highly eccentric relatives: Great Uncle Jimmy speaks to his dead wife during meals; Cousin Anne torments Michael beyond endurance; reckless Cousin Tommy secretly smokes cigars and can't wait to "kick butt in 'Nam" – and Michael watches every magical move he makes.

A few years and one driver's license later, as family alliances change and long-silent desires surface, Michael begins to understand his attraction to the double life because he's living one – at roadside rest stops, in library washrooms, and public parks. Coming out is the first step, coming to terms is the next ...

> "A simply told story of a young boy growing into manhood and evolving into himself in the midst of the contradictions, deceptions, denial, ignorance, pretensions, confusions, prejudices, and all the other weaknesses that flesh is heir to ... In one way or another this is the same world we must all find our way through and/or out of." — Hubert Selby, Jr. (*Last Exit to Brooklyn*)

A highly praised debut novel in 1993, this new edition includes a foreword by the author.

And don't miss ...

Love, the Magician: In April of 1997, Tristan Broder makes a pilgrimage of sorts from San Francisco to the prickly desert and scalped mountains around Tucson, Arizona, the place where he helped bury his partner Joe five years before. Guided by a comet that crossed the spring sky that year, he wanders toward renewal and resurrection, memory and mystery, deadly secrets and dark intentions.

There are plenty of people in the desert who still love Tristan as much as they did Joe. With open and glad hearts, they join Tristan to help him make a memorial to the whole-souled man he loved. Yet, despite the fact that they are all bound, like Tristan, by the memory and love for the saint who once lived among them, every one of them is hiding something.

ଓଃ

**If you enjoyed this book,
please help spread the word
by posting a short,
constructive review at
your favorite social media site
or book retailer.**

**We thank you, greatly,
for your support.**

And don't be shy! Contact us!

*For more information about current and future releases,
please contact us:*

E-mail: *requeeredtales@gmail.com*
Facebook (Like us!): www.facebook.com/ReQueeredTales
Twitter: @ReQueered
Instagram: www.instagram.com/requeered
Web: www.ReQueeredTales.com
Blog: www.ReQueeredTales.com/blog
Mailing list (Subscribe for latest news): https://bit.ly/RQTJoin